A QUEST OF BLOOD & STONE

A QUEST OF BLOOD & STONE

THE SEOD CROI CHRONICLES

BOOK 1

S. USHER EVANS

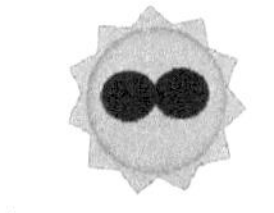

Sun's Golden Ray
Publishing

PENSACOLA, FL

Version Date: 9/23/25

© 2022 S. Usher Evans

ISBN: 978-1945438509

Cover Design by Bianca Bordianu | www.bbordianudesign.com
Cover Typography by Sun's Golden Ray Publishing
Map Designed by Frederick Kroner with Stardust Book Services
Line Editing by Danielle Fine, By Definition Editing
Proofreading by Lisa Henson, Capitol Editing

Sun's Golden Ray Publishing
Pensacola, FL
www.sgr-pub.com

For ordering information, please visit
www.sgr-pub.com/orders

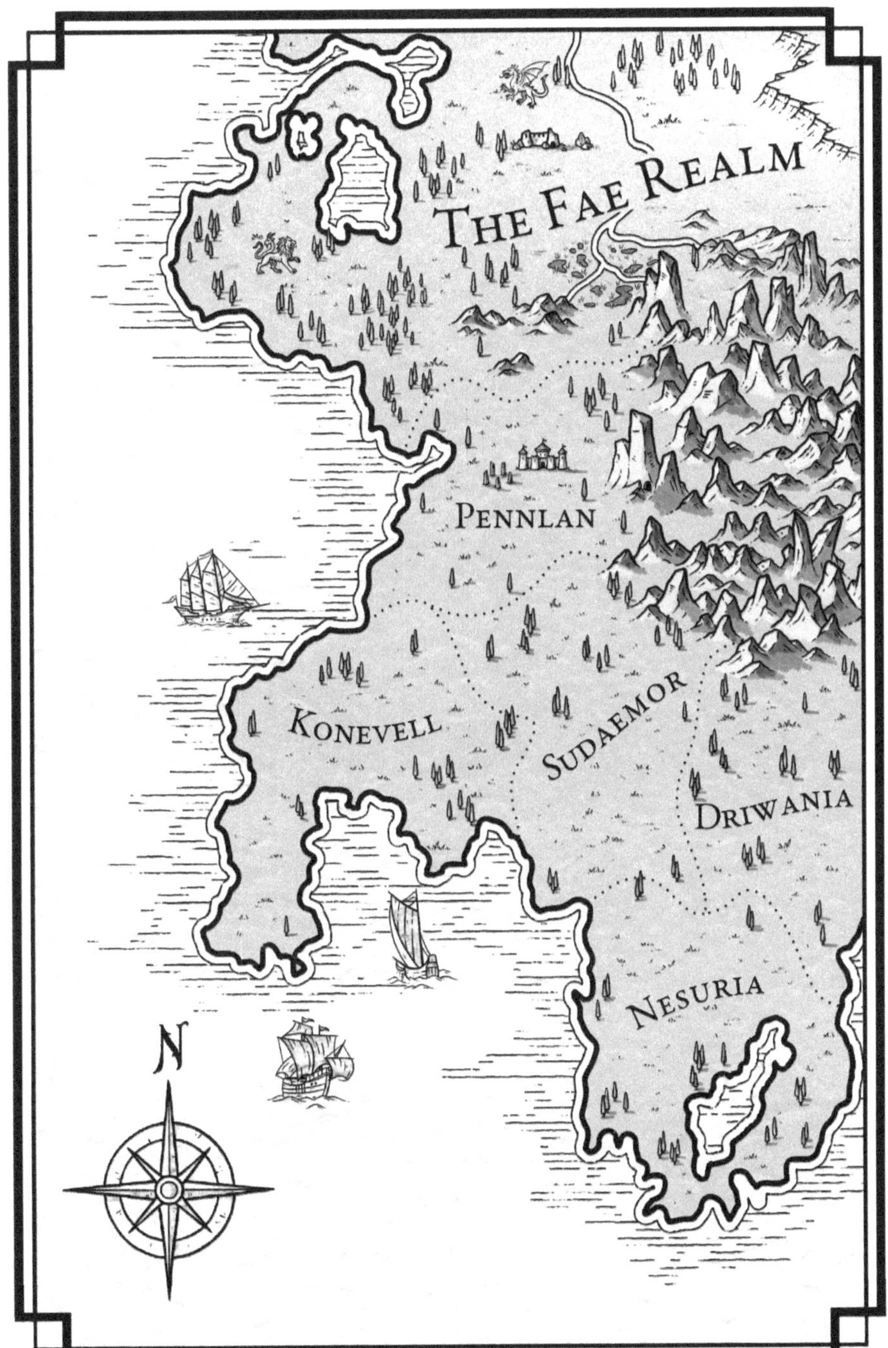

THE FAE REALM
PENNLAN
KONEVELL
SUDAEMOR
DRIWANIA
NESURIA
N

To MJS,

May you never lose your sense of adventure

CHAPTER ONE

AYLA

"Three fae were arrested yesterday in Críoch."

"*Three*?" I tried to hide my concern, but Eoghan would see through it anyway. My wizard advisor kept his tone light, but that was perhaps to keep me from worrying. "How many is that?"

"Ten in the past few weeks."

"The Erlking is getting bold," I said, flexing my fingers to keep from picking my thumbnail. "Why do you think they've started crossing the border more often?"

"Perhaps testing you prior to your coronation," he said. "But don't worry, we've put them in Caecarcem. The iron will hold them until we can interrogate them."

Caecarcem was the mysterious prison tucked away in the northwestern corner of the country. I'd always worried it wasn't enough to keep our magical enemies away, but to my knowledge, no fae had ever escaped.

"Then what?" I asked.

"We'll dispose of them."

I exhaled softly. Three fewer fae in the world would certainly help me sleep better at night.

Eoghan cast a warm smile in my direction, as if sensing my unease. "You're safe here, I promise."

"What about everyone else in the country?" I asked, more to myself.

"That we caught them is a testament to the commander's strategy in Críoch," Eoghan said. "He's very familiar with the creatures, and knows how to keep them from causing too much trouble."

Críoch had once been the last human town before travelers crossed into the fae realm, back when trade was free, and we weren't always looking over our shoulder. Now it was the first and last line of defense against the monsters to our north.

"Speaking of the border guards," Eoghan said as we turned the corner in the castle, "have you been down to see Captain Gabhann lately?"

I shook my head. "Why?"

"She's found herself another new recruit—this one from Críoch, actually. I believe his name is Ward."

"He must be impressive if he captured the captain's attention." The commander of my most elite forces regularly toured the country in search of new recruits.

"He's young, too." Eoghan cast me a sideways look. " Around your age. I think he'll flourish here."

My heart lightened at the thought of *someone* in this castle younger than middle age. Every other guard Gabhann had found across the country was at least forty, and while they made for interesting conversation partners, young blood was definitely welcome.

"Was that intentional?" I asked, pursing my lips. "Cade leaves, you bring me a new playmate?"

"My apprentice isn't gone yet."

"But he will be."

"Of course," Eoghan said. "It's part of the wizard tradition."

Considering Eoghan and Cade were the only two wizards around, I had to take his word for it. "And you won't give me *any* hint about what this trial will entail? Or when you'll send him away?"

"No." He smiled. "But the mystery will be revealed soon enough."

I pouted. Cade was almost of age, and per Eoghan, would have one final challenge to overcome before he was officially a full-fledged wizard. And once he was…he would be sent to one of the other four kingdoms. I was excited for him to step into a new phase of his life, but inconsolable at the thought of losing my best friend for good.

"Are you still thinking you'll send him to Driwania?" I asked, a little desolately.

"That or Nesuria," he said. "But my mind changes with the breeze. It could be Konevell, too. I want to ensure that wherever we send him is the most strategically advantageous for Pennlan." His gaze landed on me again. "Of course, you could also assist in that effort."

"Not this again…"

"It's important to the kingdom that you forge alliances. No better way to do that than to marry a close ally of the throne in one of the other four kingdoms. You should seriously—"

"Consider marrying shortly after my coronation," I parroted with a hearty roll of my eyes. "Or marrying at my coronation. Or marrying before. I hear you, Eoghan."

I would become Pennlan's queen in six short weeks; it was hard to avoid counting the days on the calendar every time I passed it. Time seemed to be moving ever faster, like a runaway horse toward a cliff. To add the choice of a lifetime partner when I hadn't even reached my eighteenth birthday… It seemed too much to handle all at once.

"The merchant from Sudaemor is looking forward to our dinner tonight," he said. "I hope you'll be on your best behavior."

"Aren't I always?"

He pursed his lips. "You have a tendency to let your tongue get away from you."

Perhaps because Eoghan's choices of dinner companions weren't all that great lately—and I was growing increasingly worried that he was bringing them here as potential marriage options.

"I'll be good," I said.

"And on time?"

"And on time." I cast my gaze at him. "And when do *I* get to schedule my own dinners and with the guests of my choosing?"

"As soon as you can prove to me that you can make decisions that are in the best interests of the country, and not merely the ones you want."

I deflated. I'd started asking him to include me in more of the day-to-day running of the kingdom, but his answer was always the same. "In six weeks, you won't have a choice. I'll be queen and all the decisions will fall to me."

He lifted his shoulder in a shrug that somehow made me feel worse about myself. I decided to change the subject. "What should we do about the fae? Could they be planning something? Perhaps wanting to disrupt the coronation?"

"I wouldn't put it past them," Eoghan said as we walked into the throne room. "We have given our guards at Caecarcem instructions to extract information, but the fae probably won't betray their kind. So in the interim, I have—with your blessing—asked Captain Gabhann to double our store of iron-tipped arrows and the number of scouts patrolling the castle border."

"Thank you," I said with a nod. I stopped as we passed a plaque behind the throne—a shield with the Pennlan crest and a place for a large gemstone. Perhaps with that stone around my neck, I might not have felt so hopeless against the fae. It had been gifted to my ancestor hundreds of years ago, allowing anyone in the king's bloodline to wield unbelievable magic—more than any wizard, fae, or other magical creature.

But when I was barely a toddler, the fae had sent an envoy—Leandra—to Pennlan. She'd bewitched and befuddled my father, who was vulnerable and still mourning the death of my mother. Leandra's aim wasn't just to become queen; she wanted the stone. She killed my father in pursuit of the stone, but once the last breath left his body, ownership of the stone came to me. If it hadn't been for Eoghan, she would've killed me as well. But he'd intervened, and she escaped, taking the stone with her.

"You don't think they still have it, do you?" I asked, staring at the empty slot where the stone had been.

"It is as useless as a diamond to them," he replied. "As long as you're still alive."

I smiled weakly.

"Don't worry, the fae know better than to attempt anything," Eoghan said, offering the same warm smile that could untangle any knot in my chest. "You will ascend the throne without trouble and become a magnificent queen. I have the utmost confidence in you."

At least one of us does.

⇥ ⇥ ⇥ ⇥

My footsteps echoed on the stairs as I descended toward Eoghan's so-called "vault." It had once been the Pennlan dungeons, but Eoghan had transformed it into a magical training space for himself and his one apprentice. There was a large sparring ring, residences for himself and Cade, and a magnificent library I'd spent hours getting lost in.

I pushed open the heavy, wooden door, peering inside to make sure there were no spells flying about. But all was quiet, save the scribbling of quill on paper. Cade had his back to me, his silky black hair touching the edge of his white shirt as he hunched over the table. Every so often, he would stop and look at the book, running the tip of his feather quill along the words and murmuring to himself before scribbling more.

Wizards were incredibly rare; Eoghan had to search far and wide for Cade, traveling to a faraway continent across the ocean from Nesuria. Even after almost a decade of living here in Pennlan, Cade still had the slightest lilt of an accent, and when he was frustrated, he'd curse in his native tongue. His skin was a deep, rich golden brown, and over the years he'd grown taller and taller until he towered over nearly everyone in the castle. He never quite seemed to know what to do with his long limbs, an awkwardness that belied the powerful magic coursing through his veins.

I almost hated to interrupt him, but he sat up and stretched, tilting his face up toward the ceiling and yawning.

"Cade?"

He nearly fell off the bench, turning around with wide, dark brown eyes. "Your Highness?"

He scrambled to his feet, as if to bow, and I giggled, putting up my hands. "It's just us."

"Damn, Ayla," he said, his shoulders sagging as he ran a hand through his hair. "Don't scare me like that. I could have hurt you."

"You would never," I said, unable to keep a smile off my face.

He sat down. "I might."

"Your staff was on the other side of the table," I said, nodding to the lightly colored wooden walking stick.

"Fair."

I plopped down next to him. "What are you doing?"

"Reading. What else?" He sighed and leaned onto his elbow. "Waiting to hear what sort of crazy thing Eoghan is planning for my trial."

"Any idea what it might be?" I asked.

"No. The only thing I know is to be ready at a moment's notice."

"Probably part of his plan," I said with a solemn nod. "Maybe the challenge is just you being on edge for the next month."

He snorted.

"Do you think it's something incredibly dangerous, like fighting a dragon?"

"He'd have to find one first."

"He could do it."

"He's been hinting that he might send me on a journey," Cade said, glancing at the withered map on the wall. "Maybe he'll have me find my own dragon, bring it back, and slay it."

I followed his gaze, taking in the sight. Most of my maps were concerned with Pennlan, the other four human kingdoms, and the fae realm to the north. But the continent was expansive. The fae controlled a territory nearly the size of the human realm, with as many clans as there were kingdoms. To the west, past Driwania, an impassable mountain range that scraped the sky. And at the bottom of the map, more islands, countries, nations to the south, where Cade had come from. The world was so vast, yet I'd only seen the walls of this castle.

"I wish I could leave," I said, a little wistfully.

"Where would you go?" Cade asked.

"No idea," I said. "Maybe Konevell to sit by the shore. Just to see more of this world before I'm chained to my throne."

"I'm sure you can leave once you're queen," Cade said.

"If he assigns you to one of the other kingdoms, I damn well better," I said with a little grumble. "Do you think he'll send you away immediately after you finish your trial?"

He sighed, finally meeting my gaze. Even in the scant light, his eyes shimmered with a small hint of gold.

"Would you miss me?" he asked.

"I mean, who else is going to help me raid the kitchens at midnight if you're gone?" I said, a smile coming onto my lips.

He snorted and broke my gaze, looking down with something unreadable on his face.

"Hey," I said, nudging him. "It's gonna be…fine."

"Is it?" He cast me a glance.

"I mean…" I couldn't pretend. "Maybe."

"Yeah." He tilted his head back toward the map. "I think Eoghan's going to send me there."

My heart seized in my chest. "Cade, he wouldn't send you to the fae realm."

"He might." He rested his hand on top of mine. "If he does, I promise you, I'll be fine. As long as I have my staff."

The ash staff sat to his right, and although I'd seen him do magnificent things with it, how that magic would fare against an entire country of bloodthirsty monsters was a mystery.

"I even have a new trick," he said, releasing my hand and standing. His hand hovered inches above his staff and he concentrated, a furrow forming in the middle of his brow. After a moment, the staff shook then flew into his hand. "See?"

I couldn't help the unladylike squeal that came from my mouth as I clapped. "Cade! That's amazing!"

"It's taken me weeks, but I think I finally cracked it." He beamed, showing off the dimples in his cheeks as he walked back over to me. "Eoghan wants me to practice farther distances, but that may take me a few months. He can summon his from across the room." He shook his head. "Sometimes I don't think I'll live long enough to be as good as he is."

"You will," I said with an affirming smile. "Just cast an immortality spell on yourself."

"As soon as I find one, I'll do that." He smiled. "Do you want to see what else I've learned lately?"

"Is that even a question?" I leaned onto the table. "Why else do you think I'm here?"

Cade beamed.

Chapter Two

Ward

I dreaded every step as I walked down the gloomy stairs to the wizard dungeon. I'd drawn the short straw, and tonight, I was to stand at attention at a dinner and try to stay awake while the diplomats discussed the lives of the civilians they oversaw. But first, I was instructed to retrieve the princess from the depths of her castle and ensure she was dressed and ready for dinner.

Why a guard in her elite service was assigned such a job, I had no idea. It was probably part of Captain Gabhann's desire for all of us to know everything there was to know about the castle, and who lived there. I should've probably listened to her, as she'd served two kings and the princess, but I was still adjusting to her leadership style versus the looser one in Críoch.

At the time of my selection, I'd been elated. Here was my chance to prove myself in the most prestigious guard in the entire kingdom. No longer walking along the border in the dead of night, looking for fae and finding nothing except the occasional drunken fool. But ever since I'd arrived, it had been nothing but learning the castle schematics and practicing my vacant stare as I stood at attention. Now, tonight, I would put all those very important lessons into practice as I escorted the princess from the wizard dungeon to her bedroom, then waited for her in the dining hall, standing guard while they ate and drank for hours. It was all so…riveting.

But this post had come with a sizable income increase, and if I played my cards right, I might just save up enough to make my own way someday. Then I'd be the one at the table, and someone else could stand at attention and watch me eat.

I reached the bottom of the stairs and came face to face with a thick, wooden door. It didn't budge when I twisted the handle, but I'd been warned that the wizards had put enchantments everywhere.

I knocked on the door three times, aiming for stern yet respectful, then waited, putting my hands behind my back.

There was chatter from inside, a female and a male voice, along with a twitter of laughter. I steeled myself to face the princess for the first time, having only seen paintings of her up until now.

The door swung open, and my heart stopped beating.

She was hands-down the prettiest thing I'd ever seen in my life. Her auburn hair fell in thick strands around her alabaster face, where her pink lips were open in surprise. Her eyes were like emeralds, shimmering even in this low light. I realized I'd stopped breathing, so I inhaled deeply, but still couldn't do anything but stare in awe.

"Um…" She smiled, and somehow, she was even more gorgeous. "Hi. Can I help you?"

My tongue stuck to the roof of my mouth. "I, uh, er…"

"Are you unable to speak?"

The wizard's voice snapped me out of my reverie, and I straightened. "I'm sorry to disturb you, but I'm supposed to be escorting you to dinner."

"Damn," she said, turning to the wizard, who hadn't taken his suspicious gaze off me yet. "Sorry, Cade. I suppose your demonstration will have to wait."

He narrowed his eyes at me but said nothing, and the princess walked out, brushing by me in the cramped space. She smelled of lavender and something else I couldn't place, and I held my breath until she was past me so I wouldn't be tempted to lean in.

"Well?" she asked at the top of the stairs. "Are you escorting me or not?"

"Y-yes, ma'am," I muttered, scrambling after her.

>+>+>+>+

Once we reached the main level of the castle, we walked side-by-side, but that was more her doing than mine. I tried to slow my pace to remain behind her, as was protocol, but she kept dropping back as well.

"I haven't seen you around before," she asked, her voice carrying in the empty hall. "What's your name?"

"W-Ward, m'lady," I said then remembered what Gabhann had drilled into my head. "Your Highness, I mean."

She stopped and turned to look at me, an amused smile on her face. The fading sunlight cast an orange glow, reflecting beautifully in her eyes. "Are you…scared of me or something?"

"N-no, of course not," I stammered, knowing I wasn't helping my case. "I'm not scared of anything."

"You look scared," she said, but there was no malice anywhere in her smile. "How long have you been in the castle?"

"Three weeks," I said. "I've just come from Críoch."

She nodded. "That seems to be Gabhann's new plan to inject fresh blood into the castle guards. Pluck the best and brightest from all over the kingdom to train and learn here."

"Yes, ma'am—Your Highness." I cursed myself and my tongue for not functioning correctly.

"Ayla is also an option," she said, tilting her head to the side and smiling at me with those beautiful lips.

"Absolutely not," I said, horrified. "Do you know what the captain would do if she heard me address you in such a way?"

"And I would tell her that I asked you to do it."

I snorted before I could stop myself. "If you say so."

Her smile widened. "There you go. Now you aren't so nervous."

Indeed, the knot in my chest had lessened, and I let myself relax a little. "Is it your general rule that no one should be nervous around you?"

"There's no need for it, so I don't see why you would be," she said, resting her hand on my arm and sending bolts of electricity straight to my heart. "I don't have a family, so I've come to think of everyone here as my surrogate one."

I nodded, remembering what Gabhann had said about the sordid history of the princess's father and stepmother. "I don't have a family either. Not really."

"Tell me about yourself," she said, looping her arm through mine, causing my pulse to gallop in my chest. "Ward of Críoch. Were you born there?"

"N-no," I said. "I'm from a farm outside the city. We used to be very prosperous, until the border closed…"

"That seems to be common up there," she said with an understanding nod. "It's one of the things I hope to fix once I'm queen."

"You'll reopen the border with the fae?" I asked, almost stopping.

She laughed. "Absolutely not. But there must be some way I can help revive Críoch without having to trade with those murderous creatures."

"I'm sure there is," I said, though I knew nothing of politics or economics.

"But I'm sorry," she said, surprising me. *Why is she apologizing?* "You were telling me more about yourself. What was your farm like?"

It had never really felt like home, not since my brother had taken over and turned me into a stablehand rather than a family member, but telling this beautiful girl about my childhood felt right somehow. She asked questions, curious about the livestock, life on the farm, and how we managed. When I told her I'd left at fourteen to seek employment at the border, she nodded.

"And then you were so impressive, you were selected for the guard?"

"I don't know about impressive," I said, as we came to her bedroom door.

"You certainly had to have impressed Captain Gabhann," she said.

"Otherwise, you wouldn't be here."

I found myself smiling at her, staring into her green eyes and forgetting for a moment that she was a princess, and I was just a lowly guard. If she were anyone else, I would've asked her to join me for a picnic on the greens, to get to know her better. Perhaps even chance a kiss under the blue sky.

But with a start, I remembered our situation and did my best to rid my mind of those ridiculous notions.

"I suppose I'd better get inside," she said with a half-hearted gesture to the door beyond. "Eoghan will yell at me if I'm late."

I furrowed my brow. "But doesn't he…work for you?"

"In a manner of speaking," she said, not moving to open the door. "Sometimes it feels like it's the other way around. But he did practically raise me, so…"

I nodded, waiting for her to leave, but she didn't. I'd thought, perhaps, her interest was cursory, or even just her general niceness. But something in the back of my mind told me she wanted to prolong this conversation.

"I go riding sometimes," she said, breaking the awkward silence. "Are you a good horseman?" She laughed, covering her lips with her delicate hand. "I don't even know why I asked. You told me you raised them on the farm."

"I did," I said, enjoying how her cheeks turned rosy. *Is this common? It couldn't have been.* "You like to ride?"

"It's better than being cooped up in the castle," she said. "But… perhaps tomorrow, we could go riding together. I'd love to hear more about the farm, about Críoch, about everything." Her cheeks grew redder. "I mean, it's just…"

The door swung open, revealing a very harried-looking maid, who clamped down on the princess's arm and dragged her inside as she squeaked a goodbye. Before the door shut, she flashed me another dazzling smile, leaving me staring at the door and actually excited that I'd get to see her this evening.

>—» >—» >—» >—»

By the time I arrived in the dining hall and took my spot along the wall, some of my giddiness had faded. I'd remembered I'd have to stand at attention for at least the next three hours. I held my wrists behind my back and watched the servants come and go as they set up the room for dinner. Once they'd cleared the room, the telltale sound of conversation echoed from the door beyond.

Eoghan was there with the guest of honor tonight, the brother-in-law of the king of Sudaemor. The wizard looked like just a man, somewhat tall, with dark hair and pale skin, perhaps from spending all his time in the basement with his apprentice. But something about him had set me on edge, ever since Captain Gabhann had introduced us last week.

I did my best to ignore the details of their conversation, not wanting them to think I was eavesdropping, but I couldn't help but gaze at the wizard in curiosity.

"If you think she will be amenable…"

Eoghan rested his hand on the merchant's shoulder. "I think if you present your case, she will be. She's nothing if not understanding."

The merchant nodded and sat down, though he didn't start on his food. Eoghan took the seat to the right of Ayla's chair and waited as well, glancing at the clock. Princesses were supposedly never late, but as the moments ticked by, my concern grew.

Finally, at half-past the hour, I heard her slippered feet rushing down the hall. She stopped a few feet from the door, and I spied her collecting herself, smoothing her hair and taking a long breath. She was dressed in a blue frock, undoubtedbly designed by the most skillful artisans, and her hair had been pinned and curled. But if I had my choice, I'd take the way she'd looked in the hallway over this.

She stepped into the room. "Good evening," she said, her voice like music. "I do apologize for being a few minutes late."

The merchant and Eoghan rose and bowed as she joined them at the table. Almost immediately, servants emerged from the kitchens to plate the first course, working quickly and silently as Ayla engaged the merchant in some pleasantries.

"I hope your trip was quick, Lord Weymouth," she replied. "Tell me, is it faster to travel by sea or by land from Sudaemor?"

The merchant chortled. "It is a shorter distance by land, Your Majesty. Surely, you know your geography."

But Ayla just kept her gaze level, a kind smile on her face. "It may be a shorter distance, but given the right conditions at sea, a case could be made to travel a longer distance at a faster speed. Surely, a merchant with fleets of ships at his disposal understands that."

I couldn't help the snort and pretended to cough before resuming my position. Luckily, those at the table were so used to guards and soldiers that they barely noticed my presence.

Eoghan glared at the princess. "She certainly has her opinions, doesn't she? Would you like some more wine?"

At first, I frowned at the patronizing tone, but after the merchant was two glasses in, his demeanor softened considerably. Perhaps that was the wizard's plan, though the princess still wore a look of discomfort as she tried to get a word in edgewise. But Eoghan kept cutting her off, pouring more wine into the merchant's glass. Finally, she seemed to give up, sitting back and pursing her lips in annoyance.

That was, until her bright eyes met mine. Her lips parted in surprise, and it seemed a smile lingered at the corners of her mouth. It was hard not to reciprocate, but I wrenched my gaze away to look forward, feeling her attention but not wanting to give in to it.

"I'm very interested to see about this wizard apprentice you have," Weymouth said. "Is he quite powerful?"

"I could give you a demonstration, if you like," Eoghan said, reaching for his staff.

I held my breath—I'd never seen magic before. The soldiers talked about it, of course, and the fae just beyond the border breathed it, but I'd never been so lucky. The wizard's staff glowed a dark orange color, then returned to normal. I frowned; that wasn't the sort of magic show I'd been hoping for.

"He'll be right up," Eoghan said.

Chapter Three

Cade

My staff clicked against the stone staircase as I hurried toward the great hall. I'd been engrossed in reading when it had lit up—my master was calling. I shouldn't have been surprised. He'd grown fond of showing off my power to various merchants, visitors, and envoys who stopped in to see Ayla.

I paused and conjured myself a mirror with my staff, the magic glowing bright gold as it formed a reflective surface in front of me. I smoothed my hair down, adjusted my tunic over my undershirt so it was straight, and made sure nothing else was out of place. Then I strode confidently into the dining hall.

My gaze first landed on Ayla, and I couldn't help the smile that came to my lips. She was a vision in blue tonight, her hair swept out of her face, showcasing those beautiful green eyes framed by dark lashes. Her maids had dressed her up with a little makeup that made her look more like a young woman than my best friend, but the way she grinned at me warmed me from my toes to my forehead.

"Ah, good, Cade," Eoghan said. "Come in, come in. Have a seat. We'll have a demonstration after we finish this meal." He snapped his fingers. "Bring my apprentice a place setting."

The activity was furious, clearing the decorative place setting next to the merchant and replacing it with an empty plate. I sat, resting my staff against the table, and murmured my thanks, knowing it was better to keep quiet until I was called on to show off.

"As I was saying…"

The talk of politics was boring, so I snuck a glance at Ayla. She was at the head of the table, gently pushing the vegetables in her soup from side to side instead of eating them. Her gaze drifted to the wall more often than to her food, so I followed it to see what could be so interesting.

It was the boy who'd interrupted us in the vault. Eoghan had told me there was a younger knight from Críoch—hand-selected, in fact. He didn't appear to be anything special. He had an average build that filled out his uniform and was shorter than me—though that wasn't hard. His black curly hair had been shorn close to the scalp, and his skin was almost the color of clay, a dull brown that lacked any excitement. His dark eyes held a little mischief as he fought to keep a smile off his face.

"Princess?" Eoghan said, catching us both by surprise. "Lord Weymouth asked you a question."

"I'm sorry," she said, a little blush coming to her pale cheeks. "I wandered off for a moment."

"Does this happen often?" Weymouth asked, snatching his glass off the table. "A queen must always give her guests her undivided attention. Or else someone might find it rude."

Ayla's gaze narrowed, and the hair on the back of my neck rose as I sensed she was about to let loose on this guy.

Luckily, Eoghan stepped in. "Apprentice, it might be time for you to give us a demonstration."

"Yes, of course." I walked to the space beside the table, standing with my hand on my staff and my gaze on my master. "What would you like to see today, Master Eoghan?"

"Let's let the merchant decide," he said. "What would you like him to do?"

I inwardly sighed. I wasn't a trained animal, but sometimes it felt that way.

"Conjure me some gold," he said with a hearty laugh. "Let's make this trip worthwhile."

"Impossible," Eoghan said, saving me the explanation. "The magic can only conjure and create organic matter." He leaned in with a smile I knew was forced. "Otherwise, I wouldn't be sitting at this table. I'd be down in the whorehouses."

Ayla rolled her eyes at his crude joke, and I kept my face passive, awaiting instruction. The guard against the wall who'd caught Ayla's eye had found it funny, though. I was starting to dislike him already, for reasons I couldn't put into words.

"Then surprise me," the merchant said, sitting back. "Show me your most impressive spell, boy."

I bristled—I was nearly eighteen—but turned toward the space and gathered magic in my staff from the corners of my body. It always felt like I was scraping the bottom of the barrel, leeching my very essence from my bones to conjure even the simplest of tricks. Eoghan had said it would come with age, but I wasn't sure.

Still, impressive to the non-magical usually meant a light show, heavy on the theatrics and light on the actual power. And this merchant was so drunk, he might not notice anything but something bright and shiny. So I created some fireworks, exploding them above the table and letting them sprinkle down harmlessly. Ayla's awed smile was gracious, even though she knew this was nothing special. For her, I'd show off a little more.

With my golden magic, I drew the Pennlan crest above the table then formed an eagle made of light to circle around it before dipping onto the table and snatching the small date from Ayla's hand. She giggled and clapped as it squawked and zoomed around—and perhaps I was a little pleased when the knight jumped out of the way when it came too close to him.

I felt my master's magic before I saw it and quickly erected a shield around myself as his spell slammed into me—much harder than was perhaps safe in these close quarters. I glanced at Ayla, and that blasted guard had moved closer to her and had his hand on his sword. As if a sword would do anything against—

"*Damn.*" I just barely noticed the second barrage and got up another shield in time. Ayla and her stupid knight were distracting me, and I'd hear about it later if I didn't pull myself together.

I glared at my master. What did he want me to do? I couldn't retaliate, not with him sitting so close to Ayla and the merchant. I didn't have enough control to attempt something like that, and he knew it.

A flash of disappointment crossed Eoghan's face. But when he lowered his hands and turned to Weymouth, he was all smiles.

"You see, he's quite powerful. Nearly ready to take his wizard trial and break out on his own." He waved his hand at me. "You may stand down, Cade."

I nodded, feeling like I'd done something wrong. But that always seemed to be the case around Eoghan. Over a decade learning from him, and I still had no idea what was going on in his mind.

⤜ ⤜ ⤜ ⤜

I ate my dinner in silence, casting furtive looks at Ayla. By the time we finished our dessert, Lord Weymouth was practically falling over. But Eoghan invited the three of us to join him for an after-dinner drink, which meant there would be more magic required on my part. But we'd be upright and mobile, and thus I could speak with Ayla alone.

The small sitting room was right off the dining hall, and before long, we each had a glass of brandy.

"To Sudaemor and Pennlan, may their alliances continue to grow stronger," Eoghan said.

"Hear, hear!"

I raised my glass, as did Ayla, after which, luckily, the merchant asked to inspect the tomes that had belonged to Ayla's father. Eoghan led him there, and blessedly, Ayla sidled up next to me.

"He's a boor," she muttered under her breath.

"You seem to be doing well against him," I replied with a half-smile.

"Mm." She turned behind her to the closed door and sighed. "I wonder if I can ask to take my leave yet."

"Having that much fun?" I asked. "You look absolutely riveted by his company."

She snorted and downed the rest of her brandy in one gulp, so I decided to change the subject.

"What's with that knight?" I asked, keeping my eye on Eoghan and Weymouth in case we were called to their side. "He seemed interesting to you."

Her cheeks pinked, earning a frown from me. "I don't know. He's kind of handsome."

"H-handsome?" I sputtered, a little louder than I'd meant to. "He's a guard."

"He's a member of my *elite* guard," she said with a knowing look. "Freshly arrived from Críoch and chosen by Gabhann because of his skill."

"Still," I said, hoping it was an observation and nothing more. The last thing Ayla needed was to get her head twisted by some guard from the middle of nowhere. Perhaps he was only here for a few weeks.

"What do you care anyway?" she asked, a mischievous grin on her face. "I'm allowed to look at men, am I not?"

"He's not a man. He's a boy."

She scoffed. "He's as old as you."

I glanced behind me at the closed door, wanting another look at him. "You got to know him pretty well, did you?"

"As well as anyone in fifteen minutes," she said. "And he looked so nervous, bless him." She ran her finger around the rim of her empty cup with a secretive smile on her face. "I've never made anyone that nervous before. It was kind of—"

"What? Fun?"

She dropped her finger and pursed her lips at me. "I was going to say thrilling. You can't blame me for flirting—there's nobody half-decent to look at in this castle—let alone anyone half-decent who isn't twice my age."

I glared at her pointedly. "Excuse me?"

"I mean, besides you, but I look at you all the time."

"I—"

"Cade, another demonstration," Eoghan said, interrupting our conversation. I wasn't sure if he'd overheard it, but I knew it wasn't over. If anything, I'd have a talk with Gabhann about her new guard and make sure she knew he was putting foolish thoughts into the princess's head.

"Yes, master," I said, remembering the title almost too late. "What would you like to see?"

"We've just been discussing our fae problem to the north," Eoghan said. "I would like you to demonstrate the magic we can use to control them."

I nodded, though I was a little confused. "But there are no fae here."

"No, but you can surely showcase the technique."

"Shame we don't have one of the devils here to play with," Weymouth said. "I'd like to show them what's what."

"Indeed." Eoghan nodded. "Cade, if you will."

I turned around, facing Ayla, who was leaning against the wall with a sour look on her face. But I did my best to ignore her as I gathered power in my staff to Eoghan's narration.

"I've devised a way to use wizard magic to take hold of their power, the same way we do for all inanimate things, and mold them to our will. As you can see," he gestured to the spell that floated from my staff, "this is what would go inside a fae to compel them completely. And at that point, they would be as obedient as a dog."

"Brilliant." Weymouth clapped. "Surprised you didn't march into the fae realm and take over that bastard King Birch for yourself."

"The level of control depends on the fae," he said. "Someone like the Erlking would be difficult to spell for a long period of time. And I haven't yet mastered how to split the magic across multiple fae."

Weymouth snorted and sat back. "And you came across this great discovery *after* the fae bitch killed your king? Your timing is impeccable."

Ayla shifted uncomfortably, and I sucked the magic back into my staff, glaring at Eoghan and waiting for him to say something. But he didn't.

"It's high time that Pennlan share their wizards with the rest of us," Weymouth said, now several glasses of wine in. "It's not fair to keep all the wizardry for yourself. Like that bloody stone your father misplaced."

I could've marched over and punched the merchant in his rosy face, but Eoghan was faster.

"Careful, Weymouth," Eoghan warned. "If you should offend my soon-to-be-queen, I will have to send Cade to Konevell."

"We had a deal, my good man," Weymouth said. "You'd send us the wizard and the queen, and in return, we would allow a larger tax on our goods."

Ayla sucked in a breath. "I'm sorry?"

Eoghan cleared his throat. "I don't believe we *agreed* to that, only that I would listen to it." He glanced at Ayla, whose cheeks were growing rosy with anger. "And we aren't sending you the queen, of course. She will remain here and simply marry—"

"And *why* is my marriage a bartering chip?" Ayla barked.

"Because *you* are the queen, and your marriage is of national importance," Weymouth replied. "Goodness, Eoghan, haven't you taught her anything?"

Ayla's fists clenched. "He taught me proper manners when addressing a sovereign, which you clearly—"

"Ayla." Eoghan snapped, cutting her off with a look. "I believe it's time for you to go to bed."

"I'm not a child," Ayla snapped.

"You're certainly acting like it."

She narrowed her gaze, and I gently rested my hand over hers. "Maybe he's right," I said softly. "You should—"

"Don't touch me." She ripped her hand from mine and marched out of the room, leaving the three of us staring at the space she'd left.

"Please forgive her," Eoghan said. "She still needs to grow into her role. But we will be sure that by her coronation, she'll be ready to accept the crown and all its responsibilities."

"I should—*hic*—hope so."

I watched the space she'd left, torn between following her and knowing I would be called back if I attempted it. Once I was dismissed, I'd bring a slice of cake to her room and we'd talk about it. But for now, I turned back to my master, counting the seconds until I was allowed to leave.

CHAPTER FOUR

WARD

My legs were falling asleep, and my head was bobbing as I stood at attention outside the drawing room where the four diners were taking their sweet time. I didn't know how long these fancy events lasted, but now that Ayla was inside the room, I was bored and eager to get things moving. I wouldn't get a reprieve from a long day of drilling and training in the morning, and the longer they lollygagged in there, the more I'd hate them tomorrow.

The door blessedly opened and Ayla came storming out, her face red and eyes wet. I expected the rest of the party to come after her—or least her wizard friend—but the door shut behind her, and she stood there, breathing heavily and fighting back tears.

"Your Majesty?" I said, softly. "Are you all right?"

She looked up, seeing me for the first time, and quickly wiped her cheeks, as if embarrassed that I'd seen her in such a state. Clearing her throat, she plastered a very fake smile on her face and beamed at me.

"Ward, I think I'm ready to go to bed now."

"Of course." I bowed my head. "I'll follow your lead."

As before, it wasn't long before we were walking side-by-side, though her gaze was unfocused and distant. I wanted to press more, to ask what was on her mind, but I didn't know if it was my place. Still, I wanted to help.

"Can I do anything for you?" I asked after a moment.

"No," she said. "Not unless you can tell all the men in my life to stick their damn staffs up their asses."

I barked a laugh that I tried to cover with a cough, but she giggled and slowed her pace as we passed a window overlooking the gardens below. She turned to it, pressing her hands to the stone sill and looking up at the moon, taking a few long breaths.

"I'm sorry they're not living up to your expectations," I said, after a moment. "But if you don't mind me asking, why don't *you* tell them to stick their damn staffs up their asses?"

"Because when I do, they tell me to go to bed because I'm being a child," she said with a long sigh. "And I'm just…"

I waited patiently for her to complete her thought, but she stayed where she was. I wasn't sure if she was praying or merely trying to delay the inevitable.

"Do you want to take a walk with me?" she asked, not looking at me.

"Where?"

"Out there," she said. "It's a nice night, and I could use some fresh air. Otherwise, I'll just…be mad all night and get no sleep."

"We can't have that," I said. I might get in trouble, but I didn't care. "Shall we?"

>⇥ >⇥ >⇥ >⇥

She led me to the gardens, stepping out into the moonlight and looking like a creature from one of the magical realms. The blue light of the full moon reflected off her skin, and she tilted her head upward to breathe in the air. I attempted to keep my distance, but she found my arm and threaded hers through it. If I hadn't known any better, I would've thought it a proper date. But considering how distraught she'd been, I let her take control.

"The brooklime are blooming," she said.

"Is that a flower?" I asked, dumbly. Of course it was a flower. "I'm not very well read in botany."

"It happens so quickly that I didn't want another day to go by without seeing them," she said. "They say it was my mother's favorite flower, so my father planted the garden full of them."

I nodded. "Do you remember her?"

"No, she died shortly after I was born," she said softly. "My father was inconsolable."

And yet, he'd married that fae woman, Leandra, within a year. But I didn't want to bring that up right now. "I'm sorry you didn't get to know them."

"You told me you were raised by your brother," she said. "Do you know your parents?"

"No," I said. "I don't even have an idea what they looked like, though I've heard I resemble my father."

She half-smiled. "I've stared at their painting in the great hall for more hours than I can count. I have my mother's coloring, but my father's eyes, for sure. And his face, somehow."

"You are beautiful," I stammered, the only thing I could think to say. "And they would both be very proud of you."

"I'm sure the same could be said of your parents," she said, squeezing my arm with her other hand. "Come, let's check on the butterfly bushes. They're around the corner."

We walked slowly and in silence, but I enjoyed the way her hand felt on my arm, the way her body brushed against mine every other step. It felt natural to be here with her, to be strolling through the gardens late at night under the moon. I could tell her everything and anything, but I'd be just as happy in silence.

Our circuit around the garden ended where it began, and I expected her to continue back to the castle.

"Shall we keep walking?" she asked, her voice soft and emotional.

"Your Highness?" I prompted. "Are you all right?"

"It's just us," she said softly. "Please, call me Ayla."

"I would get in mountains of trouble—"

"It's just us." She turned to me, her eyes wide and pleading. "And I swear to you, I won't tell a soul."

I loosened a breath. "Very well. Ayla."

"I like the way you say it." She smiled, her eyes twinkling.

My stomach felt like it was going to fall out of my body. "The question remains: are you all right?" I asked, my voice shaky. "You seem… I don't know you very well, but something's wrong."

She dropped my arm and shook her head, walking to the bench tucked into the butterfly bushes and sitting down. I hesitated for a moment before following her.

"There are times when I feel like I know what I'm doing. And others I feel like Eoghan has his own plans that he'll let me know about when he feels like it." She shook her head. "I know he has my best interests at heart, but there comes a point when the counselor must let the queen rule."

"Have you talked to him about this?"

"He always has some reason for why it's not quite right yet, something that makes me feel…" She sighed and tilted her head up toward the sky. "Stupid."

"You are certainly not that," I said. "You put that merchant back in his place."

"And then got yelled at for it."

"Which I don't agree with. You're the sovereign. You get to set the rules." I felt as if I were walking on thin ice, speaking so boldly. But after seeing the way she'd been coddled and berated at dinner, I felt compelled to remind her what a strong woman she really was. "And they can pound rocks if they feel differently."

She snorted and turned to me, a little smile coming into her eyes. "Pound rocks? Is that a saying from the border? Or is it from the farm?"

"The soldiers here, actually," I said. "But I think it fits. You shouldn't let them boss you around. You're the queen."

"Not yet."

"Queen enough," I said.

Her gaze dropped to the grass beneath our feet again and she swung her dangling legs, barely touching the greenery. "I'd always hoped there would be this switch, that one day I'd feel like a queen. But the closer we get to the coronation, the more I feel like… I'm just going to be the same old me but with a heavy piece of metal on my head. Eoghan will still make all the decisions, and I'll just be an ornament."

"Somehow I don't think you're capable of being an ornament."

I didn't get the smile I'd hoped for, but she did soften somewhat. "I also… I don't know if I'm capable of ruling *without* Eoghan's guidance. I know I should be. But… As you saw tonight, I still can't seem to keep everything straight. Maybe it would be for the best."

I glanced down at her hand, resting on the stone bench, then gently moved mine to cover hers, taking a chance. She looked up at me with wide eyes, but didn't pull away. There was an innocence there, and something told me that this might've been the first time she'd asked a guard to accompany her to the gardens.

"I think I know what you should do," I said, softly.

"What?"

"Abdicate."

Her brow furrowed, and she yanked her hand from mine in horror, rearing back until she perhaps noticed my mischievous smile. "That is *not* funny," she said. "If I abdicate, there would be no one left to protect our kingdom, our people."

"Sorry. But you looked so forlorn, I didn't know what else to say," I said, ducking my head in an attempt to show humility.

She settled back down, resting her hand next to mine once more. "You don't look sorry. You look like you thought it was a wonderful joke."

"Because…" I turned toward her, reclaiming her hand with mine. "Because I think the fear you have is somewhat unfounded. After all, you've been preparing for this your entire life. This kingdom will flourish under your rule, even more than it has in the past." I held my breath and lifted her hand, bringing it to my lips. "You wouldn't let it be otherwise."

Her cheeks had turned beet red, but she made no move to remove her hand from mine. She licked her lips, and her gaze dropped to my mouth. If I hadn't known better, I would've thought she was expecting me to kiss her. And damn it all if I didn't desperately want to.

"I should get you back to your room," I said.

"Or we could stay here a little longer," she replied with a soft smile. "I like listening to you tell me I'm not going to ruin everything. I might even start to believe you."

I straightened, inching closer. "Is there anything else you'd like me to say? You're the princess. You can command me."

"I'm not that kind of princess," she said, mirroring my movement and leaning in. "Though it would be—"

"Here you are."

I jumped so fast I practically landed in the bushes behind me and Ayla stood up quickly, smoothing the folds of her dress with a bright red face. The wizard's apprentice stood in the clearing, a scowl on his face. I kept a wary eye on that staff of his, expecting him to use it on me at any moment.

"C-Cade," Ayla said, her voice high. "What's the matter?"

"Bronwen said you hadn't made it to your room yet, so I went searching for you." He turned in my direction, glaring at me.

"I asked Ward to take me out to the gardens for fresh air," she said, a little hotly. "I don't think I'm bound by any schedule, am I? Least of all one set by my maid."

Cade softened as he looked at her. "Of course not, but we do worry when you disappear. You should've told someone."

"I was here with a guard," she snapped. "I was fine."

"Clearly." His angry gaze turned to me again, and I found myself wondering just how quickly I was about to be sacked. The princess might vouch for me, but her handlers seemed to have other ideas about what should and shouldn't go on in the castle.

"Cade, please," Ayla whispered. "It's been a long night."

He held out his arm. "Then let's get you to bed and we can talk about it."

"Cade," Ayla said, a little more forcefully. "I will head to bed in a moment, I promise."

"I would feel much better if I took you myself."

"*Fine*," she huffed, grabbing the front of her skirt and marching forward. She barely acknowledged the wizard as she passed him, but she did offer me one final, longing look that told me she might not have been so opposed to a kiss after all. And that was worth whatever trouble the apprentice caused for me—even if it meant orders back to Críoch.

"Fascinating."

I spun on my heel to face the apprentice's master. Eoghan had his chin in his hand, observing me as if he were making a decision about something.

"Sir," I said, swallowing hard. "I can explain—"

"No need," he said, waving his hand. "But I do need you to come with me."

CHAPTER FIVE

CADE

I'd known that guard was trouble the moment I'd laid eyes on him. I'd intended to find Ayla in her room, to try to explain Eoghan's thinking. But when she wasn't there, I had a hunch she'd absconded with that damn scoundrel. I was just grateful I'd gotten there when I did.

Ayla, however, didn't seem to share my sentiment. "I can't believe you just did that, Cade. I'm *fine.*"

"Oh, yeah?" I scowled. "What were you doing with him?"

She gave me a very stern look. "That is *none* of your business."

It was, because that damn knight had been making eyes at her the entire night. I'd thought my princess smarter than that. He wasn't even of noble birth, having fought and wooed his way into the elite guard by brute strength and intellect. But his ambition was concerning. I wouldn't put it past him to be clamoring for the throne—using any means necessary.

"Stop looking at me like that," Ayla said. "Ward is… Well, he's sweet. And he's fun to talk to."

"You can talk to me," I snapped.

"I did," she said, turning on me. "And you dismissed me."

I furrowed my brow, my mouth dropping open. "I did not."

She shook her head, exasperated, and kept walking.

"I merely suggested that you might be better with a cooling off period," I said. "Eoghan knows what he's doing. That merchant wasn't going to listen to you."

"He would if Eoghan would get out of the way and let me handle things, for *once.*"

I bit my tongue instead of reminding her that calling a dignitary from a neighboring kingdom a boor wasn't exactly "handling" things. "Ayla." I jogged forward to take her arm gently. "I'm sorry you felt like I was ignoring you. But that doesn't mean you should go around making out with random guards."

"I didn't *make out* with anyone."

"Yeah, because I got there in time."

She yanked her arm from my grip and kept walking.

"Do you like him or something?" I asked.

Her face turned the color of a tomato, clashing with her auburn hair. "I told you, that's none of your business."

"So yes."

She let out a hiss and stomped away, slamming her bedroom door behind her. She wasn't usually so childish. Obviously, a princess and a knight were incompatible, and I was glad she at least knew that a relationship between them wouldn't be allowed to continue. No matter what that ambitious knight thought.

⤛⤛⤛⤛

I couldn't wipe the image of Ayla and that damn guard from my mind, no matter how much I tried. Although we'd been friends for years, she'd *never* looked at me like that, never seemed so ready to be kissed. It burned at me to know someone could just swoop in and confound her.

Eoghan was waiting for me in the vault, standing over the table in the center of the dungeon with my scrolls and notebooks still scattered about. "How familiar are you with the Pennlan stone?"

"As familiar as anyone, I suppose," I replied, knowing my master's penchant for mind games. "The fae call it the *seod croi.* It was gifted to the Pennlan king by a wizard then stolen by the fae queen after King Bresel died."

"And you know it's very powerful."

I nodded. "Not that anyone's used it in a few hundred years, but they say it's something to behold." I paused, furrowing my brow. "Does this have to do with my trial?"

Eoghan smiled. "Cade, you've been ready to leave us here for months now, but something has been holding me back. The fae have been becoming more brazen, and I felt more comfortable with two wizards protecting our princess."

I was somewhat flattered by his confidence in me, though I didn't think I was more of a deterrent than he was. "So my trial has to do with the fae."

He put his hand on the table, releasing a weary sigh. "I will let you in on a little secret, my dear apprentice. I'd never planned to stay long in this castle."

"What?"

"When I arrived here, there was a young king with an heir on the way, and he took me in and gave me a place to stay," Eoghan continued. "Up until then, I'd been traveling the lands in search of a place for my talents. Wizards are not known for staying long in one place, historically. But I was so taken by the generosity, I changed my mind.

"And when the king was dead, his young daughter without counsel, my desire to stay increased. It has been my absolute pleasure watching Ayla flourish from a precocious girl to a wise and steady ruler. But the itch to leave has grabbed me once more." He looked at me, his eyes full of mirth. "You see, it's not you I'm planning to send to another kingdom. It's me. I would like to venture to the other kingdoms, find their problems and solve them, the way I've done for Ayla."

I swallowed, my hopes lifting to the sky. "And me?"

"You could stay, if that's what your heart desires," Eoghan said.

Did it ever. Perhaps I could even convince the princess I was worthy of being more than her friend. Unlike that knight, I had something to offer my queen. Protection, magic. And most importantly, loving her not for what she was but for who she was in her heart.

"I could be convinced," I said, after a long pause.

"I thought as much," Eoghan said. "But there remain dangers at our borders. I firmly believe that if I left, the fae would take the opportunity to encroach onto our lands. You, alone, as powerful and skilled as you are, would not be enough. We need to arm our soon-to-be queen with the powers that are her birthright."

"The stone," I said softly.

"Your task is to find it and bring it back for Ayla. Once you've done that, I will officially give this role to you and move on to another adventure."

His words rang in my ears. It was hard to keep myself from jumping for joy. Everything, *everything* would be resolved if I just... ventured into a dangerous enemy land full of magical creatures hell-bent on killing me and retrieved a stone that no one had seen in sixteen years.

"Where do I begin?" I asked.

He smiled and straightened. "There are three fae our soldiers recently arrested in Críoch. I gave them orders to hold them until you arrive and can interrogate them." His face grew serious. "To use the spell I taught you on a real fae, not just a theoretical one."

I swallowed. "I will do my best."

"You'll need to leave tonight. We can't be sure there aren't fae spies in the castle, or even some from our allies. If anyone asks where you are going, you are venturing to complete your trial."

"Very well," I said.

"There is one more thing."

He swung his staff and the door opened, revealing the damn knight who'd almost kissed my princess. "I've asked Ward to accompany you."

I couldn't help scowling. "Why?"

"He's from Críoch," Eoghan said. "And can lead you there quickly. Besides that, he's the best swordsman in our guard and will ensure you reach the border swiftly."

I exhaled loudly, swallowing whatever arguments I had at the ready.

Eoghan perhaps hadn't fully disclosed our mission, so after we reached Críoch, and I managed to extract the information from the fae, we would part ways and I could continue by myself.

"I have the utmost faith in you both," Eoghan said. "But good luck."

>⇥ >⇥ >⇥ >⇥

I returned to my room, packing a small bag with just the essentials. Críoch was at least a week's ride from here, and after that, I might venture into fae territory and have to carry what I'd brought on foot. I'd have to leave my personal library of well-worn books behind, unfortunately.

But before I continued, I realized that I wouldn't be able to say goodbye to Ayla. She was probably asleep, and I could already hear what she'd say when she found out I'd left without seeing her one last time. I walked over to my bedside table and picked up the book that was sitting on top. I'd finished it the night before, and had been hoping to share it with Ayla so we could talk about it. But perhaps our conversation would have to wait until my return.

I scribbled a note on the first page, along with an apology for not delivering it in person. Using my staff, I transported the book from my desk in the vault to Ayla's in her room, several floors above. I wished I could transport myself there to tell her goodbye in person, but this would have to do. Such things were beyond wizard magic.

With a heavy heart, I tossed my bag over my shoulder and headed up toward the stables. But I hadn't gotten to the first landing before there was a very unwelcome sight waiting for me.

"Ready to go?" the knight asked.

I took a moment to scrutinize him. Up close, my initial suspicions were confirmed—he really wasn't anything special. Why Ayla thought he was worth spending a few moments with in the garden, I had no idea.

As I passed him, he turned militarily and began to climb after me. "Clearly, you don't like me."

"What gave you that impression?" I snapped, keeping my pace quick. "Why are you really coming? Is this some kind of punishment for you for almost kissing the princess?"

"I didn't almost kiss her."

I whirled around, my staff glowing gold as I prepared to blast him into next year. "You *kissed* her?"

"No." He smirked. "Have you?"

Instead of answering, I turned around and kept walking, forcing the magic back into my body so I wasn't tempted to use it on him.

"Eoghan gave me the job of protecting you until we get to Críoch," Ward replied. "And that's what I'm going to do. You don't have to like me. But you should know that I will be upholding my duty."

"I don't need *protection*," I snapped.

"Then are you familiar with the roads and cities we'll be encountering along our way?" he asked.

I slowed my gait. I…actually wasn't. I'd spent my entire life in the confines of this castle, barely even venturing into the rolling meadows outside the castle walls.

"And what's in it for you?"

"It's a direct order."

But he could pretend all he wanted—I saw right through him.

The stables were quiet at this hour, and it irked me how very comfortably the soldier walked into a stall and prepared a horse for himself. I wasn't a novice by any means, but horseback wasn't my favorite mode of transportation, and I had to use a little magic to lighten the saddle as I put it on the steed I chose. I worked as fast as I could, but the knight was still ready before me.

He kept looking around, as if waiting for someone. When I guided my horse up to meet his, he said nothing as he kicked the barrel of his horse and took off toward the front gates of the castle. I exhaled softly, hoping that the weeklong trek to Críoch would take half that, and followed.

Chapter Six

Ayla

I wasn't sure what exactly came over me in the gardens the night before. Perhaps the wine and brandy had made me brave, or perhaps I was just in need of some comfort. Or, maybe, I felt like I needed to control something in my life, and that knight was the handsomest thing to walk through the castle doors in years.

Not only that, but he was… I sighed happily. He was sweet. He listened and seemed genuinely interested in what I had to say. His faith in me was unwavering—perhaps only due to my position as his sovereign, but there was an earnestness about him. It made me want to share every one of my deepest, darkest secrets with him. And when he looked at me, I was ready and willing for anything.

Then Cade ruined it.

I knew he was being protective; that was his way. But how he'd even *found* me in the gardens, I had no clue. If he'd just been five minutes later, I might've known what it was to be kissed. Then I would've been waking up with a smile, instead of scheming how to get that knight alone again without anyone the wiser.

Bronwen arrived to bathe and dress me, braiding my hair and readying me for another day. I was so distracted that I barely remembered to mark the day on the calendar. For the first time, my impending coronation wasn't the only thing on my mind.

I ate my breakfast in my room, as usual, watching the blue sky out my open window along with the occasional bird that fluttered by. It was a beautiful spring day; perhaps I could break away from the castle to take a ride in the countryside. And I knew just the knight I'd ask to escort me.

"Ma'am?"

I jumped, stuck in my daydreams, as Bronwen appeared in the doorway. "Yes, Bronwen?"

"I was just checking to see if you'd finished your breakfast."

I shoveled three more unladylike spoonfuls of the gruel and berries into my mouth and nodded, not wanting to make her wait around because I was daydreaming. I wiped my face and sucked down my juice, earning a chuckle from my maid.

"Don't choke, please," she said.

"I'll try," I replied, taking another spoonful as I finished the meal. "Thank you."

She took the tray and walked out of the room, and I finally noticed something new on my desk. An old book with a red cover and a spine broken from use—definitely one of Cade's. Perhaps a peace offering?

But when I opened the cover and read the inscription, my heart sank to my stomach.

That little…

I slammed the book shut and grabbed the hem of my skirt, stomping off in search of my wizard for an explanation.

⤞⤞⤞⤞

"Good morning, Your Highness," Eoghan said before squinting at me. "Do you—"

I waved him off. "Has Cade left for his trial?"

"He has."

"And neither of you thought it appropriate for him to say goodbye to me first?"

Eoghan closed the book he was reading and rose slowly. "Time was of the essence. But I expect him back, victorious, in a few weeks."

"A few…weeks." I swallowed, my heart sinking to my stomach. "Do you think…?"

"I don't think anything could keep him from your coronation," Eoghan said. "But I couldn't wait any longer. We had an opportunity we haven't had in a while, and I thought it the best time to send him."

"What, did you find a dragon or something?" I snapped.

He chuckled. "Not so much. Shall we take a walk to your office so we can speak in private?"

I would've rather just yelled at him in public, but I followed, swallowing my anger. Eoghan always had ulterior motives, and they usually ended up being some brilliant political strategy that made everything work out just fine. If he had his reasons for sending Cade, I would have to trust him.

My office was a short walk, but I kept my pace quick, eager to hear the truth and perhaps stop worrying that Cade had been sent to almost certain doom. I didn't even sit at my desk, turning to cross my arms over my chest.

"Well?"

Eoghan shut the door. "The three fae we had arrested in Críoch weren't just any fae. One was a cousin of Leandra, a nephew to King Birch himself. I sent Cade to interrogate them." He smiled. "I have a feeling they may know where Leandra hid the stone."

"And if there's information?" I asked, a little breathlessly. "Will Cade continue into the fae realm?"

"I have given him instructions to return," Eoghan said. "Hence my confidence he'll be back. It would be entirely too dangerous for him to go to the fae realm by himself."

I sat back, relieved. Críoch was a one-week ride, so he'd be back within a fortnight, if he rode quickly.

"See?" Eoghan said with a smile. "Nothing to worry about. And perhaps if we get the information we're looking for, we might be able to retrieve the stone for you, and your coronation will be cause for extra celebration."

"I don't even know what to do with it," I said.

"It's in your bloodline," Eoghan said. "I'm sure you'll figure it out." He glanced at the clock behind me. "Now, Lord Weymouth has asked to meet with you this afternoon."

I groaned.

"The weather is so nice, I thought it might be a good idea to go for a ride. It might put him in a better humor than he was last night—as long as you keep your tongue."

It was less a warning than an order, and all I could do was dutifully nod.

>→ >→ >→ >→

When I arrived at the stables, I already had two guards waiting, and neither of them were Ward, which soured my mood further. I didn't feel comfortable asking after him, as I didn't want to arouse suspicion or get him in trouble. So I dipped inside the stables to avoid being seen—and delay the inevitable as long as possible.

Two horses poked their noses out to see me, and I patted them warmly. But I stopped outside an empty stall where Cade's horse should've been. I already missed him, as mad as I was that he'd interrupted my moment with Ward. Eoghan hadn't mentioned what would happen when Cade returned, but perhaps I should get used to his absence, as he would no longer be mine to boss around.

I kept walking toward the stalls until I noticed another horse missing. I doubled back to the front of the stalls, counting the horses. Two were waiting for myself and Lord Weymouth, another two for the guards who'd accompany us. Cade's was gone. As was…a sixth.

I walked out to the two waiting guards, ready to ask where the horse had gone, but to my chagrin, Lord Weymouth had finally arrived. His pristine white riding breeches were somewhat ridiculous yet paled in comparison to his velvet overcoat. I glanced at the sun overhead. It was a nice day, but after even thirty minutes under the sun, he would be sweating. I would have to stay upwind.

"Shall we?" I asked, mounting my horse. "There's a lovely pond nearby with plentiful waterfowl and tree cover. It's my favorite place to ride."

"I would rather see the local farms."

I bristled, debating if I should be a gracious host or the queen of this kingdom, and in the end, I deferred to grace. "Then let's ride."

What started as a quick pace slowed almost immediately, as Lord Weymouth didn't seem very comfortable on a horse. The two guards behind us wisely kept their silence, and I couldn't help but think about what Ward might say. The night before, I'd heard a guard snort when Lord Weymouth had been put in his place, and I had a hunch it was Ward. It had been a small victory before—

"I daresay, child, are you listening?"

I cursed myself for being distracted. "It's hard to hear over the hoofbeats," I said, innocently, as I tugged the reins to slow my mare. "What did you say?"

"I asked if you made it out to see the townsfolk often."

"Not too often." Eoghan had wanted to err on the side of caution, as I was the only one left in the Pennlan bloodline. "Hopefully I'll increase my visits when I'm queen."

"What will change when you're queen?" Weymouth asked. "Will you finally step out from under the shadow of your wizard overlord?"

I bristled. "That's unfair. Eoghan has been my guide since I was a child." But he was still somewhat overprotective. "I believe that the whole country will release a collective sigh of relief when a crowned monarch is back on the throne."

"And when there's another heir."

Another heir… I turned to him, frowning. "You mean, *my* child?"

"I don't see how another heir could be made."

I turned away from him, a slimy uncomfortable feeling crawling up my back. "I would surely have to be married first."

"And isn't that your first act as queen?" Weymouth asked. "After all, you said yourself that the country has been holding its collective breath. It might be easier when you are married with several children to take the mantle should something unfortunate happen to you."

It took everything in me not to stop my horse right there. "Let's hope nothing unfortunate happens, then," I said, after a long pause.

"Eoghan has certainly discussed marriage prospects with you, hasn't he?" Weymouth pressed. "You will be expected to forge a union with one of the four other kingdoms."

"I should think that decision would be mine and no one else's," I snapped, perhaps a little too heatedly. "And as it stands, I don't think marriage is the only way alliances are forged. There's something to be said for diplomacy and…" I probably shouldn't have finished my thought, but I couldn't help myself. "And tact."

He bristled and made a face. "Perhaps, princess, you should take your own advice. It wouldn't do to make enemies of your only human neighbor. Considering your history with the fae, you don't want them to be your only ally."

"And do you, Lord Weymouth, speak for your sovereign?" I snapped. "Are you so powerful that you can wield his good favor like a cudgel?"

"I have his ear—"

"Then perhaps I'll try the other one." I jerked on the reins, and my horse slowed to a stop. "I think this concludes our ride. I will leave a guard here to guide you home."

And with that, I turned my horse and galloped back toward the castle, not caring who followed.

CHAPTER SEVEN

WARD

When the wizard Eoghan had beckoned me down into the dungeon, I'd been absolutely sure I was about to be turned into a toad or become his latest experiment. But then he'd started talking about the stone, about how it was Ayla's only hope to reclaim Pennlan's former glory. Unsaid was that if *I* were the one to retrieve it from the dangerous fae realm for her, I would no longer be merely a guard in her employ. I would be a national hero.

That had been enough for me, and I'd readily accepted this task, even if it meant traveling with the surly wizard apprentice. After a morning of riding, it was clear he was completely lost outside the castle walls, perhaps spending too long holed up in his library and not enough time out in the countryside. More than once, I had to veer us back on course, which earned me more scorn.

But I kept to my purpose, thinking of the reward—monetary and otherwise—that would be waiting at the end. Besides that, we'd only be together for a week. The wizard would get information from these fae then return to the castle. Meanwhile, I would continue on in search of the stone. Eoghan had told me a human could move more discreetly in their realm, not attract as much attention as the wizard would. But he'd been very clear:

"Cade will not accept that I've given you this task instead of him," he'd said. *"So it is imperative that you not discuss this with him."*

I had my doubts the wizard apprentice would last longer than a week, especially when he was already slowing us down with his need to break after every hour.

"Let's rest the horses," he called to me.

My horse was fine—we were at a slow but consistent pace—but I led her to a small lake and tree cover, one of many that dotted the countryside. I dismounted and allowed her to drink and rest, before diving into my saddle bag. I'd not been given much time to pack, but I'd thought ahead to bring provisions like dried meat, one extra set of clothes, and a pouch for water. The wizard hadn't even brought a canteen —a decision he clearly regretted based on the way he was slurping the pond water.

"How far until we reach the first city?" he asked, wiping his mouth.

"Depends on how much we stop. It's not my preference to sleep in the open, but if we must, we must." I tore off another bite of the dried meat. "The farther we get from the castle, the more we'll have to contend with bandits and the like."

"And we'll be riding for seven days?"

Again, I nodded. "Give or take. If we get up before dawn each day, we can make better time and perhaps make it in six."

The wizard's stomach took that moment to release a loud growl, one that might've been heard back in Pennlan Castle. I swallowed my smirk. "Did you bring any food?"

"I thought we'd reach a village by now," Cade said. "But I'm sure we'll be there soon, right?"

"After nightfall."

He cursed and looked away, and I finally gave in. Ayla would want me to make sure her dear friend didn't die of starvation. "Here. This will tide you over."

The wizard looked at the jerky and begrudgingly took a piece, devouring it in one bite. Based on the look on his face, he wasn't sated.

"Are you ready to go?" I asked.

"We're resting the horses," he replied.

But I'd seen how gingerly he'd gotten off his horse. "Very well. Once your *horse* has recovered, we will continue."

He scowled at me. "I'm the one who gets to decide when and where we leave. This is my task, remember? You're just here as an escort."

I resisted the urge to bow. "Of course. But know that if we don't get going, we won't reach the next village before nightfall. We may not have a room to sleep in, and we may miss dinner." I rested my hands on my hips. "Just something to consider."

>—» >—» >—» >—»

We were on the road fifteen minutes later.

He wasn't pleased to keep going, but he kept his complaints to himself as we continued into the afternoon. What had started out as a nice morning had quickly turned into a hot one, and the sun was ruthless on the back of my neck. My canteen, which I'd filled up at the pond, quickly emptied. I was certain the wizard was dying of thirst.

My suspicions were confirmed when he spotted another small lake in the countryside and turned his horse in that direction. I didn't like that we were stopping again, but as he'd made *abundantly* clear, I wasn't in charge. At least not until we parted ways in Críoch.

A long, *long* six days from now.

He dunked his head into the water and drank loudly, sitting back and letting the water drip down his clothes. "Why is it so hot out?"

"You should buy a canteen when we reach the village," I said, dipping mine into the water. "Might help us avoid stopping."

"Buy?" He blinked. "With what money?"

"You don't..." I licked my lips carefully. Eoghan had given me a pouch of money for the journey, but I'd assumed he'd given the wizard the same amount. "You don't have any coin?"

He shook his head. "Do you..." He actually looked uncomfortable to be asking. "Do you have coin?"

I nodded. "Eoghan gave me some to pay for our journey."

"Why didn't he give me any money?" he said, more to himself.

"Did you ask him for any?"

"No."

"Then how were you going to eat?" I asked, tilting my head to the side. "Or where were you going to sleep?"

"I suppose…I didn't think about it."

Didn't think… I released a loud sigh. This poor sheltered soul. The other soldiers in Pennlan had said that he and the princess never got out of the castle, but I'd at least thought he had *some* idea of how things worked. Then again, he did have magic…

"I suppose you could just conjure yourself a bedroll," I said.

"That's not how magic works," he scoffed, as if *I* were the idiot. "You can't just make something from nothing."

It sure looked like he was making something from nothing back in Pennlan. "I see."

"I don't expect a human such as yourself to understand," he said, getting to his feet. "Shall we?"

"You're in charge."

>⇥ >⇥ >⇥ >⇥

Multiple stops pushed our arrival time later than I would've liked, but there was still light when our horses padded into the village. I was looking forward to a hearty meal and perhaps a tankard of ale to wash away the day. By the looks of the wizard, he was feeling the same.

Our late arrival also meant the rooms were scant, but there was one left with two beds. I paid for it out of the coin Eoghan had given me, as well as one meal for the wizard.

"Here's your bowl," I said, shoving the bowl into his hand. "Go get yourself something to eat."

"Where are you going?"

"To buy you a canteen and some provisions so we don't have to stop as much tomorrow," I said. "Don't wait up."

Unfortunately, the shop I'd eyed when we'd arrived half an hour before was already closed. I supposed it was just as well, as the wizard would probably have some other excuse as to why we needed to stop tomorrow.

Instead of returning to the inn, I took a loop around the village—and found a bustling tavern. I settled in, paying for my ale out of my own stash of coin (significantly less than the one Eoghan had given me) and took a long sip. It was warm and watery, but it was more appetizing than eating with the apprentice. And when it was done, I ordered a second.

Knowing we had another long day, I took my time with it, contemplating my situation while watching the suds dance along the top.

I envisioned what might happen when I returned to Pennlan with the stone in my hand. They might shut down the kingdom to celebrate my accomplishment. I'd be awash in riches beyond my wildest dreams—more than anything a boy from a ramshackle farm outside Críoch should've dared to hope for.

And if I was exceptionally fortunate, I might get more than a stolen moment in the garden with Ayla. I let a smile grow on my face at the thought. Everything I wanted was in my grasp, as long as I kept my mouth shut and the wizard apprentice happy for six more days.

Though the latter might be harder than anticipated. I hadn't expected a smooth trip, but he was utterly hopeless. No wonder his master had asked me to accompany him. I'd be shocked if he could make it back to Pennlan without me once we parted ways. But that wasn't my worry.

I took another sip then paused, the hair rising on the back of my neck. Someone was watching me. I put down the tankard and did my best to look unbothered but cast a furtive glance to my left and right. Everyone seemed lost in their own ales. I made like I was stretching, tilting my head back, and I spotted the watcher—a man in the corner who looked down just as I saw him.

My pulse quickened. The telltale pointed ears, just visible under the hood, the smooth skin, the golden eyes. *Fae.* So close to Pennlan castle?

I turned around again, taking another long sip of my ale, steadying my breath. I had a choice to make: engage the fae, which would potentially bring out his friends but stop them from continuing to Pennlan and Ayla, or remain as I was and keep a low profile, as Eoghan had instructed. Somehow, I didn't think the wizard had anticipated a fae this close to Pennlan.

I paid another copper for my second ale and rose, purposefully ignoring the fae in the corner to see what he might do. I waited outside the front door of the tavern, hiding in the shadows to see if the creature might follow me. Ten minutes after I'd left, he emerged from the tavern, casting his suspicious gaze around. Up close, he was breathtakingly perfect, but I'd been told such a thing was usually due to magic.

I kept my distance, just enough to prevent him from noticing I was there, but not enough so that I'd lose him. But perhaps he sensed my presence, because he moved quickly, cutting through alleys and side streets. Finally, he slowed between a pair of taverns, coming to a stop in the middle of the alley.

"Show yourself, human."

His voice was velvety and deep, and there was something ethereal about it. I stepped out from the shadows into the moonlit alley and rested my hand on my sword, ready for anything.

"What is your business in Pennlan?" I asked.

"I could ask you the same thing," he said. "A knight from the princess's guard and her wizard, traveling together toward Críoch." He flashed a knowing grin. "I wonder what for?"

My pulse quickened. *How did he know*? "Fae aren't allowed in Pennlan. You're a long way from the border."

He just stared at me, his golden eyes shining in the dark. "And your so-called quest is a sham."

I pulled my sword. "I'm sure."

He cracked a smile. "Is this what you want to do, human boy? Have you ever fought a fae? Is whatever hatred you have toward our people worth your life?"

Instead of answering, I ran toward him, lifting my weapon and bringing it down. The fae moved too quickly for me, and my blade hit air. But I'd had my share of dirty fights, and this monster didn't deserve my honor. I pulled a small knife from a holster under my shirt and lunged at the fae.

This blade was true, and the fae gasped in pain as my knife slit his arm. He took two or three steps backward, looking at the red blood in his hands, before disappearing in a puff of…butterflies? They fluttered up to the night sky and disappeared, leaving nothing but blood on my knife.

I stared at it, unsure if it was a dream or I'd actually fought the fae and won. But one thing was sure—I needed to go get that damn wizard.

CHAPTER EIGHT

CADE

It had never dawned on me how very privileged my meals were until I had to sit down and eat common food. The stew was mostly water, the meat gristle, the vegetables sparse. The bread that came with it was days old, perhaps, and had started to mold. But after riding all day with nothing else to eat, I powered through. And when my bowl was empty, I rose to get myself seconds.

The cook, or whomever it was ladling out the food, gave me a look. "What?"

"I would like some more," I said.

"Do you have coin to pay for more?"

I opened my mouth, feeling somewhat foolish that I hadn't considered that. "No…?"

"Your traveling companion only paid for one meal. So that's all you get."

And with that, he slammed the top on the pot and dragged it back to the kitchen. I stared at the space he'd left, shocked that someone could be so rude at such an innocent question. When I turned around, I noticed that the others in the room were staring at me. I brought my bowl back to the table and sat down, scraping it for the final bits of anything I might eat. My stomach felt completely empty, and I doubted I'd be able to go to sleep with it grumbling so loudly.

Not only that, my ass was sore, my skin raw from being in the wind and sun all day, and every joint screamed in pain with the smallest movement. I was already dreading tomorrow's return to the torture; if the knight was to be believed, we'd be up and gone before the sun rose. Then we'd do it again and again until we reached Críoch—a week's journey.

I rubbed my face, scouring my brain for the litany of spells I'd learned as an apprentice and coming up with nothing that could ease the journey. Though Eoghan thought I was ready to venture out on my own, I still felt like magic came secondhand to me. I felt it, deep in my bones, but the practice of channeling through my staff was one I still hadn't gotten used to.

Perhaps this was part of Eoghan's plan. Shove me out of the nest to fly or fall on my own merits.

At this rate, falling seemed like the more reasonable outcome. How in the world did he expect me to face a country full of dangerous fae?

My stomach gurgled again, and I stared at my bowl. I supposed I could hunt down the knight and demand he give me more coin for dinner, but that seemed like…defeat? I hadn't handled money in my life —everything I needed was brought to the castle—but surely, *surely* I should've thought to prepare more. That might've been my first test of this trial, and I'd failed.

I scraped the empty bowl once more, annoyed at it, and the knight, and everything else in this tavern.

"Can't you conjure up a bedroll or something?" Idiot knight.

And yet…I straightened, mentally slapping myself. I couldn't create something from nothing, but I could surely create something from *something*. If I hadn't inhaled the food, and left a little in the bowl, I could've cast a multiplication spell on the meat, potatoes, and broth and made more.

Instead of sitting here pouting, I could've solved my problem.

Good grief.

The knight was right to be so dismissive of me—I might've had magic, but if I didn't have the intelligence to back it up, I wouldn't last one day in the fae realm. Forget watery stew and gristle, I would have to come up with my own food and shelter in the thick of enemy territory. If I was already whining now, I'd be dead in days once I crossed the border.

So I had two choices: either continue to stubbornly ignore and hate him for making a move on Ayla or put aside my ego for the next six days and learn from him. After all, it wouldn't matter how many sweet words he whispered to my princess. She'd forget about him as soon as I returned with the stone in hand.

>→ >→ >→ >→

The knight was nowhere to be found when I walked into the small room we'd be sharing, but perhaps that was for the best. I wasn't going to sit around and whine about my present circumstance anymore. I would toughen up and live with it, or I'd use the talents I was born with to make things easier for myself.

Starting with the bed. It smelled of dirt and body odor, and the sheets hadn't been changed in some time. But instead of complaining, I cast a cleaning spell on the sheets. I'd used it for clothes in the past, but it would work for this purpose. Gold magic slid from the top of my staff, curling over the grimy sheets and wool blankets, agitating dirt and bugs from the individual fibers. When I was satisfied, I sat down on the bed and winced—it was hard as a rock.

But not for long. I considered my litany of spells in my arsenal and opted for a multiplication spell on the stuffing in the mattress, taking what was there and making more of it until the seams were about to burst. I did the same for the threadbare pillow then laid back down on the bed.

It still wasn't as comfortable as my bed back at the castle, but it would do.

A yawn broke free as my eyes closed. Tomorrow, I'd cast more. Tonight, I'd be grateful I found my head.

Hurried footsteps echoed from the hallway outside, and I sat up quickly, grabbing my staff as the knob turned. The knight came barreling in, concern on his face.

"What's wrong?" I said, standing.

"I need you to come with me."

"Why?"

"Don't ask questions. And bring your stuff."

"Are we leaving?" I asked, a little mournfully. "What's going on?"

He ran his hand over his face. "I found a fae. Here, in town."

"You…*what*?" I blinked, sure I'd misheard him. "You found a fae? So close to Pennlan?"

He nodded.

"Well, did you kill it?"

"No, it escaped."

"Why'd you let it do that?" I barked, perhaps louder than I should've. There was a fae a day's ride from Ayla, and it was only because I remembered Eoghan was there protecting her that I didn't run back to the stables and return to Pennlan myself.

"It wasn't intentional," he said. "I stabbed it, and it disappeared into a puff of butterflies."

"Butterflies?" I leaned in, scenting a little ale on his breath. "Are you sure you saw what you think you saw?"

He pursed his lips and yanked a knife covered in blood from beneath his shirt. "I don't walk around with a bloody knife on the regular."

I was about to argue with him when my fingertips touched the blood. Immediately, the scent of honey filled my mouth as the magic in the blood buzzed on my skin. It was the oddest sensation, and I rubbed my fingers together, mesmerized for a moment at the way I could *taste* the creature at just the touch of its blood.

"Well?"

"Well, what?" I said.

"Well, what should we do? You're the fae expert."

I opened and closed my mouth, realizing he was *actually* looking to me to have the answers here. "Tell me what happened—exactly," I said, to buy myself some time.

"I was at the tavern," he said. That explained the light scent of ale on his breath. "I felt like someone was watching me—it was a fae. I left to see if he'd follow. When he didn't, I waited around until *he* left then trailed him. He knew I was following him, and he knew who we were."

I tilted my head. "He did?"

"He knew you were a wizard and that we were headed to Críoch." He put his hands on his hips. "He said our quest was a sham."

"Obviously, that was a lie."

"Fae can't—"

"They absolutely can twist the truth," I snapped. "Then what?"

"We got into a scuffle. I nicked him, he disappeared into butterflies. Damndest thing I ever saw." He shook his head. "Do all fae do that?"

I honestly had no clue, so I changed the subject. "And instead of coming to get me, you thought you'd engage him yourself? Even though you have no magic?"

He swallowed hard. "I didn't think I'd need magic to fight him."

"Faced many fae in Críoch, have you?"

His gaze darkened, telling me all I needed to know. I couldn't help but feel a little superior to him; although I hadn't faced a fae, either, I *had* studied them extensively. And after the miserable day of fumbling through basic tasks, it was nice to have a leg up on the knight for once.

"We have training," he said. "I thought it would be enough."

"Clearly, it wasn't," I said, earning a look of scorn from him.

"Yes, clearly." He shifted. "Well? What are your orders?"

I had no idea. Eoghan had said it was important to get to Críoch as quickly as possible, and he wouldn't be pleased if we headed back to Pennlan. We could scour the village for the fae, but he was probably long gone by now. At least, I hoped he was. If his final destination *was* Pennlan, Eoghan would see to it that he was properly disposed of—better than I could, in any case.

The knight's gaze was focused on me. Unless I wanted him to think me a complete weakling, I would have to project a little strength.

"In the morning, we will send a letter to Eoghan to let him know what we saw," I said.

"That's…it?" Ward said with a frown. "I found a fae, you're going to just…let him continue to Pennlan? To Ayla?"

I jumped at the *familiar* use of her name. "*Princess* Ayla will be fine as long as Eoghan is there. We will let him know to improve the defenses around the castle."

"Through a letter?" He shook his head. "Don't you have some kind of magical something that could do it instantly?"

I did, but I hadn't attempted it at such a distance before. I didn't want the knight to know that, though. "There are too many charms on the castle to get through. So the human way will have to work."

"I worry if we wait until it goes through the post, it'll be too late," Ward said. "We should return to Pennlan tonight."

"Absolutely not," I said, earning a look of surprise from the knight. "Look, you have no idea what sort of magic Eoghan has. He makes me look…well, amateurish. The Erlking even fears him. The castle is protected by all manner of spells to keep the fae out."

Ward didn't seem impressed. "I still think we should act quickly—"

"I told you," I said with all the confidence I didn't feel, "this is my task. You asked for an order, and I'm giving you one: we will rest here tonight and continue in the morning."

He clenched his jaw, the argument resting on the tip of his tongue, but his training seemed to kick in. "Very well. Good night."

Without another word, he blew out the candles, marched over to the bed, and lay down, ignoring the smell and sweat and dirt on his mattress.

As I returned to my bed, stretching out on the comfortable mattress and staring at the dark ceiling, I second-guessed my decision to stay in a town with an injured fae lurking about. But that thought was lost in seconds as sleep overtook me.

CHAPTER NINE

WARD

I hated making mistakes. All night long, I tossed and turned on the lumpy mattress, thinking of what I might've done differently. I certainly *had* thought I could take on a fae; every guard in Críoch had been taught how. But faced with an actual creature, that training was about as useful as the wizard's thinly-veiled criticisms.

Before we left the village, Cade wrote a letter to his master to tell him what had happened and to keep an eye out. I was sure the letter would be an embellished version of my failures, but hopefully Eoghan still had faith that I could carry out the task he'd given me.

Neither of us were in a mood to chat, so I spent the morning ruminating. Even though I'd grown up a stone's throw from their lands, I knew very little about our neighbors beyond the wall. As children, we would sneak across to retrieve flowers as proof of our idiotic bravery, but we were never caught—at least, not that I knew. There very well could've been fae in the trees that allowed us mercy *because* we were children. I doubted I'd get the same when I ventured into the fae realm this time.

At the very least, I needed to know the extent of their abilities and what assumptions I had to throw out the window. My brief interaction with the fae had taught me more than I'd learned in my entire nineteen years. The wizard would certainly be a useful asset—if he'd get off his high horse.

"The only thing you need to know about the fae is that if you see one, leave them alone and come find me."

That'll be hard when I'm in the fae realm and you're on your way back to Pennlan castle. "Surely, there's something you can tell me. You said their magic is different from yours, right? How so?"

"It's complicated."

Damn it all. "I'm not a simpleton. You can tell me."

"What do you know about wizard magic?"

I paused. *Nothing.* "A little."

He seemed pleased with my answer and didn't say anything else.

But perhaps if I tried a different tactic… "I clearly don't know anything about this, and you are the expert. We have a long ride, and you may need my assistance one day in a fight. At least tell me how to kill them if my sword won't do it."

He remained silent for a while, and I was sure he would ignore my question.

"They're tricky, and they don't play by any rules," he finally said. "They can heal themselves and fly away and do all manner of things that even we don't know."

"So there's no defense against the fae?" I asked. "I should simply roll over and die if we encounter one again?"

Cade released a loud sigh. "Iron."

"What?"

"Iron is their weakness. It's why Caecarcem is an iron prison. Strips them of their powers—and why we've stocked the armory in Pennlan with iron arrows." He glanced at me. "I don't suppose you brought any with you, did you?"

I shook my head. All I had for a weapon was my sword and my wits.

"It's just as well," he said with a smug smile. "The next time you see a fae, come get someone who can actually do something about it instead of mucking things up yourself."

It was all I could do not to throw my sword at his head.

>→ >→ >→ >→

As before, the wizard wanted to stop every time we saw a pond, but he'd somehow rustled up a meat pouch and canteen identical to mine. Unfortunately, it didn't seem to make our journey go any faster.

The next village on our path was only half a day's ride, so we arrived mid-afternoon. Due to the early hour, the only inn in town still had two rooms available, and the wizard ventured up to rest before dinner. I perhaps should've done the same, but I wanted to see about additional provisions. I doubted there would be anywhere to purchase iron weapons here; most likely, I'd be doing my final shopping in Críoch, but it didn't hurt to check.

I circled the village three times, which wasn't hard; there couldn't have been more than ten buildings in the collection at all, and most were dedicated to farming supplies. There were still several hours until dinner, so I leaned against a wooden fence and watched a field full of goats and chickens in front of a small, ramshackle house. It was so familiar that it almost made me homesick—almost. My childhood wasn't rough by any measure, but it hadn't been the stuff of nostalgia. I'd gone to bed hungry more nights than I could count until I realized I could make my own way.

"Looking for a job?"

I glanced at my left where an old woman had appeared out of nowhere. She had to have been at least seventy, with stringy white hair and a face that looked like it had been in the sun for most of her life.

"Not particularly," I said. "Just watching."

"Hope you aren't planning on stealing anything. You look like the kind of man who could."

I snorted. "I used to be, but not anymore. Found out pretty quickly I could make more coin preventing crime than causing it."

She nodded, looking me up and down. "You're a guard, aren't you?"

"I am. In Her Majesty's service."

"Long way from Pennlan."

"On a special mission," I said. "We're in town for the evening. Any recommendations on things we should see?"

She snorted and reached into her apron to feed the chickens. "Not much to see here. Just a sleepy town that travelers pass through. Nobody really pays much attention to what we need here."

I furrowed my brow. "What do you need?"

"The usual needs of farmers. More rain, more feed, more hands." She chuckled. "But at the moment, we have a griffin problem."

"A gri…Griffin? As in the fae creatures?" I blinked. "That's impossible. They're only in the fae realm."

"And they have great big wings they can use to fly over that stone wall," she said with a surly laugh. "A nest of them has settled in a forest nearby and they come here to pick off our livestock."

I licked my lips. Every so often, one of the border guards would swear he saw a griffin in the sky above the wall, but we'd all assumed he'd had too much to drink. Surely, someone would've noticed if a whole pack of them had left the safety of the fae realm and settled here.

"Perhaps you could help?" she asked. "Find the nest and eradicate it so we can stop losing cows and sheep and goats."

We had another mission, one that would benefit me much more than helping out a bunch of farmers. But there was something that made me feel for this woman. I knew what it was to have an unfair hand dealt my way, especially out here.

"I'm not sure what I could do," I said, after a moment.

"I might be able to give you something in return," she said. "A chicken, or even a goat."

"We're traveling," I replied with a sad shake of my head. She was surely desperate if she was offering me such a thing.

"What about iron?"

I blinked, turning to her quickly. "Beg your pardon?"

"They're fae creatures, aren't they?" she said with a knowing look. "You'll need something to kill them. Back when the fae were allowed in these lands, my father would keep a stash of iron arrows around in case they would come to call. Never trusted those devils, you know."

I nodded, a little dumbly. Was it serendipity that the one thing I was searching for was here? Or was there something else?

I scrutinized this woman carefully and could find no fault with her. She seemed an honest woman working her land and in need of a problem-solver. "Where can I find the nest?"

She pointed to the east. "Keep going along that road until you reach the large hill, then you'll see a tree line. They're in the dead center of the forest. But you won't find them until nightfall—that's the best time to strike."

Nightfall, perhaps not great for me to be out and about, especially considering the long ride we had in the morning. But if I was to venture into the fae realm, iron would be crucial to defend myself. Iron arrows would be even better, as I was an expert marksman.

"Well?" she asked. "Will you help me? Or keep to your travels like everyone who's come before you?"

I exhaled loudly. She was laying the guilt on thick. "Fine. I'll help. Where are the arrows?"

⤞ ⤞ ⤞ ⤞

I followed her into an old barn in severe need of repair. I was surprised it was still standing with that much rot in the walls. Everything inside here seemed to have been in its prime twenty years ago; rusted plows sat in the corner, and old scythes and axes hung on the wall. One weathered saddle was perched on the wall next to a horse that was probably born before I was.

"You've seen better times," I said.

She grunted. "We all have. Things haven't been right since we closed the border to the fae."

"I thought you didn't like them."

"I didn't say I liked them. I just said it was better when we had open trade. The other human kingdoms don't trade as well with Pennlan.

69

They have their own farmlands and industry. The only thing our kingdom had was access to the fae and their wares."

My suspicion was aroused once more; she was talking an awful lot of politics for a simple farm hand. My brother couldn't even tell me who was on the throne in Pennlan, let alone discuss economics.

"The arrows?" I prompted, resting my hand on my sword, just in case.

"Hold your horses," she said, walking to the corner where a large pile of hay rested. She began to dig, and for a moment, I thought she was just mad, but then a large trunk became visible. Once all the debris was cleared, she unlocked it and struggled to lift the heavy top but managed it before I could step in to help her.

Inside, there were moth-bitten quilts and old family heirlooms, including a solid gold necklace that might fetch a nice price. But the real treasure was buried at the bottom. A quiver full of black-tipped arrows, and a bow made of dark wood.

"Will these do?" she asked, handing them to me.

The arrows were heavier than the flint ones I'd become accustomed to, but with practice, I might be able to adjust. And if all else failed, I could just jab them into whatever fae I came across.

For a moment, I considered just walking out with the arrows and never returning. But this barn, her plight, even her face was familiar and tugged at my memories. I'd always wanted to help my brother more than I had; he wasn't a bad man, just struggling.

I shook myself. Why I was being nostalgic, I had no clue. But the fact of the matter was, I could probably take a few hours from my journey to help this woman with her griffin problem. Then, in the morning, I'd continue to Críoch with a quiver full of arrows and a sated conscience.

"Well?" she asked, looking at me. "Will they do?"

"They will." I pulled the quiver strap over my shoulder. "I'll bring you good news later this evening."

"You'd better be done before my bedtime or I won't answer the door."

Chapter Ten

Cade

I managed to clean the mattress and make it more comfortable, as I'd done the night before, but sleep wouldn't come. The sun was bright outside the window. My stomach was still grumbling and tired of the dried meat I'd conjured from what the knight had brought. Instead of lying there for the next few hours, I got up and took a walk.

Small was certainly an apt description of the village. The persistent smell of manure and livestock made my nose twitch. It was the sort of town where people seemed to know everyone, and anyone new was most assuredly a traveler. But the people seemed nice, waving at me as I passed.

I reached the end of the town and my gaze drew to a shop. Was that...

Was that a library?

I opened the door and a small bell dinged above my head. There was no one at the clerk's table, but the smell of books drew me toward the stacks. The shop was a single room, every inch filled with some kind of book imaginable.

I walked the length of the store, greedily drinking in every title and wondering what might lie between the covers. Some titles I recognized from Eoghan's library, but others were brand new. I hadn't tackled even a fraction of what was in the vault, and yet, here I was, eager to add to my collection.

I missed my books back in the castle, and not having them to read before falling asleep was a hardship I hadn't gotten used to. But perhaps I might find something lightweight I could take. I had room in my satchel, and if I was clever enough, I could magic it to a smaller size so it wouldn't weigh me down.

The word *wizard* caught my eye and I pulled a book down from just above my head. It was titled *A History of Wizards in the Modern Age*, though based on the age of the book, modern might be a stretch. I carefully leafed through the pages, curious that such a book existed. Literature on wizards was scant because wizards were so rare, so Eoghan told me once. Though my master wasn't as interested in books as I was, he would surely find something like this of value.

"Oh, someone did come in." The clerk was an older woman with gray hair balled onto the top of her head. "Can I help you?"

I lifted the book to show her. "I would like to have this book."

"Three silvers."

I looked back at the book, and only then remembered I had no money of my own. I considered the book. It wasn't necessary, but the knight had some coin I could borrow. Perhaps I'd offer to replenish his food stores again…or do something of the sort.

"Give me five minutes."

I handed her the book and left, making a beeline back to the inn. The knight wasn't in the dining room yet, nor was he in the room he'd reserved for himself. But after some searching, I found him in the stables, brushing down his horse.

"Can I have three silvers?" I asked.

He stopped, turning to me. "Why?"

"Because I need it."

"For what?"

I scowled. "None of your business."

"Whores cost more than three silvers, if they're good." He turned back to the horse.

All I could do was stutter. "It's not for…*that*. And how do you know how much whores cost?"

"Then what's it for?" he asked, keeping his back to me. "This money was given to me by Eoghan for the purpose of paying our way to Críoch. It's not for idle nonsense."

I scowled. "Fine, it's for a book."

He snorted and put the brush down, grabbing a pick. "So it is idle nonsense. The answer is no."

"Do you even know how to read?" I snapped, narrowing my gaze at him.

"I do," he said, without the faintest trace of annoyance. "But more importantly, books are heavy. It's not as if we have a whole lot of space to carry things that we don't need."

I clicked my tongue. "I have magic, you dolt. I can make it weightless if I want."

"The fact remains: we don't have the coin for this."

"How about if…" I hated having to barter my magic for money, but this book was too good to pass up. "If you give me three silvers, I'll make sure your store pouches don't go empty until we reach Críoch."

He surveyed me for a moment then returned to his horse. "Tempting, but no."

It was then that I saw his sword—and a new quiver of arrows slung over his shoulder. "And where did you get those arrows?"

"I've been offered a small job," he said, turning to me. "In exchange for iron arrows."

"By whom?"

"Local."

"What kind of job?" I crossed my arms over my chest. "And I thought we don't have time for idle nonsense? If we have enough money to last us to Críoch—"

"The job is in exchange for these arrows."

I blinked. "But you…have the arrows. Why not just take them and run?"

"Because that's what a coward would do," he said, finally finishing with his horse and looking at me. "Are you done yet? I was hoping for a few hours without having to hear your nagging."

I narrowed my gaze. "Do you want help on this job?"

"I'm perfectly capable of managing on my own."

He began to walk out of the stable, but I put my staff in his way. If he got to go off on some heroic side-quest, I wanted my book. "Give me the three silvers."

"*Fine*, you utter child." He reached into his pouch and pulled out three silvers. "Here. Go buy your damn book. I don't want to hear another word about it."

><»><»><»><»

I returned to the store just as she was closing and purchased the book, happily carrying it back to the inn with a smile on my face. It would be hard to keep myself from staying up all night to read, but I'd have a few hours to get through a good chunk of it.

By the time I returned, dinner was being served, so I got my bowl and settled in at an empty table in the corner, gingerly opening the cover of my new treasure and diving in.

> **This book is a compendium of legends, lore, and spoken traditions across the human and fae realm of the deeds and conquests of wizards of the past five hundred years.**

Off to a brilliant start. I finished my stew in minutes and dove back in, skimming the introduction as it was a wordy background on the creation of wizards and how…

> **It is estimated that for every ten men born, there will also be one wizard.**

I frowned. Ten men to one wizard? That was…no longer accurate.

It was more like ten thousand humans to one wizard these days. I was the only wizard born in the past twenty years, so Eoghan had told me—and why he'd traveled all the way to the southern isles to retrieve me for training.

How old was this book anyway? I carefully scanned the first few pages, hoping for some sign of a date, but came up empty. I decided to keep reading. The first wizard described predated the publication by five hundred years, but I'd never heard of him. Same for the second wizard, who had successfully killed a dragon terrorizing the kingdom of Driwania, near the mountains. Ten more wizards, and I realized that my wizard history education might've been lacking. It wasn't as if we didn't study it, but Eoghan's knowledge was somewhat limited in this area. Another good reason for me to have bought this book.

"Idle nonsense." That knight was a moron. He would've left this knowledge behind because he didn't see the value in education. I did actually doubt he could read—it probably wasn't taught wherever he was raised. And clearly, he wasn't wholly focused on our mission, as he was off helping locals with whatever problems they had in exchange for iron arrows.

I frowned. Then again, having some iron on hand might not be a bad idea. We'd already encountered one fae on this journey, and although I hadn't seen any others, we might find more. And I'd definitely have to deal with my fair share of them once I left the knight in Críoch.

Hm. Maybe the old woman would have some more arrows she'd give me if I helped him.

I closed the book and, when no one was looking, magicked it back to my room. Then I performed a small location spell on the knight and followed the trail.

>–» >–» >–» >–»

Dusk had fallen, and the knight was on the road leaving town, his sword and the quiver on his back. I had to jog to catch up to him, but I made it.

"What do you want?" he asked, looking at me. "Don't tell me you're back for more money."

"No," I said, panting a little from the run. "I thought you could use some help."

"I don't."

"Don't you?" I asked, straightening. "What sort of job is this, anyway?"

He sighed and turned to keep walking. "The old lady said there's a nest of griffins nearby that have been picking off her livestock. She wants me to go to this forest up ahead and kill them."

I about tripped over my feet. "Griffin? Like the fae creatures?"

"Yeah."

"And you believed her?"

"Why wouldn't I?" he said. "She had no reason to lie to me."

But I wasn't convinced. Something was off here. "So you happened to come across an old woman who happened to have iron arrows after we discussed the weapon today. And she wants you to venture into a forest and kill fae."

"That's about the long and short of it."

I couldn't help the incredulous chuckle. "And again, you believed her—even though griffins haven't been seen south of the border in years."

He slowed his steps. "What are you saying?"

"I'm saying that something smells fishy—or more importantly, it smells like fae trickery." I held out my hand. "Let me see those arrows."

"What? No." He pulled the quiver higher on his shoulder. "Go back to the inn."

But I used my staff to pluck one of the arrows and bring it to me. The moment it touched my skin, I smelled it—that sweet honey smell. Fae magic was all over it. I concentrated to clear the enchantment, and the iron-tipped arrow morphed into a single strand of hay.

"W-what the hell did you do to it?" Ward barked. "Change it back!"

"These iron arrows aren't that, and the old woman was a fae," I said, throwing the hay to the ground. "You were tricked." I smirked. "Again."

His mouth opened and closed like a fish as he blinked at me. "You're…you're joking."

I summoned the entire quiver and performed the same spell, reducing all the arrows to strands of hay. His eyes bugged out, and he let out a filthy curse that seemed appropriate for a soldier of his upbringing.

"Fae are wily," I said, a little smugly.

"But for what purpose did that fae send me into the forest?" he asked. "If there are no griffins there…"

"My guess?" I leaned on my staff, somewhat enjoying this moment of superiority. "They probably had a cage or trap in there that you would've fallen into. Perhaps they even thought I might join you."

"But *why*?" Ward shook his head. "I still don't understand what the fae's goal is."

"Obviously, to stop us."

"If they wanted to stop us, the fae would've put a dagger in my heart that first night," Ward said, his gaze on the forest beyond. "I think they want something else."

He did have a point. I followed his gaze, smelling the air for any sign of the fae, but it was just the usual lingering scent of grass and manure. "Whoever they are, they aren't around anymore. Perhaps they meant to return in the morning to claim their prize."

"I'm not a prize."

"Well, I'm going back to the inn to sleep," I said. "But if you do decide to venture into any more fae traps, please be sure to give me the gold so I can continue without you."

CHAPTER ELEVEN

AYLA

I feigned illness to get out of having another meal with Lord Weymouth, and to my great pleasure, he left the next morning. Whether planned or due to my abrupt cessation of our conversation, I didn't care. As long as he was on his way back to his kingdom.

"Will you finally step out from under the shadow of your wizard overlord?"

His words had settled uncomfortably on my skin, and as much as I tried to tell myself they didn't matter, they echoed in my memory as I lay awake, watching the shadows dance on the ceiling. I knew that by allowing myself to be rattled, I was letting him win. But as soon as I turned to think of something else, they would come back and the spiral would begin anew.

I came up with a thousand different comebacks, rationalizations for why Eoghan had been so essential to this kingdom and my own upbringing. He was the one who'd found my tutors, who'd taught me what it meant to be a leader. His steady hand on this kingdom for nearly my entire life and was the only reason it hadn't fallen to ruin, either thanks to the fae or the other kingdoms that were now vying for my attention.

In the morning, I ate my breakfast slowly, hoping to postpone Eoghan's lecture about decorum and politeness and treating our allies with respect. And then, instead of being the queen I was supposed to be, I disappeared out into the greens, eager to get some fresh air and clear my mind.

The sky was blue, the wind cool, and soon the tight ball of nerves that had settled in my chest loosened. Above me, the royal guard patrolled, waving to me when they spotted me out and about. I'd been so busy with Weymouth, I hadn't had a chance to look for Ward again.

Although it might've been more discreet to search for him, I decided to go straight to the source—Captain Gabhann. She was a stalwart woman, getting on in years as she'd been old when my father was crowned. She had been another constant presence in my life, much like Eoghan. When she saw me coming, she turned and whistled at her guard to drop whatever they'd been doing and come to attention.

"Good afternoon, Captain," I said with a smile. "How are my guards today?"

"Your Majesty," she said, bowing at the hip. "Very well. Shall I gather them for a demonstration?"

"No, please continue with your usual drills," I replied, looking out across the green and searching for that familiar face. Ward wasn't amongst them. "I was wondering if you could tell me a little more about our newest arrival from Críoch?"

"Who? Ward?" I remained stoic in the face of her curiosity, but blessedly, she didn't ask for a reason. "Good find. Very adept with a sword, bow and arrow, and general weaponry. Very strategic-minded, too. I'm sure that's why Eoghan asked him to accompany Cade to Críoch."

My stoicism vanished. "I'm sorry, *what*? Ward went with Cade? Why?"

"Eoghan merely asked for my permission. I don't make it a habit to question his methods." She lifted one shoulder. "Don't worry, Your Highness. Your wizard is in good hands."

I nodded. "Thank you. Please, carry on."

>→ >→ >→ >→

I returned to the castle to seek out my wizard counsel, trying to keep my temper at bay. Why Ward? Had Cade said something to Eoghan about our moment in the garden? Nothing had happened, and if anything had, it wouldn't have been anybody's business.

Wizard overlord.

I winced, rubbing my face to clear Weymouth's words. Surely, there would be a reasonable explanation for this. It wouldn't be prudent to lose my mind before I spoke with Eoghan—something I was having to remind myself of more and more often.

I found my counsel in his basement library, reading a book. It was startling to be in the vault without Cade's presence.

"Ah, there you are," he said, closing the book. "I was wondering when I would see you today."

"You sent a guard with Cade?" I asked, realizing the question was quite stupid. What did I care who came and went from my royal guard?

And damn it all, Eoghan smiled knowingly. "I sent the knight Ward, yes. Does that trouble you?"

I chewed my tongue, thinking of how to worm my way around the conversation. "I—"

"It's no use. I know you're fond of him," Eoghan replied. "You're great at many things, but hiding your emotions isn't one of them."

My face grew so hot I thought it might catch fire. "Is that why you sent him away? Because I like him?"

"Yes, but not for the reason you're insinuating," Eoghan said. "I thought, perhaps, his affection for you might make him a good candidate to accompany Cade to Críoch. He would make sure the mission wouldn't fail."

"So you don't care that I…" I cleared my throat. "Well, you know."

"Do I think it's an advantageous match? Absolutely not," Eoghan said. "But you have been denied so much of your childhood, I won't step in the way of your crush." He cleared his throat. "However… We do need to discuss Lord Weymouth."

I braced myself. "I know I was wrong—"

"On the contrary, the guards told me how he spoke to you, and it was absolutely uncalled for," he said. "And you showed strong backbone by leaving the conversation."

I exhaled, relieved. "Thank you. I couldn't see… I shouldn't have to let some lord speak to me that way in my own kingdom."

He smiled warmly. "I'm sure he will return to his king speaking ill of you, but from what I hear of Weymouth's reputation in the Sudaemor court, it will presumably fall on deaf ears. You might actually earn more respect by his derision of you."

I opened my mouth, confused. "Was that…your plan when you let us ride alone?"

He shrugged in his noncommittal way. "He may be the king's brother-in-law, but he's not the only one with his ear. I'm sure there will be others from Sudaemor who would seek an audience with this fascinating princess of Pennlan and try their luck."

"Try their luck how?" I asked.

"Isn't it obvious?" He smiled at me the way he did when he was explaining simple concepts. "Weymouth was here to ask for your hand."

My brows shot up and my mouth fell open as a peculiar mix of disgust and shock melded in my mind. "Are you…serious? He's twice my age. And…well, we've already established his personality leaves a lot to be desired."

"In my experience, the more mediocre a man, the larger his ego," Eoghan said. "He considered himself a good match because of his connection to the king. My guess is he was hoping to ask on your ride, but unfortunately, his aforementioned personality got in the way before he could."

And a good thing it had—I wouldn't have been able to stop laughing if he'd dropped to one knee and started singing my praises. "And you think there'll be others like him?"

"Perhaps not like him exactly, but there have been other inquiries, and there are others making plans to visit," Eoghan said with a small chuckle. "But when I've been asked to provide some idea of your preferences, I've requested the kings to send their youngest and most handsome options."

I shifted uncomfortably. I trusted him, but when it came to matters of my heart, anyone knowing my secret thoughts was unsettling. Not only that… Weymouth's harsh words came back with a vengeance. If it was my hand that was being asked for, perhaps I should be the one providing permissions and preferences.

"Is something wrong?" Eoghan asked my silence.

"The truth is… I don't think I'm ready for this conversation. And I don't…" I struggled with how to phrase it without hurting his feelings. "I don't want you discussing my 'preferences' with anyone. Those will be conversations I have when I'm ready to seek a partner to help me rule. But I should think I'm perfectly capable of doing it by myself for at least a couple of years."

He glanced at me, as if inclined to disagree. "As you wish, Your Majesty. Unfortunately, Driwania, Nesuria, and Konevell are preparing to send their own envoys as we speak. I've had a devil of a time trying to space them out so they aren't on top of one another."

Your wizard overlord.

"Perhaps then, you should leave the correspondence to me?"

"Are you ready for the responsibility?" he asked.

The question was open-ended, but something about his tone made me doubt myself. I *should* be the one sending letters to the other kingdoms, but what if I made a mistake? What if I accidentally scheduled two dignitaries at the same time, or caused an international incident?

"How about this," he said, after another long pause. "Let's get through the coronation, then I will hand over all correspondence to you." He smiled. "I don't want to overwhelm you too early."

"I doubt letters are going to overwhelm me," I replied.

He reached into his jacket pocket and pulled out an already opened letter. "Are you sure? This one might."

It was addressed to me, but the seal was already broken. I pulled out the letter from the envelope and scanned it quickly.

To Her Royal Highness, Princess Ayla of Pennlan,

I am writing to offer my congratulations on your upcoming coronation and the hopes we can reopen communication between our two nations. It has been many years since our nations were on friendly terms...

Many years… My gaze skipped over the paragraphs until they reached the final line and the signature.

I hope this letter finds you in good health. Best wishes for a long and fruitful reign as queen.

Sincerely,

Birch, Erlking of the Fae Realm

My heart leapt into my throat and it was all I could do to keep myself from tossing the letter out the window. "The nerve of him."

"You can see why I'm hesitant to give you every letter that comes to your door," Eoghan said, gently.

I nodded, though perhaps I should be stronger about these sorts of things. My father had been dead for years, and I barely remembered him or the woman who killed him. But the betrayal was fresh. Even now, with Cade on the road to Críoch to find information about the stone, her actions were reverberating through my life and my kingdom. That he thought he could just pen me a letter, acting as if nothing was wrong while he kept my family's property hidden away in his castle… After he'd sent his daughter to seduce and destroy my father…

"Ayla?" Eoghan asked. "Are you all right?"

"Fine," I said, taking the letter and balling it up. "I don't think this merits a response."

"Indeed, it doesn't."

"But any…*other* correspondence should probably start coming to me," I said. "From the kings or anyone interested in…my hand. I would like to handle those myself."

"If I may," Eoghan began slowly, "you've never worried about this before. What's changed?"

I averted my gaze. "Something Weymouth said rubbed me the wrong way."

"Something else?"

"He said I was…" I swallowed, not wanting to hurt his feelings. "He called you my wizard overlord."

Eoghan chuckled. "I'm not surprised. He's a man who would seek to control you, and that would be very hard to do with me around, reminding you of your own power."

I opened my mouth, not having considered such a thing. "Oh."

"Don't worry, my dear. As soon as you're ready, I promise I will step aside with gratitude. After all, it was only happenstance that a wizard was the one to step in when your father passed. It's not my natural place to manage a kingdom, and I will be grateful to never do it again."

Chapter Twelve

Ward

I couldn't believe I'd been so easily hoodwinked by that fae, yet again. I couldn't figure out what, exactly, their game was. Fae weren't just mischievous for no reason, that wasn't their style. There was strategy and danger and *something* I wasn't seeing. I almost hoped we'd see them again, so I'd have one more piece of the puzzle to put together.

The wizard, however, had become absolutely unbearable. For someone who was so woefully inept at the simplest of tasks, he was surely acting as if he were the superior man. I had half a mind to just take off without him the next time we stopped, if only so I didn't have to hear him make intellectual noises every time he pulled out that damn book.

"You know, we'd probably get to the next city faster if we weren't stopping for you to read," I barked during the third stop of the day.

"The horses—"

"Are fine. They can travel the length between the cities without stopping, if we wanted to," I snapped. "You just want to rest your ass."

"If there's an ass that needs to give it a rest, it's you."

I blinked at him, torn between ripping out my sword to challenge him and just getting on my horse and leaving. After a moment of staring at him, I opted for the latter—and begrudgingly, the wizard followed behind.

⸻

When we arrived in town, we headed straight to the inn, speaking to or acknowledging no one else. I gave the wizard the coin to purchase the rooms so I could deal with the horses and get a reprieve from him. I brushed them down, picked the mud from their hooves, and made sure they had fresh hay and water for the night. The act did a lot to soothe my temper, and I was looking forward to a hot meal and a long night of sleep.

I found the wizard in the dining hall with two bowls, one of which he was eating out of. I snatched the other and went to get my food, but I was given a stew of mostly water—along with an apology and a recommendation that if I wanted more, I should be more prompt to dinner.

"I'll keep that in mind, thanks," I grumbled.

When I turned, there was nowhere else to sit except for the table where the wizard had a chair for me, so I walked over and plopped down, digging into my meal and trying to convince myself it wasn't that meager. Tomorrow, we'd be one day closer to Críoch. Tomorrow, things would look brighter.

The wizard was reading the book, and his bowl was still flush with meat and vegetables. If he were a decent man, he would've offered me some. I did my best to ignore him, staring into my bowl, but the meal was gone in moments, and my anger at the wizard reignited. It wasn't his fault I'd eaten too quickly, but I sure felt like blaming him. There wasn't any ale for sale, and I hadn't seen a tavern on our way in.

"You don't have to be so cranky about being hoodwinked by the fae," he said, breaking the silence between us. "It used to happen more often when the border was open. You should feel lucky that nothing worse happened."

"I'm sure."

"Seriously." He closed the book. "The fae must've known that you would be swayed by tales of woe from a farm, with your upbringing."

I narrowed my gaze at him. "How do *you* know I grew up on a farm?"

"Ayla told me."

I sniffed, though I was secretly pleased I'd made a big enough impression to have come up in conversation. "What about that book?" I said, nodding toward him. "You're awfully interested in it. What's to say the fae didn't coerce you into taking it?"

"Because I can sense fae."

"How?"

He sighed. "I can…" He cleared his throat. "Taste them."

"I'm sorry…what?"

"It's like a scent on the air that lands on my tongue," he said with a grunt. "But the fact of the matter is, their magic tastes a certain way. I knew it the moment I touched those fake arrows. This book has none of it."

"And you're sure the fae didn't just *happen* to leave it where you could find it?"

"For what purpose?" he said. "This is a book on the history of wizards. Why would a fae have such a book, and why would they want me to have it?"

"Why would they want to entrap and not kill me?" I countered. "None of this is making sense."

He shrugged and dipped his spoon into his bowl that was…still full. Odd, considering we'd both been sitting here a while, and I'd heard him slurp. But then I noticed the faint glow of his staff.

"Ridiculous," I muttered.

"Did you say something?" he asked, looking up innocently.

"You heard me," I snapped, too worn, cold, and hungry to keep my opinions to myself. "You've been making this trip easy for yourself, haven't you? Didn't cross your mind to help the man taking you to the border."

"Didn't think you needed help," the wizard said, looking down at his bowl. "And keep your voice down. We don't want anyone knowing who I am."

"Oh, of course not, the precious wizard of Pennlan," I said, enjoying the way his eyes widened. "Nobody cares out here. You're just another traveler."

"And you're just an idiot," he replied. "Now shut up before I shut you up."

"You can't—" But something had happened to my voice. I could no longer speak at the same volume. I glared at the wizard, pointing to my throat. "Fix it," I croaked.

"Not until you calm down."

"I'm calm," I snapped, growing angrier when my quiet voice didn't match the fire in my belly. "Don't use your wizardry on me—"

"Weren't you just complaining that I wasn't?" Cade asked.

I threw my hands in the air then slammed them on the table. At least that sound echoed.

"Give me my room key."

"Just one problem," the wizard said. "There was only one room available."

Great. "Fine. Give me the key."

"And..." He winced. "There was only one bed."

I stared at him, now very close to knocking his pointed nose flat. "Then I suppose I'll sleep with the horses. See you in the morning."

Whatever he said after that, I didn't hear, as I made my way out to the stables.

⤞⤞ ⤞⤞ ⤞⤞

Unsurprisingly, I slept poorly. My mood was quite sour when we set off at first light, and I purposefully ignored any and all comments or requests to stop from the wizard. The sooner we reached the next city, the better, and the dried meat in my pouch was starting to taste like dirt.

But midday, the wizard told his horse to slow. I turned in my saddle as he dismounted and led his horse to a small pond near a couple of trees.

"What are you doing?" I asked. "I said we aren't stopping."

"You can keep going. I'll catch up." He purposefully pulled his book from his bag. "I'm taking a break."

"And you think you'll be safe out here by yourself?"

He gestured to his staff and leaned against the tree as he opened the huge tome in his lap. "I'm sure I'll be fine. Please, continue on to the next village."

I almost did, except I knew he'd probably get lost along the way and I'd have to double back to find him. So with a huff, I dismounted and led my horse to join his.

"I told you—"

"I was given a task to lead you to Críoch," I said. "Can't do that if your ass is sitting here under this tree. So whenever you *decide* you want to leave, we will continue."

He slammed the book shut and rose, grabbing his staff. "And if you think I don't know the real reason you took this *task*, you must think me an idiot."

"What's that supposed to mean?"

"It means I know you're here because you're trying to improve your station in life," he said. "It's why you decided to sneak out to the garden with Ayla."

I couldn't help the hearty eye-roll. "You should be grateful. It's only because of her that I'm putting up with you."

"What happened to, 'it's a direct order?'" he asked with a smirk.

"One I'm following because I believe my princess would be very cross with me if I allowed her childish little wizard friend to be robbed by thieves—or worse."

"If you hadn't put the moves on her, she wouldn't have even noticed you exist."

"For the last time," I barked, marching over to him. "She *asked* me to join her in the gardens. I was merely following her lead, as a good soldier does."

"A very convenient story. Ayla doesn't just ask random guards to the gardens, and she's not the type of girl who invites that sort of attention, either."

"I'm not saying she is," I replied, a smile curling onto my lips. "I'm saying she just wanted to sneak into the gardens *with me.*"

"You've spent all of half an hour with her," he snarled. "You have *no* idea who she is or what she wants."

I let out an incredulous laugh. "Oh, yeah? I know she was pissed at you. Whatever happened in that dining room sent her marching out in tears, and you were nowhere to be found."

"If she'd waited five minutes, I would've followed her," he snarled back. "But no, you decided to sneak her out to the gardens and have your way with her."

"For the last time, I absolutely did *not* do anything she didn't ask me to," I said, my hand coming to my sword. "She asked me to accompany her out into the gardens. *She* asked me to stay."

"And you took advantage."

I threw my hands up. "Maybe—and this might come as a shock to you—Ayla is a woman capable of deciding what she wants."

"I know she's capable of deciding what she wants," Cade sputtered. "But she's easily persuaded—"

"To my eyes, it seems like that's entirely the problem she has with you and your master," I said, leaning toward him. "Both of you coddle her and treat her like she's a damn child when she's going to be *queen* in a few short weeks. What do you think will happen when that time comes?"

He licked his lips. "Eoghan will step aside and allow her to rule. It's what he's always wanted."

"Is it? Because from where I was standing, he looked like he was in command of that room and in no hurry to give it up." I shook my head. "But what do I know? I'm just a bystander who listened to her while she poured her heart out to me because her so-called best friend ignored her."

He stared at me, the wheels spinning in his head, and I fully expected him to turn me into a toad and step on me. But I was not going to stand by and let him think I was some sort of predator, especially where Ayla was concerned. My honor was my most prized possession.

"Well, we'll just have to see who she chooses when we get back to Pennlan," he said, after a long pause. "Won't we?"

"We will." I smirked. "Get on your horse. You've rested enough."

Chapter Thirteen

Cade

I glared at the back of the knight's head, envisioning all manner of spells I could cast on him and debating if I should once we reached our destination. After all, it wouldn't be any skin off my nose if he never made it back. They might just say he'd deserted his post. One soldier going missing wouldn't do much.

I couldn't stand anyone besmirching my master. Eoghan had found me, raised me, and taught me everything I knew about magic. If it hadn't been for him, I would've remained on the small island where I'd been found and perhaps never known about the beautiful gift that lived inside me.

Besides that, his presence had been a blessing to Ayla, not a hindrance. He was the one who'd fought off the foul Leandra and prevented her from killing the baby princess. Then he'd stayed behind and kept a steady hand on the kingdom until she came of age. He could be a little overbearing at times, and perhaps nearly sixteen years of ruling in Ayla's stead had made him used to making the decisions. He would have to step aside, of course, but it seemed he didn't feel that Ayla was ready to take on the responsibility.

Then again, Ayla *had* been mad at me when I'd left. But that was her usual bluster. Eoghan wasn't necessarily unfair to her, not that I saw. The merchant from Sudaemor was a blowhard, and Eoghan was merely trying to smooth things over to keep our alliances secure. Ayla was still somewhat green in the realm of politics.

But the knight didn't know any of that. All he saw was a vulnerable girl in need of comfort, and he was more than happy to give it. He could hide behind his fake honor and indignant assertions that he'd done nothing wrong, but I saw right through him.

The storm clouds gathered overhead mirrored my mood as we plodded over the plain. I doubted we'd stop if the skies opened, but at least I had my staff to keep me dry. And I might enjoy watching the knight get waterlogged and covered in mud while I stayed warm.

I didn't think we would stop at all, but he silently led his horse to a small pond and dismounted. He didn't say a word to me as he stretched out under a tree and fell asleep before I was even off my horse.

"So I guess we're stopping," I muttered.

I walked around to the other side of the tree and sat, pulling out my book. I was about a quarter of the way through it, and still hadn't been able to decipher when or where the book was written. The wizard legends were becoming a little repetitive, too. Big danger to humanity, wizard saves day, wizard is canonized in lore and given a great sum of riches. On and on.

But then, I turned the page.

The wizard Laughlan and the Seod Croí

"Oh."

The seod croí, a powerful stone, was created by an alliance between the wizard Laughlan and the fae Aoibheann. The stone contained the magic of both the wizard and fae, and was considered the strongest magical object ever created.

However, due to the danger of the stone's existence, it was decided that it would be given to a human king of Pennlan and his descendants, to keep the magic from falling into the wrong magical hands.

I stared at the book, my brow furrowed. I'd known it had been given to Ayla's familial line, of course, but the details of the stone's creation hadn't ever been shared with me—nor what kind of power it contained. I searched the book, but all it gave me was the barest detail. I wanted more.

I reread the passage, paying special attention to the mention of the fae. It was…surprising that a fae had helped in the creation of the stone then just given it to the humans. It seemed out of character from what I knew about the creatures. Why would they willingly give up something so powerful—and why would *they* give it to the Pennlan king?

A snore echoed from the other side of the tree, and I sighed. What I wouldn't give to have an intellectual conversation with someone, instead of having this boorish knight as my companion. By my count, we'd passed three cities, which put us at the halfway point. Tonight, we'd reach number four then two more nights before we reached Críoch.

Not as if I'd find any intellectual conversation there, but at least I'd be on my own.

The first raindrop landed squarely on my nose, followed by another, and within seconds, the deluge began. The knight snorted and woke up, cursing loudly as he scrambled to his feet. He sighed and muttered to himself as he walked to the horses.

Just as I'd thought. No rest for the weary.

⤜ ⤜ ⤜ ⤜

The rain continued to pound around us, and it was only thanks to my magic that I was able to see more than a few feet in front of me. How the knight was managing, I hadn't a clue, but I hadn't yet forgiven him for what he'd said, so I didn't offer any assistance.

Up ahead, there was a large forest, and my heart lightened. If my map-reading skills were any good, this forest was something of a halfway mark between Pennlan and Críoch. And there seemed to be a road already cut through the forest to ease our passage.

The knight twisted in his saddle and frowned, looking at the sky. "Do you know what time it is?"

I shrugged. It was hard to see anything under the thick clouds. "Why?"

"I don't want to be in the forest after dusk. We should stop."

I scoffed. "Why? Afraid of the dark?"

He turned to me, perhaps noticing for the first time that I was dry. "The forest is notorious for thieves who pick off travelers at night. I would prefer to avoid them if possible."

"I can handle a bunch of human thieves," I said, drawing my horse even with his. "I say we press on."

He glared at me and shook his head but urged his horse forward. The forest provided little cover from the pouring rain, the dirt road was all mud, slowing the horses somewhat, and it was getting harder and harder to see. My staff glowed gold, partially for the light, but also to deter any ne'er-do-wells who might have an inkling to attack us.

"I think it's nighttime," Ward called back to me, resting his hand on his sword. "Be on your guard."

We continued to plod through the forest uneventfully, and I increased the glow of my staff to illuminate the surrounding area as the rain lessened to a mist. More than once, I thought I saw movement in the trees around us, but it must've just been the shadows.

Every bend in the road we took, I hoped we might see the end of the forest, but there were just more trees, more rain, more mud. We turned a rather sharp bend in the wood and had to stop. A tree had fallen in the road, and it was too big for our horses to maneuver around or over.

The knight let out a loud sigh. "Perfect."

"I can move it, you know."

"Stay where you are," he snapped, looking around suddenly. "This —"

The arrow came out of nowhere, whizzing by my face by mere inches. Ward swore and pulled his sword, standing at the ready. I gripped my staff, waiting and looking into the darkness around us.

Movement drew my attention, and three men came out, holding crossbows.

"Your coin, travelers, and we will let you pass."

"I think not," Ward said. "Put down those crossbows and see if you can't earn my coin, thieves."

Well, that was stupid, there's no way…

To my surprise, the thieves put down their crossbows and opted for their swords and clubs instead. Perhaps something about the challenge had spoken to their egos. Or they weren't that smart.

"Stand down," I commanded, getting off my horse as my staff grew even brighter. "Or suffer the consequences."

The thieves grinned at each other. "What is this? Fae magic?"

"I'm a wizard, you dolt," I snapped, pointing my staff at them. "And if you don't—"

The air left my chest as a force hit me from behind, and my staff went flying. I fell face-first into the mud, twisting to look up at the burly man lying on top of me. He was missing four teeth as he grinned at me.

I turned back, the wet ground squelching under me, as I struggled against his grip. My staff was too far from my fingertips, and I couldn't focus with the air being squeezed from my chest. I saw spots, and I pushed everything I could into summoning my staff. But without the conduit, the magic in my bones was limited.

Cold steel pressed against the side of my neck. "Quit squirmin' down there."

I froze, fear starting to creep across my consciousness. I was defenseless, the knight was having to fight off who knows how many thieves, and if I made one wrong move, this brute would end my life without a second thought. I began to silently bargain with my magic to work just this one time without the help of the staff. But it remained stubbornly in my veins, and the blade at my throat pressed even harder.

"I said—*Oof!*"

The weight lifted from my chest, and I rolled onto my back, gasping for precious air. When I got my fill, I lifted my head off the ground.

Ward was covered in mud, his sword in one hand and a knife in the other, his stance tense and furious as he faced down a man three times his size. The others were on the ground, some unconscious, some bleeding quite profusely.

Had he managed to fight off three thieves by himself?

"Are you going to help or just lie there, you colossal idiot?"

I turned back to Ward, who was trapped in a headlock. I scrambled across the ground and grabbed my staff, the connection akin to breathing air again, then sent one giant fireball toward the burly man. It might've had a little too much oomph behind it, because the man went flying into a nearby tree.

"Any others?" Ward said, heaving as he looked around.

"I don't see any," I said, gingerly getting to my feet.

We stood in awkward silence. I was a mix of emotion—mostly shame and gratitude. Ward could've very easily taken care of the three thieves, hopped on his horse, and left me for dead. Instead, he'd come to my aid, even after all the arguments between us.

"Look," I said, after a moment.

"Why didn't you step in sooner?" he barked. "Just thought it would be fun to let me do all the work?"

"No," I said with a blink. "I lost my staff."

"Oh." He rubbed his face, smearing mud. "Why'd you do that?"

I snorted, looking down at my staff and shaking my head. "I won't do it again. I promise you that."

"Horses are still here. That's good," Ward said, limping to his steed. "Let's keep moving. Make sure to keep that staff handy in case anyone else gets any ideas."

"Ward," I began. "Thanks."

"I have a job to do," he said, climbing onto his horse.

That was true, but out here, a lesser man might've just let the worst happen. So after I mounted my horse and magicked the mud and muck off myself, I turned to the knight and cast a spell to rid his clothes of the mess.

He jumped, staring at his clothes as they moved of their own accord, then perhaps realized what I was doing. He turned in the saddle and nodded at me.

"Let's go. We shouldn't be far from the next village."

Chapter Fourteen

Ward

"I lost my staff." So my initial suspicion was correct. Once that staff disappeared from his hand, the wizard was as useless as a newborn babe. I perhaps should've offered to teach him how to defend himself, but what was the point? Three days and we'd part ways.

The storm had brought with it colder weather, but thanks to the wizard, my clothes were at least dry. It was clearly his attempt at a peace offering, and perhaps tomorrow, I might be more eager to accept it. But for now, I wanted a hot meal and bed, in that order. The thieves had gotten a few good hits in, and I was sure I'd find bruises whenever I peeled my clothes off.

But when we reached our village, the first inn was full, as was the second. The third could, yet again, offer us just one room—and there was no dinner to be had.

"Are there any other inns in town?" I asked, a little edge in my voice.

"No," the clerk said.

"We'll take it," the wizard said behind me.

I sighed, praying that my exhaustion would at least help me get a better night's sleep in the stables. Was this torture was worth the glory that finding the Pennlan stone would bring?

Yes.

"Here." I handed the key to the wizard. "I'll see you in the morning."

"Where are you going?" he asked.

"To sleep, obviously."

"Where? In the stables again?"

"Yes."

"There's no need for that." Cade motioned to his staff. "Come with me."

Annoyed, I followed him up the narrow staircase to a row of doorways. As expected, the room we'd rented was barely big enough to fit the small single bed.

"So what, you're going to let me have this?" I asked. "Because I'm not cuddling with you all night."

He put his staff on the ground and gold tendrils seeped out from the bottom, crawling along the floor and…expanding it. Where one floorboard had been, now there were two, three, four. The wood creaked and moaned as the walls moved backward. Whether those in the rooms next door felt it, I didn't know, but I was mesmerized.

The magic stopped and the room was twice the size it had been. And with another wave of the staff and a puff of gold magic, the single bed duplicated itself—right down to the same pillow. There still wasn't much room between them, but I'd never seen anything so welcoming in my life.

"This is…" I shook my head, but before I could finish, two steaming bowls of stew appeared on the table next to the washbasin. But unlike the previous few nights, this was full of vegetables and big chunks of meat. My mouth watered immediately.

"I gave the dinner offering downstairs some help," he said, handing me one of the bowls.

My suspicions were aroused as I debated diving into the meal. "You're being awfully nice. What do you want in return?"

"Maybe just for you to accept my apology," he said with a sigh. "You saved my life today. I've been something of an ass."

"You would've gotten out of there, I'm sure," I said, sitting down on the mattress.

"Once he found out I had no coin? He would've left me for dead," Cade said with a shake of his head.

"Probably." I stared at the bowl, my stomach growling. "Don't worry about it. I told you, it's my job to get you to Críoch. And I just assume that means in one piece."

He deflated, but I ignored him as I inhaled the food. Magical or no, it was magnificent—heartier than anything I'd had in the past. And when it was empty, the bowl magically replenished itself, so I had a second— then a third. When a fourth serving appeared, I waved my hand.

"Enough," I said. In an instant, the bowl was gone.

I chanced a look up at the wizard, who had long finished his meal and was sitting on the bed, reading that book he'd procured in the last village. It must've been something special if he wanted to lug it around.

"Is that thing any good?" I asked.

"What do you mean?"

"You're always reading it," I said. "What's it about?"

"History of wizards," he replied, turning the page. "I found something of interest, but it wasn't very detailed, so I'm hoping there's more later in the book."

I waited for him to say more. When he didn't, I padded to the bed and took off my boots, stretching out and tucking my hands behind my head. The bed was soft and the pillow smelled fresh. That it had taken him *four* nights to offer this courtesy was a little annoying, but I was grateful for it now.

"Night."

><del>→ ><del>→ ><del>→ ><del>→

I slept like a baby, waking at first light feeling refreshed and ready for another day. The wizard was still fast asleep, and I wasn't quite ready to listen to him yet, so I rose and padded to the wash basin. The mirror was dirty, but in my spotted reflection, I ran my hand over the coarse black stubble that had grown in the past few days. I pulled my knife from the sheath under my arm and carefully scraped my cheeks until I was somewhat happy.

The wizard stirred by the time I finished, sitting up and blinking heavily. "Oh, is it morning?"

"Yep," I said, grabbing my scabbard and hanging it around my waist. "Onward."

Since it was dark when we'd arrived, I hadn't noticed that the landscape had changed until we set off on the main road that morning. The chill from the rain hung around, but it wasn't solely because of the weather. The farther north we traveled, the colder it would become. I could only imagine how cold the fae country would be.

"We'll take this road all the way to Críoch," I said, when the wizard asked. "Up this way, there are more villages along the main trade route with the fae." I paused. "Or what used to be the trade route."

"The fae realm is closed to trade, though."

"It wasn't, for a few hundred years," I said. "Trade with the fae used to be Pennlan's primary industry. This road goes southwest toward Driwania, and all these villages served as overnight stops for fae travelers looking to trade with kingdoms south."

He drew his horse even with mine as we plodded by a carriage full of wool driven by an old man who waved at us as we passed.

"And now, I suppose, they trade with the human kingdoms," Cade asked. "Right?"

"Lots of people have left, and those who can't just..." I shrugged, thinking of my brother. "Do what they can."

"Críoch is a thriving city, isn't it?"

"Used to be. Now it's just a border town full of soldiers and not much else."

He glanced at me. "You said you're from there? Do you still have family there?"

"My brother. But I'm not planning on paying him a visit, if that's what you're asking."

"Why not?"

I glanced in his direction; he looked genuinely curious. "I wasn't really welcome once he took over, and he didn't pay me too many visits when I lived at the garrison. We aren't what you'd call close. But there are others in town who'll be glad to see me—including the garrison commander. He and I had a..." I smirked. "Unique relationship."

He snorted, and we passed a family who were walking the road on foot, their belongings strapped to their backs and onto a sad-looking donkey. Probably headed south to seek better fortunes.

"Everyone up here looks so sad," Cade said, once they'd passed out of earshot. "I don't know if Ayla knows how dire it is up here."

"I doubt there's anything she can do, other than open the border," I replied.

"She would never."

"So there's nothing she can do."

"It can't be all or nothing, though," Cade said, twisting in his saddle to look at the family who'd walked by. "She's smart. She'll figure something out."

Your wizard master hasn't yet. I bit my tongue. We were having a pleasant conversation, and I didn't want to ruin it. "What about you? You're not from Pennlan, are you?"

"No." He faced the front. "I'm from a small island you've never heard of, past the southernmost tip of Nesuria."

"How did you end up here?" I asked. For someone who was woefully inept at being on his own, that sounded like a journey.

"Wizards are rare," he said. "So when a human boy starts using magic, word travels. Eoghan showed up one day, and a month later, I was in Pennlan castle. I must've been..." He shrugged. "Five? Hard to tell. I'm not exactly sure how old I am today. I couldn't understand anyone—the southern isles have their own language, you know."

I didn't know. "Must've been lonely."

"It was, for a while, but Ayla was there," he said, his voice lightening with the mention of her. "She'd been the only child in the castle until I showed up and was delighted to have a playmate, even if I couldn't communicate with her. I'm pretty sure she's the one who taught me how to read and speak clearly. We spent our entire childhood getting in trouble together."

The rest of his thought remained unsaid, but I heard it loud and clear. No wonder he was so protective of her; she was the only friend he had. I could sympathize with him, but at the same time, his concern for her well-being bordered on overbearing. They were friends, but he didn't own her heart.

And there was no denying the way she'd looked at me in the garden. I doubted she'd ever looked at him that way—and it perhaps drove him mad.

"She seems like a good friend," I said, after a long pause.

There was a little ice in his gaze when he turned to me, but he said nothing more.

>-» >-» >-» >-»

This close to the border, we had our pick of villages to stop in, so we opted to ride until the sun was almost gone. Our inn was one of the dingier ones we'd found so far, though it had once been nice when trade was plentiful. The wizard did his magic to my bowl of food, and I thanked him nicely. It seemed we'd managed to come to an understanding, and that would at least make the next two days more pleasant.

Tonight, we had separate rooms, so I crawled into the bed and was almost asleep when there was a heavy knock on my door. I grumbled and grabbed my sword in case it was someone intending to rob me, but it was just the wizard.

"What?" I said, rubbing my face.

"Come with me."

"Why?"

"Don't ask questions." There was something in his gaze that

stripped me of my arguments, so I rose and followed him into the chilly night.

He led me around the inn, not once, but twice, and just as I was about to tell him I was going back to bed, he stopped, his staff lighting up. Before I could say another word, he fired off one of those magical orbs of light toward a nearby building.

A loud cry of pain echoed from the roof, and a dark shadow fell to the ground, landing with an unceremonious thump in the center of the alley.

"Who the hell is that?" I asked.

The wizard's gaze was firm, his staff still bright gold, as if ready to fire off another shot. "Get up."

The shadow lifted their hands into the air while still on the ground. "I'm not here to harm you." Her voice was young, but there was something about it that set me on edge. Something familiar.

Cade's staff was bright gold once again, ready to fire. "Get. Up."

"Do I have your word you won't blast me again if I do?"

"Get up and we'll see."

"Cade…" I said with an eye roll. "Yes, just get up and show us your face."

The shadow put her hands on the ground and pushed herself up, coming to stand a head shorter than the wizard or myself. When she lifted her gaze to meet ours, I was surprised Cade was so concerned. She seemed barely older than sixteen, with raven-colored hair that reflected in the moonlight and green eyes made brighter by the color of the wizard's magic.

"Why are we harassing a young girl like this?" I asked the wizard.

"Take off your hood."

She swallowed and slowly put her hands to the hood, lifting it and drawing it down, revealing a pair of pointed ears.

"That's why," Cade said. "She's fae. The same one who's been following us since we left Pennlan."

CHAPTER FIFTEEN

CADE

I'd known from the moment we'd set foot in the city that she was here—though I hadn't been sure she was a she until just now. The taste of magic had been faint, but when a middle-aged man had walked into the inn, it had become much more pronounced. He'd watched us without buying dinner, perhaps hoping to be discreet. I'd wanted to wait until the knight had finished his food, to be sure, but once we got up to leave, the man had mysteriously vanished.

Yet I could still find that taste on the wind, and when we'd come outside, I'd practically been able to see the creature in the dark.

"Is this your real face?" I asked.

"Yes," she said, sounding much younger than I'd expected. Her pale skin glimmered in the moonlight, and her eyes, a very unique shade of green, were cautiously watching me. Those pointed ears, though…

"Why have you been following us?" Ward snapped.

"My name is Riona," she said, after a moment. "And I'm here to help."

"Help with what?" I asked. "Because all you've done so far is try to veer us off our quest."

She swallowed, looking at my staff, then back to the knight. "Tell the wizard to stand down, and I'll tell you."

I narrowed my gaze. "And then you'll attack us."

Her nose twitched, as if she were resisting a scowl. "And if I do, I assume you'll blast me into next week with that wizard magic of yours. So what are you so afraid of?"

I wasn't exactly sure. She was very young, but could have glamoured herself to look that way so we would lower our guard. But perhaps she was right. I did have the upper hand. And at the very least, she might offer something of value. I pulled my staff upright and absorbed the magic back into my body.

"Speak," Ward snapped. "You told me our quest was a sham. What do you mean by that?"

She licked her lips. "The fae you've been sent to interrogate in Críoch aren't there."

Immediately, my staff lit up, and the knight had pulled his sword. "What are you talking about?" we asked in unison.

Riona let loose a small chuckle, holding up her hands in surrender. "Don't be touchy. I told you I'm here to help."

"Forgive us if we don't trust a fae to tell us the truth about anything," I snapped. "Especially considering your track record."

"We can't lie," she said with a knowing look.

"You can twist the truth," Ward shot back. "Like you did with the griffins. What was the point of that, anyway?"

"I was trying to get you away from the wizard so you'd listen to me," she said. "But unfortunately, he's meddlesome."

"I've had enough of this," I said, gathering my magic in my staff. First, a containment spell, then, I would attempt the—

But before I could fire off the first spell, she vanished in a puff of butterflies that swarmed toward us, blinding me for a minute. I waved my staff to clear them, and by the time I regained my bearings, there was no one in the alley except the knight and myself.

"Thanks," Ward said, wiping his face as if there was a butterfly on it.

"For what?"

"Interrupting my interrogation."

"I was about *to* interrogate her, in case you didn't know what I was doing," I barked. "I can use magic to coerce her into speaking."

"As long as she stays still," Ward replied. "But she was about to tell us what she wanted from us."

"She was about to lie."

"She can't lie."

"Twist the truth, then," I said with a disgruntled sniff as I looked up. "She's gone. I can't find her anymore."

"And now we have no idea why she was so hellbent on speaking with me," Ward said.

"She wanted to dissuade you from the quest," I drawled. "Clearly, if she's lying about the fae being in Críoch."

The knight shook his head. "That was a fairly clear statement. Fae can't out-and-out lie like that."

"They could be in the garrison outside Críoch. Not *in* Críoch technically." It was the sort of wordplay fae were known for.

"No." He squinted at the sky, perhaps searching for her. "As much as I hate to say it, I think we should pack up and head out. If we keep a steady pace, we can be there in a day and a half. Then we'll know for sure if she's telling the truth."

I didn't love the sound of another all-night ride. "Or we could remember that she's been quick to use magic to play on our emotions. This could just be another fae trick."

"If it is, we'll be in Críoch that much quicker," he said. "And if it isn't..." He put his sword away. "Make sure you're ready to use that staff should the need arise."

>–» >–» >–» >–»

We set off under the moonlight, and for once, I was as twitchy and nervous as the knight. I was caught between two dueling ideas: that the fae knew of our quest and that she hadn't tried to harm us. I doubted she thought we'd give up on our mission so easily, which made her attempts all the more curious. If she wanted to sway us, why not be more persuasive?

The sun rose behind us, and we passed right through the next town, stopping only to feed ourselves and the horses. I was exhausted, but the threat of the fae after us kept me going. Once the horses were ready, we were back on the road.

Our pace was somehow slower than before, but consistent. The knight and I took turns catnapping while the other kept watch for the fae or anyone else who might want to bother us. Every so often, I'd catch a taste of her, but it was so faint I couldn't pinpoint where it was coming from.

We reached the sixth town at midday and kept riding. By now, I was barely able to keep my eyes open, dreading another long night on my horse. But Ward insisted we'd get to Críoch around sundown—and head straight to the garrison to speak with the commander.

"And you're sure she's following us?" Ward said when I mentioned it while we rested the horses. "You said you can smell her?"

"In a manner of speaking," I said. "But I'm sure she's around somewhere. It's unmistakable."

He took a bite of his dried meat. "Say she's right and the fae aren't there."

"They're there," I snapped. "Eoghan wouldn't have sent us on this seven-day journey if he didn't have full faith and confidence in our mission. Remember, this is part of my wizard trial—the last thing I need to do in order to strike out on my own."

Not to mention the fae supposedly held the key to knowing the stone's location. If we got to Críoch and there was nothing there, I'd have to continue into enemy territory blind. I didn't even want to consider the thought.

"I wouldn't listen to a thing she says," I said, more to myself than the knight. "The fae have a way of twisting facts to suit their needs and convincing you of insane things. Remember Birch was able to send Leandra to the castle and convince Ayla's father to marry her."

"I thought that was political," he replied.

"Depends who you ask," I said. "Some in the castle thought that Bresal was as enamored with Leandra as he was his first wife. And they said she was a doting stepmother to Ayla, giving her everything she could want by magic or by purchase. That's why it was…" I exhaled. "It was such a shock when she killed him."

"That seems like a lot of effort for the stone."

"The legend is centuries old," I explained. "There's so much that was lost to time, including the specifics. The only thing that survived the years was that it was given to Ayla's ancestors by a wizard and the stone could only be used by a member of the monarch's immediate family. Whether that meant by marriage or by blood was unclear. Leandra and the fae thought they'd try their luck."

Ward pushed himself off the tree and shook his head. "But they have magic. Why did they need more?"

"Power-hungry people always want more," Cade said. "Eoghan thinks it's because Birch wanted to expand his reign beyond the fae realm borders. If he had the stone, he would be unstoppable. Not even a wizard could stand up to him with that power."

"Then why did a wizard give it to the Pennlan royal family?"

I shifted, remembering the vague description in the history book. "No one knows for sure. At least Eoghan doesn't, and he knows more about the stone than anyone," I said. "But my guess is that although we have magic, wizards still come from human parents. Perhaps the wizard lived in these lands a long time ago and wanted to give something to his king to keep the fae in check."

The knight was silent for a while. "Was Leandra able to use the stone?"

Cade smirked. "No. Once Bresel was dead, the role of sovereign fell to Ayla. Leandra still took it, though. Probably to make sure no one could use it on *her*."

"And nobody knows where? The fae realm is a big place."

"I think if we did, we would've retrieved the stone by now." He shifted in his saddle. "My theory is that the stone is sitting in the hands of King Birch as a trophy piece. A reminder of how he nearly bested the humans."

"Great," the knight muttered.

"You said it."

>→ >→ >→ >→

I knew we were getting close to Críoch thanks to the long wall that stretched from one end of the horizon to the other beyond the village we headed toward. My pulse picked up at the thought of being at the end of this journey—until I remembered it was only the beginning.

As Ward had predicted, we arrived at sundown and continued straight to the garrison where we'd find the captive fae. We left the horses in the stable out back with a silver to the stable boy and headed toward the main building. Ward walked inside the brick building with confidence, but we were stopped before we got too far.

"Well, look who's back?" the guard said. "Did you get kicked out for being a street rat, boy?"

"Actually," Ward said with a tight smile, "I'm with the Pennlan wizard on business from Eoghan. We need to speak with the commander immediately."

He barked a laugh and glanced in my direction. "This kid? A wizard?"

I tapped my staff on the ground and the tip lit up gold. "Yes, indeed. My name is Cade, and Ward is telling the truth. Now if you don't step aside and allow us to pass, I will have to use this thing on you. And you won't enjoy it."

The guard looked at Ward for a moment before turning around and unlocking the door behind him. He gave me a wary look as I passed, and I simply smiled, which somehow terrified him more.

We came to the end of a long hall and a pair of wooden doors. Ward raised his hand and knocked confidently, and we waited.

The doors opened to reveal a young, pretty woman. "Can I—Ward?

Is that you?" Her cheeks turned pink. "What are you doing back?"

"Just need to speak with the magistrate," Ward said, his smile melting into the most charming one I'd seen on him yet. "How ya been, Saoirse?"

"Better now that I've seen you," she said. "You aren't in trouble again, are you?"

"On the contrary." He gestured toward the room. "May we?"

She allowed us entry inside, and finally I saw him—Commander Eithne. He was an older man wearing a nice overcoat and seated behind a vast desk covered in papers. He looked up when we walked in, and his brow furrowed.

"Now, here I thought I was rid of you."

"And you will be again," Ward said, holding up his hands. "On official royal business today."

"Oh?" He sat back in his chair and looked at me. "Who is this?"

"My name is Cade," I said, not wanting to hear how the knight would introduce me. "I'm the apprentice to the wizard counsel Eoghan. He's sent us here to speak with the three fae you captured at the border."

Eithne leaned forward and put his hands on his desk, a perplexed look on his face. "What in the world are you talking about? We haven't captured any fae in decades."

Chapter Sixteen

Ayla

Against my better judgment, I did read the letter from the fae king. I read it probably ten times, just to make sure I wasn't missing anything. I wanted him to mention the sordid past between our kingdoms, to even acknowledge what the fae had done, but he didn't. His was merely a request to open the borders between our lands, as the trade routes had made both our countries rich once, along with an offer to send an envoy to my upcoming coronation as a first step.

The entire thing was a slap in the face, the audacity so brazen… What could've gone through the fae king's mind? Knowing he'd sat down to write a letter—a *long* letter—to me was…unsettling. The flowery words, the praise, the genial well-wishes. As if nothing in the world had transpired between our two nations.

And to send an *envoy* when every fae who'd set foot in these lands had been arrested and sent to prison… He was either drunk, senile, or evil from his head to his toes.

After the tenth read, I accepted I'd get nothing more from this letter. So I placed it in my hearth and lit it on fire with my candle, secretly hoping the fae had cast some kind of spell on it and would know what I thought of his nonsense.

But I didn't mention the letter to anyone. Eoghan was already treating me like a delicate flower, wilting at the sign of anything difficult, and perhaps I'd allowed him to think that way of me. I needed to be stronger if I was to be a good queen.

When I completed my breakfast and ventured down to my office for the morning, I found a stack of letters waiting for me, along with a note from Eoghan.

Call on me if you need any assistance.

I smiled and pushed aside his note, picking up the first letter. It was addressed to me, with a flourished pen, and seemed very official with a wax insignia I recognized as the Driwanian royal family's. I used the letter opener to slice the top off and pulled out the letter.

It was a request to attend my coronation as an envoy, signed by Prince Domnall. The second was a similar request, but from a duke from the kingdom of Konevell. His name was unfamiliar, but based on his title, he was someone close to the king.

In fact, every single letter on my table was a request to attend my coronation. We had begun assembling the attendees, starting, of course, with the local lords, dukes, and merchants who fueled the industry of the kingdom. But as to who we'd already invited from these other countries, I had no clue—perhaps a problem.

I rose and rang the soft bell at my door to call my attendant. Bronwen appeared after a few moments, bowing and smiling.

"How can I help you, Your Majesty?"

"I would like the official list of invited attendees to my coronation," I replied. "And I'm not sure who would have that information."

"Lord Eoghan has taken to managing your coronation, I believe," she said. "Shall I fetch him?"

"No, just the list," I said with a tight smile. No wonder Eoghan had said he was eager to give me all the responsibility—between managing the country and my coronation, it was a wonder he even had time to mentor Cade.

I walked to my window and stared out onto the plain, counting the days since Cade left. Four. Had he forgiven Ward for the moment in the garden with me? And Ward… Had he managed to see past Cade's high walls to the genuinely sweet wizard with a thirst for knowledge? They might come back best friends, for all I knew. And perhaps then, Cade might not be so cross with me for wanting to spend time with the knight.

Then again… My heart sank a little. The *marriage* conversation had come up more often than I liked, and I doubted that I could entertain a short dalliance with a knight when I was supposed to be looking for a husband. If I became attached to him, I wouldn't want to give up something wonderful, even if it was for the good of the kingdom.

And yet, I couldn't help but daydream about the way he'd looked at me, not as a princess of his sovereign, but simply a girl who was ready to be kissed for the first time.

"Your Majesty?" Bronwen was back. "I apologize, but Lord Eoghan said he's still finalizing the list and will have it to you in the next few days."

I turned, frowning. "It should've been finalized ages ago."

She hesitated. "I can only tell you what he told me. He also wanted me to inform you that you will have a dinner guest, Prince Hamish from Nesuria, this evening and to be sure you're punctual."

>-» >-» >-» >-»

By the time my hair was brushed and dinner shoes were on my feet, I had a speech prepared for Eoghan about why he should give me the coronation preparation activities. After all, if all the correspondence I was receiving was related to that activity, it just made sense. Eoghan would offer me some reason that would seem obvious, as he always did, but I would stand firm.

I arrived on time to dinner, where I found Eoghan waiting with the guest of honor. I had been hoping for a younger man, perhaps someone who might tempt my eye away from Ward, but the prince was even older than Weymouth, and a head shorter than I was.

"Ah, our fair princess has arrived," Eoghan said with a smile. "May

I present Prince Hamish of Nesuria."

I nodded, forcing a genial smile onto my face. "It is very nice to meet you. Shall we sit?"

"In a moment," Prince Hamish said, turning back to Eoghan. "So as I was saying, it seems somewhat silly for you to be charging us three copper per crate, especially considering your trade route to the fae isn't what it used to be."

Eoghan glanced at me, then nodded to him. "Yet, we are your largest importer of corn for our people. The taxes you pay pale in comparison to the money you make."

Hamish laughed. "You know so much about the costs of shipping halfway across the continent?"

"Nonsense, it's two weeks by boat. Barely a blip. Not nearly as expensive as Nesuria's trade with Konevell over land."

I bounced on my toes, ready to offer my opinion, but it didn't seem I could get a word in edgewise. Every time I'd open my mouth to comment, Eoghan would interject and make the comment for me. We were saying the same thing, so I assumed it was fine, but I still wanted to be the one to knock that prince down a few pegs.

"My merchants can barely make a profit based on your rates."

"I think we disagree on that. They get a whole gold coin for every crate."

"But you must consider the costs—"

"The ships can carry four hundred crates. That's hardly a hardship."

"Especially considering that those tariffs maintain the docks that are used by those ships, and we've constructed new ones to accommodate their larger sizes," I added.

Eoghan and Hamish turned to look at me as if they'd both forgotten I was there.

"I would let the adults handle the conversation," Hamish said. "You haven't seen enough years to know what you're talking about."

My mouth fell open in shock, and I looked at Eoghan for his

assistance. But he didn't appear to be on my side, either, turning toward the prince to continue arguing his point.

I sat back, folding my hands in my lap and staring at them, fighting the tears that had come, unwelcome, to my eyes. Crying was definitely not queen-like, so I kept my composure until the danger passed, focusing my gaze on the tips of my nails. When I finally lifted my gaze, the conversation had moved on to other matters, and it seemed the disrespect Hamish had shown me was forgotten.

Whether from spite or strategy, I kept silent the rest of the meal, just to see what would happen. I was never called on for my opinion, nor was I acknowledged in any way. I might as well have been invisible.

But while I was annoyed at Prince Pompous, the object of my ire had shifted to the wizard counsel dominating the conversation. It was his time to step aside, so why did it seem like every time I inched forward, he pushed me back into my box?

The dinner was excruciatingly slow, and I kept glancing at the clock on the wall, sighing in relief when the next course appeared. After the final plate of dessert was cleared away, I was practically bouncing in my seat to leave, but the two old men decided to continue their conversation for at least half an hour afterward.

Finally, I could take no more. "I believe I will take my leave. Good evening, Prince Hamish."

"Ah yes, excellent idea," Eoghan said. "Hamish, there are some books in my vault that you professed some interest in. We should retire to my study for a nightcap."

"Perfect!" As with Weymouth, the prince had imbibed far too much and needed assistance standing.

"Just give me one moment to speak with Her Majesty, and I will be there."

I almost protested, arguing that I didn't need to speak with him about anything, but I doubted I'd get a choice in the matter. So I followed him out, ready for the lecture and armed with my own retort.

"That was certainly something," Eoghan said. "What's gotten into you this evening? You were pouting like a child the entire time."

I narrowed my gaze at him. "Because the one time I spoke up, Prince Pompous bit my head off—and you did nothing about it."

"Why didn't you?" Eoghan asked. "You have a voice, the same as me. You just need to be more assertive. That's perhaps why Prince Hamish thought you so easily quieted."

I chewed my lip, unsure what to say to that.

"I know you're worried about the coronation, and your upcoming responsibilities, but you have to remember that I've been guiding in your stead for years. These personalities are used to my calm hand. Especially someone like Hamish. Nesuria is one of our closest trading partners, as they've got access to the southern islands. Hamish is the queen's brother, and he has her ear and attention." He paused. "Surely, you remember that from your studies."

I nodded. "That doesn't give him the right to be disrespectful."

"It doesn't, but unfortunately, depending on the ally, it's better to allow them to walk over you than risk it. We can't grow as much corn this far north—"

"I know, I know," I said, waving my hand.

"You seem annoyed about something else," Eoghan said, tilting his head toward me. "What is it?"

I hesitated again, unsure if I wanted to keep complaining, but it needed to be said. "The letters I received today were all about invitations to my coronation," I said. "And as I don't have the most recent list of invitees or even the plan for the coronation, I can't possibly respond to them. So…" I cleared my throat. "I would like to take that on."

"I would love to give it to you, trust me, I would," Eoghan said. "But based on what happened this evening, it doesn't seem prudent. A coronation is a delicate thing—assigning seating based on the particular personalities is a tricky art."

I crossed my arms over my chest. "I know the personalities."

"You do, but not as well as I do. One day, you will know all of them."

"In a little over a month, this will all be my responsibility," I replied, a little hotly. "So—"

"Ayla." He gave me a stern look I hadn't seen in a few years. "Let me do what's best for you. I promise everything will be fine once the crown is on your head." He straightened. "In the meantime, it might be best to resume your studies with Lady Enid."

"Are you serious?" I'd finally rid myself of that old windbag weeks ago. "I don't need to study more. I need to do the work."

"When you're ready," he said, turning to walk away. "And in the meantime, Lady Enid will be in your office tomorrow at ten sharp. Please don't be late."

And with that, he left me in the hallway, open-mouthed and wondering who was the sovereign and who was the supposed counsel.

Chapter Seventeen

Ward

The words hung in the air and the wizard let out an incredulous laugh. "There...has to be a mistake." Cade looked at me. "Is there another place they could be?"

"No, this is the only..." I leaned on the desk. "Are you sure you have no fae here? Eoghan told us he was the brother-in-law of the fae king."

My former commander, a grizzled, straight sort of man, shook his head, a glimmer of confusion in his eye. "Ward, you've been too long in that castle. We haven't seen a fae in years."

That was true, but I'd thought this was... I honestly didn't know. A special situation? Shame and embarrassment—and a little anger—crept up my neck. I hadn't even questioned the order or thought about whether it fit within what I knew of the garrison here. I'd just accepted the mission, and the implied glory that would come with being successful, and set off.

Cade was trying to reason with Eithne, but I was too far in my own mind. Where had the miscommunication happened? Had Eoghan gotten bad information? It was entirely possible, considering the distance between Pennlan and CrÍoch. It seemed preposterous that a wizard would send his apprentice and one of the guard's new recruits on a mission to nothing.

Unless... No. This had nothing to do with being in the garden with Ayla. The wizard was a powerful man. That sort of behavior was beneath him.

More importantly, without the fae, I had no leads to find the stone in the fae realm. The wizard would presumably turn around and head back to Pennlan, and perhaps have some choice words with his master. But even though this particular part of the task was a dead end, I still had my part to play.

Vaguely, I heard the wizard thank the commander for his help and turn to leave, and I followed. Saoirse tried to call my name, and once upon a time, I would've stopped to flirt with her. But today, I just didn't have it in me.

Night had fallen when we walked out of the prison, and we stood for a moment, the both of us in shock.

"I suppose you'll head back to Pennlan now?" the wizard said, after we'd stood there for a few minutes.

"Me?" I blinked. "You."

"Why me? I…" He cleared his throat. "Eoghan told me that your mission was to bring me to Críoch only and return to Pennlan."

I licked my lips, turning to him fully. "Eoghan told *me* that *your* mission was to interrogate the fae and return to Pennlan. Where the hell…" I let out a sigh, glancing at the sky. "He told you to get the stone."

"Well, obviously," he said, a flush starting on his cheeks. "What? You think he would let a human like you take on such an important task?"

I quirked a brow. "Yes, actually. He told me I could travel easier and attract less attention than a wizard."

The wizard's jaw dropped. "That can't be true. Why would Eoghan give us the same mission and not tell us?"

"Because he's a liar."

I turned quickly, grabbing the hilt of my sword as the wizard's staff came to his hand. The fae girl who'd been following us stood right behind us, her hands raised in surrender and her hood pulled over her head. In the light, her youth was even more apparent. But I remained on my guard.

"Put down your weapons before someone notices," she said, glancing around furtively. She had taken a risk to show herself here—what she had to say was probably important.

"Cade," I said, dropping my hand. "Let her speak."

"Absolutely not," the wizard snarled. "We needed a fae to interrogate, so let's interrogate her."

"Or, alternatively," she said, her hands still raised as she kept looking around for someone to notice her, "I can help you find the stone."

The wizard straightened then barked a laugh. "So you're telling me that you, a fae, want me, a wizard, to trust you to bring us into your homeland and get us the stone that one of your kind stole from us?"

"Yes," she snapped, her cheeks turning a little red.

"And why would a fae do something like that?"

"Because it belongs to your princess," she said. "Ayla can use it to defeat that damned wizard who's been lording over her for years."

"Careful," Cade said, his staff still lit up and ready to attack. "That damned wizard is my master."

"And clearly, he lied to you," she said, keeping his gaze. "Or did I mishear the conversation you just had?"

She had us there, and I was a little more inclined to believe her at the moment. "Why did he lie to us?"

"I don't know, exactly. I don't pretend to understand how evil thinks," she said, venom in her words. "But my guess is that he expected you both to continue on to the fae realm and get yourselves killed. It didn't matter to him how—he just wanted you out of the way."

Cade straightened, disbelief plain on his face. "He spent the last decade and a half training me. Why would he want me dead?"

"Did you miss the part where I said he's evil?" she snapped. "All he cares about is getting the stone for himself."

"He can't use it," Cade said, matter-of-factly. "What he cares about is getting the stone back for Ayla, to protect Pennlan from creatures like you. He told me he wants to leave the castle and let me remain as its protector."

"How is getting us out of the way getting him the stone?" I asked.

"Look, I told you, I don't pretend to know how evil works," she stammered, her cheeks flushing more. "But he sent you on this quest knowing full well that you two would fail. Let me help you, and you can actually *find* the stone and bring it to Princess Ayla."

"We can find it just fine," Cade said.

"It's not in Birch's castle," she said. "He's not so stupid that he'd put something so dangerous there."

"Then where is it?" I pressed.

She smiled. "You don't expect me to just tell you? Besides that, you two know nothing about the fae realm. You need a guide. Let me be that guide."

Cade just laughed, but I considered her offer. "What do you want in return?"

The wizard spun on me, his jaw falling open. "You can't be serious?"

"I am," I replied, waving him off. "You say you'll take us to the stone. What's in it for you? The wizard has a point. We've been enemies ever since you betrayed King Bresal."

She licked her lips. "That story might not be as cut and dried as you've been told."

The wizard grabbed my sleeve and dragged me away to have a private talk. "This is dumb," he said. "She's clearly trying to trick us into following her because she thinks we're desperate."

"We are desperate," I said, removing his hand from my shirt.

"She just wants to lead us away from Birch's castle. Send us on a wild goose chase and in a year or so, we'll finally make it back."

I glanced at her, as she pretended to ignore our conversation. "Then why not just kill us?"

"I don't know how fae think." He narrowed his eyes. "Maybe they can't kill me, and they just want to distract me while they attack Pennlan."

"You?" I snorted. "Why just you?"

"You're inconsequential. A mage like me only arrives once in a generation," Cade said. "And with Eoghan and myself at the castle, it's protected. But if I were to wander off into the fae realm…"

It took everything in me not to laugh. The wizard who'd nearly pissed himself when thieves had attacked thought he would be any help against an advancing fae army? "Then I'll go, and you go back to Pennlan and find out why Eoghan lied to us."

"But… But you can't…" He sputtered, shaking his head.

"After all, I'm inconsequential," I continued, a smile on my face. "Not to mention human. Seems like the most logical solution to our problem."

"And what happens when she betrays you?"

"Then either I'll die or she will, but either way, Pennlan won't lose its *main protectors*." I tilted my head. "I can't see why you're so averse to this idea."

And yet, I could. The wizard had the same lofty ideas as I did about retrieving the stone and becoming Princess Ayla's hero. Forget his so-called wizard trial, his prize at the end of this was her love, and I doubted he'd go down without a fight.

"Do you really think this girl is worth trusting?" he asked, after a long pause. "So much that you're willing to bet your life?"

I turned to the girl again, who was watching the ground as she kicked it. There was an earnestness about her words, almost like she was trying to prove something. It was the same look I'd had when I'd convinced the commander to take a chance on me after he'd caught me stealing for the fiftieth time.

"Here's the alternative," the wizard said, turning on her. "I can just take her under my control, force her to tell us where she 'kind of' thinks the stone is, then go get it without her."

"You…" She took a step backward, a flash of fear crossing her face.

"Cade, wait—"

Before I could get out what I wanted to say, the girl disappeared into a flight of butterflies again and was gone. I exhaled loudly, staring at the sky and resisting the urge to clock the idiot.

"Great job, wizard."

"That wasn't my fault."

"She was *literally* about to agree to help us."

"But we don't need her help if I can coerce her to speak," Cade said, waving his staff. "If she were under my control, she could lead us all the way to the stone, and we wouldn't have to wonder if she was tricking us."

I sighed, squinting in the direction the butterflies had gone and wishing I had that magic. Then, without another word, I walked away.

"Where are you going?" the wizard called after me.

"My orders were to get you to Críoch," I said, turning to walk back to him. I reached for the pouch under my shirt and handed him the whole thing; I doubted I'd have use for it in the fae realm. "Here. This should be enough to get you back to Pennlan safely."

"But—"

I clapped him on the shoulder. "Good luck to you, wizard."

Chapter Eighteen

Cade

I was torn between several thoughts as I wandered aimlessly around Críoch. The first was fury that we'd come all this way for nothing. The second was confusion—Eoghan wasn't the sort to get things like this wrong. Perhaps…perhaps he'd fabricated the whole thing to get me out of the castle. But if that were the case, why give the knight the same mission as myself?

And more importantly, why not just come out and tell us?

Eoghan always had a master plan, something that was so plainly obvious once it revealed itself, but I struggled to figure it out until then. He'd sent me this way for a purpose, and I trusted my master much more than some meddlesome fae girl.

Ward could do what he wanted, but I would continue to the fae realm without him. I just needed to get beyond the wall. It didn't take me long to find what had once been the main gate. Near the garrison, the wall was split by two large wooden doors nearly the size of a city block. Once upon a time, they'd been open, allowing trade between the two nations. Now, they were covered in thick vines and rust.

Guards stood at lax attention, so I approached two of them, waving at them with a smile on my face. "Good evening."

"What d'ya want?" one barked at me.

"I wondered if you could open the gate for me," I said with a confident look. "I'm here under royal orders."

They looked at each other then burst into laughter.

I gripped my staff as I waited for them to stop, pursing my lips in annoyance.

"That gate hasn't been opened in almost twenty years, you moron."

"Sure, we'll just go upstairs and turn it on, like magic."

"Oi!" One of them turned to a nearby guard who'd grown interested in the commotion. "This guy wants us to open the gate! Can you believe him?"

"I believe I said I was under royal orders," I said, calmly.

"I don't care if the queen herself came down here and told us to open the gates," the first said, wiping a tear from his eye. "Unless the garrison commander tells us to, we aren't budging. Go get his approval, and we'll do it."

I considered blasting the three of them into next week, but I merely nodded. "Thank you. I will be back."

>→ >→ >→ >→

The commander was still in his office when I let myself into his office. He jumped when I opened the door, but recognition dawned.

"Story's still the same," he said, returning to the papers he'd been working on. "No fae."

"I understand," I said. "But what I'd like is a signed letter from you informing your guards at the gate that I should be allowed to cross the border."

He glanced up from his work then lifted his head. "You want me to…what?"

"We may not have found any fae here, but I still have a task from Princess Ayla herself to complete," I said. "And it requires me to cross the border into fae country."

"And you want me to open the gates—the gates that haven't been opened in twenty years?"

I was starting to get a headache from the repetition. "The very same."

"No." He went back to his papers.

"No? You can't tell me no. I'm the damned wizard apprentice of Pennlan," I said, coming to my feet. My staff glowed menacingly, but it didn't seem to faze the commander at all.

"I'm saving your life, wizard apprentice. The fae realm is no place for anyone, let alone someone like you."

I scoffed. "What do you mean, someone like me?"

"You look like you haven't seen a hard day's work in your life," he said. "And the fae realm is… There's things there that will sooner eat you than let you walk by. Everything is dangerous there, even the trees and rocks."

"But you'll let someone like Ward go?"

"I wouldn't let *anyone* go," he snapped. "And Ward's smart enough to know what's over there. Caught him sneaking across the border enough times."

I paused. "I'm sorry?"

"He grew up here, you know?" He grunted. "Fell into a rough crowd for a couple months before we got it into his head he could do more than steal from farmers. Half the time, we caught them trying to sneak through the weak parts in the wall."

Interesting. "I see. How often do you catch humans crossing?"

"Not very often. Usually just kids." He tilted his head. "But as I said, it's dangerous over there. More than once, a kid slipped through the border and didn't come back. If the fae find you, it's over."

I doubted the street urchins of this town had magic. "Understood. I'm merely trying to understand what goes on here so I can give a *good report* to my master and princess."

But he was either impervious or too dumb to get my insinuation. "Do what you want. Just don't attempt to cross."

I rose to leave but couldn't help my curiosity. "You said Ward was a thief as a child? I thought he grew up on a farm?"

"He had a brother on the outskirts of town, but after the tenth time coming to bail him out, he stopped coming." The commander pulled another paper from the stack and began reading. "But Ward had promise, so we recruited him. Clearly, we made the right call, as he was chosen to serve at the castle."

"Chosen how?" I asked.

"Royal recruiters pass through once a year, see if anyone stands out. Ward got it into his head that he wanted out of here, so he got real good at swordplay, archery, whatever else they'd be testing on. Blew everyone else out of the water." He scrawled his signature on the page then grabbed another one. "I bet that boy could fly to the moon if he wanted it bad enough."

I smiled at the thought, but inwardly, I was relishing my own instincts. I'd accurately pegged him from the beginning. He wasn't interested in Ayla for any other reason than her position, and what she could give him. This task—the stone—was merely to advance his career and personal wealth. I was sure he expected a hefty reward when he was victorious.

Which meant I had to make sure he wasn't.

"Thank you for your time," I said, walking to the door. "I'll bring a good report back to Pennlan."

⤙⤙⤙⤙

When I left the commander's office, it was dark, but I was oddly wide awake. I perhaps should've found an inn to rest for the night, especially since I had the bag of Ward's money around my neck, but I could move easier in the dark. I'd rest once I was through and could find safe haven.

I purposefully avoided the main gate this time, but still made a beeline for the wall. If the commander was to be believed, children were able to pass through. That meant there was at least one weak spot in the wall. Certainly I could make some adjustments to the wall to slip across myself.

I could've done a locator spell on the knight and asked him where the breach was, but I doubted he'd tell me, plus he was probably elbows deep in his third tankard of ale. He hadn't given me all his money, after all, just what Eoghan had provided.

I let my thoughts wander as I walked the length of the stone wall. It was…just stone. No iron, no other armaments. Just a basic wall that stretched above the city. It seemed woefully inadequate to keep out magical creatures like the fae. When I returned to Pennlan, I would make it my mission to fortify this wall with iron so that all creatures would stay where they belonged.

Every few feet, I'd tap the stone with my staff, searching for a weak spot. If I had to guess, it would be far from the city center, but not so far that the local children couldn't reach it after a short journey. The houses were starting to look more run-down, so I hoped I was going the right way.

A shadow moved ahead of me. I quickly dimmed the light on my staff, hiding myself in the darkness of the night. I held my breath as I squinted—was it the knight?

Son of a bitch. He was making his crossing tonight. I supposed I should've known. An ambitious man like him wouldn't let a little thing like the fae realm stop him. I picked up my staff and hurried after him, keeping my distance and casting a silence spell around my feet to keep my footfalls silent.

The clouds shifted and moonlight flooded the street once more, revealing Ward's face. He glanced up at the border wall then quickly dashed to the safety of the wall, pressing himself flat. Not two seconds later, two border guards walked by, talking loudly.

Once they'd passed, Ward took a moment to survey the area, making sure no other danger was around. I thought he might've seen me, but I was well-hidden in the darkness of an alley. He peeled himself off the wall and kept walking, albeit at a much faster pace.

Twice more, he had to flatten himself against the wall to avoid being seen by a pair of guards walking the streets. Finally, he stopped abruptly, sliding his fingers around a large stone, which, to my surprise, came loose. Based on its size, Ward should've been straining to hold it, but the way he carried it told me it was a fake. The hole it left behind was small—perhaps only children could get through it.

Just as I assumed he might give up and try somewhere else, he took off his sword and traveling bag and pushed them to the other side. Then he crawled head-first into the hole, wriggling like a fish. I was dead sure he'd get stuck, and I'd get to gloat and offer aid. But then he managed to disappear, his boots the last thing I saw.

I moved forward then stopped when he reappeared and reached down to grab the stone that he'd removed, pulling it back into place behind him to seal off the hole.

"Hm."

I waited a few minutes, not wanting to alert Ward to my presence. I glanced at the wall above and the streets, making sure there weren't any guards walking by. When the coast was clear, I crossed the street to the wall, running my hand along it. The stone itself was no different in size and shape than the others, but when I touched it, my mouth was filled with the most peculiar taste—like sweet vinegar.

Fae magic. This stone was covered in fae magic.

I swore, shaking my head and wishing I could walk right down to the commander's office and bring him here to show him what he'd allowed. But there wasn't time for that.

Even though I surrounded the stone with my magic to move it, that taste still filled my mouth and I was glad to put it down. The hole it left behind *was* rather small, and it was amazing Ward had been able to contort his body to fit. I was much thinner, but I had my doubts.

That was, until I rested my hand on the outside and got another taste of fae magic. This thing *was* small, but it would expand to fit whoever was crawling through. Would it let a wizard pass? That was the real question.

I took off my pack and pushed it through, but I didn't want to give up my staff. Placing it on the bottom of the hole, I gripped it for dear life in case this whole wall decided to collapse on top of me, but nothing happened. I ducked my head and crawled into the darkness, my pulse pounding in my ears. So far, so good.

I reached the other side and tumbled out in a heap on the ground, and clutching my heart and being thankful that whatever fae had charmed this place hadn't thought to put an anti-wizard charm on it. I rose and dusted myself off, sliding my traveling pack over my shoulder again and steadying myself.

My magic slid through the fae-made hole and surrounded the stone I'd removed on the human side, pulling the stone back into place. Then I closed my eyes, concentrating until I found it—the tendrils of fae magic that surrounded the hole and stone themselves. It resembled something like ivy tangling around an object, though invisible to the naked eye. With my magic, I broke up the connections, releasing the magic from the wall and the stone itself, and leaving them both impenetrable again.

"There," I said, satisfied. "Should solve that problem."

"So you thought it a good idea to get rid of our only way back to the human world?"

Chapter Nineteen

Ward

I'd know the wizard had been following me for a while, and I was curious how far he'd go. But when I saw him standing at the stone, that damn staff glowing, I knew what he'd been up to—and I wasn't pleased.

"You could've mentioned to…I don't know, *anyone* that there was a weakness in the wall," Cade said, turning the conversation. "Perhaps during your time growing up as a thief or in the local garrison."

I couldn't help but smile. "You've been talking to the commander."

"I have, and I pegged you correctly from the beginning," he said, sounding very pleased with himself. "You're nothing but a social climber, and you don't care who you step on to get to your end goal."

"Which is what, exactly?" I asked, crossing my arms over my chest. "Because where I'm standing—which is, might I remind you, a dangerous territory filled with deadly creatures without a map or a way of knowing where I'm going—I'm taking great personal risk to retrieve an object for the ruler of my kingdom. Doesn't seem like the sort of thing a social climber would do."

"It is absolutely—"

His voice had begun to echo, and I quickly shushed him. "Do you want to draw all the fae to us? Keep your voice down, you colossal moron." He scowled at me and I shook my head. "Look, you can think whatever you want about me, I really don't care. Our partnership is at an end."

He stared at me, almost as if at war with himself. "You know, it might be better to work together."

"Oh?"

"Two heads are better than one, after all. One of us can sleep while the other keeps watch. That sort of thing."

I crossed my arms over my chest, amused. "Or are you just scared to go off on your own?"

"I'm not scared," he said, but the look on his face was telling. "But if we're going the same—"

"I'm good," I said, cutting him off.

He snorted. "Fine. Be that way. Have a good life, for however long it lasts in this country."

Blessedly, the wizard turned in a different direction and within minutes, the glow of his staff had disappeared over a hill. The moon overhead offered light every so often, and more than once, I considered stopping to rest. I bargained with myself that I would get at least a way from the border, lest I be seen by either the humans or fae guarding it. Then I'd rest until sunup, get my bearings, and press on.

On this side of the border, the world didn't seem so different from Críoch. The ground was still rocky and sparse, the trees scraggly. There were roads and bridges and villages, so said the old folk in Críoch who used to trade with the fae, but how they differed from the human realm remained unknown. I would immediately stick out there, so it was probably best to avoid them unless absolutely necessary.

King Birch lived in a castle on the northeast side of the fae realm, supposedly only a few days' ride from the border gate at Críoch. When the sun came up, I would find the road—which I hoped still existed— and keep close to it. Without the trade with the humans, it might have fallen into disuse, perhaps even become overgrown. That might bode well for me as there wouldn't be any fae traveling along it.

But I would have to be careful. The old folk in Críoch also said that everything had its own mind in this land, from the rocks and grass to the birds and trees. Nothing could be trusted to be real, either, due to their use of glamour and magical tricks. The fae girl had shown us what she was capable of, and I just hoped she showed herself once more now that the wizard was gone.

After walking for roughly an hour, exhaustion finally caught up with me. I found a small hiding spot in an outcropping of a rock, hoping that the rock itself wouldn't crush me in the night, and settled underneath it, stretching out and trying to find a comfortable spot. It certainly made me miss all the lumpy mattresses back in the human world.

The moon appeared from behind the clouds again, revealing the empty plain I'd just walked down and the border wall stretched across the horizon. Críoch lay just beyond, barely visible in the darkness. It was, perhaps, the last time I'd lay eyes on the human realm and something about it made me homesick. Perhaps I should've taken a moment to stop in on my brother.

But just as soon as the city appeared, it was gone again in the darkness. And I closed my eyes and let sleep take me.

>→ >→ >→ >→

Squawk!

I opened my eyes slowly, my mind still caught in sleep's embrace. But there was…a thing sitting on my chest. Three eyes stared down at me, as well as a beak.

"Shit!" I scrambled to my feet, awake in seconds.

What I'd considered a monster in my half-awake state was just a crow, jumping around on the ground and cawing at me. I put my hand to my chest to soothe my pounding heart and reached down to grab my sword and scabbard by my side.

"Peace?" I asked the crow. It looked at me with its three eyes blinking blankly and snapped its beak. Then it unfurled giant wings and flew off into the pink and purple sky.

I leaned back on the rock I'd been sleeping under and shook my head, rubbing my face. I was in need of a wash basin and a mirror to shave, but here in this world, I'd get neither. Maybe a pond. But for now, there was nothing to do except have some breakfast then start my journey.

I reached for my meat pouch and opened it…only to find it empty.

"What the…?" I turned it over, my brow furrowing. "That little…"

He must've stopped the spell on my bag. And clearly, I hadn't been carefully rationing my food.

Ignoring my gurgling stomach, I swung my traveling pack onto my shoulders, put my scabbard around my hips, and got to walking. The border wall wound and curved across the land. I'd walked northwest from the gate, but I could make out the remnants of the road that terminated there. If I walked due east, I would hit the road then get on track.

I rested my hand on my scabbard, keeping my eyes to the sky and ears open for anything approaching. The sun was up, warming the land from the somewhat cool morning that had settled on my skin.

The farther I walked, the more I began to worry I was leaving too much to chance by being in the open like this. If I came across any fae soldiers, there would be nowhere to hide. Not that there seemed to be much in this part of the country, other than the errant three-eyed bird.

In fact, that damn bird was following me.

It could've been a different crow, of course, but something told me it wasn't. Midday, when I stopped to rest, it landed within a few feet, cawing at me.

"What?" I asked. "You want some food? Because I don't have any."

It snapped its beak and hopped closer.

"You know, those three eyes are disconcerting," I replied.

To my horror, the eyes rotated…*rotated*…on its face.

"That's worse," I said, suddenly put off from the dried meat for a moment. "Don't do that again."

It hopped up onto the rock I was sitting on and cawed at me expectantly, so I pulled out the empty bag to show him I had nothing.

"See? Damn wizard left me with nothing. Now unless you know the way to the fae capital, get a move on."

It unfurled its wings and flew away.

"That's what I thought..."

>→ >→ >→ >→

Mid-afternoon, I was starting to miss my horse. I'd left her in the garrison stables and given the stable boy explicit instructions on her care. The commander would hopefully ensure her well-being. Hopefully, she'd be there when I returned. But for now, I was stuck on my own two legs, which had begun to ache with every hill I ascended and descended.

It had been hours since I'd seen the wizard, and I was starting to wonder where the fae girl was. Surely, enough distance had passed that she felt safe coming to find me. But without the wizard around, I didn't really know if she was watching me. For all I knew, she could've been that three-eyed crow.

Speaking of: my friend returned mid-afternoon, crying out in a nearby tree. And this time, he'd brought a friend. Six eyes stared down at me as I walked by.

"Okay," I said, stopping. "I have nothing for you. So you can just forget it. Go forage or do whatever you were doing before."

The original crow hopped forward and opened its mouth to cry out, but instead, a horrifying sound came out. I cried as my ears hurt like nothing I'd ever felt before. I covered them quickly, but it didn't do much good. The sound was deafening.

The crows' eyes turned blood red, and they spread their wings, taking off together. Instead of flying for the skies, they flew directly for me. Their sharp beaks pierced my clothes, pulling and tugging at it.

"Hey, back off," I said, waving my arms to keep them off me. But they were too many, and seemed to multiply. I cried in pain as one reached my flesh, ripping a piece off and...eating it.

"Uh oh."

I reached for my sword and swung it at whatever I could. Three birds dropped, but by now, there was a flock of them, flapping their wings and waiting for their turn at the food. Me. I swung more, hitting as many as I could, circling around to the ones pecking at my back and neck but gaining no traction.

Finally, I did the only thing I could think of—put my sword away and ran like hell.

The birds were momentarily surprised by the change in tactics, but they were right behind me. I grabbed my knife from my holster and kept it ready to slice at any bird who got too close, my heart pounding in my chest.

Up ahead, I saw a thicket of trees—perhaps my saving grace. I doubled my speed and dove into the shade of the trees, flipping over, ready to attack any crows that had followed.

But they remained on the edge of the forest, gathering and squawking. Their eyes had returned to the soulless black they'd been before and I heaved a sigh of relief as I checked myself for injury. They'd managed to carve a few chunks out of my arms, and my neck was wet with blood, but it wasn't too bad.

"That'll teach me to feed the locals," I muttered, reaching into my pack to see if I'd been smart enough to pack bandages to stop the bleeding. The cloth of my sleeve was caught in a nearby thorn bush—I hadn't even noticed it when I'd dove in. I tugged at it to free it, ripping my shirt in yet another place.

"Perfect." I sighed. At this rate, I'd have no shirt left. I dug in my pack, but then noticed my left arm was now caught. I rolled my eyes and went to stand up, but my legs were caught.

No, they weren't caught—the vine had *wrapped around them.*

"Does *everything* in this place want to eat me?" I said, pulling my knife out and cutting the vines. But just as soon as I was free, more vines slapped around my arms, and my knife fell to the ground. I reached for it, but the plant was stronger. Now, I had all four limbs under its control, and realized it had begun *pulling* me backward.

And to my horror, a low growl echoed from the darkness.

Chapter Twenty

Cade

The knight was a bastard, and I wouldn't be sad if he only lasted a day. Let the fae come for him. He'd be an excellent distraction. As I walked along the empty plain, I considered that might've been Eoghan's plan all along. It was one plausible explanation for a situation that still made very little sense to me.

It was daylight now, and I regretted not stopping to sleep. But this land was filled with magic—everything was filled with magic—and I probably wouldn't have been able to sleep if I'd tried. I wasn't sure what to expect once I passed through to the fae realm, but the almost overwhelming sense of *aliveness* humming around me was strange and unsettling.

I would acclimate, I hoped, then get back to focusing on the task at hand. While the knight would stumble around and probably get lost, I had the benefit of a locator spell in my arsenal. It was one of the many I'd practiced in my preparation for my trial and, once cast, the magic would guide me in the direction of something I was looking for.

The spell, however, seemed to be struggling—or I was. There was so much interference here it was hard to think straight, let alone use my magic with any sort of clarity. It was almost as if I was back to my early childhood, carrying this staff and trying to figure out how to do the simple tasks Eoghan asked of me. I'd spent days unable to wield magic correctly, sensing the magic in my veins but unable to communicate with it. Then, as now, I was merely throwing my desires out there, and hoping something would stick.

Compounding this was my extreme exhaustion. Finally, around midday, I gave up and decided to rest under the shade of a small tree. I was able to conclude the tree itself held no magic of note before setting my staff and bag down beside me and stretching out. I didn't even have the energy to make the rock under my head more comfortable as I closed my eyes.

But just as soon as I was nearly asleep, I was awoken by a loud growl from my stomach. I reached into my meat pouch for a small snack, but to my horror, it was completely empty. Not even a crumb to cast a replenishment spell on.

I turned the bag inside-out in a bit of panic, wishing I'd at least thought to purchase some actual provisions for the road before barging across. Now, all I had was regrets and trepidation. I didn't relish the idea of finding some animal, killing and skinning it, and making my meal that way, but if it was what I had to do, so be it. If that damned knight could fend for himself, so could I.

This time, I used my locator spell—with difficulty—to find something I could eat, and it seemed to work a little better, confidently guiding me toward the west. My mouth watered at the thought of fresh meat—as much as I could stomach. I'd devised an elaborate plan where I'd eat half of it, dry the rest, then use the pelt for a satchel to take with me, like the knight had.

But when I saw what was waiting at the end of the spell, my heart fell into my very empty stomach.

It was a nest of tiny creatures covered in brown fur, squeaking and whimpering in a small nest of twigs. They had pink eyes and webbed feet with claws, and long snouts that ended in little wet noses. They moved slowly, as if blind, and stumbled and crawled over one another in the comfortable nest.

I frowned. They were almost too adorable to kill. But my stomach insisted that their cuteness would only make them more delicious, so I raised my staff and girded myself.

"Sorry, little friends."

I released a bolt of lightning toward the closest one, but it jumped out of the way. I frowned and released another one, then another one—all of them missing.

"Okay," I said, shaking myself. "I can do this."

But no matter how hard I tried, my lightning bolts wouldn't land true. After a few minutes, I sat down and sighed, defeated.

"Find me more food," I said to my staff. The magic landed three feet from me in the small nest of beautiful creatures. "Not them. Something else."

It circled the area then landed three feet away once more. Annoyed, I rolled onto my back and slapped my face a few times.

"Get yourself together, Cade," I muttered. "Kill the damn things and eat them so we can keep going."

I raised my staff yet again, but then there was a loud noise—a roar of sorts. I looked up at a giant version of the adorable little furry monsters. Where the little ones had minuscule teeth, this thing had fangs the size of my arm, dripping with drool and blood as it carried prey in its mouth.

"Whoa there," I said, scrambling to my feet.

It was at least as tall as my waist and weighed probably five times as much as I did. It let loose another feral growl, and I backed away slowly, holding my staff up, ready. This would be more meat than I could possibly eat in one day, but perhaps it could…

The thing opened its jaw and let out the loudest roar I'd heard in my life, the force so great it sent me flying backward. I would've landed hard on a nearby rock, but at the last minute, my magical survival skills kicked in and stopped me in mid-air. I righted myself just as the creature opened its mouth for another round.

I held up my staff and formed a shield, but even still, I skidded backward a few feet. It was then that the little babies came crawling out of the nest and opened their mouths, sending smaller versions of their mother's roar. Individually, it might not have done much, but together, it was just as powerful.

So, like any self-respecting wizard, I turned tail and ran.

>→ >→ >→ >→

As much as I hated to admit it, I perhaps needed the knight to survive in this damn place.

I cast another locator spell—this one working perfectly—and found the knight some half an hour's walk away. I practiced what I'd say, my hunger promising me that groveling was much less horrible than my brain said it was. I could prove myself useful if need be. Or I'd just throw myself at his mercy and beg for his help.

Hunger had made me a humble man indeed.

I crested the hill where I'd find him and stopped short. There was no sign of him, but a flock of birds sat expectantly around a large thicket. I came closer, both curious and hoping that they'd make excellent meat, when I heard the distinct sounds of struggle from inside the forest.

"Ward?" I called into the forest. "Are you in there?"

"W-wizard?" came the strangled response. "*Help!*"

The thicket was covered in fae magic, and inside was a very peculiar mixture of earthy wood and blood. Whatever had the knight was going to eat him.

"I'll get you out," I said, but the forest somehow grew thicker as I tried to approach. But through the thickets, I spotted Ward splayed out on the ground and covered in vines that were tugging him closer to a dark fae monster. He struggled against the binding, but they replaced themselves as soon as he pulled them off.

"Stay still," I called.

"Easier said than done," he barked back.

I licked my lips, taking a deep breath. It was one thing to fail to conjure when I was just hungry, but if I failed now, Ward would die— and I'd really be alone. Panic seemed to calm my racing brain, and I conjured a lightning bolt, casting it into the darkness. It landed true, severing the vines at once and I let out a little cheer of relief.

Ward didn't wait around, scrambling to his feet and dashing out to the plains beyond. Once he was at a safe distance, he fell to his knees, then his hands, then rolled onto his back, staring at the sky and huffing and puffing.

"Seems like that forest didn't like you very much," I said, standing over him. "Are you all right?"

He closed his eyes and nodded. "What are you even doing here anyway?"

"Clearly, saving your life."

He cracked one eye open to glare at me. "I was fine."

"I fail to see how you were going to get yourself out of that one," I said, leaning on my staff. "But…perhaps it was foolhardy to split up. I find that I'm not quite as adept at walking in the open plain as I thought."

He grunted as he came to his feet. "You may have a point. Everything in this place wants me dead, so it might be nice to have someone watch my back."

Relief spread across my chest; I'd feared he would be stubborn and refuse my assistance. "I feel the same way. I've got a locator spell on the castle. We should be there in four days."

There was an awkward silence between us, one I hoped was the beginning of an actual partnership of choice and not just by circumstance.

"You know," I said, clearing my throat, "this journey may go a lot easier if we're nice to one another."

He rolled his eyes and started walking. "Just when I thought you weren't going to be an ass."

"I meant that for both of us," I said, scrambling to catch up with him.

"I'm sure."

"Ward." I finally noticed the chunks of flesh missing from his neck, arms, and legs. "Let me fix you. All that blood might attract more predators."

He gazed at me somewhat curiously then nodded. My staff lit up and knitted together the punctures and scratches in his skin, clearing the blood from the fibers of his clothes and mending the tears. I frowned when I found a rather large chunk taken out of his neck.

"What the—"

"Crows," he said, rubbing the back of his neck. "Don't ask. And don't feed anything here."

"Noted."

"We should look for food, though. My bag—"

"Shut up."

A breeze had blown a mixture of scents by—fae scents. I tilted my head up toward the sky and spotted a large dark cloud floating this way.

"What is it?" Ward asked, following my gaze.

"I think we've been seen," I said, looking around. There was nowhere to hide, not unless we wanted to duck back into the forest that had just tried to eat Ward. My staff filled with magic as I readied myself for our first tussle with the dreaded creatures we'd been hoping to avoid.

The moths drew closer, landing in pillars that surrounded us and transforming into ten fae warriors wearing leather armor and holding various weapons—swords, spears, bows and arrows. One even had an axe. They were as tall as I was, thin and willowy with pointed ears and golden eyes.

One drew my attention, perhaps because his armor was slightly shinier than the others. His hair was white-blond, odd against his deep brown skin, and his countenance was decidedly unfriendly. But I couldn't blame him. We were a human and wizard in a place we certainly shouldn't have been.

"State your purpose in the lands of King Birch, intruders."

Chapter Twenty-One

Ayla

"And in the fifth century, the queen of Nesuria married the second cousin of the king of Sudaemor, and thus created an alliance and the Morgan line."

It was hard to keep my eyes open, both from the hot air in the room and the droning of Lady Enid. I couldn't believe I was back here, listening to her go on and on about the ancient web of royal families that stretched back a thousand years. I didn't think it entirely necessary for a queen to know who'd married whom in the fifth century, especially since, two hundred years later, the entire family line would be wiped out by a massive plague.

But I had to sit here, had to pretend to be interested, to take notes. I would probably be quizzed on it at the end of the day, knowing my tutor and the damn wizard counsel who'd put me here in the first place. I'd hoped he was joking, but when Bronwen came to retrieve me after breakfast, she'd led me here.

"Pay attention, Your Majesty, this is important."

"Of course," I said with a thin smile. As a little girl, these lessons had been the bane of my existence. I wasn't keen on sitting still for this long, and now, I still felt the urge to fidget, to stretch my legs, to venture out into the beautiful day and breathe in fresh air and freedom.

"And who was the offspring of Queen Doireann and King Malcolm?"

I turned to Lady Enid, my mind going blank. "I..."

"You need to pay attention," she said, her wrinkled lips pursing in displeasure. "Master Eoghan has insisted on restarting your studies so you'll be prepared to assume the throne."

Was that the reason or was he trying to bore me to death? I wasn't sure. "I have told you, I don't think it's necessary. It would be better for me to return to my office to deal with the business of the kingdom—"

"And make another colossal mistake?" She tutted. "Now, as I was saying, Caointiorn and Dierbhile gave way to King Fíne, and his wife Ailish, who was from the Driwania kingdom."

⤳ ⤳ ⤳ ⤳

Lunch provided a well-deserved break, and I was grateful to get out of the classroom to stretch my legs. There was a guard waiting outside the classroom, and I almost lost him as I walked briskly through the castle. I should've felt bad, stopped to chat with him about his wife and new baby, but I was in a mood. It was perhaps better for both of us if I remained silent.

My meal was served in my chambers, but I wished I'd had the foresight to tell Bronwen to pack it up so I could go riding. I was scheduled for another session with Lady Enid, and I would've preferred to have gotten on horseback and not stopped. Perhaps I could've caught up with Cade and Ward, victorious from their interrogation of the fae in Críoch. By now, they should've arrived. I hoped the fae broke easily and told them everything they needed to know.

Then what? Some part of me wondered if perhaps Eoghan had spared me the reality of their quest—that he'd sent them not just to Críoch, but to the fae realm to act upon the intelligence they'd gathered. If so, I'd be furious at him for keeping such important information from me. I wasn't a child, no matter what he might think. Sure, I'd be sad if Cade wasn't by my side when the crown was placed on my head. But if he returned a week later, victorious, I wouldn't say a word against him.

If he does return...

My heart squirmed a little. Once he came back, Eoghan would

probably send him away again—this time for good. I would only see my best friend on the off chance he was sent to travel on behalf of his new sovereign or could get some time away. Our friendship would turn into letters received every so often, and we would grow apart as his life took him in a different direction. It hadn't even happened, and I was already almost in tears about it.

I left half of my lunch on the table, no longer hungry, and walked to the window. Perhaps it was just as well that I hadn't gone riding as the sky was an ominous gray. A perfect match to my mood.

With a sigh, I crossed the room to the door to accept my fate when I realized no one was there. Perhaps the guard thought I would take longer to finish my meal, or perhaps it was a temporary lapse. Still, something tickled in my mind to take the opportunity.

It was childish, but if Eoghan was determined to treat me thusly, I wouldn't disappoint.

It had been at least a month since I'd been allowed to go anywhere without a guard. Eoghan had said it was because the threats against my life were growing more numerous, but something told me he just wanted to keep tabs on where I was at all times. I'd made the best of it, as it had allowed me to get to know the guards I'd seen from a distance my entire life. But today, my footsteps were light as I rushed down the hallway. How quickly would I get caught?

I wasn't even halfway down the hall before I heard voices around the corner. Not wanting my game to end just yet, I turned to the closest room and let myself inside, softly closing the door. I pressed my ear to the wood and bit my lip as I recognized the voices of two guards. They resumed their posts, not realizing I'd slipped past them in their moment of laxness.

Still, I'd gone all of one room away, and with them standing there, I couldn't exactly venture off by myself. But when I turned around, my heart sank as I realized whose room I'd let myself into. White sheets covered the furniture except for the expansive four-poster bed that sat in the middle, stripped of blankets and pillows.

My father's room. The place where he'd been murdered.

As a child, I'd been scared even to walk by it, worried that my father's ghost was hiding in the wardrobe. Even now, my heartbeat pounded. Those childhood fears still held me in their grasp. But I swallowed and peeled myself off the door. Ghosts weren't real, and if they were, my father wouldn't harm me.

I hoped.

I hesitantly ventured into the room that smelled of dust and disuse. I lifted one of the sheets, revealing an intricately carved table with two chairs next to it. Perhaps where he'd taken his meals. Under another was a chest of drawers that had been emptied of clothes. I leaned in to see if I could still smell him, but there was just that same dusty smell.

Next to the window, I found a large desk and chair. I removed the sheet and sat down in the cool leather, leaning back in the chair and looking out onto the expansive plains beyond. My room had a similar view, but this window seemed built for a sovereign.

I closed my eyes and imagined the painting of him come to life, sitting here and doing the sorts of things a king would do.

Certainly not playing hide-and-seek from his guards.

Dismissing that thought, I gingerly opened the desk drawers, finding them surprisingly still full of trinkets and stationery. My father's crest had been dutifully stamped atop all the letters, and envelopes stood ready to receive the wax seal. In another drawer were various small knickknacks and children's toys—perhaps mine? But in the bottom, I found a stack of opened letters, all addressed to my father in a feminine, flourished hand.

I pulled out the first one and my heart stopped in my chest.

Your Majesty,

News has reached us of the loss of your wife. On

behalf of the Erlking and the entire fae country, I wanted to express my sincere condolences. Had we known she was ill, we would have sent our best healers to aid in her late pregnancy.

We are so grateful to hear that your daughter has survived, and hope that her presence is a balm in these horrible times. Please let me know if we can be of service during this time.

Sincerely,

Leandra, daughter of the Erlking

Express my sincere condolences? Had she expressed those same condolences when she murdered him not three years later?

His response letter was in the fae kingdom, most likely, but the next one on the table gave me some insight as to what happened next.

Your Majesty,

We are saddened to hear your daughter is still so very ill. I would like to personally offer my assistance, as I have a special fondness for caring for sick children.

I can be there in a week.

Sincerely,

Leandra, daughter of the Erlking

I put down the letter. I'd been sick? No one had ever mentioned such a thing to me.

I'd never understood why my father had let a fae into his castle, but perhaps his fear of losing his only daughter might've made him foolhardy. I doubted a fae could've healed me any better than Eoghan, but she'd arrived and done her best to ingratiate herself into the kingdom.

The next letter was from a different hand, but no less regal and formal. It took me a moment to recognize the Erlking's particular flourish.

Your Majesty,

I am humbled by your request, and while my daughter's happiness is of the utmost importance, I would implore you to consider if your affections toward my daughter are not merely the loneliness of a widower and a father in need of a mother for his child. If that is the case, I hope you will look amongst the well-qualified princesses of your human counterparts for such a woman.

As well, I would ask both of you to fully understand what you would be undertaking, should you marry. Any child born of such a marriage would be half-fae, and our kind has never been welcoming to such creatures—even one born from a human king and the daughter of the Erlking.

If, after all this, you and Leandra are still as madly in love as your letters would indicate to me, then I wholeheartedly give my blessing on your union and wish you much happiness.

Sincerely,

King Birch

Erlking of the Fae Realm

Fae couldn't lie, but the Erlking's letter was full of twisted truths and caution. How very *generous* of him to think of my father's well-being so soon after my mother's death. More likely, he was merely trying to play the doting father, offering warnings of what sort of monstrosities would appear from such a union, but not standing in the way of his daughter's happiness. When in reality, he and his daughter were planning a betrayal of the worst kind. Leandra was no more *madly in love* with my father than she was with me.

I reread the letter three times, anger boiling in my veins. *Madly in love.* I couldn't wipe that phrase from my mind. The way this letter was penned, my father and Leandra were like two besotted kids begging a father for his blessing to marry. The only image I had of my father was the stoic man in the painting in the throne room—serious and regal—and it baffled me to think of him as anything but.

My daughter's happiness is of the utmost importance to me. Happiness or ambition? There were times I thought I might remember her. I had flashes of a woman with raven hair and golden eyes. I distinctly recalled being fascinated by the shape of her ears, pointed and beautiful. In my nice dreams, she was a warm figure, who'd sweep me into her arms and hold me to her chest like a mother would. But in my nightmares, I envisioned her standing over my small crib, wielding her fae magic as she tried to end my short life.

It had been only thanks to Eoghan that I'd been spared. I sighed, feeling guilty for being so ungrateful toward him. He was looking out for my best interests; he always had. And if he felt like I needed to study to become the best queen, the sort of queen that would've made my father proud, then perhaps I should stop acting like a child.

Rising from the desk, I stacked the letters in my hand. There was a flint and half-used candle on the desk and I smiled. I walked to the unused hearth and placed the letters there, using the flint to light the candle then the candle to light the letters. The Erlking and Leandra's handwriting disappeared in an orange glow, drifting to the ash heap as the fire spread across the old paper. I'd hoped it might make me feel better, but all I felt was cool numbness under my anger.

When the ashes were out, I smoothed my dress and readied myself for another afternoon of drab history lessons. I'd perhaps had enough excitement for one day.

Chapter Twenty-Two

Ward

"I said, state your purpose, intruders. What are you doing on King Birch's lands?"

I put my hand on my sword, but something told me I wouldn't be able to draw it before they magicked me into oblivion. Out of the corner of my eye, I saw the wizard's staff glow gold, but he didn't make a move. Perhaps ten fae against one wizard were terrible odds. Or perhaps he was just a chicken. Either way, the only way we'd get out of this one was if I could manage to charm or convince them to let us go.

"Are we in King Birch's lands?" I said, feigning ignorance. "We must've taken a wrong turn, then."

"I find that hard to believe considering your kind has erected a twenty-foot-high stone wall," he said, before his golden eyes landed on Cade. "And you have a wizard with you."

I waited for Cade to say something, but his face was a mask of uncertainty. What was he waiting for?

"Well?" the fae prompted. "What do you have to say, wizard?"

"I have nothing to say to the fae," he said, his staff glowing brighter. "And I suggest you leave us before I have to make a mess."

"I would like to see you try. One wizard against all of us. There's a reason your master is too scared to set foot on these lands," he said with a smirk. "Perhaps we'll let the Erlking have his fun with you."

The staff was now a bright gold, and I held my breath. Wizard versus fae—I'd finally see who was more powerful.

But before the melee could begin, a flutter of butterflies passed right by my face, landing between us and the fae soldiers. The fae girl had finally reappeared, it seemed, and she held out her hands toward the wizard and her fellow fae as if to keep them apart.

"Stand down, both of you," she demanded.

The fae warrior snorted, and some of the others joined in as well. "You have no business here, Riona. Go back to the castle."

"You go back to the castle," she said, her voice full of confidence. "King Birch sent me himself."

"Did he now?" A condescending smile grew on his face. "And what job could he have for you that has anything to do with these two trespassers?"

She paused for only a moment. "This human is an envoy from Princess Ayla. King Birch wrote to her asking to resume relations and she sent him," she stuck her thumb out at me, "to start those negotiations. I was supposed to meet them at the border, but I got a little waylaid."

She's lying. Based on the confused look on Cade's face, he was thinking the same.

"Seems rather forward to send a wizard into our lands," the fae said. "Considering."

"The wizard was merely to help the envoy reach the fae lands until such time that they met up with me," the girl, Riona, continued. I was amazed at how easily the falsehoods rolled off her tongue—but then again, it wasn't *exactly* false. That had been my mission from Eoghan. "The wizard will promptly turn around and return home. Her Majesty knows exactly what we think of his kind."

"And *you* are the one who will be escorting this human?" He lifted his chin to glare at her down his nose. "Why did the Erlking give *you* this job?"

"The human can't travel quickly, so it will take some time to reach the castle," she replied. "And as you've made clear many times, I'm inconsequential and won't be missed if it takes me a week to arrive."

She smiled, and there was a little cheekiness to it, daring him to contradict her. I couldn't help but be impressed, especially as these other fae stood head-and-shoulders taller than her.

The lead fae considered her for a long time, and I held my breath, waiting for him to ignore her and give the order to attack. When a cruel smile curled across his thin lips, I knew the time had come and my grip on my sword hilt tightened. Instead, he dipped his head in a nod.

"Very well, Riona. I look forward to seeing the human at the Erlking's court within the week."

She swallowed and nodded. "Then you will go on your way?"

"We shall," he said. But even as he spoke the right words, his tone left me uncomfortable. There seemed to be more here than I understood, and just because he was leaving us didn't mean we were in the clear.

"And the wizard?" she asked, glancing in Cade's direction. "Do I have your word that he will be allowed to return unscathed?"

"I don't see why that should be necessary. One fewer wizard in the world will benefit everyone."

"Because if you kill him, we will lose our ability to negotiate with the humans," Riona replied, inching in front of Cade, to his surprise. "He's one of the princess's closest friends. Killing him would further fray our relationship."

How does she know that? My suspicion increased tenfold, but now of this fae girl.

"Fine, I trust that you will see this task to completion," the fae said, with a hearty eye roll. "But if I see him again, we will kill him. This is your only warning."

"Fair," Riona replied, casting me a look. "He will return as fast as he can walk."

"And as for you, human envoy, you had better travel as quickly as your frail body will allow," he said to me, his gold eyes piercing me to my core. "King Birch has waited a long time to open the borders between our lands once more. He will not wait for much longer."

The leader dissolved into a cloud of moths and took off toward the sky, and his warriors followed one after another until we were alone on the plains. The fae girl watched the cloud disappear, not moving until they were completely gone.

"That was close," she said, her entire body slumping.

I cleared my throat. "I suppose we should—"

She whirled around, her cheeks growing red with anger. "What in the *hell* were you two thinking? Just waltzing around in the open."

"I…" My mouth fell open. "I don't—"

"There are *eyes* everywhere," she said with an exasperated sigh. "Do you know anything about the fae realm?"

Considering the last day of haphazard discovery, I had to laugh. "No, I can't say that we do. You….do know I'm not an envoy, right?"

"Obviously," she snapped. "And I'm not taking you to Birch's castle. That's not where the stone is anyway." Her green eyes landed on Cade, and he actually jumped in surprise. "But the wizard can turn around and head back to the human realm. You're no longer needed."

"Like hell I'm not," he snapped. "I'm not afraid of the fae."

"You should be," she said. "Had I not shown up and saved your ass just now, you'd be dead. Aldrick wasn't kidding when he said he'd kill you if he ever saw you again."

"I'll kill him first."

"You were doing a lot of killing when I showed up to save your skins," she replied, and I had to admit, she had him there.

"How did you know I was friends with Ayla?" he asked.

She shook her head. "It doesn't matter."

"I actually think it does," I said.

"We keep tabs on what happens in Pennlan, obviously," she said, though there was something in her gaze that told me she wasn't telling me the whole story. "But it worked to convince Aldrick to keep you alive for another few hours, so that's all that matters."

"Who was that guy, anyway?" I asked.

"That was the second son of King Birch, and guardian of the border. He wants to take over for the Erlking when he steps down one day. He'd be keen to have *your* head hanging on a mantle to prove his worth as king of the fae," she said, pointing to me.

"How did he find us?" Cade asked.

"I told you, they have eyes everywhere."

"We've seen no one," I said.

"Fae spies don't look like you and I," she said, a little impatiently. "Aldrick has all manner of beasts at his disposal. Birds, bugs—you name it." She glanced around. "You can't be too careful."

I followed her gaze, seeing nothing in the landscape. But the thought of a bug watching me, taking information back to the fae…that was certainly unnerving.

"I'm still trying to figure out why you're so inclined to help us," Cade said. "If you know where the stone is, why not just go get it yourself?"

She sighed, as if debating whether she wanted to give up some secret. "Because if the rumors are to be believed, Leandra put an enchantment on the stone when she hid it away. She was afraid of someone taking it who wasn't…well, who wasn't worthy. I think the only person who can actually take the stone is…" She looked at me. "Him."

"Me?" I blanched. "Why me?"

"Because you're human, obviously." She turned back to Cade. "Which is, again, why *your* services are no longer needed, wizard."

"I think not," he replied. "If, as you say, the only person who can retrieve it is Ward, then what's to stop you from killing him the moment he does?"

She tutted her tongue. "I'm not having this conversation with you anymore. I don't trust Aldrick not to send a spy to figure out if I was telling the truth."

"I thought fae couldn't lie?" Cade asked.

"We can't, but I didn't really lie, did I?" she replied, crossing her arms over her chest. "You two were headed to King Birch's castle on behalf of the princess. King Birch did send your princess a letter. You," she pointed at me, "were told that he," she pointed at Cade, "was to head back to Pennlan as soon as you reached Críoch." She shrugged. "I just patched together a story."

"Fae trickery," Cade muttered under his breath.

"Yes, we're the worst," she said with a scowl before looking at me. "Are you coming or not?"

"I want to know what's in it for you," I said, after a moment. "Why do you care if someone gets the stone back to Ayla? You're fae. What happens in Pennlan is none of your concern."

She pursed her lips, narrowing her gaze. "I want peace between our countries. The border opened."

"Pennlan seems to be doing just fine with it closed."

"Are they?" Riona replied. "Críoch and the other towns in the north are dying because they no longer have a purpose. If our scouts in the other countries are to be believed, they're losing their interest in trading with Pennlan because they no longer have access to the fae."

"And the fae? Are they suffering from a lack of trade?" I asked.

She nodded. "You won't hear anyone like Aldrick admit to it, but… There's only so much magic can grow. We need real food that comes from the southern, human lands. So the sooner we put the stone back where it belongs, the sooner we can get back to our normal trade relations."

There was something else she wasn't telling us, but for the moment, I believed she could be trusted. "Then lead the way."

"You know," Cade said as we turned away. "You just told a very powerful fae a bald-faced lie. My guess is you're going to avoid him as much as possible. Considering he already seemed tired of your antics, I wouldn't put it past him to kill both of you for your insolence. You need my help."

"He won't kill me," she said softly, but it wasn't as sure as it should've been.

I surveyed her for a moment before shaking my head. "I like my chance with two magical users instead of one. Cade comes."

"Excellent," Cade said with a smug smile.

Riona, however, wore a scowl. "We don't need him."

"Then Cade and I will go back to Pennlan."

It was something of a bluff, but I wanted to see how convinced she was that I was the necessary key to her plans. After a long moment, she let out a cry of frustration and shook her head.

"*Fine.* I will allow it, but on *one* condition." She turned to Cade, fury plain on her face. "You give me your *word* on your beloved princess's head, that you will *never* use that disgusting spell to compel me. You will not breathe a word of its existence or your ability to do it." She looked at me. "And if he does, you give me your word that you'll kill him."

I opened my mouth in surprise. "I'm not going to promise that."

"Then the wizard goes—"

"Fine." Cade stepped forward. "As long as you give us your word, on the Erlking's head, that you will not betray us or lead us into danger —"

"You were in danger the moment you set foot in these lands," she drawled.

"More danger," Cade continued with an impatient wave. "Then I will not use my magic to compel you."

She surveyed him for a long time, the distrust plain on her face. She glanced at me once then nodded. "I suppose that will do."

"Great." Cade nodded. "Shall we?"

I ran my hand over my face. This was either the start of a beautiful partnership or a disastrous mistake. "Let's go."

CHAPTER TWENTY-THREE

CADE

The fae girl led us in a more northerly direction than we'd been heading before. Ward kept pace with her while I was three steps behind, my staff ready at a moment's notice to attack anything that came for us. But there wasn't much out in these lands.

I didn't trust our stroke of luck for one second. That the fae warriors would simply *believe* her, that they'd trusted me, a wizard, to turn around and walk back to the human realm. That they trusted Riona to bring Ward to the Erlking's court. What would happen in four days when they didn't show up?

And her reasons for wanting to help us…absolutely false. I didn't care if the fae supposedly couldn't lie, she'd already demonstrated how easy it was to, as she called it, "patch together a story."

But from the beginning, she'd been interested in the knight and the knight alone. Every one of her tricks had been to separate him from me, from the fae warrior in the village to the old woman at the farm. But that scent—the sweet honey smell that had been on the air since she'd arrived—was the same every time.

I was now sure it had been her all along, especially after encountering the other fae. Each of them had their own distinct flavor, some sour, some sweet, some musky, some earthy. Hers was unique amongst them, and now familiar after sensing it the entire trip.

There were still so many questions—who she was, why she could persuade that fae and his guards to leave us be, to leave *me* to walk back to the border, how she knew about my relationship with Ayla. We had escaped entirely too easily from what should've been a disastrous encounter. And until the other shoe dropped, I wouldn't relax.

But my gumption slowly drained as the afternoon wore on. At this point, I'd been going nonstop since the night before, and even before that, Ward and I had rushed through the countryside to get to Críoch. I was starting to will the sun to move faster toward the horizon, but no matter how much I tried, it remained firmly in the sky.

"Keep up, wizard," she barked at me. "We need to make it to the first village before nightfall. You won't find much pleasant out here in the night."

"He's not a quick walker," Ward said with a smirk back at me. I thought it odd for him to be speaking so plainly, especially considering he'd just asked me to come along. But perhaps he didn't trust the fae girl as much as he'd let on. A good call on his part.

I cast a spell on myself for strength. It was a pathetic imitation of what I could've cast in the human realm, and barely gave me enough to keep going. Once I had a chance to catch my breath, I would examine my staff and figure out why I couldn't seem to cast right in this land.

It was part of why I hadn't immediately fired off warning spells against the fae who'd surrounded us. I couldn't seem to gather enough magic to make a potent fireball, let alone ten of them. What should've been easy was growing increasingly difficult. I hoped it was just a by-product of exhaustion and not something more sinister. Otherwise, I would be in trouble.

The strength spell allowed me to catch up with my traveling companions, but I kept behind them, eager to listen but not to engage—hoping the girl would spill something that would clue me in to her real reason for helping us. But so far, ours was a silent party.

Mid-afternoon, Ward finally dropped back to keep pace with me. "You look like death."

"Thanks," I said with a grimace. "How much longer until we get to this village?"

"No idea. She won't tell me."

"Is she telling you anything?"

"Not a word. And it's not as if I haven't tried," he said. "I think she still doesn't trust you."

"I don't trust her."

"That makes two of us."

"So why are we following her?" I asked, stopping and leaning on my staff. "Why not just continue along the way we came?"

"Because you'd be going the wrong way." She'd appeared beside us in a column of butterflies. "I told you: the stone isn't at Birch's castle. He wouldn't put his people in danger like that."

"Danger from whom?" Ward asked.

She cast a furtive glance at me. "People."

"Wizards," I said.

"You said it, not me."

"So if it's not with Birch, where is it?" Ward asked.

She put her hands on her hips. "I'm taking you to it, if you two would quit talking and get to moving."

But Ward didn't move, folding his arms over his chest. "I think we've demonstrated that we're going to follow you, but we at least need to know where we're going."

"Right now, we are walking until we reach a village," she drawled. "At which point, you'll use some of that gold and get us rooms for the night," she said. "We rest, then we continue in the morning. Depending on how much of it you have, I might be able to get us a beast or two to travel on."

We shared a curious look. "The fae use human coin?"

"Of course they do," she said with a little giggle. "You two really know nothing about the fae realm, do you? It's a good thing I found you."

"After that, where are we going?" Ward pressed. "Where exactly is the stone?"

"Do you even know what the fae realm looks like?" she asked. "If I told you a name, would you have context for it?"

"No," Ward said with a knowing smile. "But you can explain it to us."

She let out an impatient sigh, sounding like a petulant teenager. Then she conjured some of those butterflies in her hands and released them into the air. Instead of flying away, they created a circle that formed what looked like a map with borders. But the countries were names and words I'd never seen before.

"So right now, we're in the lands of the *daoine maithe*," she said, pointing to a large country in the southwest of the map. "This is Birch's domain."

"Birch doesn't rule everyone?" I asked.

"Yes and no," she replied. "Birch is Erlking, ruler of all the fae, but there are other fae and clans that rule themselves, too. He's the leader of the *daoine maithe*, though."

"What's that?" Ward asked.

"The most powerful fae," she said. "Like me."

I snorted, and Riona shot me a dirty look.

"There are other fae, too," she said. "They have different levels of power. Some clans have their own domain inside another clan's. It's all very convoluted. But they defer to the Erlking for final say on all matters, which is all the humans ever cared to know about. When he speaks, he speaks for everyone." She made a face. "Most of the time, anyway."

"Where is the stone?" Ward asked.

One of the butterflies fluttered madly up in the northeast of the map. "Here, in the *sidheog* lands. They're close cousins of the *daoine maithe*. But it's a long way to get there. We'll need to travel this way." The butterflies gathered in a small path leading from the bottom of the map, through a thick forest, until they reached the realm marked *Sidheog*. But it kept winding, terminating at the very northern end of the world.

"How…far is that?" I asked, my stomach turning.

"Several weeks," she said. "And I'm not sure the stone is in that exact spot, either. It's just in the lands, so I've been told."

I felt Ward's gaze on me, and he was thinking the same thing I was. There was no way we'd get all the way up there and back to Pennlan for Ayla's coronation.

"I'll try to get you there as quickly as I can," Riona said. "As long as we can avoid any more of Birch's children."

"How many does he have?" I asked.

"A lot. Birch is perhaps…four hundred years old? He has twenty children, mostly sons, but a few daughters."

"Including Leandra," I said.

She tripped over her feet and looked back at me, almost guilty. "Yes. She was his youngest."

"So Aldrick is her brother?" Ward continued.

"Half-brother." A pause. "The fae don't usually stick to one partner."

"And he's some kind of guard?"

"Keeper of the border, yes," she said. "But he has ambitions to become the Erlking one day, so he's always sticking his nose where it doesn't belong."

"And who are you, exactly?" I asked, unable to keep the question to myself. "One of Birch's children?"

"If I were, Aldrick wouldn't dare talk to me that way," she said with a scoff. "I'm a distant relative. My parents were cousins of the Erlking, and when they died, I was sent to live in his castle. I'm just important enough that it would make sense he tasked me with retrieving you."

A lie that could easily be disproven, especially with the speed with which the fae seemed to travel. "And what will happen when we don't show up in Birch's court?" I asked. "Or what happens if Aldrick's spies are in the village?"

She sighed, looking tired for the first time. "We hope that doesn't happen."

>–» >–» >–» >–»

"Bad news—"

"You saw his spies in the village?" I said, cracking open an eye. It was dusk now, and Riona had decided to send one of her butterflies ahead to make sure the coast was clear. After attempting to conjure myself a bed, I gave up and stretched out on the cold, hard ground. I was sure I'd wake up covered in dirt and mud, but I didn't care. I was just glad we weren't walking anymore.

"Yes, his whole unit is there," she said, putting her hands on her hip. "Bastard."

"Are you surprised?" Ward asked. "I would've thought it obvious. This is the closest town on our way."

She shook her head. "Not if we were going to Birch's castle. So he must suspect our true intentions."

"Or perhaps he sent word back to Birch and realized you were lying," I offered.

She shook her head. "Fae can't lie."

"You keep saying that," I said with a snort. "I don't understand why he's not just showing up and murdering us. Not that I want him to, but…why all this trickery and waiting around? Seems like it would be easier just to deal with the problem and drag you back to the Erlking to face your punishment."

She glared at me. "Do you want that?"

"No, but I'm trying to be logical here."

"There are forces at work neither of you can understand," she said. "The point is, we will have to be much more careful from now on. I don't think…" She shook her head. "We'll have to make camp tonight and every night until we reach the Cernonn forest."

I wasn't really looking forward to sleeping in the dirt, but it was perhaps safer than attempting a fae village. "Is here fine? I've made this particular patch of ground comfortable."

She nodded. "There are creatures that roam the lands after dark. One of us should stay up and keep watch, at least."

"You first," I said to Ward as I yawned.

Within seconds, I was asleep.

CHAPTER TWENTY-FOUR

WARD

"Thanks for your help..." I said as the wizard passed out on the ground. "What are we planning to do for food?"

"I can find some roots, I'm sure," she said. "If you'll gather firewood."

"Roots?" I blanched. "Can you use that magic of yours to at least make it into a stew?"

"No. Roots will be fine raw." She rose and disappeared into a puff of butterflies.

I scowled. "Could've stuck around to gather the firewood since it's so easy for you."

With a sigh, I pushed myself up to stand and scoured the area, gathering what I could. But as there weren't many trees, there weren't many fallen branches. Hopefully, the fae girl could conjure something the way the wizard could.

I put the sticks on the ground, amused at the snores coming from the wizard. I could've probably thrown the sticks in his face and he would've stayed asleep. Instead, I put them on the ground and used my flint to start a small fire. I left a few pieces of kindling out, just in case, but the light it put out was enough to compensate for the disappearing sun.

"Sleep now, buddy, I'm waking you up for your shift in two hours," I said with a chuckle.

The butterflies returned, and Riona appeared with a handful of long, white roots in her hand. She looked down at the firewood and quirked a brow.

"That's it?"

"I figure you can do something with it," I said.

The faintest color of pink appeared on her cheeks. "No."

"But you can turn into butterflies."

"I don't…" She chuckled. "It's merely the expression of my magic. Everyone has their own version. Some like to change it every so often." To my questioning look, she added, "I use it to gather my essence and move from place to place."

"Could you turn us into butterflies so we could move faster?"

"No," she said with a little laugh. "We'll have to walk."

"Great." I nodded at the roots in her hands that she'd begun slicing. "What is that anyway?"

"Ferrick root. Full of protein." She conjured a couple of butterflies to pick up slices and bring them across the meager fire to my waiting hands. "Should sate us for the evening."

I took a bite and almost gagged. It tasted like dirt. Suddenly the stews in the inns felt much less meager. I chewed slowly, my jaw hurting from the effort before I could finally swallow.

"I suppose I should leave some for the wizard," she muttered.

"He's not wholly useless," I said. "Seems to be able to smell the fae."

She blanched. "*Smell?*"

I shrugged. "He knew where you were the whole time."

She shivered. "Perhaps not the whole time."

"The whole time."

She pursed her lips at me. "You still fell for my tricks."

"And why did you try to trick me?" I asked, tilting my head sideways. "What was the point of the old farm woman and the warrior in the village?"

"I was trying to tell you that your quest was a falsehood.

Obviously."

"By trapping me?"

"By getting you away from the wizard. He never would've believed me had you not gone to Críoch and seen for yourself that Eoghan misled you." She took another bite of the root.

"And you thought I might?"

"I had hope. But it's just as well. We're together now, so I suppose it was all wasted effort." She sighed, shaking her head. "Once we get out of these lands, things will improve. I know the Cernonn forest like the back of my hand."

"How are you planning on getting two humans inside without being noticed?" I asked.

"Glamour," she said. "I can at least make you look fae."

"The way you changed your appearance?" I asked. "You seem fairly good at that."

"Had to learn quickly," she said with a small sigh. "Are you taking the first watch?"

I nodded. "What should I be watching for?"

She unhooked her traveling cloak and spread it out on the ground. "Anything that might want to eat or capture us." She yawned. "I'm sure you'll figure it out."

Then she was still, and I was left alone with my thoughts. I stared at the small fire. It would be out before too long and my eyelids were already drooping. I got up to look for more, but as before, the pickings were slim. So I returned to the fire and wrapped my own cloak tighter around myself, settling back against the rock that had become my spot.

I mulled over the day, the girl's words and how there was still something missing from them. But as I cast my gaze over her, already asleep, something about her vulnerability gave me pause. After all, if she was willing to sleep around us—around Cade, specifically—perhaps there was something truthful to her words.

>→ >→ >→ >→

When I could stay awake no longer, I kicked the wizard awake and made sure he was fully coherent before settling down. I slept soundly until the light of dawn reached me. Cade was still up, staring at the dwindling fire with a sleepy look on his face, and the fae girl was still asleep.

"Why didn't you wake her?" I asked.

"Don't want to touch her," he replied with a scowl.

"That is extra dumb," I said, rubbing my face. "Especially considering you were in such a fine mood yesterday."

"I'll be fine," he said, looking down at his staff and sighing. "I think."

I couldn't help the curiosity. "What's wrong?"

"Ever since we set foot in this land, my magic isn't working the way it did before," he said. "It's like I'm having to relearn what it is to wield it. I'm not sure if it's my staff or if it's me..." He shook his head and pointed his staff at the pile of sticks I'd left for him. After a moment, the tip turned gold, and the sticks split into two duplicates of each other.

"You did it?" I said with a curious look.

But within seconds, the new stick disintegrated.

"It keeps doing that," he said with a sigh. "Don't tell the fae girl."

"She has a name," I said.

"Are you two getting along well?"

"Fairly well, considering," I said. "I suppose it's time for another day of walking, hm?"

"Makes me miss our horses," Cade said as I crossed the campsite to wake the girl. She looked quite innocent, sleeping with her mouth slightly parted, and allowed me to shake her without so much as a moan. Blinking her eyes, she looked up at me, confused at first; then, perhaps remembering her surroundings, she shook herself.

"Did I sleep all night?" she asked, looking at the wizard. "Why didn't you wake me?"

"Apparently, he didn't want to touch you," I said, answering for him. "Tonight, I'll take the middle shift. Can't have half our party falling asleep in the middle of the day."

She glared at Cade, a little hurt on her face, but then gathered her things. "There are a few pieces of root left if either of you wish to have some breakfast before we depart."

"What root?"

I plucked the white slices from the ground and showed them to Cade. "They're not bad, if you can get past the dirt taste."

"Eating fae food?" Cade said with a dismissive snort. "Good luck."

"Oh, that's a false rumor," she said. "Humans used to live in this realm alongside the fae." She smirked. "Wizards, too."

I expected him to contradict her, but he narrowed his gaze, perhaps asking a silent question of her. "It's getting light. We should get moving."

>→ >→ >→ >→

We gathered our meager things and set off to the northwest, the same way we'd been walking before, and at a quick pace. The wizard dropped behind once more, but I realized it wasn't because of his lethargy —he was observing. How long would he be wary of her? It was probably getting a little exhausting to hate everything about her.

I dropped back once more to walk with him. "Any sign of Aldrick's spies?"

"No," he said. "The only fae in miles is her."

"How far does that sense work anyway?"

"No clue." He cracked a wry smile. "But the closer the fae are, the stronger the scent. I've finally gotten used to her stench."

I hoped after a few days on the road, they might be less inclined to hate one another, but when we stopped to rest at midday, they continued glaring at one another. I might've had more patience for it had my entire supply of meat not dried up. I didn't mention Cade's magical issues to Riona, as requested, but I could tell she was confused by his unsuccessful attempts to transfigure a rock.

Then, though none of us wanted to, we were off again, walking over rocky, sparse terrain and keeping our eyes peeled for fae spies and other dangers. Perhaps it was the mere presence of a fae in our group that kept most of the lesser predators away, or perhaps she'd just led us away from danger, but we didn't encounter any more man-eating forests or three-eyed crows.

But when we crossed over a rather large hill, my eyes widened. The valley before us was filled with the oddest sort of beast. They were the size of cows but covered in woolly fur. Some of them had large horns that seemed heavy to carry. There were at least a few hundred surrounding a small creek that ran lengthwise across the valley, feeding the green grass they were eating.

"What are they?" Cade asked.

"*Tarroo*," she replied. "We'll have to go around them."

"No, wait," I said, holding up my hand. "Do you think we could slay one for some food?"

She quirked a brow at me. "Why?"

"Because a man cannot survive on fae root alone," I said, my mouth watering at the thought of meat over the fire tonight.

"We don't have time to stop and let you carve up an animal," she drawled.

"If he kills it, I can process it quickly," Cade said, stepping forward. "It won't take long."

"Very well." She took a seat on a nearby rock. "Have at it."

Cade followed me down the hill, and I waited until we were out of earshot to ask, "I thought you were having problems."

"I'm not having *problems*," he spat. "But this… I think I can handle this."

"Do you think you can conjure me a bow and arrow?" I eyed the nearest beast—he was almost as tall as I was and thick with muscle. It would take a kill shot through the eye to do it quickly. I could then use my knife to start the carving. Unless… "Unless you want to just use one of those magical fireballs and knock its head off?"

"I don't know if I can do that." He adjusted his tunic. "My last attempt to kill for meat didn't go so well."

"Fine, I'll do it," I said. "I think our guide is going to leave us if we waste too much time."

"Let's get this over with," Cade said, his staff glowing gold as he furrowed his brow. "I need something to transfigure."

I plucked a blade of grass and handed it to him. He exhaled loudly and stared at it, and I was sure it would catch on fire from the intensity. It began to vibrate, and my heart lifted. But then it stopped.

"Damn it all," he muttered.

"What's…wrong with it?" I asked, hesitantly.

"I just need to concentrate," he snapped, gritting his teeth and narrowing his gaze more. The blade vibrated, grew in size, then transformed into a large bow that fell to the ground.

"Brilliant!" I cheered, hoping positive reinforcement would aid in resolving whatever confidence issue he was having. "Now for an arrow? Maybe two?"

"Think you'll miss?" he asked wryly, plucking another blade of grass and a pebble from the ground.

"It's a big beast. I might need two," I said.

As before, he struggled, but he was able to form two arrows. I tested the heads, finding them a perfect sharpness for what I needed.

"Okay, let's do this," I said, turning to the nearest *tarroo*. He paid me very little mind but lifted his head to stare at me as I aimed my arrow. Before I had time to think, I released the arrow, and it hit him square between the eyes. It let out a cry of pain before falling headfirst to the ground. It shuddered as the life left its body.

"What's happening?" Cade whispered, horror on his face.

"You haven't killed anything before, have you?"

He turned to me, shocked. "Have *you*?"

"I grew up on a farm," I said plainly. "Obviously."

"R-right." He licked his lips as the beast stilled. "Is it… Is it dead?"

"Should be," I said, picking up the other arrow. "Next time we stop, make me some more and a quiver to carry it in. Might be useful to have."

He nodded and slowly approached the still animal. "So…how do I start carving it?"

With his back turned, I chanced an impatient look at the sky. "Start with skinning it, then I'll help you carve off the pieces of meat. It's close enough to a steer. Parts should be more or less the same. Then you can use that magic of yours to dry it out."

I had to help him along, explaining how I would use my knife to separate the meat from the skin, and he did a passable job. Before long, we had a skinless carcass on the ground, ready for carving and drying.

"Boys…" Riona's voice echoed from above. "You might want to hurry it up."

"Why?" I asked, craning my neck toward her. "Is it Aldrick?"

But the answer came as a shadow flew overhead—and a cry of fear echoed from the hundreds of wooly beasts surrounding us. I turned to tell Cade that we needed to reach higher ground, but just as I opened my mouth, the strangest beast I'd ever seen—with clawed feet and fur on most of its body, but a bird's head and wings—landed in front of us, blocking our path.

Chapter Twenty-Five

Cade

I recognized the griffin from the history of wizards book—there had been a painting of one. Apparently, a few hundred years ago, Siofra the Wise had taken on an entire nest of them and fought them back with his wits and a little grace, though the details were scant.

I wasn't sure why I was thinking of that right at this moment when said beast was prowling closer to us.

"I think it wants our dinner," Ward muttered, his hand on his sword.

"I think we should give it to him," I replied, taking a hesitant step backward.

"What? Really?" He glared at me. "Absolutely not."

"If it doesn't take our dinner, it will most likely eat us instead," I said, backing up more. "Let it have the meat. We'll just have to make do without it."

"Absolutely not," Ward said, nocking his remaining arrow. "We'll just kill it, too."

He fired off a shot, but just as the arrow reached the griffin's head, it transformed back into the rock and blade of grass it had been before, landing harmlessly at its feet. The golden eyes seemed to understand that we had just made the first move, and it lurched toward us threateningly.

"I think that was a mistake," I said lightly. "This isn't some dumb beast—"

"What are you two doing!" Riona's shriek came from above. Her face had gone white, even from this distance. "Get away from that thing!"

"But our food?" Ward called with a frown.

"Better go hungry than forfeit your life!" She waved us up. "Come on!"

We backed up more, and the griffin seemed to accept our retreat as it walked over to the felled beast and dug its sharp beak into the flesh, tearing and swallowing large chunks of what should've been a few weeks' worth of dried meat for us. Ward let out a whimper, and my stomach chose that moment to turn uncomfortably. But Riona was right; we had no chance against this monster.

Chills fell down my spine as I heard another griffin's telltale screech. It wasn't just one, though. There were at least ten in the skies above. The herd had begun moving, bumping into one another as their panic grew. The griffins were still circling above, but they'd begun diving into the crowd, perhaps picking off the weakest amongst them. And, to my surprise, the griffin who'd been chowing down on our dinner raised its head, unfurled its wings, and took off.

"Now's our chance," Ward said. "Grab as much as you can and let's —"

But the words died in his throat as the ground began vibrating beneath our feet. Rocks jumped on the ground, and the beasts let out frenzied cries as they bumped and moved against each other—and us.

"We need to get out of here before we get trampled," Ward said, nearly losing his footing when a large shoulder knocked him from behind. I turned around to leave but he stopped me. "*The food, you idiot!*"

I couldn't believe he was thinking of such a thing at a time like this, but I turned with my staff glowing. I concentrated, imagining the magic separating strips of meat, but my heart was pounding too much. I shook my head, thinking about how hungry I'd be if I had to go another day without eating, as I wasn't going to touch anything that fae girl brought me, and somehow found my gumption.

I managed the shoulder before a force knocked the wind out of me, sending me to my hands and knees. I had mere seconds to realize there was a bovine about to step on me before rolling out of the way. I rose and grasped for my staff—only to find it missing.

Fear sank deep into my bones as another wooly creature pushed me to one side then the other. Their speed was picking up as they had more room to run. And it seemed they were all coming this way.

"Cade!" Ward's voice was far away. "Get the hell out of there!"

"I lost my staff!" I called back, refusing to leave until I found it. I would be defenseless; I would be lost. Dead by this evening, probably. There was no other choice—I just had to hope the beasts didn't snap it in two.

I shoved through the moving animals, getting pushed backward more often than forward. It was hard to keep my feet and search for my staff at the same time. Then, I saw it, far in the distance. I redoubled my efforts, avoiding the sharp horns of the moving creatures and forcing myself to move forward instead of backward. In the distance, the fae girl and Ward called my name, but I kept moving, walking—and more importantly, digging deep into my psyche to summon the staff to me.

"C'mon, *c'mon*," I whispered, reaching out. But it seemed my magic was confined to my skin, unable to break free without the staff to guide it. Damn this stupid fae realm and all its strangeness.

Finally, my foot touched the ash wood, and I kicked it up, grabbing it with my hand. Just in time to see a pair of horns come for my face.

Without thinking, I cast a protective spell around me and thankfully *it worked like it was supposed to*. The animals were still charging toward me, but they harmlessly moved around the large, gold bubble I'd made for myself. I released a sigh of relief, pressing my head to my staff and thanking whatever luck I had that I'd managed to save my own skin.

"We need to have a discussion about your performance," I said to myself, much the way Eoghan would do when I'd fail at a particular task he'd set me.

"Cade!" Ward's voice was a little closer. I looked up and blanched;

he was practically floating above me, buoyed by the fae girl's butterflies. "There you are, you moron!"

"So you can fly now?" I asked, looking up at him.

"For a few minutes. Just wanted to make sure you hadn't been crushed." He actually looked relieved. "See you got your staff back. You gotta quit dropping that thing."

"Yeah." I turned to the side where the carcass still remained, untouched. "I'm going to finish what we started."

"Really?"

"I worked hard for this meat," I barked. "And I'm not letting it go to waste."

⤛⤛⤛⤛

Thankfully, I was able to carve the meat and dry most of it without any problems, as well as leave a chunk or two that I cast a cooling spell on to keep fresh until we stopped for the evening. Maybe whatever mental block had been keeping me from accessing my magic had disappeared, but something told me I wouldn't get that lucky. Even though I *was* able to do it, the effort took far more concentration than before. Still, baby steps.

We only had three or four hours of daylight before we had to stop and make camp for the night. I was able to conjure a large fire and a vessel to cook our meat, and Ward and I ate very well.

"You sure you don't want any?" he asked the fae, who was sitting apart from us, a permanent scowl on her face.

"I'm fine. Roots will sustain me."

"Suit yourself." Ward swallowed the piece he'd offered her in one bite. "Cade, I'm so glad you decided to come."

"You're only saying that because you have a full belly," I said, but I couldn't help but share his mood. "How much longer until we reach the border?"

"Longer now that you two screwed around."

I shared a look with Ward. He shrugged and patted his belly. "You

180

want the first shift?"

"Sure," I said.

"Good." He stretched out, closed his eyes, and was snoring in seconds.

I felt someone watching me and met a pair of green eyes glaring daggers at me from across the fire.

"What?"

She sniffed and looked away.

I sat back and scowled at her, my good mood evaporating. "You know, you could've stepped in to help if you're so eager to get us moving. It's not like I wanted to walk around a stampede of wild animals looking for my staff."

She furrowed her brow. "What happened to your staff?"

"I dropped it, obviously," I snapped.

"How?"

I blinked, confused and a little angry. "It fell out of my hand. How else?"

"No, I mean…" She leaned forward, a little hesitantly. "From what I understand of wizards, the staff is part of them. It's not something that can just fall out of your hand."

"You read wrong," I said with a huff. "They're objects like anything else."

But she didn't look convinced. "Where'd you get it? Your staff?"

"Eoghan gave it to me. It's made of ash wood—"

"Obviously," she said. "But…where did he get it? It's not like ash is very prevalent in the human world."

"He said it belonged to an old wizard who died and bequeathed it to him," I replied, looking at it. "He'd hung on to it, hoping another wizard might be born. When I came along, he gave it to me."

"Oh, well…" She giggled. "That's your problem. It's not your staff."

I narrowed my gaze. "What the hell are you talking about?"

"Don't..." She shook her head. "Never mind."

"No, what?" I leaned forward. "What do you know about wizards?"

She opened and closed her mouth, as if debating if she wanted to share. And I could've chalked this whole conversation up to fae trickery or her messing with my head. But something tickled in the back of my mind that asked me to consider believing her.

"Perhaps you should read more of that book you're carrying around," she said, after a long pause. "It might give you the answers you're looking for."

"It's a compendium of old wizards."

"Is it?" She yawned and unhooked her cloak, spreading it out along the ground and lying down. "You might want to check again."

As she stilled, I glared at her, then reached into my bag. I told myself I was going to read anyway, that it had been a while since I'd cracked open the tome and read a few pages—not that I was making sure she was right. I set the tome in my lap and opened to the last page I'd read a few days ago.

But to my...surprise, the book's pages had shifted. It was no longer just about wizards of yore...the page I was reading was about a *fae*.

I closed the book and opened it again, rubbing my eyes and making sure I wasn't just seeing things. But no, something had happened to this book when I'd crossed into the fae realm. Some kind of deep magic I hadn't been able to detect that had been masking the true purpose of this book.

Even the title had changed. It was no longer just *A Book of Modern Wizards*, but now was *A Book of Magical Beings in Modern Times*.

I looked up at the fae girl, desperate to ask her how she knew, what she knew, and what else. But instead, I sat back and began to read the new words now available to me.

Chapter Twenty-Six

Ayla

I was dutiful at attending my lessons and not complaining. I even received high marks for my memorization of the royal family of Nesuria when Lady Enid quizzed me. But that itch to do something more, to be *useful*, was starting after only a few days of good behavior.

I hadn't seen Eoghan since our disastrous dinner, but I felt it time to speak with him about regaining control of my affairs once more. I felt confident I could study while also taking on correspondence and was hoping to convince him of such.

However, when I asked for him, I was given a peculiar answer.

"Master Eoghan has left."

I furrowed my brow. "He…left? To where?"

"I believe he's taken the Lord Sloani for a tour of the close-in villages," Bronwen said with a bow. "He told us to expect him late this afternoon."

"Lord Sloani is in town?" I asked, recognizing the name as brother to the king of Driwania. "Is Eoghan planning on inviting me to dine with him?"

She cleared her throat. "Not to my knowledge."

I sat back, staring daggers out my office window. And yet—a new thought entered my mind. If he was gone all day, that meant I didn't have to ask permission for anything. A smile crept across my face.

"Your Majesty?"

"Can you let Lady Enid know I won't be attending lessons today?"

I said with a little smile. "And please have my lunch sent to my office. I'd like to work on my correspondence today."

"Yes, Your Majesty."

Unfortunately, the correspondence that was delivered to my office was as confusing and unworkable as the last time I'd attempted to review it. Lots of requests for my time and self-invitations to dinners and my coronation. At least I had a little better idea who was who, thanks to Lady Enid, so my first order of business was to put the letters into piles based on their kingdoms. From there, I'd triage them in terms of rank then perhaps decide who to respond to. But I still needed that coronation plan. And since Eoghan wasn't around to keep it from me…

But all my scheming came to an end when Bronwen appeared with a frown on her face. "My apologies, Your Majesty. It appears the wizard's vault is locked," she said. "So I was unable to retrieve the information."

"Locked?" I frowned. "Why is it locked? Don't we have a key to get in?"

"It seems to be…" She squirmed a little. "Magically locked. Our keys don't work on it."

Eoghan *locked* his vault? That was unacceptable. There shouldn't have been anything in there he'd want to keep from me.

"Thank you," I said with a smile I certainly didn't feel. "That will be all."

"Yes, Your—"

"Oh, one more thing," I said. "Can you leave the key?"

She pulled the key from her ring, bowed, and left. I was sure she thought me quite mad, but before I lost my temper at my wizard counsel, I wanted to see for myself.

I walked with purpose, barely remembering to smile at the people I passed along the way. The guard who'd been assigned to trail me was new, and I promised I would ask him about himself later, but I was on a mission. I pushed open the door to the vault and continued down the stairs, the cool, musty air of the dungeon doing little to dispel my mood.

Footsteps echoed behind me, and I remembered my guard. I turned and smiled at him. "No need to follow me down here."

"Your Majesty?" He swallowed. "I was given a direct order."

"Then perhaps you could wait upstairs?" I asked with a little wince. I didn't want an audience for this. "I promise there's no way out from here, and I'll be up in ten minutes."

He hesitated for a moment then nodded, turning and leaving. I sighed in relief and continued down until I reached the bottom landing, coming face to face with the nondescript wooden door with an iron bar across the top and bottom.

Just to be sure, I turned the knob, but it didn't budge. I stuck the key in the door, and it fit perfectly, turning the gears inside the door, but when I pushed at the knob, it still didn't move. Magically locked, indeed.

Cade had never mentioned such a thing, but I'd picked up enough about magic over the years to know a little. It was a mental game, about confidence and saying the right words as much as about the raw power in one's veins. I didn't have such power, but I had confidence aplenty.

I stared at the door, putting my hand on it. "Open."

Twisting the knob did nothing.

"I said, *open.*"

Again, nothing.

"I, Princess Ayla, sovereign of Pennlan and soon-to-be queen, demand that you open for me."

It was almost mocking me now. I paced the small landing area, rubbing my chin and thinking of all the things Cade had told me about magic. There should've been a provision in his charm for me to gain access. I tried three more versions of my demand to the door, starting to sound silly for yelling at a door that was clearly not going to budge.

Fine, I thought to myself. *We'll do this the hard way.*

>→ >→ >→ >→

"You want us to what?" Captain Gabhann said.

"I want you to break the door down," I snapped, my cheeks flushed from all the running around. It had taken me a while to find her.

"You want us to break down the door to the wizard vault?" She rubbed her chin with uncertainty. "Pardon my curiosity, but...why?"

"Because I think he's hiding something from me," I said. "And there's no reason any door in this castle should be locked to the queen." I paused, clearing my throat. "Soon-to-be queen."

"I agree, but..." She eyed the door. "I'm not sure what we can do. But we will try our best. Please, stand aside."

Within minutes, the staircase was filled with soldiers, each carrying different weapons. I waited to the side as they hacked at the door with swords, axes, spears. A normal door would have shattered under the effort, but the magic imbued in the wood kept it together. Instead, the ground was littered with twisted and mangled metal and the soldiers disappeared to nurse their bruised arms.

"We can try something else?" Gabhann said, looking at me. She probably would've rather me left it alone, but we were in too deep now.

"What are you thinking?" I asked with a smile.

Ten minutes later, more soldiers appeared, this time with a log they had to work to get down the stairs. Two on either side stood at the ready to swing it forward.

"Ready?" Gabhann said, looking at me.

I nodded. "Do it."

They swung, but the log sprang backward when it hit the wood, nearly flying out of the soldiers' hands. They fell backward in a heap and I winced.

"Let's try that again," Gabhann said.

They gathered themselves, tightening their grips on the log, and took a collective step back. Then with a loud roar, they hurtled the thick log at the door. But this time, instead of flying backward, the log itself splintered and exploded into a million pieces.

I let out a scream and fell to my knees, covering my head. When it was over, I rose, praying no one had been seriously hurt. Some cuts and bruises, but otherwise, everyone looked all right.

"Shall we—"

"No," I said, finally admitting defeat. "That's enough for now. Thank you all for your efforts."

>→ >→ >→ >→

I had my dinner in my office, watching the sunset and waiting for Eoghan to show up. I'd given Captain Gabhann instructions to send him straight to me. I'd rehearsed what I would say to him all afternoon, going through several revisions before settling on the right words. Even now, my palms were sweaty as I prepared myself for the fight I was about to have.

Finally, just as the last light of day was dwindling, I saw a pair of horses down the main road that led into the castle and my pulse quickened. I read through my speech once more, reminding myself that *I* would be queen in a little over a month. *I* needed to stand up for myself. *I* had every right to know what was in that vault.

The lock to my office door turned over, and I hastily wiped my hands on my skirt, lifting my chin and readying myself.

"Good evening." Eoghan walked inside and closed the door behind him. He wore a genial smile on his suntanned face, as if he were amused to be summoned like this. "I hear you've had a busy day."

"I hear you've been keeping things from me," I replied, lifting my chin and trying not to glance at the writing on my desk. "First of which is that Lord Sloani is in town."

He opened and closed his mouth, confused. "I told Bronwen to inform you. But I didn't tell you myself because he's…not great company. I've been trying to keep him out of the castle to spare you his boorishness." He made a face. "The man was more interested in the local whorehouses than our economic policy. It's not something I thought you should lower yourself to entertain."

Some of my anger deflated. "Well, I suppose that makes sense." I leaned forward. "Then why was your vault locked?"

"It isn't. At least, not to you," he said.

"It was."

He smiled, again without any hint of malice. "Come with me, and I'll show you how to unlock it."

He led me downstairs once more, remarking at the splintered logs the soldiers had used to try to break down the door with amusement. My face burned with embarrassment that my antics were so clearly on display for him to mock. In hindsight, a bunch of soldiers against a wizard's magic was exceptionally foolhardy, but I hadn't been interested in thinking rationally.

"So, what did you try?" he asked. "Surely, Cade gave you some tutelage on how to speak magical incantations."

"I asked it to open." I gestured toward the door. "It wouldn't."

"Try this," he said, standing behind me. "I, Princess Ayla, sovereign of Pennlan and soon-to-be queen, demand that you open for me."

I spoke the words exactly as he said them, and to my annoyance, the vault door opened with a click.

"You have to speak the words exactly," he said, holding the door to allow me to walk inside. "Now, what was it that you needed from in here?"

"Nothing," I said quietly.

"Lady Enid was most upset that you skipped your lesson today," he said softly. "Any reason you opted for this assault on my vault instead of learning your history?"

"Because..." The reason sounded idiotic in my mind. *Because I thought you were lying to me, keeping things from me, and locking your vault. Because I don't want to study this stuff anymore, I want to rule.*

I sounded like a petulant child.

"Well?"

"I don't know," I said, wishing my face didn't burn so hot. "But I'll be back with her tomorrow."

"Good girl." He nodded. "And if you would like to dine with the boorish Lord Sloani and hear about all the women he's bedded, I'd be happy to set up such a dinner with you."

"No," I replied, fighting back tears of shame. "No, I'll pass. Thank you."

He let me walk back up the stairs, alone, perhaps to sit and stew in my mistakes. The voice in my head that sounded like him was hard at work berating me for acting without thinking, for causing such a disruption in everyone's day because I'd had a wild hair. I was clearly not ready to be queen if this was how I acted when the *slightest* hint of distrust entered my mind. More like a tyrant who'd be content to send her country into ruin instead of listening to reason.

And yet…as I walked back up to my room to hide for the rest of the evening, I couldn't help but feel like I *had* said those exact words and it hadn't worked.

But perhaps I was just being silly.

Chapter Twenty-Seven

Ward

We set off the next morning, and it seemed Riona was intent on making up for lost time. I didn't mind, as dinner the night before had refilled my energy stores, and even Cade was able to keep pace with us, though he seemed lost in thought for most of the day.

All in all, we were a quiet traveling party through a mostly empty land, which perhaps suited Riona, who kept glancing at the sky. I was sure she thought Aldrick might fall out of a tree and attack us, but it had been several days since we'd seen him. Whether that was a good sign or not I didn't know.

"I'm sure it's fine," she said when I pressed her on the matter. "I'm unimportant. He probably forgot all about it."

"But we aren't," I said. "A wizard and the envoy from Ayla going to meet the Erlking? Surely, that merits a follow-up or two."

"It would, if he knew where we were going," she said. "But clearly, he has no clue or else we'd have seen him."

I made a noise of distrust. "I don't—"

"Think about it," she said, turning to look at me. "The *daoine maithe* lands are as big as Pennlan. Even with the fae magic, it would take time and effort to comb every inch. We are staying out of the villages, off the roads. It would be hard for him to find us out here."

"So you think he's looking for us?"

"I think…" She licked her lips. "I don't think he wants to be."

"What does that mean?"

"It means what I said."

And that was the end of that conversation.

>⇥ >⇥ >⇥ >⇥

That night, we stopped to make camp and assumed our usual roles. I went to gather firewood, Cade performed a little magic on the dried meat to plump it back up for cooking, Riona scoured the land for those roots she insisted upon eating. I returned first this evening, setting the fire while Cade had two large strips of meat ready for roasting.

"I need to talk with you about something," he said. "While the fae girl isn't here."

"She has a name," I drawled. "But what's wrong?"

"It's…the book," he said, keeping his voice low as he glanced furtively around. "It *changed*."

"What do you mean, changed?"

He summoned the book with his staff, and it floated over. "In the human world, it was about wizards. But when I opened it last night…it was different. The words were different." He ran his hand over the cover. "All of them are. It's an entirely new subject matter."

"Really?" I frowned. "Is that a thing that can happen?"

"I've never seen it before, no." He shivered. "There's so much about this realm that sets me on edge. And now I'm wondering if perhaps this book was *planted* for me to read."

"By whom?"

"My guess?" He nodded to the space Riona had left.

I narrowed my gaze. "So why not just ask her about it?"

"I don't want her to know I know that she planted it."

That made no sense to me, but the wizard looked absolutely convinced. "Why not just toss it then?"

"Because I want to suss out the reason she gave it to me," he said. "But so far, it's just a long history of fae and wizards together—"

"Maybe her hope was to teach you that your kinds can get along?" I offered. "I don't know. But I think you're looking too far into this.

Chuck the book, ask her about it, or stop being so suspicious."

"Ssh." He straightened and a moment later, the puff of butterflies returned. Riona stood at the edge of the campsite holding only one root, a frown on her face.

"I only..." Her eyes narrowed at us. "What are you two scheming about?"

"Just trying to plan dinner," I said, walking around to finish building the fire. "Find enough roots?"

"Not enough. I think we're getting too far north for them," she said with a frown. "The sooner we get to the forest realm, the better."

⤜⤜⤜⤜

But two more days passed in the same fashion—long walks through empty country, short breaks, and nighttimes spent under the stars with one of us keeping watch. The wizard's nose was in his book every time we did stop, though I thought it funny that he was so hell-bent on reading something he thought was so evil. If it were me, I would've destroyed the book at the first sign of danger. He also made no attempt to ask Riona about it, even though she clearly knew he was reading it. The whole scene was downright comical.

Still, I was starting to get restless and eager for a change in scenery. It had been five days since we'd left the border, and although we were at a much slower pace than if we'd had horses, I felt we still should've seen some sign of this mysterious forest realm she kept talking about. But every time I asked how much longer, I would get the same snippy answer.

"Soon."

"That's not an answer," the wizard said, also clearly annoyed with her lack of transparency. "Conjure up that map again. Tell us where we are on it."

"No."

He let out a growl of frustration and marched quickly to pass her, standing in her path with a furious look on his face. "That's not an answer either."

"I think it's a complete sentence," she replied with a sweet smile.

"Riona," I said, coming to stand next to them. "Please. Just give us some hint. We've been dutiful in following you without question. Reward our faith."

A flash of uncertainty crossed her face before she masked it. "I promise, it's coming. As long as we keep heading to the northwest, we will get to the end of the *daoine maithe* lands."

"How will you know?" Cade replied.

"I'll know." She turned her back to us. "Quit complaining and let's keep moving."

The wizard looked at me for support, and I shrugged. "You heard her."

"I don't think she knows where we are," he muttered under his breath. "Mark my words."

>↠ >↠ >↠ >↠

Another day and night passed, and I was starting to think Cade might be right. Compounding the problem was the utter lack of villages, landmarks, roads—any sign of civilization. Once, I thought we might've passed some old stone ruins, but they turned out to just be curious rock formations. If I were to describe the fae realm based on our journey so far, I'd have thought it completely void of people.

Finally, we crested a hill and found a large lake, fed by what appeared to be a river. Riona announced proudly that it was a river that flowed from the *sidheog* lands, through the forest kingdom, and ended in this lake.

"If we keep following the river, we'll make it to the forest realm," she said with a smile that showed a little more relief than it probably should have. "I give us two more days from here."

"What lives in that lake?" I asked.

"I don't know," she said. "Fish? Why?"

The wizard came to stand next to me, and he practically read my mind. Neither one of us had bathed in weeks, and although I was used to long stretches, I also knew when to take the opportunity.

"Going to stop for a minute to refill the canteens and wash up," I said. "Trust me, we'll be less likely to attract attention when we don't smell like a pair of humans."

"I don't really want to stop for long," Riona replied, glancing at the sky.

"We've been going nonstop for days," I said. "I'm sure we can afford an hour to wash our clothes. It'll help us avoid detection."

She made a face. "Fine. Make it quick, though."

She disappeared into a puff of butterflies and flitted off into the sky.

"Brilliant," Cade said, finally wearing a smile. "How cold do you think it is?"

"Based on the air? Frigid." I grinned. "Race you."

I dashed down to the water, stripping my clothes off and wading in. The water was ice cold, but I didn't care. I washed my body first, scrubbing weeks of dirt, sweat, and grime off my skin and hair. I turned to see if Cade was coming, but he remained on the shore, an uncertain look on his face.

"What?" I asked.

"I don't know what's in there."

"Damn precious wizard," I muttered, shaking my head. "Look, it's fine. Just go in waist-deep and if something comes up to bite you in the ass, jump out."

"You may want to keep your eyes on your clothes," he said, nodding toward me.

I spun around just as my undershirt was floating away. I dove for it, but it zoomed out of the way. "Crap." I wasn't eager to keep going north without it, so I sloshed through the water as I went to follow it. But just as it was within my grasp, it sped away again. I cursed as it inched closer and closer to a marshy area, not really where I wanted to go in the fae realm.

But when the rest of my clothes followed suit, dashing past me at a quick pace and disappearing into the reeds, I had no choice.

"See?" Cade called.

"You could use that wizard magic," I called back. "Maybe help me?"

"I don't know what's under there," he said. "Don't want to summon a dragon."

I doubted a dragon would emerge from these murky waters, but perhaps he just enjoyed watching me struggle while he was proven right. I still had my knife holster slung around my bare shoulder, so I pulled the blade out and walked cautiously toward the marsh.

"Give me back my clothes," I barked, pushing aside the reeds. One of my socks was caught, and I plucked it out of the water, revealing a small little creature with brown skin and webbed feet—and wings, strangely enough. It sputtered some high-pitched squeaking sound at me then jumped off my sock and dove back into the water.

I put my sock on my shoulder for safekeeping, finding the various pieces of my wardrobe stuck in the reeds. Some of them had the small fae creatures on them, others had been left alone. But my shirt, it seemed, was lost.

"Fine," I barked to them. "Hope you enjoy the taste of sweat and grime."

A bubble floated up from the bottom, followed by another, and I took a step backward, holding my knife out at the ready. But what came after it was just my undershirt, now sporting a lovely hole in the right arm. I scowled as I plucked it from the river and hoped the wizard could mend it as well as he'd mended my other tears and cuts.

"Thanks. Hope it was worth it, you little bastards."

Something shifted in the air, and I began to think perhaps I'd said the wrong thing. A few dozen sets of eyes appeared between the reeds, and a loud hissing sensation echoed off the water. I took a hesitant step backward, clutching my clothes in one hand and my knife in the other.

"S-stand down," I said.

A wave of brown creatures sped out of the water, dive bombing me with their open mouths. I saw a few pairs of razor-sharp teeth and that was enough. I turned tail and dashed out of the reeds, crying out in fear as they attacked me, sinking their little teeth into my flesh. One or two might not have hurt, but twenty was like a thousand sharp needles digging into my back. I did my best to shake them off as I ran on shore, dropping my clothes and dancing around as fast as I could.

"What the hell is going on?"

I stopped, as did all the biting on my back. Riona stood ten feet from me, a confused look on her face. But her gaze dropped, and her brows shot up to her hairline, her pale face turning bright red. I hastily grabbed my clothes from the ground to cover myself as I straightened back up and loudly cleared my throat.

"Something attacked me," I said, trying to sound serious and brave.

She giggled. "What?"

"A giant lizard," I said, clearing my throat. "Just came up out of nowhere."

"Ah." She danced on her toes as she looked behind me. "Is that why there's a river sprite back there cursing you out?"

"A what?" I turned to find one of those creatures sitting on a nearby rock, shaking his fist at me and squeaking in a high-pitched voice. "What's he saying?"

"It's not nice," she said. "But if you've finished…er…cleaning yourself." Her gaze dropped once more, and I adjusted my clothes across my waist. "We should get a move on. Where's the wizard?"

"He was right here," I said with a frown. "I'm sure he's not far."

She sighed. "Fine. Let's see what water creature *he* pissed off."

Chapter Twenty-Eight

Cade

While Ward had stupidly waltzed into an unknown body of water in the fae realm, and summarily got his clothes stolen by some tricky fae creature, I'd opted for another course of action. I'd been able to cast cleaning spells on myself and my clothes along the way, so I wasn't as dirty as he was, but I still thought it might be nice to dunk my swollen feet in the cool water for a change. I'd walked along the river until I found an overhanging rock. Carefully, I slid my boots off and inched toward the edge of the rock, finding immediate relief as my feet plunged into the icy depths.

I exhaled loudly. No amount of magic could replace a sensation like this. As much as I wanted to bathe, after seeing Ward dash off in search of his stolen clothes, I opted to remain as I was and merely refresh my achy, swollen feet and read more of this damned book.

I'd been poring over the pages for days now and was still no closer to understanding how I could've missed such clear fae magic when I picked it up in the human realm. I analyzed every page, searching for double meanings and hidden messages within the drab history of fae and wizard interaction, which was curious in and of itself. If this book was to be believed (and I didn't quite believe it), the wizards of yore had a lot to thank the fae for. It was a fae who had found the first wizard and taught her how to wield the latent magic in her veins using the wood from an ash tree. While Eoghan had told me all wizards used staffs, this book claimed there used to be all manner of vessels to channel magic, from wands to carved talismans and more.

Familiars, they were called. I'd never heard my staff called such in my life.

The book also said the fae had planted a grove of ash trees in the Erlking's castle and would bring wizards into the realm to have them select one to take for themselves. This book made it sound like the process was unique to each wizard, and that a wizard was nothing without the correct staff.

It had caused me to second-guess—momentarily—my own staff. Eoghan had given it to me when I'd arrived in Pennlan and there hadn't been any choice in the matter. It was the staff he had available, ergo, it was given to me. And to my eyes, it worked just fine.

I could hear Eoghan's voice in my head, chiding me for carrying a fae artifact around and reading it. But for some reason, I couldn't put it down. And at the rate we were moving farther away from Pennlan, I'd probably get to the very last chapter before we even reached the human realm again. The thought made my insides twist with despair.

I jumped when I heard rustling in the bushes nearby. Narrowing my eyes, I placed my hand on my staff and gathered my magic, ready to fire off a warning shot at anything that thought it might try its luck with me—and hoping that my magic would cooperate this time.

Instead, what hopped out of the bushes was a small creature. She— at least, I thought she was a she—had long, gray hair and leathery skin to match, with spindly fingers and a long, hooked nose. Her black, beady eyes were trained on me, and a giddy look spread across her face.

"Hello," I said, lifting my staff. "Do you know what this is?"

She nodded and let out a low giggle. All the hair on my body stood upright, and I had the distinct feeling that this...*thing* wasn't good news. Whether she planned to grow and eat me, hypnotize me, or do some other horrific fae trickery, I had no idea.

I raised my staff. "Be gone, vile creature."

She hopped from one foot to the other, cackling more. My insides began to squirm, but somehow I knew it wasn't her doing. It was dread—something was wrong here.

"Wizard?"

Riona's voice echoed from the distance, breaking me from my trance. The small creature looked behind me and dashed back into the bushes, leaving behind the feeling of unease in my chest and the silence around us. Riona and Ward, whose clothes were dripping wet, rounded the corner and the fae girl actually looked relieved to see me.

"Here you are," she said. "It's time to leave."

I turned to the lake once more, searching for that small creature. I didn't even feel comfortable turning my back on it.

"What's wrong?" Ward asked.

"I saw something…" I said, unsure why I was so spooked. "It was a small little thing, but it felt like…"

"Small things can be terrifying," Ward muttered with a serious look behind him.

"We don't have time for the two of you to be screwing around with the lesser fae," Riona said. "For people who have a timeline to get back to Pennlan, you do like to take your little breaks."

"Sorry," I said, barely listening to her as I rubbed my chest. "It just…that little woman was freaky. I've never felt anything like that before."

"Little…woman?" I turned at Riona's concerned tone. "What did it look like?"

I described her, and Riona let out a curse. "That's not good."

"What was it?" I asked.

"A *bean-nighe*," she said. "It's a river fae, but more importantly… It's a bad omen. They like to show up around people who…" She cleared her throat, clearly trying to regain her confidence. "Never mind. It's just a fae children's tale."

"People who what?" I asked, a drop of fear sliding down my spine.

She looked up at me through her thick, black lashes. "People marked for death."

"That's ridiculous," Ward snapped. "First of all, a creature can't just know who's marked for death. Cade is clearly very healthy and not about to drop dead any time soon. And second of all—"

"It's as I said," Riona said, straightening, but not quite looking me in the eyes. "A children's tale, nothing more. But perhaps we should consider moving somewhere else before we set up camp for the evening."

I nodded swiftly. "Agreed."

"Oh, good, the first time the two of you agree on something, it's about a tiny little goblin," Ward muttered. "Fine. Let's go."

>-» >-» >-» >-»

We used the dwindling light to make progress along the river, but Riona wanted to camp far enough away that we couldn't hear the water, and I, once again, agreed with her. I didn't know how far that little imp could travel, but I wanted her as far from me as possible.

Marked for death. Even if it weren't true, I could understand why people would feel like it could be. That creature must have some sort of emotional manipulation magic. And perhaps then someone who believed in that sort of thing would be so unnerved that they suffered an episode and died. That thought made me somewhat more comfortable as night fell around us.

"Well, are you taking the first shift?" Ward asked.

"Yes," I said.

"Sure you can handle it? Don't want you to get scared by little witch women," he said.

"It's not a laughing matter," Riona snapped from the other side of the fire.

"Okay, how many people have died from a *bean-nighe* then?" he asked, putting his hands on his hips. "Ten? Fifteen?"

"We obviously don't have a number," she said.

"Then how do you know it's true?"

"Because unlike you, I happen to be well-read on the creatures of this land," she snapped. "And the fae lore is always steeped in reality, even if it is embellished. There are things out here that don't make sense, even to the *daoine maithe*." She shivered. "Since there aren't a lot of fae out here, many of the lesser beings have migrated down from the wildlands."

"Wildlands?" Ward asked. "What's that?"

"It's the land to the east of the forest realm and northeast of the *daoine maithe* lands," she said, conjuring her map using her butterflies. I had to hide a smirk—she knew where we were now, so she was more confident in showing off her geographical knowledge.

She conjured a butterfly that fluttered wildly on the bottom of the map, right next to a river that started in the lake where we'd just been. The river twisted up into what was clearly a patch of forest, but she was more concerned with the land that ran parallel to it.

"The civilized fae live here in the west," she said, gesturing to the map. "The *daoine maithe*, the forest realm, the *sidheog*, a couple others. But this here." She pointed to a spot just north of where we were. "Is full of creatures like the *bean-nighe* and the small sprites that stole your clothes."

"They weren't that bad," Ward muttered.

"The point is that this land," she gestured to the wildlands, "is full of dangerous creatures that would sooner eat a fae than have a conversation."

"They listen to the Erlking though, right?" I asked.

"Sort of," she said. "I don't want to test their loyalty, though." She shivered and wrapped her cloak tighter around herself as she lay down. "Let's just be glad we don't have to go that way."

⇀⇀ ⇀⇀ ⇀⇀ ⇀⇀

Even when it was my turn to sleep, I didn't really rest much. My dreams were plagued by that *bean-nighe* creature popping out from behind rocks and trees to remind me I was *marked for death*. The worst was when I dreamed the creature came to visit Pennlan, showing up in Ayla's bedroom and whispering curses over her sleeping form. I woke up in a panic, filled with dread that somehow she was in danger, and I'd made a horrible mistake in leaving her alone. But as I came down, I remembered Eoghan was there, and she was safe with him.

The next morning came too soon, and I groggily followed the others. Riona didn't want to keep too close to the river, just in case Aldrick had his spies, but she was confident she could navigate now.

"Now?" Ward asked, trying to share his annoyance with me. But I was too tired, still on edge. And I didn't mind being far from the water, either.

Midday, we crested another large hill, and instead of more plains and emptiness, there seemed to be a field of raised hills, almost like a burial ground. They were covered in the same scrappy grass that had been underfoot for the past few days, but something about them was unnatural —giving me that same creepy vibe the *bean-nighe* had.

"Is that the forest I see?" Ward said, squinting. "Yeah, that's it over there. Just due northwest of here."

But Riona didn't share in his joy. "We've gone too far west. We need to turn around."

"W-what do you mean?" He threw his hands in the air. "The forest is right there. All we need to do is cross this valley—two, three hours tops of walking. Why the hell would we want to turn back?"

"Because I'm not setting *foot* in there," she barked, pointing at the little hills. "We call it the *aos sí*, it's the site of a terrible fae battle gone wrong—and filled with spirits." She shook her head and backed up three steps. "We'll head south then west until we reach the forest."

She didn't wait for us to argue with her, turning on her heel and walking as fast as she could the other way.

"I'm starting to get annoyed with her cryptic answers," Ward snapped, looking to me. "That bean whatever thing yesterday and now this? She can't possibly be that superstitious."

"You weren't the one marked for death."

He tossed his hands in the air. "I can't believe you bought into this crap. You're a wizard—you don't trust a word out of her mouth. Now you believe you're cursed or whatever because she says so?" He pointed to the cemetery. "I see the forest right there. Let's just go, and she can catch up with us."

But every fiber of my being told me that if I set foot in that valley, something horrible would happen to me. "I'm going with Riona."

"So she has a name now?" Ward called after me.

Chapter Twenty-Nine

Ward

I didn't know much about magic, but I couldn't believe Cade and Riona were being so ridiculous as to make us go the way we'd come before going north once more. Riona, I could perhaps understand—fae were notoriously worshipful of their superstitions and lore. But Cade? Mr. "I hate everything fae"? That didn't make a whole lot of sense to me.

But I'd been overruled, so we dutifully walked back the way we'd come. I hated backtracking, especially when we were so close to reaching a place where I could get a proper bath and sleep in a real bed.

The sun was high in the sky when I finally saw the forest again. It was massive even from this distance, stretching from one end of the horizon to the other. I could see why it was considered its own realm— from the sparse land of the *daoine maithe* to this was a change.

"Things will be different from here on out," Riona said as we picked up our pace. "The forest is thick, so we'll need to take the roads. That means we'll be around more civilized fae, so the two of you will have to watch what you say. I can glamour you, but I can't help you if you say or do something stupid." She looked behind her at Cade. "And you absolutely can't use that staff."

He sighed. "Fine. I suppose that makes sense. We won't need magic when we're walking along safe roads."

"I didn't say they were safe. I just said they were roads." She turned back as she walked under the tree line. "Let's just say human thieves have nothing on fae ones. Especially with the gold in your pocket—it's like a beacon to them."

Cade shifted, putting his hand over the pouch that hung around his neck. "And you're sure I can't use my magic?"

She shrugged. "A wizard would draw attention and news would travel fast. Might attract more trouble."

He looked at me with a frown. I just patted him on the back. "I'll protect you from the fae thieves, don't worry."

"Thanks."

The road beneath our feet was dirt, but the wagon wheels and hoof prints were the first sign of civilization in days. I was eager to get a glimpse of the first fae village, to walk amongst the creatures I'd only heard stories about—and perhaps to see how this fae glamour worked.

However, when we turned a rather sharp corner on the road, the three of us stopped short. There was a bright green cloud covering the road. No, not just the road—it permeated the thick foliage on either side of us.

"What…is that?" I asked as we inched toward it.

"No idea," Riona said. "Never seen anything like it before."

"Wizard?" I asked.

He seemed as perplexed as the rest of us as we approached the cloud. It didn't have a smell, and it moved and shifted as if it were buffeted by the wind, but I felt no such breeze. I reached my fingers toward it, but before I made contact, Cade slapped my hand away.

"Do you always touch things without knowing what they are? What if it sucks you inside and kills you?"

"Then I'd find out what it was, wouldn't I?"

"Stop," Riona said, walking up to the cloud so she was almost nose-to-nose with it. Then, with a sigh, she stepped through to the other side. The cloud cast a green glow on her body, but she seemed no worse for the wear. She turned around and shrugged. "No idea why this is here. Let's go."

"You heard her," I said to Cade as I approached the barrier and walked into it.

Not through it—*into* it.

It was still a vapor cloud of sorts, but to me, it was as solid as a wall. I couldn't even push a single finger through.

"Quit screwing around," Riona said, coming to stand in front of me. She easily passed through the barrier back into our side. "Just walk through it."

"I'm trying, dear Riona," I said, impatiently. "But..." I placed my hand flat on the vapor cloud, demonstrating the effect. I turned behind me to the wizard, who was watching with a curious look on his face. "Any ideas?"

"It seems to be a magical barrier," he said, after a moment.

"You think? How do we get around it?"

He stepped forward with his staff lit up gold and released a tendril of magic toward the wall. It penetrated the cloud, farther than I got, and for a moment, I thought it might do something. But the cloud vibrated angrily and spat the spell back out, nearly taking the wizard's head off as it flew by, before landing in a tree and leaving a deep gash in the bark.

"You okay?" I asked as he straightened and adjusted his traveling cloak.

"Barely," he said. "Let me try that again."

He took a moment to concentrate, and the tendril of magic seemed a bit more potent than before. It was yet again sucked in, considered, then flung out. This time, Riona had to dive out of the way to avoid being obliterated by it.

"So let's not do that again," she said, as I helped her to her feet.

"Well, do you have any other ideas?" Cade asked. "It's fae magic."

She licked her lips and put her hands on her hips. "I don't know. I've never seen anything like this before. Maybe it's just on this road for some reason... I'm sure if we turn around—"

I let out a groan. "No more backtracking."

"Well?" She gestured toward the barrier. "I could just continue on by myself, but that kind of defeats the purpose, doesn't it?"

"Maybe there's an opening somewhere deeper in the forest," Cade said. "Perhaps we can try a different road. Surely, there are multiple paths that lead into the realm. A barrier like this has to end eventually."

"You would be wrong, wizard. This magical barrier encircles the entire realm."

The deep velvety voice made us all jump. I drew my sword, the wizard had his staff lit up with a spell, but Riona...Riona merely paled.

Aldrick stood on the other side of the barrier, tall and powerful even at this distance. He seemed to be alone. I cast a nervous glance at Cade, who seemed as shaken as the rest of us. Perhaps this magical barrier had hidden Aldrick's scent from him.

"You look like you've been traipsing through the mud," he said with a dismissive smirk. "But I suppose that's exactly what you've been doing, considering no one has seen hide nor hair of you in nearly a week. I'm honestly impressed—I didn't think you could manage without your nanny."

She shifted, pink appearing on her cheeks. "Who's been looking for me?"

"Why, everyone, little Riona," he said with a smirk. "The Erlking is incensed. He's got half the court scouring the countryside for you."

Cade and I shared a look. It didn't sound like they were looking for all three of us—just her. In fact, Aldrick hadn't even acknowledged us. We might as well have been invisible.

She swallowed. "Can I be so lucky as to count you amongst those concerned for my welfare?"

"Of course not," he said. "I told the Erlking what you told me about escorting the two lesser beings to the border. He was…shall we say, less than pleased with your half-truths?"

"And I'm sure you found a way to weasel your way out of punishment," she snapped.

"I wouldn't call it weaseling. More an understanding of how the

Erlking thinks. Something you might find out if you live long enough."

"Stop with your stalling," Riona barked. "Are the rest of your minions on their way? Are we about to be surrounded?"

"That depends on you," he said. "This barrier was erected per the request of the Erlking to the *Cernonn* chief. The fae clanleaders have such power, you know. The Erlking wants you to stay in his lands until he finds you. My guess is, the moment you passed through, the *Cernonn* knew it and is sending his flocks of sprites and various beings to make sure you stay put."

"And you won't help them?" she asked, a little curiously. "I should think it would be in your best interests to let me get captured."

"On the contrary, I would *much* rather you continue your journey," he said with a cruel chuckle. "Which is why I'm here with some, shall we say, friendly advice?" He cast his gaze to the two of us. "The Erlking has managed to get the *Cernonn* to erect a barrier, but the wildlands…they're so much less civilized. If you truly wanted to finish this all-important task you've set your mind to, I would head up that way."

Riona licked her lips. "The…wildlands?"

"I suppose it's a choice then: venture into the most dangerous part of fae country or face the wrath of the Erlking for your disobedience." He spared us another glance. "Your friends would probably fare the same either way."

"And you won't bring us in?" I asked, speaking for the first time. "You would defy your Erlking?"

He seemed to think I, a lowly human, was beneath him, because his gaze slid to Riona. "It's your choice. But I can promise that the retribution would be swift and harsh should the Erlking find you."

Then he disappeared in a puff of moths and fluttered up into the trees.

"Well," I said, after a few minutes of stunned silence. "That was interesting."

"Very," Cade said, eyeing Riona with renewed suspicion. "So the

Erlking has made provisions to keep us in his land while searching for us?"

Searching for Riona, I thought curiously. If I were him, I would've wanted the wizard and trespassing human found first. But the way Aldrick had phrased it…

"Strange he hasn't come across us in the fields," I said to her silence. "But then again, it sounds like he was expecting Riona to stick to villages."

"Either way, I do believe Aldrick when he says fae creatures are headed this way," Cade said. "So unless we want to be caught, we should move."

"Back to the *aos sí*?"

He blanched. "Absolutely not. We'll go another way."

"There is no other way," Riona said quietly. "Either we give up on this quest or we go through the graveyard…and on to the wildlands."

I waited for Cade to argue, but the wizard had simply grown ashen and stared at the ground.

"So you're telling me you believe this guy?" I said. "He makes a big fuss catching us at the border then shows up here to tell us how to continue the quest. How does that make any sense?"

"He was merely putting on a show at the border so he could tell the Erlking he performed his duty," she said. "He knew I wasn't going to the castle, and he was content to let me go."

"And just now? Why help us?"

"Because he wants me dead," she said, lifting her gaze to mine.

I started. "Why does he want you dead?"

"Politics."

I couldn't believe that. She was barely sixteen—hardly capable of causing the kind of trouble that would warrant such a threat from a full-grown fae.

"How does helping you now hasten your death?" Cade asked.

"It's not…" She sighed. "He knows what's in the wildlands—

what's in the *aos sí*—and he doesn't expect us to last."

"The question I keep coming back to is why Aldrick is going through so much trouble to get you out of the way," I said. "Are you in line to succeed the Erlking or something?"

"No."

"Then why?"

"I told you. Politics."

I made a face. "That's not an answer."

But she didn't respond, merely walking out into the sunlight of the plain with a nervous, but resigned, look on her face. Cade sighed heavily and followed, having added nothing to the conversation. And since I had neither magic nor the desire to continue by myself, I let out a loud grunt of frustration and marched out of the forest.

Chapter Thirty

Cade

I didn't like the idea of going back to the *aos sí*, but I'd read that magical barrier in ways the knight hadn't. It wasn't just impermeable, it was all-encompassing. In the brief moments my magic had been inside it, searching for a tear I could exploit, it had revealed itself to me. Even if my magic had been at its best, I wouldn't have been able to overpower it.

Ward seemed insistent that there was more to the Aldrick story than she'd let on, but I could very clearly see the fae's thinking. The Erlking clearly wanted her back in his castle. Aldrick couldn't defy him openly, but if he merely offered advice and enough rope, Riona could hang herself with it. It was a very fae move.

"What do you think 'politics' means?" Ward asked.

"No idea," I said. "But I'm sure we'll find out sooner or later."

"I'm not walking back over this plain again, so we'd better actually cross through this time," Ward said with a meaningful look to me. "No more freaking out over what a little goblin told you."

I nodded, but the closer we came to the *aos sí*, the more I remembered why I'd been so against crossing it in the first place. There was some sort of deep, foreign magic—something that made my insides squirm. But Ward was right. I couldn't delay us more because I was afraid of a little ghost story.

But that was easier said than done when we crested the hill and came to the vast, misty field of overgrown mounds. Riona let out a shaky breath next to me, and I tried to keep her nerves from affecting my own.

"We should camp before—" she started.

"No," Ward snapped. "We'll keep going until we reach the other side."

I set off behind him, but when I reached the bottom of the hill, a deep chill entered my bones. Something very magical lived here—though lived might not be the right term. Existed, perhaps. Nothing seemed alive, save the grass that covered the mounds.

"Creepy." Ward tossed a look over his shoulder. "Oh look, she's decided to join us."

I followed his gaze to where the fae girl was making her way down the path we'd already walked. Her face had gone paler than usual, almost an ashen gray, and her hand remained on the small knife at her waist.

After the first hour of walking, I acclimated to the feeling of the magic on my skin and the tension in my shoulders loosened. The fae girl was now three steps behind us, so I assumed if we were heading in the wrong direction, she would let us know. But she hadn't made a peep yet, which was something of a blessing.

"What is this place, anyway?" Ward asked.

"A long time ago," she said, her voice barely above a whisper, "the fae didn't get along as well as they do now. There was no Erlking to serve as arbiter, so fae just killed one another. At the time, there was a fae by the name of Laughlan who ruled this realm with an iron fist. His people went to the *daoine maithe* clan leader and begged him to step in. So they did." She gestured to the surrounding mounds. "This was the site of the battle. Every mound is a soldier dead—all of them Laughlan's."

Laughlan, that name sounded familiar. A cool breeze whipped across the land and cut through my shirt, raising goosebumps on my skin. "So there's just a lot of dead fae here, that's all."

"No," she said. "Laughlan's people...well, they became part of the *daoine maithe* and the clan leader who defeated him became the Erlking. Obviously, that made Laughlan's spirit vengeful."

Ward snorted. "Obviously."

"The legends say his soul split into a thousand pieces, forming revenants that…" She licked her lips. "That prowl these lands in search of *daoine maithe* blood."

"Oh, good."

We kept quiet after that, our footfalls the only sound. There had been a constant chatter of birds overhead on our journey and without them, the silence was eerie. Shadows danced over the mounds that flanked us on either side, organized like perfectly lined soldiers waiting for their orders. There were no markers or descriptors on the graves, just raised earth.

The sun, which had somehow disappeared behind clouds as soon as we'd set foot in this place, was setting, as the light was becoming scarcer.

"How much longer?" I asked, breaking the silence.

"No idea," Ward replied. "Riona?"

She didn't respond. I cast a look over my shoulder, and she was chewing on the nail of her thumb, her eyes wide and fearful.

I stopped and turned to her. "How much farther do we have to walk through this place? It's getting dark."

"Yes, it is," she said, her voice barely above a whisper. "That's why I didn't want to attempt this so late in the day. We can't possibly camp here. We should continue until we reach the other side."

Ward shared an annoyed look with me, but I also would've rather left this spooky place before attempting sleep for the night. So I turned and kept walking.

Within an hour or so, it was getting hard to see. My footfalls were sure with my staff poking the ground first, but once the light disappeared completely, we'd be walking blind.

"Anyone got a lamp?" Ward asked.

"I can—"

"Absolutely not," Riona snapped. "That'll draw them to us."

"Except we've been in this place for hours and haven't seen a single thing," Ward drawled. "So maybe it's all in our heads, eh?"

"We shouldn't have come," she whispered.

"Let me at least light the way," I said. "We can't see anything."

"I agree," Ward said, and I heard his feet shuffle over something. "We don't even know where we are."

She protested, but I ignored her, sending magic into the tip of my staff and illuminating the graveyard with a soft light. I exhaled a little in relief that there wasn't a large hulking monster waiting in the shadows, and based on the knight's expression, he felt the same way. We picked up the pace, still eager to get out as quickly as possible. But as the minutes and mounds passed, the end seemed nowhere in sight.

Another cool wind blew by, and I got the taste of something disgusting on my tongue. It was rotten, like refuse or old meat, and drew a disgusted look onto my face as I coughed, trying to clear it.

"What's wrong?" Ward asked.

"I think…"

Riona inhaled a sharp breath, turning behind her. "We've been spotted."

We stood still, Ward's hand on his sword and my staff ready to jump into action. But nothing was there…just the foul taste on my tongue. Still, I'd been around enough fae in the past few days to know it wasn't just my mind. There was magic afoot.

"T-there…" Riona whispered.

I followed her gaze as one of the mounds next to us began to shift. At first, I thought it might've been a trick of the light, but no… something was emerging. My instinct was to run, but I couldn't find it within me to move—and neither could anyone else in my traveling party.

A guttural sound emerged from the darkness as the creature stood, and my heart fell into my queasy stomach. I'd never seen such a creature as the one in front of us. It was three heads taller than I was, with a skeletal head that had remnants of gray skin stretched taut, revealing bare teeth with fangs. The one ear it had was pointed—it had definitely been fae at some point. The threadbare clothes that hung from its frame were grimy and had long since lost whatever color they'd had.

"What…the hell…" Ward breathed beside me.

"You said it," I replied, looking to the fae girl. "What do we do?"

But she'd gone stark white, and before I could say another word, she screamed and took off running away from the monster. Before she got three steps, another monster burst from the mound, blocking her path and growling in her direction. She backed up until she reached us, shaking her head and muttering words I couldn't understand.

I turned back to the revenant, magic coming into my staff. "I will do my best to destroy them. Ward—"

"Yep." He pulled his sword out. "Riona, keep an eye on our backs." But there was no response from her. "Hey, are you—"

She'd collapsed into a ball on the ground, her hands covering her head as she whimpered to herself.

"I guess she's no help," I muttered. "We've got to handle this ourselves."

"How's your magic doing?" Ward asked.

I swallowed. "Let's hope it behaves."

We each took a creature, leaving the fae girl between us.

"Okay, monster," I said, twisting my fingers tightly around my staff. "Let's see what you're made of."

I sent a small magical spell in its direction, and it harmlessly bounced off the creature's skin—but it did earn me an otherworldly chuckle from the creature.

"*Wizard,*" it hissed from somewhere deep inside.

"That's me," I said, hoping that didn't mean something worse for myself. But this…this was never covered in any of my training. I'd always trained one-on-one. But perhaps this was part of the trial he'd hoped I would endure.

I tossed my staff into my other hand, thinking quickly through my knowledge. But before I could say or do anything, it came toward me at a speed I hadn't thought possible, and took me in its bony hands, knocking the staff from my hand. I cried out in pain as it began to squeeze—reaching out with my magic for the staff that was a foot away.

"*Arg*!" I cried as the revenant squeezed harder, spots clouding my vision. But the pain cleared the fear from my mind, and I could feel my staff once more. It flew into my hand, and I released a stronger spell toward the ghoul. It dropped me and I fell to my hands and knees, gasping for air.

I scanned the monster, searching for something that looked vulnerable, but the whole thing *looked* like it was barely held together. With a deep breath, I gathered magic into my staff and fired off another spell, this time straight for the monster's head.

It exploded into a giant spray of dirt and dust, and the body dropped to the ground.

"Got one!" I called.

"Great," Ward said, backing up as he faced a second monster. Behind him, the ground began to move.

"Look out!" I ran forward, sending another gold fireball whizzing by Ward's head, barely missing him. It landed squarely in the mound that was moving, and earned another cry of anger from a revenant about to make its escape. But it wasn't the only one.

All around us, the mounds had begun shifting... This entire cemetery would be up and moving if we didn't get out of here.

"We need to run," I said.

"No arguments here," Ward replied. "But which way is out?"

I spun around. In the chaos, I'd lost our trail and direction, but that wouldn't stop me. I put my staff on the ground and whispered a spell for direction.

"Cade..."

"Give me a minute."

"I don't think we have a minute."

I opened my eyes to a gathering storm of monsters—from all sides.

"What now?" Ward asked.

I'd killed one of them by aiming for the head, but I needed something a little faster than one at a time. Taking a step forward, I dug my staff into the ground, gathering magic from every inch of my body. I'd never attempted anything like this before, but I could see it fairly clear in my mind. Somehow, being on the cusp of death was the key to mastering my scattered focus.

I inhaled and exhaled as the magic built in my staff, and the wood grew hot under my fingertips. The revenants were coming closer, and Ward's worried tone echoed in my mind, but I kept my eyes closed as I gathered magic. Almost…ready.

One of the monsters was right in front of me, but I released the magic from the top of my staff toward the sky. It flowed out of me, illuminating the entire graveyard with a bright gold glow. The magic coalesced in the sky above, gathering into storm clouds.

"What—"

With a cry, I split the magic into lightning bolts and shot them toward each of the revenants, easily visible under the illuminated sky. Their otherworldly voices melded together in a cacophony of pain before growing silent. I stood at the ready, waiting for more, but the cemetery was once again silent.

"Wow…" Ward breathed beside me. "So you could've done that this whole time?"

"I didn't know… I wasn't sure how I did that," I said a little breathlessly.

"Are they…" Riona's quiet voice came from the ground. "Are they gone?"

"Yes, they're gone," Ward said, putting his sword away as he reached down to help her up. "Are you all right?"

She nodded, some of the color returning to her face. "We shouldn't stay here. We need to keep moving."

I stared at her, dumbstruck. That was all she had to say after that?

"Is there anything else in this land we need to be worried about?"

Ward asked.

"There may be more revenants out there, but perhaps your magic has scared them away," she said. "Once we leave here…there will be different dangers. So we'll just have to be on our guard."

"What could be worse than those things?" Ward asked, disbelief on his face.

"Let's hope we don't find out."

Chapter Thirty-One

Ayla

It had been a few days, and I was still smarting from my disastrous attempts to get into Eoghan's study. The more I thought about it, the less I could believe I'd acted so rashly. It was no wonder Eoghan was hesitant to give me the reins. He probably thought it better for the country—and it probably was.

I vowed to be better, to think before I acted, and to no longer give anyone in my circle cause to think I wasn't fit to rule.

In any case, I had something else to distract myself from my idiocy. If my math was correct, Cade and Ward had reached Críoch and should've been on their way back.

"I have faith they will be here within the next day," Eoghan said with a kind smile as we walked around the gardens. "And then, hopefully, they will know where we can get the stone."

"Will you retrieve it?" I asked him.

"It depends on what they say. My own theory is that Leandra brought the stone to her father," Eoghan said. "If that's the case, it makes it a little more tricky. The fae might recognize a wizard if one walked amongst them. We may have to send a soldier who was exceptionally brave and cunning, and who knows much about the fae realm." He tapped his chin. "Perhaps even the one I sent along with Cade."

I licked my lips. "Do you think he'd accept such a mission? It sounds dangerous."

"Very." He cleared his throat. "Especially if it meant he would be getting it for you."

My face flushed at the insinuation. "*Eoghan.*"

He chuckled, as if enjoying the way I squirmed. "And on that note, Konevell is sending an envoy to meet with you. I think he might be the best of the bunch so far, so I ask that you meet him with an open mind."

"Always, but..." I tilted my head up at him. "I still don't see why it's necessary for me to marry so quickly. So many monarchs in history have ruled solo for years—decades, even. As I've recently re-learned thanks to your mandatory history lessons."

"Our alliances have frayed," Eoghan said. "It would be prudent to strengthen them quickly by marrying someone from one of the other four kingdoms."

"I can strengthen alliances in other ways," I said, stopping mid-step and turning to him fully. "Marriage isn't the only way."

"I know you think that," he said, smiling down at me. "But it is the best way. I promise you, we'll find you someone as handsome as that knight and who'll also help guide you."

"This isn't about Ward," I said with a dismissive wave of my hand. "I've been waiting to rule my entire life, and now that it's here, I don't want to give it away to a stranger from another land through marriage."

"Is that what you think marriage is?" he asked. "A trap?"

"I won't have autonomy," I said with a frown.

"Of course you will—"

"You *just* said that you'll find me someone to 'guide me.' What if I want to guide myself for once?"

His smile had become somewhat patronizing, and I was sure I sounded like a child to him. "In due time. But you still have a lot to learn. In the meantime, will you at least dine with the envoy from Konevell?"

"Of course I will," I said with a huff. "An envoy is an envoy."

And with any luck, I could prove to Eoghan that I was every bit as capable of forging an alliance *without* having to give up my authority.

>»‑»‑»‑»

The next evening, I ignored the suggested attire Eoghan had sent up. It was light and pastel and very innocent-looking. Tonight, I was preparing for battle, so to speak, so I opted for a dark navy dress paired with my hair down my back. I pinched my cheeks to help them not look so round (it didn't work), and practiced a fierce expression in the mirror until I was retrieved by my guard—Donnegan, one of the oldest in my personal staff.

"You look lovely this evening," he said with a kind smile. "Is that a new dress?"

"Just one Eoghan doesn't often suggest I wear," I said with a smirk as I dropped back to take his arm in mine. "Trying something new tonight. How's your daughter doing, by the way? Has she had the baby yet?"

"Last week! A boy. Healthy as an ox."

I grinned. "Please, do tell me everything."

Donnegan left me a few steps from the door, nodding his goodbye and assuming his position outside the door. I continued through the small hallway to the dining room and pushed open the door. Inside, Eoghan was seated with…not the sort of person who should've been a suitor. He was at least as old as Eoghan, skinny, with ashen skin and sunken-in cheeks. I didn't want to be morbid, but I didn't think he'd live past the summer.

"Ah, pr…" Eoghan's brow furrowed. So he noticed I wasn't wearing what he wanted. "Princess Ayla. Good of you to join us."

The envoy, Duke Guinnein, coughed into his napkin and slowly rose, taking my hand and kissing it. I wanted to dunk it in water after, but I merely hid it behind my back as I wiped it discreetly. We made small talk about the journey from Konevell, which was nestled between Nesuria to the west and the mountains to the east, and he indicated it was a tiring journey. I bit my tongue instead of mentioning that it seemed most journeys would be for such a frail man.

Eoghan watched me for the entire conversation, and I could practically predict the lecture that would come after. *He was only trying to protect me, why did I insist on stepping outside of the lines he'd drawn for me, one mistake could ruin the kingdom forever.* But my confidence could not be swayed.

The envoy seemed to feed off my energy, gaining more life as the dinner continued. He actually wasn't that awful to speak with, mild-mannered with a keen interest in reading and sciences. If he wasn't twice my age, I could see the potential for a marriage alliance. But that was quickly dashed every time he hacked into his napkin.

"It's late," I said with a genuine smile. "You should return to your room for the evening and rest after your journey. How long will you be in town?"

"Just for the evening," he said with a frail smile. "I was told of your intellect and beauty and wanted to see it for myself."

I smiled demurely. "A long trip for a short visit. I implore you to stay a few days and regain your strength—"

"I'm," he hacked into his napkin, "perfectly fine. But I appreciate your concern."

⇥ ⇥ ⇥ ⇥

The dinner did end shortly after that, thanks to a coughing fit that left him red-faced and wheezing. I asked for two guards to make sure he made it to his room safely, and he declined them both. Eoghan waved his hand to dismiss them, and they returned to their posts.

Once the door shut behind him, it was just Eoghan and me.

He twisted a fork in his hand, not meeting my gaze. "So."

"Are you going to lecture me because I didn't wear the outfit you'd picked out for me?" I asked, raising my brow. "Because I think you should save your breath for something more interesting."

He said nothing, just kept twisting that fork. This was a game he liked to play, to stay silent until I could stand it no more. But I wouldn't give in this time. I wouldn't.

I did. "How'd I do?"

"Would that topic of conversation be interesting to you?"

"Eoghan," I said with a sigh.

"I don't think he will write to offer a marriage contract, if that's what you're asking," he said. "Duke Guinnein prefers a wife who'll be quieter, more in line with his own tastes. I don't think you fit the bill this evening."

"I don't think I fit the bill ever." I smoothed the dark folds on my dress. "You said he would make a good husband—"

"I said to keep an open mind."

I pursed my lips. "To consider him for marriage."

"Which you made very clear you didn't want." He tilted his face toward me, his expression unreadable. "Is that why you acted the way you did tonight? To prove a point?" He shook his head. "You should make up your mind whether you want to marry or not. I can't seem to keep up."

I opened and closed my mouth. "I don't, but…" I struggled to find the right words. "I wanted to at least make a good impression so we maintain relations with Konevell."

"An impression is only as good as the person delivering the news about it. I don't think Duke Guinnein had a great impression of you, and thus…"

I frowned. "I don't think—"

"In the morning, I will be leaving for Sudaemor to meet with their king," he said, rising. "I don't expect I will be gone very long."

Sudaemor, perhaps a week's ride south. "Are you sure that's wise? I thought you said the fae—"

"Cade should be returning any day, as I've said," he said, twisting the wine glass. "And he will be adequate protection until I return."

"I see." I fiddled with my skirt again. "Are you mad?"

"Of course not." But he didn't meet my gaze. "I will probably not see you in the morning. Be sure to keep to your studies. And if you decide to try to break into my vault again, please take care not to use the entirety of the guards' time and to clean up after."

He rose and left me there. I frowned as tears came to my eyes. I wasn't even sure why I was so hurt by his brusqueness, but sitting there in my dark dress and the ruins of my confidence, my chest began to hurt. Before I showed anyone else my weakness, I hurried back up to my room and prayed Eoghan was right about Cade's return.

I could've really used a friendly ear.

Chapter Thirty-Two

Ward

It took several hours, but when the moon was high in the sky, we reached the other side of the *aos sí*. Even then, we didn't stop walking until we were at least another mile from the mounds and misty air. By the time we collapsed to the ground, no one wanted to volunteer to take the first shift, so I did it, knowing I wouldn't be able to sleep without seeing those monsters in my dreams.

I watched the small fire Cade had conjured and kept my ears open for the sounds of approaching predators. We were in the wildlands now, and Riona had promised more danger and unpredictable creatures. I just hoped she was up for the task of fighting them.

I could understand why she'd been so scared. The creatures were otherworldly, so perhaps she had some fae-driven fear of them that I didn't know. But on the other hand, I was also terrified to the point of nearly wetting myself and I still managed to rise to the occasion. Even sheltered Cade, who was more apt to lose his staff in a fight, had found it within himself to blast them into oblivion. I had yet to see Riona demonstrate any sort of defense with her magic—or any magic other than glamour and that butterfly thing she did.

As much as I wanted to, I couldn't get what Aldrick had said out of my head. *Surprised you made it this far without your nanny.* There had been a few instances where her absence in helping had been conspicuous. Namely, when Cade had nearly been trampled by the *tarroo* beasts and she'd just let him figure it out on his own. At the time, I'd thought it was because she would rather the wizard died, but now… Now, I wasn't sure.

I glanced across the fire to where Riona was sleeping. It was her shift next, but I wasn't sure I could sleep when she was supposed to be watching. Not when I wasn't sure she could protect us in the event of an attack. But eventually, my own tiredness got the better of me and I rose, waking her softly. She jumped, looking at me as if I were one of those revenant creatures then softened, swallowing hard.

"Sorry," she said, blinking heavily. "Is it my shift?"

"It is," I said, sitting down next to her and making sure Cade was fast asleep. "But I thought we could have a little chat first."

"About what?"

"What do you think?"

She licked her lips and looked away. "Can we just not? It wasn't my finest moment."

"Yes, but…" I tilted my head at her. "How old are you anyway?"

She exhaled and looked as if she'd swallowed something disgusting. "How old are you?"

"How many fights have you been in?"

"Enough."

"So none." I couldn't help but laugh, earning a scowl as her cheeks flushed bright red.

"Is there a point to this?"

"I'm curious why someone who's never been in a fight and who barely has enough magic to protect herself volunteered to take us through this dangerous land." I paused, glancing at her. "Considering that you don't have the blessing of the Erlking, either. Did you…" I snorted. "Did you run away or something?"

"Don't forget, I can still hurt *you*, human," she snapped. "Besides that, I'm the only one who can bring you and the wizard to the stone. So you still need me."

"I didn't say we didn't," I replied lightly, noting she'd avoided answering my question directly. "I just want to know what sort of fighter you are, since you haven't shown us much of what you can do. Are you able to use sword? Knife? Bow and arrow?"

"Of course not," she said. "Why would I do that when I have magic?"

"That you've only used to turn into butterflies and glamour yourself," I said, tilting my head. "What else can you do?"

"What I can and can't do is none of your business."

"I think it is, considering I'm putting my life in your hands every time we encounter something that wants to kill us, and we're about to walk into a land full of them." I sat back on my hands. "I just need to know that you're up to the challenge."

She glared at me. "Of course I am. I just had a brief moment of panic and lost my head for a minute. It won't happen again."

Won't it? "What kinds of creatures will we see in the wildlands anyway?"

"Hopefully none."

"But if we do," I said. "I'd like to be prepared."

She licked her lips. "There's the Clurichaun, they're solitary creatures who would rob us of our weapons and gold. But I think they'd only come if we had drink on us."

"Good thing I left my ale behind," I said with a wry smile. "That doesn't sound too bad."

"The *ellén trechend* are three-headed birds that eat corpses," she said. "They've become rarer since the fae stopped killing each other. We'd definitely see a *fachan* coming—they're as tall as a mountain. The *dullahan*, that one might be a problem—changelings, too." She shifted. "But hopefully, we won't encounter any of them."

"And if we do?" I pressed.

"We'll handle them."

We. "You, too?"

"Damn it, human, I said I was sorry!" she barked, her voice echoing in the clearing.

The wizard snorted and blinked before falling back asleep. I couldn't help but laugh; Riona resembled a very irate child and not the fearsome creature she was hoping to convey.

"If you aren't going to get your rest then please let me go back to sleep," she said with a scowl.

"I'm going, I'm going."

⤔ ⤔ ⤔ ⤔

That I got any rest that night was a miracle. Most of the time, I kept waking up to make sure Riona hadn't either left or there wasn't another of those revenant creatures creeping up behind us. But I caught a few minutes here and there, and too soon, it was light, and time to continue.

Riona didn't say much, and she kept her distance from us as she led us over the land. Where the *daoine maithe* had at least been grassy with pockets of thick trees, this land was darker, more barren. I was grateful for the dried meat in our pouches because I had a feeling Riona wouldn't be able to find any of those roots.

For being "dangerous," there seemed to be as many monsters waiting for us here as before—which was to say not many. There was the errant owl the size of a hawk, a small furry creature that seemed very interested in Cade's coin purse when we stopped to rest midday, and the distant chirping of birds, but nothing too scary came wandering by.

Riona was back to acting confident, declaring that she knew where she was going with nearly every hill we crested. I didn't know about Cade, but I could sense her overcompensation. She knew I was onto her, and she was going to prove to me that she wasn't just useful, she was *necessary*.

Still, my own sense of direction was in line with hers. If her map was right—and that was a big if—and we kept northwest, we would hit the *sidheog* lands eventually. Too far west and we'd run into the forest realm again and have to cut north.

"I don't care, as long as we get there," Cade said when she

explained it to him.

"We will."

Even with all her bluster and confidence, I wanted to learn more about her, to find out exactly how much trouble we were in with her as our guide. So when we stopped for another break, the wizard left to relieve himself, and I sensed my opportunity to reopen the conversation.

"How many days do we have in the wildlands?" I asked, trying to keep my tone casual.

She snorted and didn't answer.

"I mean, just your best guess," I said.

"I think you know the answer to that question."

"Do I?" I tilted my head. "You said you knew where you were going."

"I know the direction in which we need to walk," she said, looking up at me. "But exactly how far it actually is, I don't know." She looked at the ground. "The forest is roughly the same distance, but it's different—more villages to stop in, more people. More…" She shrugged. "Out here, we don't have a true path to follow, but as long as we keep to the north and northwest, we should hit the *sidheog* lands eventually."

Eventually. "That doesn't sound encouraging."

"If we keep moving and cut at the right angle across the land, we might shave a few days from our journey." She shook her head as Cade came back through the bushes. "But I don't think you'll be back in time for her coronation."

"How exactly do you know when her coronation is going to be?" Cade asked.

"Because I do." She rose and began walking. "If you two are done, let's get moving."

I rested my hand on my sword as Cade came to stand beside me, a confused look on his face.

"What was that about?" Cade asked.

I sighed, deciding it was time to share my thoughts. "I have a suspicion our guide isn't as well-equipped to handle what lies ahead as she'd have us believe."

He clicked his tongue. "I was afraid you'd say that. I've been curious about what happened back in the *aos sí*, and I was hoping it was just a fluke."

"I don't think so," I said. "I think she's a kid who ran away from home and is pretending to be some kind of savior."

"But why?" Cade shook his head. "Why would she do something like that?"

"That's another mystery. But the more important question is what do we do about her *now*?" I made sure she was far enough away that she couldn't hear. "It doesn't help us if we come across another real monster."

"Then we leave her behind," Cade said. "We know the way we're going—northwest. I'm sure I can use magic to find the stone once we reach the *sidheog* lands. If she's not going to benefit us, why should we continue to travel with her?"

"Because we'd be two very obvious humans in the fae realm," I said. "Unless you can do that glamour thing."

"I mean…" He bristled. "I don't know that kind of magic. I don't even know if it's part of a wizard's abilities." He pointed his staff at her back, which was fifty steps ahead of us by now. "But even still, why should we keep her around just because she can glamour us? She's pretty much dead weight."

So was he, at the start of our journey. "I don't think we should take that drastic a step, or even know if she'd let us. If anything, she's taken great personal risk to help us up until now."

"That doesn't mean we should take the same risk."

But I couldn't stomach the idea of telling her to get lost, especially as the only way back was through the cemetery. "She stays. We can figure out what we want to do when we reach the *sidheog* lands. But for now, it's better to stick together."

He snorted. "Whatever. You'll have to step in and save her ass if we get in trouble because I won't do it."

I couldn't help myself as I slapped him on the shoulder. "You know, I could've said the same thing about you a few days ago. If you can get better in a fight, so can she."

He stopped and sputtered at me.

"Will you two quit whispering and start walking?" Riona barked from a distance. "We don't have all day."

CHAPTER THIRTY-THREE

CADE

Ward had developed something of a soft spot for the fae girl, obviously. Otherwise, why would he be so keen on keeping her around when she had nothing to offer us? I couldn't deny that I'd gotten in trouble a few times on our initial journey, especially when I'd lost my staff, but at least I'd kept my wits about me.

As we crossed the desolate land, punctuated by a chilly breeze every few minutes, I replayed every moment with her since we first encountered her back in Pennlan in this new light. Where my prejudice had seen a dangerous creature, hell-bent on ruining our mission and perhaps taking our lives, I now saw a mischievous child who was doing just enough to pretend she wasn't. Aldrick had pegged her accurately, and he might've been correct when he said we would all perish in these untamed lands.

Whenever she stopped to check our direction, I cast a quiet spell to ensure we were, indeed, heading in the right direction. I'd tried countless times to cast a spell to lead me in the direction of the stone, but my magic wouldn't cooperate, or the stone was too far away to locate. So I opted for just a simple directional spell to tell us if we were going northwest.

"There's no need to do that," Riona said, as the compass appeared over my staff. "I know where we're going."

"Do you?" I asked with a raised brow.

She glared at me, something uncertain in her gaze, before turning away. She hurried to catch up with the knight, whispering to him and casting angry looks back at me. I could only guess what they were talking about, but I assumed the knight was doing his best to soothe her worries.

That night, we encountered another problem: our food stores were starting to run low. The fae meat wouldn't react to my dividing spells, and the fae girl was unsuccessful in finding those dirty roots that were our last resort. Ward rationed out a little food that didn't do much to sate my hunger, and we settled in for another night on the cold, hard ground. I wasn't even in the mood to crack open my book.

Nobody spoke the next morning as we got up for another day of trudging. I supposed I should've been grateful we hadn't encountered any of the sorts of creatures Riona had been so worried about. And yet, I was also starting to wonder how sure she was that those creatures even existed. Sure, the *aos sí* had been full of revenants. But it had been days since we'd seen more than birds. This land might be void of all living creatures—and Aldrick just assumed we'd starve to death instead of being killed by something out here.

As my hunger increased, I focused my ire on the back of her head. Could we have entered the forest realm another way? Was that barrier really as bad as I'd thought? Should we have attempted to go around the barrier? The questions were a drumbeat in my mind.

"Why don't we walk parallel to the forest?" I asked.

"Because it would add to our journey," Riona replied. "I thought you wanted to avoid that."

"If we run out of food, our journey will end a lot sooner," I said.

"We're not going to run out of food," Ward said with an impatient sigh. "I'm sure we'll come across something soon that we can kill, cook, and eat."

But another day passed, our rations were even more meager than before, and I was starting to lose my patience.

"How much longer until we reach the *sidheog*?" I snapped.

"We'll get there when we get there," she replied. "But feel free to use that magic of yours to help out, if you're so eager to move us along."

I felt a cruel smile form on my lips. "Why don't you? Oh, that's right—because you're just a kid who led us out here without provisions or a plan."

Her eyes widened as hurt flashed across her face.

"*Cade*," Ward growled from her side. "Enough."

She balled her fists and kept walking, but Ward remained where he was until I reached him. He held out his hand to stop me from moving forward, pushing me back with a glare.

"I don't know what's gotten into you, but you need to knock it off," he said. "We're all hungry and miserable, and it doesn't help for you to be a dick to Riona."

I thought it might, but I kept my opinion to myself.

>→ >→ >→ >→

Now, I had two objects for my anger, and every time they spoke or even looked at one another, my dislike for them grew. It was probably a good thing I was along, else Ward might forget his allegiance to Pennlan and throw in his lot with the fae. I began to suspect the girl had bewitched him somehow, and made plans to cast a few test spells on his mind to make sure it wasn't swayed.

But all of that went out the window when the sound of a braying animal echoed across the land. The three of us shared a shocked look then dashed toward the sound. Riona got there first, as she cheated and used her magic to land atop the nearest hill.

It was the most beautiful sight—a herd of some kind of beasts that resembled cows, except with giant wings. My mouth watered as much as my eyes, and I thanked whatever luck we had that at long last, this ever-present gnawing in my stomach would come to an end.

"They're safe, right?" Ward asked Riona.

She shrugged. "No idea what they are. But I don't really care."

Ward looked at me, hesitation in his gaze. "Would you conjure me a bow and arrow again?"

"Oh?" I raised a brow. "So now you're interested in my help?"

He rolled his eyes and muttered under his breath. Riona glared at me from the other side of him but said nothing.

"If you would like to kill the beast, be my guest," Ward said. "We'll make other arrangements."

"Like what?" Riona asked.

But my hubris was short-lived. I still wasn't capable of killing, no matter how hungry I was. "Wait." I sighed as I tapped the top of my staff to the ground, conjuring a bow and arrow from the dirt there with a little effort. "Here."

Ward glanced at it then nodded as he picked it up. "This shouldn't take long."

He fired off a shot, and it was an immediate kill. I still wasn't used to the sight of a creature dying and looked away as it shuddered for a moment before going still. Riona caught my gaze, clearly as disturbed as I was, but turned her head up to the sky instead.

"That should last us another week," Ward said with a look at the sky. "Let's just hope there aren't any more griffins around to steal our food."

I nodded and set to work quickly. The meat was much tougher than the *tarroo* we'd had previously, but beggars couldn't be choosers. Within minutes, I had both our bags full of dried meat once more, and three large slabs that we could eat for dinner tonight.

"Thanks," Ward said, putting his pouch back in his travel bag.

"Thank you," I replied then stuck out my hand. "Sorry."

He took it and shook. "Hunger will do that to you. Let's quit talking and eat."

We made camp right there, with me conjuring up a fire and Ward and Riona scouring the land for firewood. Eventually, we had a delicious meal that even Riona couldn't complain about. The meat was tough, but filling, and the mood lightened considerably.

"What do you think those things are?" I asked, gazing at the herd that had shifted to the other side of the lake but was still within view.

They were sturdy beasts, and seemed to be well-equipped for this land—and could potentially make for a faster journey across the wildlands, especially with those wings.

"No idea, but they taste good," Ward said, licking his fingers as he sat back. "Why?"

I left them by the fire, using the dwindling light to make my way to the lake and around until I reached the rest of the herd. The closest glanced in my direction but didn't seem concerned by my presence. I closed my eyes and reached out with my magic to test them—they definitely had magic in their veins.

Did that mean I could use mine to compel them?

I gathered the spell in my staff, whispering the words that came out otherworldly on my tongue. I had only practiced it in the vault, never on a real person—as Riona hadn't ever given me a chance. The magic slid from the bottom of my staff into the ground, running through the invisible veins of magic that permeated this land. It slid up the hooves of the creature, wrapping around the thick legs, up the breast, around the neck, sliding into its black eyes. It jumped for a moment, perhaps realizing what was going on, but within seconds, it was still—and completely under my control.

I could see into its mind, look through its eyes, move its head around. I saw myself in its eyes, realizing just how rough I looked after days of crossing wild terrain. But with any luck—

"*What the hell are you doing?*" Riona's shriek voice broke my concentration and the spell, and the creature shook its head as it stumbled backward. Before I could regain my control, it unfurled its wings and flew away quickly. I turned to the others, but they seemed to wise up to my presence, taking flight as their compatriot had done.

"I was trying to get us a ride," I said, watching them disappear into the sky. "But now we'll have to walk."

"What...*spell* was that?" she seethed, giving me the impression she knew *exactly* what spell it was.

"The one you made me promise not to use on you," I replied, evenly. "And I haven't."

"But you used it on that innocent creature."

"It wasn't harmed."

"Wasn't it?" She stepped forward. "You can't just *overtake* something like that, make it your slave. Things in this realm aren't your playthings."

"Calm down, Riona," Ward said, coming up beside her and resting his hand on her shoulder.

She angrily brushed it off, walking up to me with fury etched on her face. "If I see you use that again—"

"What will you do?" I asked. "Flick a butterfly at my face?"

"Cade," Ward began.

"No, you had your doubts about her capabilities," I said. "Let's see what she can do. Why don't you fight me? Let's have a little magical spar right here, right now. I'd *love* to see what you can do when you're really mad and not just letting us save your ass."

"*Enough*." Ward stood between us, holding his hands up in the air. "Neither of you are going to get into a magical fight because that would most assuredly attract something much more dangerous, and we don't want that."

I glared at the fae girl, daring her to show me what she was made of, but she merely sniffed as she turned around and marched back to camp.

"She has nothing," I said to Ward, knowing she was still in earshot. "Just smoke and mirrors."

"Well, maybe instead of berating her, you could teach her," he snapped at me.

"She doesn't need anything from me—"

"She's a *kid*, Cade," Ward said. "A kid who has put her life on the line to help us, and who'll probably be exiled from her home and people once all this is all over. Didn't you *just* tell me that book you're reading is all about fae and wizards helping each other?"

It was, but that didn't mean I should help her. "Why do you keep taking her side anyway?"

"Because someone needs to stick up for her," he said. "And if I have to be the only adult in this realm, so be it. But if you keep speaking to her like that, I'll run you through with my sword and leave *you* behind."

I narrowed my eyes. "I'd love to see you try."

"And I would love to see *you* try to stop me," he replied, stepping closer to me. "All I have to do is knock that staff out of your hand, and you're helpless. So I wouldn't test me."

Chapter Thirty-Four

Ward

Riona was hard to catch up with, but eventually I did, coming up to walk side by side with her. She was breathing heavily, her cheeks red, and her eyes on fire. I waited a few minutes to speak with her, knowing that even if she didn't have the sort of magic that could fight Cade, she could still knock me on my ass if she had a mind to.

"I'm sorry," I said.

"No need for you to apologize for what he said."

"No, but he won't do it, so I'm going to," I said. "It was uncalled for."

She sighed, dejected, and something inside me rose to offer help.

"Look, I don't have a lick of magic, and I get along just fine."

She swallowed. "You don't understand."

"What it's like to be underestimated and undervalued? I bet I do," I said. "But instead of letting it set in my bones, it made me want to become stronger. I studied every weapon that was ever handed to me because I wanted to be the best at it, and I succeeded. That's how I ended up in Pennlan."

"Is there a point to this story?"

"I can teach you how to use that knife you carry," I said. "Or whatever weapon you want. The point is…even if you don't have a lot of skill with your magic, you can still defend yourself."

"I'm not using a human weapon." She glanced down at her knife. "And I don't want lessons."

"Suit yourself," I said. "But like I said, I don't have any sort of fireballs or lightning bolts, and I've saved the wizard's ass more times than I can count on this journey." I nudged her gently. "You know the trick, right? Just get that staff out of his hand."

"I know." She finally cracked a smile. "He does lose it easily. He's not supposed to."

"What do you mean?"

"A wizard's familiar is supposed to be an extension of themselves. A wizard losing his staff is..." Her grin turned a little wicked. "It's perhaps the sign of a lesser mage."

"Don't you start," I said with a sigh. "You know, the two of you could probably learn from each other if you stopped fighting long enough to realize it. He *could* teach you magic—"

"Absolutely not," she snapped.

"That book he's been reading?" I said. "It's all about fae teaching wizards. I'm sure the reverse could be true."

"I'm not saying it's not possible. I'm saying I don't want *that* wizard's magic anywhere near me. Not sparring, not even to charm my clothes dry." She cast him a dirty look. "It's too much temptation for him to use the compulsion spell."

"He won't—"

"He *just* did," she said. "He very clearly doesn't value any fae life. He just took that beast as a slave to carry his ass across the wildlands and had zero remorse about it. That creature..."

"Why are you so unnerved by this particular spell?" I asked.

"It..." She licked her lips. "It allows the wizard to take complete control over another magical being. It's complete submission. There's no fighting it, there's no getting out of it. You're just...a bystander to the destruction, powerless to stop the hurt you're inflicting on others."

I watched her, getting the sense that perhaps she, herself, had experienced such a thing. "Cade won't do that to you. If he tries—"

"It's not him I fear," she whispered then shook herself. "I don't want to talk about it anymore."

And with that, she increased her pace, leaving me behind to wonder who or what had made her so scared of wizards.

>→ >→ >→ >→

I spent the rest of the afternoon trying to put myself in her shoes. She'd clearly trusted me enough to confide her fears, and her dislike of Cade and wizards was understandable, considering the sorts of manipulation they could do on a fae. But I didn't accept that she was destined to be stuck with just glamour and butterflies. Even if that was the limit of her magical abilities, she could still become a skilled fighter with a blade.

We stopped for camp when the light began to disappear, and we ate the dried meat from the day before. Cade said nothing about my earlier rebuke, helping to set up camp and conjuring the fire, but he sat some distance away. Silence was better than sniping, so I left him alone. Perhaps tomorrow he would be in a better mood.

Riona and I ate our meat rations silently, and I was compelled to do something to help her predicament. She carried a knife on her side, but I'd never seen her use it. A weapon like that shouldn't just be for decoration. So once I'd had my fill of the dried meat, I dusted my hands off and rose to my feet.

"All right, let's go."

"Go?" Riona blinked. "Go where?"

"You and me. I'm going to teach you how to defend yourself with that knife," I said.

"Good luck," Cade snapped from the other side of the camp.

"Thanks," I replied with a sweet smile. "You could, of course, offer to help her get better at magic—"

"*Absolutely not.*" At least they had one thing in common.

"I'm not taking lessons from a *wizard*," Riona snapped, glaring at him.

"And I can't teach a fae how to use their unkempt magic," Cade replied. "Why would I even try?"

I sighed and looked at the stars, begging for patience from the twinkling lights above. "Because we're in the middle of a dangerous land and we only have each other."

"I don't think this land is all that bad," Cade said. "So far, all we've seen is the meat we're eating for dinner and a couple small lesser fae. The only deadly thing was back in the *aos sí*. I bet you we walk for another week and never encounter another creature."

"I wouldn't want to take that bet," I said.

"Me neither," Riona replied.

"You've been lying since we first met you," Cade said, pointing his finger at her. "So forgive me if I'm not going to listen to a word you say."

"*Fae can't lie,*" she said with a sneer.

"You obviously can."

I looked between the two of them and shook my head. "So that's it then? You're just going to snipe and bitch at each other for this *entire* journey? What if one of you needs help from the other? Are you just going to let the other one die?"

They said nothing.

I threw my hands in the air. "You two are giving me gray hair. I'm going to find more firewood."

>-» >-» >-» >-»

I left them there, some part of me hoping they'd kill each other in my absence, but also hoping maybe some time alone would get them to talk. Or just sit in silence and continue hating each other. Whatever made them happy.

The moon was a sliver in the sky, and the land was more barren here. But eventually, I managed to find enough to last us through the night. I dawdled though, hoping one or both of them would be asleep when I got back, and I wouldn't have to be the middleman in their three-week-old argument.

But when I returned, Cade and Riona were sitting quietly together, smiles on their faces as they stared at the fire. The sight was so jarring that I almost dropped the firewood, especially when they turned to me.

"Did you talk?" I asked.

"Of course we did," Cade said.

"And is all well?"

Riona nodded. "Absolutely."

I blinked, hair rising on the back of my neck. I put the pile of wood down next to the fire and settled down, uncertainty running through me like lightning. Something was definitely wrong here—even if they *had* talked, their differences wouldn't have been settled so quickly. They were both too stubborn and quick to hold a grudge, and the fear Riona had carried for Cade was ingrained deep.

"What's wrong, dear friend?" Cade asked, looking at me.

"Okay, that's it." I jumped to my feet and pulled my sword. "Who are you and what have you done with them?"

"You must be tired," Riona said, smiling at me with such a wide grin it was unnatural. "Go to sleep and we'll watch. There's no need to worry."

"I vehemently disagree," I said, pointing my sword at Cade then Riona then back at Cade. "Reveal yourselves, monsters."

Cade rose, and magic gathered in his hand—*without his staff*. A rush of wind blew past me, sending me back a few steps. Before I could react, Riona had jumped from her perch and flew toward me, her jaw unhinging grotesquely. I just barely managed to knock her away with my arm.

But my reaction was too slow; Cade had come up behind me, using his staff to take me by the throat and pulling me back into him. My sword fell from my hand as I stumbled backward, my hands coming to the staff to protect my delicate neck.

"You'll make a delicious dinner," a new voice hissed in my ear.

"I don't think so," I snapped. My hands were occupied, but I still had my feet. I stomped down hard with my left foot, then used my right to kick backward. The staff loosened, and I snatched it from the other creature, swinging it with ease. I used it to knock Cade in the chest, sending him backward, then swung it around as Riona came flying toward me again.

I dropped the staff and picked up my sword, realizing that if I wanted to get out of this, I'd have to kill the creatures carrying the faces of my friends.

Could I do such a thing?

Was I even sure they weren't my friends, and they hadn't just been bewitched?

Riona's jaws barely missed my neck in my moment of distraction, and I kicked her away. Something wet landed on my arm—blood. But it was bright blue, and it had come from Riona. That was good enough for me.

I felt the *whoosh* of air before the Cade-monster tackled me, and my sword was pinned to the ground. But my other arm was free, and I could just reach my knife. With one movement, I yanked it from the sheath and forcefully rolled over, slicing the Cade-monster in the leg. It, too, spurted blue blood.

Without wasting another moment, I grabbed my sword from the ground and ran the creature through the chest. His eyes bulged, blood pouring from his mouth. My heart twisted in pain, even though I knew it was an illusion.

The Riona-monster let out an unearthly scream and flew toward me once more. I still had my knife in my left hand, so I threw it, hitting her squarely between the eyes.

In an instant, the camp dissolved into nothing, bathing me in darkness once more. It had all been an illusion, it seemed. I walked over to the bodies and knelt next to them. The faces of my compatriots had changed into those of unfamiliar monsters the size of small children, and my heart lightened considerably. Not as if I thought Cade would be that easy to kill—or Riona, for that matter. But still.

I looked around, sword ready, waiting for others to come for me, but none did. Perhaps it was just the two of them, then.

Or perhaps the rest of them were already attacking my friends. I jumped to my feet and ran back the way I'd come, hoping Cade and Riona would be smarter than I was.

Chapter Thirty-Five

Cade

The fae girl glared at me from across the fire as we sat in silence. Ward had been gone for a while, but I just assumed he wanted a break from our constant bickering. I was growing tired of it as well, but the solution in my mind was to leave the glaring fae behind and continue by ourselves.

She caught my gaze, narrowing her eyes. "Quit looking at me."

I scoffed. "You are such a child. I hope you aren't expecting me to teach you anything."

"I would rather die," she snapped.

"Based on how you react in a fight, I'd say that's a good possibility."

I was about to bark at her further, but Ward arrived with more firewood, and I didn't feel like hearing a lecture. The knight smiled at me, which was odd, then took his spot around the fire. He seemed to have walked off whatever anger he'd been carrying.

"I will take the first shift," he said.

"You took first shift last night," I replied. "It's my turn."

"It's my pleasure."

I furrowed my brow at him. "O…kay." I looked at the fae girl to see if she had objections but her eyes were shining.

Was she…crying?

"I told you to stop looking at me," she snapped, jumping to her feet. "I'm going to sleep."

She walked to the edge of the campsite and very loudly lay down and turned her back to me. I watched her for a moment, remembering how very terrified she'd been in the *aos sí*—and my gut twisted uncomfortably. I tried to justify my actions by saying that she was fae, that her kind had robbed my best friend of a childhood with her father— and were the whole reason for this journey.

But that had been *one* fae, not Riona. To blame her for the faults of someone she'd probably never met wasn't fair. And even if she was just a kid who'd gotten in over her head…being an ass to her wasn't helping the situation.

Ward was very focused on the fire, perhaps giving me the opportunity to do the right thing for once. With a sigh, I got to my feet and walked over to her side of the camp. "Riona," I said.

"Go away." Her voice was thick—she'd been crying. Guilt weighted my shoulders, and I swallowed hard; I'd never made anyone cry before.

"I'm sorry," I said, after a long pause. "I shouldn't have said that."

"You aren't sorry," she said, sniffing. "Leave me alone."

My annoyance roared back to life as I balled my fists. "I'm trying to apologize. The least you could do is acknowledge that."

"Why? Because it's *so hard* for a wizard to lower himself to offer basic decency to a fae?" She finally pushed herself up. "Because I'm less of a person? Because you can use that staff to coerce me whenever you get a wild hair, and you'd never lose sleep over it?"

"You've not given me any reason to use that spell," I snapped. "So why are you so afraid of it?"

"Because it's…" She shook her head. "Do you not understand what it *does* to the other person? How terrifying it is to have your body controlled by someone else? To have to watch the things they make you do—even if…" She swallowed. "Even if they're the worst things in the world."

"What are you talking about?" I barked.

"I'm talking about your damned master and Leandra, you dolt." She came to her feet. "But I don't think you're ready to hear that particular truth."

Something in my mind urged me to keep the conversation going, to defend Eoghan against her accusations, which I hadn't quite put my finger on. "Eoghan was the reason Leandra didn't kill more. He found her in Ayla's room. He *saved* her life."

She barked a laugh. "Think about it. Eoghan has the power to coerce fae. Why in the world would he *let* one escape? Especially with something as precious as the stone?"

"Because…" I worked my jaw, running through scenarios in my mind and finally landing on the one she was insinuating—a falsehood so ridiculous, I couldn't even think of it without laughing. "Are you trying to tell me Eoghan used that spell on Leandra?"

"If you are ready to hear the truth, I will tell it," she replied, crossing her arms over her chest. "But you won't like it."

I looked at Ward, who'd been oddly silent this whole time. "You have nothing to say to this?"

He looked at me, confused. "It's fascinating for sure."

"Fascinating?" I said, almost coming to my feet. "She's defaming my master, the very man who sent us on this mission. Surely, you want to say something more substantial about it."

But as I railed at him, something new wafted by my nose. A fae was nearby, a new kind, but I couldn't quite pin it. It kept changing with the breeze.

"Well?" Riona began but I held up my hand.

"Quiet," I snapped. "There's something nearby."

She narrowed her gaze, searching the periphery. "I don't see anything."

"We should investigate," Ward said, coming to his feet. "Where is it coming from?"

"I'm not sure," I replied. The scent appeared and disappeared at random, and it almost shifted. It was the same thing; of that, I was sure, but it was almost different versions of the same thing. I couldn't quite put it into words, but I knew one thing: it was dangerous.

With my staff lighting our way, we checked the immediate area around our campsite and found it clear. But the scent kept coming and going, drawing me farther from the warm glow of the fire. The hair on the back of my neck was upright, and the longer we went without seeing anything, the more nervous I became.

"Are you sure you're not imagining things?" Riona asked.

"I'm not. Every fae has a particular scent. This is how I've been able to peg every fae we've met so far." I glanced behind me. "Present company included."

"Me?" She blanched. "What do I smell like?"

"Honey," I replied, unsure why that seemed a little…intimate. I'd grown accustomed to her ever-present scent on my nose, and I'd never mentioned it out loud before. "But this smells like…" I shook my head. "I don't even know. It keeps…shifting." I turned behind us to where the knight was standing, staring at the moon curiously. "Ward, what do you see?"

"Nothing," he said, looking at me with an odd expression. It was almost…vacant.

And that was when I realized the scent was coming from *him*.

"Riona," I said. "Why don't we check this out over here? Ward, you go that way."

"I'm not going with *you*," Riona said with more venom than was probably necessary. I swore under my breath. No words would appease her or change her mind. But if she left with him, this not-Ward would most assuredly kill her.

So I decided to act.

I gathered magic in my staff, ready to fire, but something snuck up behind me and knocked me to the ground. Blessedly, my staff remained in my grip, but something scaly and blue landed on my wrist. I twisted my neck to stare up at a monster with golden eyes and large fangs that seemed eager to sink into my skin.

"Ward, what are you—" The creature dressed as Ward had clamped down on Riona's wrist and was pulling her away. She disappeared in a puff of butterflies and landed a few feet away, staring at him in confusion.

The magic in my staff was still ready, so I shot it backward, hoping my aim was true. The creature flew off my back, and I scrambled to my feet, huffing and puffing.

"Riona, are you all right?" I called.

"Something's wrong with Ward" she said, appearing by my side.

"That's not Ward," I said, holding up my staff as more golden eyes seemed to open in the darkness around us. Twenty, perhaps? "He's the fae I was scenting."

"It…" She straightened. "Changelings."

"What're those?"

"Shapeshifters," she said. "Banished from the *daoine maithe* for stealing fae children a few thousand years ago. Human ones, too."

"Thanks for the history lesson," I drawled, turning slowly with her at my back. More golden eyes—but how many were actually there and how many were fae trickery remained to be seen. "Deadly?"

"They do like flesh," Riona said.

"Great." I pushed magic into my staff, hoping for some of that focus and concentration I had in the *aos sí*. I could use my lightning—

Before I could finish that thought, every blue face before my eyes turned into Riona—twenty versions of her.

"That's freaky," she breathed. "I'm going to stay here with you."

"*Get off!*" I twisted around, finding another version of Riona behind me, twenty feet away, struggling against an untransformed changeling. She blasted him in the face with her butterflies, but it didn't seem to do much damage. Was *that* the real Riona?

"Remember, I'm the real me," said the one behind me.

"No, me."

"No, *me*."

I swore and backed up a few steps. Riona's cries of fear echoed in my ear—now doubled, as another version of her fought against a changeling. Tripled, quadrupled. They certainly weren't making it easy for me.

"Riona," I said, preparing the spell in my mind and in my staff, the electricity increasing in the air as I drew power toward me. "The real one. I need you to listen very carefully."

"I'm listening."

"Tell me."

"They're all liars, it's *me*."

"I want to know what form you took the first time we met."

A chorus of responses came toward me, none of them decipherable from the other. I shook my head, rubbing my ears from the deafening sound of them, and concentrated.

"You giant dolt, it's *me!*"

"No, it's not. How can you not see it's *me!*"

"It's *me!*"

They all sounded so convincing, they all *looked* so convincing. My pulse pounded in my throat; as much as we fought like cats and dogs, if I fired off this spell, I could really hurt her. She would have no way to defend herself.

Unless she did.

"Riona, listen very carefully. I want you to try something for me— and I'm not exactly sure that this'll work. But it's a rudimentary spell that every wizard child knows to block a magical spell. If these changelings are lesser fae, they might not have the power to do it, but I think you might."

"Tell me!"

"Show me!"

"Are you absolutely out of your mind? I'm not using *wizard magic*."

I released the spell in a bright explosion of power, hitting every Riona except the last one to speak. The smell of burning flesh permeated the area, and when the light faded, twenty smoking bodies were scattered around the clearing, with one, very terrified-looking Riona standing amongst them.

"I…" She opened and closed her mouth then narrowed her eyes. "Did you do that on purpose?"

I smirked and released a little laugh. "Would you rather be one of these changelings?"

"No, but…" A smile appeared on her face. "That was rather clever."

"I have a few good ideas every so often," I said. "Are you all right?"

She nodded but didn't really look like she was. She seemed to want to say something to me, but her jaw was clenched shut as she stared at the ground. For once, though, she didn't look angry at me—she looked angry with herself. And for the first time, I felt like it might not be the worst thing in the world for me to help her with her magic.

But before we could speak, hurried footsteps drew my attention. I turned, my staff lighting up at the ready to fight whatever new creature was hell-bent on killing us this time.

But when Ward flew from the bushes, his sword drawn and his eyes wild with fight, I loosened my grip on my staff.

"Stand down, you vile creatures!" he bellowed. "You won't fool me again."

"You found the changelings?" I drawled with a little chuckle.

"Change…" He straightened. "Is it you?"

"Yeah," Riona said, casting me a look. "We should get back to camp."

"Is that wise?" Ward spun, his wild eyes searching the surrounding area. "Are there more of them?"

I inhaled deeply. The only scent on the air was Riona's. "I think we're safe to stay here tonight."

Chapter Thirty-Six

Ayla

I couldn't recall a time when Eoghan had left the kingdom. He'd venture out to some of the cities, perhaps gone a night or two, but if he was traveling to Konevell…it would be at least two weeks. I had no doubt he'd be back before my coronation, but something about him being *out of the country* made me uneasy. Like my guard had been let down, and I was vulnerable.

He'd promised Cade would be back soon, but more days passed, and I saw no sign of either my best friend or the knight sent to accompany him, and I began to worry something might've happened to them. Cade was capable, and Ward was one of the most promising recruits, but that didn't mean they couldn't have been ambushed.

I busied myself with my studies, but I was distracted. Lady Enid kept smacking my desk with her ruler, dragging my attention back to the banal history of the five kingdoms, but it did no good.

"I'm sorry," I said after the fifth rap. "Perhaps today is not a good day for study."

"Master Eoghan insisted we continue in his absence," she said. "And thus, you will sit and pay attention."

I narrowed my gaze after she turned her back, yet again wondering who was the sovereign and who the servant.

Not a few moments later, there was a hurried rap at the door. Captain Gabhann didn't wait for an invite, barging in wearing her sword and a concerned look on her face.

"Your Majesty." She bowed low. "I'm sorry to disturb you. But this can't wait."

Lady Enid was miffed but I waved her off, standing and following Captain Gabhann out of the room. "What's wrong?"

"We have reports of fae in a nearby village," she said, her face stony. "So far, we haven't been able to confirm those reports, but we'd like to send a contingent of soldiers there to review the situation."

"This can't be a coincidence," I said with a frown. "Eoghan leaves, and suddenly we have fae roaming our lands?"

She nodded. "I was thinking the same. We have iron arrows and some swords. We will be able to defeat them if they come to this castle."

I shivered. "Master Eoghan?"

"By our estimates, three days' ride away," she said. "I can send for him now, if you want."

"No," I said with a shake of my head. "Go to the villages. See what you can find. Leave a contingent ready to fight here, should they venture that far."

"Yes, Your Majesty." She bowed her head then turned and marched down the hall to carry out my orders.

"Are you coming back?" Lady Enid stood in the doorway. "We still have much to cover today if we are to keep to our schedule."

Gabhann disappeared around the corner, and I bit my lip as I considered whether to go to my office and await word or try to distract myself with studies and fail miserably.

>₩ >₩ >₩ >₩

In the end, I chose the latter and regretted it. Every movement or sound sent me jumping, and I couldn't recall a single word my tutor said that day. My gaze was focused on the sky outside, and the small sliver of land I could see from my vantage point. I didn't know what I expected— an army of fae walking across the plain? Flying monsters? Or perhaps it would be the slithering, slimy movements of a people keen on killing through deceit and lies.

Our session concluded an hour later than normal, and I hurried down to Gabhann's office to see if there had been any word. She was gone, but her lieutenant promised me she'd provide me a full report once she returned. They were checking the closest villages first and would be back this evening.

So I was left with waiting and wasting the afternoon pacing in my office. I could do nothing more productive, the correspondences that Eoghan had left for me sat unopened and unread. I hadn't gotten any better at them than I'd been before, especially as I still had no idea what Eoghan had planned for my coronation.

Finally, long after the sun set and my half-eaten dinner was taken away, Gabhann knocked on my door. Her normally immaculate gray hair was windswept, and her cheeks were splattered with redness and freckles from being outside all day. She bowed, apologizing for the state of her boots and clothes.

"No need," I said. "I wanted to hear as soon as you got here."

"Reports have been confirmed, but we saw no sign of fae in the villages," she said. "Though we heard from at least twenty villages that they spotted pointy-eared creatures walking amongst them."

"How many?" I asked quietly.

"Hard to tell. We got different descriptions, but they could all be the same person," she said. "They do have the ability to change their appearance at will."

I nodded. "What do we do?"

"For now, we fortify the castle. I've sent a few soldiers out to farther villages, but it will take time to get there, investigate, and send word back." She smiled firmly. "Fear not, Ayla. We'll handle this without Eoghan."

I looked up at the sound of my name on her lips without an honorific. It soothed my worries, much like a favorite aunt might. If I'd had any.

"Thank you, Captain," I said. "Please, make sure you eat and rest tonight. And if anything changes, let me know."

"Will do."

⤜⤜⤜⤜

I didn't want to venture to my room, but eventually, I accepted that sleeping in my office wouldn't benefit anyone. And Lady Enid would insist upon her lessons, even if the castle was crumbling around her. How I lucked into such a…stalwart tutor, I had no idea.

I climbed the stairs, saying my goodnights to those I saw in the castle and stopping to chat with the two guards stationed outside my room. They had iron swords, a change from the usual steel, which they proudly showed off.

"If anything wants to come this way, we will stop it," Cleland said.

Donnegan smiled. "You can sleep soundly, knowing we're here."

I thanked them for their kindness and protection, and continued into my room. Bronwen was there to undress me and draw me a bath, both of which I declined. I just wanted to go to bed.

"In the morning then," she said, patting my cheek. "You look troubled. Is everything all right?"

"Hopefully so," I said.

Once I was alone in my room, I let my strong facade crack and closed my eyes as I tilted my head back. I shouldn't have been so unnerved by the mere mention of fae in my country, in the nearby villages, but I was—especially with my two wizards out of sight.

I walked to my desk where the book Cade had left for me sat unopened. I flipped to the first page, running my finger along his writing and wishing I could send him a message to *come home*. If only so I would stop worrying that he was in danger.

A new, horrifying thought entered my mind—what if he and Ward hadn't come home yet because they'd been captured by the fae?

No, I told myself quickly. Cade wouldn't allow it. He and Eoghan had been training for years against such a thing. I couldn't let myself get wound up over a hypothetical.

Instead, I tried to read some of the book, hoping it might distract me, but it was about as successful as everything else had been thus far. I gave up and dressed for bed, splashing my face with the water Bronwen had left for me and staring at my reflection in the mirror. I looked troubled, not at all like a sovereign. Perhaps confidence would come with experience.

I hoped.

I blew out all the candles and crawled into bed, staring at the canopy in the dim light out my window from the torches down below and the full moon. I doubted sleep would come, but perhaps if I just lay here, I might drift off eventually.

But movement on the canopy made me start. I remained where I was, breathing shallowly, then relaxed when I didn't see it again.

Now I was just being ridiculous.

I turned on my side and closed my eyes, ignoring whatever shadows might be lingering.

>⇥ >⇥ >⇥ >⇥

Someone was in my room.

I was still curled on my side, facing the window, so I cracked open my eyes, searching until I saw it—the tall figure standing at my window. My pulse began to race; I'd had this dream many times in my youth. Leandra standing over my bed, ready to kill me. Stopped only by Eoghan.

But this time Eoghan wasn't here.

I had nothing, no iron, no magic, not even a blunt object to protect myself with. All I had was my voice.

So with a start, I sat up and screamed at the top of my lungs, praying the sound would travel to the guards supposedly posted outside my room. The creature moved quickly toward me, and I backed up against my headboard. The face was emotionless, from what I could tell in the darkness, as it crawled slowly across the mattress. I moved my feet up to my butt, clutching my knees.

Was this how I was to die?

Somewhere deep in my heart, I found courage and dashed off the bed just as the monster lunged. It hissed at me, flashing teeth sharp as knives, and moved toward the edge of the bed as I backed up toward the wall. There was still a great distance between me and the door, but if I headed that way…

"What do you want?" I said, finding my voice.

It hissed once more, showing me once and for all how very uncivilized the fae really were. I screamed as it jumped toward me again, its long claws catching and tearing my nightgown, but blessedly missing my skin.

At that moment, the door burst open, and three soldiers came running in. "Your Majesty!"

The fae disappeared in a puff, and it was just me with three soldiers in my bedchambers. I rested my hand on my pounding heart. I might've been able to convince myself that it was just another nightmare from my youth, except for the tear in my nightgown.

There *had* been a fae here. It had come to kill me.

It was one thing to have been told how close I'd come to death as a child. But to have experienced it firsthand…I doubted I'd be able to sleep any more tonight, even if a soldier stood right over my bed.

"Your Majesty?" Donnegan asked. "What would you have us do?"

The only thing I could think of. "Send word to Eoghan," I said softly, somewhat hating my own weakness. "Tell him to return at once."

Chapter Thirty-Seven

Ward

"I've changed my mind," Riona said, as we ventured out into the early morning—and we were out of Cade's earshot. "I would like you to teach me how to use a weapon."

I couldn't say I was surprised, except that I'd thought she might ask Cade instead of me. "Oh?"

"Last night..." She swallowed. "I was... I tried to fight those changelings. I used magic, and when that didn't work, all I had was..." Her cheeks grew pink. "I don't even know how to defend myself."

Something you might've thought of before you left the Erlking's castle... "I'd be happy to show you some things. But to me, it makes more sense for you to learn to wield your magic." I motioned toward Cade. "You said wizards and fae—"

"We've been over this. No way."

"I thought you two had become friends?" I asked. "You weren't staring daggers at each other this morning."

"He saved my life, but I can't..." She shook her head. "I don't want to accept that sort of help from him."

"Why the hell not?"

"It's who he serves," she said softly.

"Ayla?"

"No."

"Eoghan?" I blinked. "Why are you scared of him?"

"I believe he's the real evil here," she said. "He's the reason Leandra took the stone out of Pennlan. To keep it out of his hands until Ayla came of age."

"Eoghan wouldn't be able to use it, to my knowledge," I said. "He isn't of the Pennlan royal line."

She lifted one shoulder, as if there were something very obvious I was missing. "It's my hope that Ayla will use the stone to destroy him once and for all. Once she sees who he is."

"And who is he?"

"A murdering, power-hungry monster who would stop at nothing to control the *seod croí* by any means necessary."

I snorted. "You're saying Eoghan, who selflessly—"

"Selfishly."

"—has stayed in the kingdom to guide Ayla—"

"Manipulate her."

"—and sent us on this quest to retrieve the stone—"

"Sent you on a suicide mission."

"—is the real villain here?"

She nodded, serious as death.

I almost laughed, but perhaps she wasn't completely off. Eoghan *had* sent both Cade and me on this quest under false pretenses. Whether he'd known there were no fae in Críoch, I had no idea, but something had felt off to me. Especially that he'd given Cade and me the same mission separately. But it was a far leap to suspect that a wizard who'd dedicated the last twenty years in service to the kingdom was as dangerous as Riona was saying—and a further leap to believe Ayla would use the stone to destroy him.

"What are you two talking about?" Cade said, stopping until we caught up to him.

"Nothing," Riona said, continuing past the wizard, leaving the two of us alone.

>⇥ >⇥ >⇥ >⇥

When night fell, we stopped for the night and quickly assembled camp, started a fire, and ate the meat from our pouches without conversation.

"Well?" Riona said to me once we'd put our pouches away. "Shall we?"

I nodded and rose, following her a little way from the fire but still within the warm glow. "What do you know about using that knife?"

She drew it and looked at the tip. "This part goes into the other person."

"Good start," I said. "What else do you know?"

"What else do I need to know?"

In quick order, I knocked the knife from her hands, grabbed it from mid-air, and pressed the blade to her throat. "How to hold on to it."

"How did you do that?" she asked, her wild eyes looking up at me as I released her.

"Practice." I handed her knife back to her. "First lesson: Expect that the first thing I'm going to do is disarm you, so make sure I don't do it."

"You just caught me by surprise, that's all," she said.

"That's the point, Riona," I said. "I shouldn't catch you by surprise. You should always be—"

Once again, my hand slammed against the fleshy part of her wrist and she cried out, dropping the knife. With my other hand, I swiped it from the air, grabbed her, pulled her to my chest, pressing the knife against her stomach.

"This isn't fair," she snapped, huffing a little as I released her. "I wouldn't be in this situation. I would just use magic to escape."

"Then why don't you?" Cade asked. He'd been watching us intently, his lips pressed into a firm line. What I thought was disapproval at first was actually something else—keen interest.

"Because that's not what we're doing," she barked at him. "I'm learning how to use my knife."

"You can use your magic, if you want," I said, though I wasn't wholly sure I should be offering myself up like that. "Again."

This time, she held on a little longer, but still didn't manage to keep the knife. By now, her cheeks had flushed once more, and she was growing angry. Still, she hadn't used any magic.

"It's hard for me to believe a fae such as yourself can't do more than disappear into a puff of butterflies," Cade said, tilting his head upward in something of a dare. "Why don't you show us what you can really do?"

"Are you asking me to kill the knight?" she said, gesturing to me. "No way." But once again, the knife fell from her hand, and she landed squarely on her butt when I knocked her legs out from under her. "And that was unfair."

"Nothing is fair," I said, reaching down to help her up. "That's the first thing you need to remember about a fight."

"I know nothing is fair," she snapped. "More than most."

Cade chimed in, "And when something is trying to kill you, you have to be ready for everything. There's no need for civility."

"I don't need your input."

I held my hands ready. "Once more."

"I'm done." She turned to walk away.

"No," I said, grabbing her hand as if I meant to subdue her. She tugged at it, fire igniting in her eyes, but I was stronger. She gritted her teeth and tried to release herself from my grip, but I held fast, knowing we were moments away from the breakthrough I was—

Before I knew what was happening, a column of butterflies appeared from nowhere, shooting up from the ground and carrying me twenty feet away, dropping me on the ground unceremoniously.

She wore a horrified look, her hands covering her mouth. "Are you all right?" she asked, taking a step forward. "I'm sorry, I didn't mean—"

"You did mean to," Cade said, rising from his spot. "Well done."

Riona stared at him, distrust in her gaze as if she knew exactly what he was trying to do. And I realized, with a start, that between the two of us, we'd goaded her into demonstrating something of a new skill. Me, very unintentionally, but perhaps Cade had an ulterior motive.

"Tomorrow, you get to be her partner," I said, getting up slowly.

"I thought I'd made it clear that I don't want the wizard's help," she snapped. "Even from afar."

She walked back toward the camp and promptly lay down away from us, ending the conversation. The bruise at my back warmed, as if more blood were rushing toward it. I pressed my hand to my chest then looked at the wizard, whose staff had lit up bright gold.

He rose and came to join me on the far side of the camp. "I think that was an excellent first attempt."

"First attempt at what?" I asked.

"I think she has more power than she lets on," he said. "She just doesn't have the focus required to harness it—perhaps the confidence. If we can get her to overcome both obstacles, she could be fearsome."

"I thought you wanted to leave her behind?" I asked, giving him a once-over.

He adjusted the staff and cast her a curious glance over his shoulder. "Maybe I've been too harsh with her."

"You think?"

He scowled at me. "At least I understand more of why she might hate wizards so much. She believes Eoghan used a compulsion spell on Leandra to take the stone. I'm not sure if the Erlking was merely trying to cover his tracks or spin a wild tale. But if she believes such a thing, it explains a lot."

"She called him a 'murdering, power-hungry monster who'd stop at nothing to get the stone,'" I said.

"I'm sure," he said with a laugh. "But Eoghan raised me. He's not the monster she says he is, and he would *never* use the compulsion spell to cause harm to the Pennlan royal family."

Cade was convinced, but some nagging voice in the back of my mind was skeptical. It wasn't too far out of the realm of the possible for him to have done the things Riona was accusing him of. But Cade would never believe such a thing, and I didn't think it useful to argue about it.

"So I suppose tomorrow night, I'll be the one getting beat up by the fae girl?" I asked with a forlorn look back at camp.

"Just depends on how stubborn she is," he said. "Don't worry, I won't let her hurt you. Badly."

➤➤➤➤➤➤

The next night, Cade didn't need to step in, because Riona seemed to have gained a handle on her magic and resisted using it—perhaps to spite the wizard. Even as she lost her knife time and time again, and the anger was building behind her eyes, her magic remained hidden.

"If you stopped holding back, you might be able to hang onto that knife," Cade called.

"This is none of your concern," she barked back as the knife fell from her hand again. She growled angrily and snatched it from the ground, holding it ready.

"He's right, you know," I said, tilting my head. "It might be too much for you to keep your magic at bay and hang onto the knife."

"It's not," she snapped. "Let's go again."

The following evening was much the same—Riona refused to show even the faintest butterfly, she couldn't hang onto the knife, and she was growing more visibly frustrated. Cade kept his mouth shut, which seemed to make her even angrier.

"Stop watching me," she barked at him. "I know what you're doing."

"Which is what?"

She turned back to me, her face flushed with frustration, and I held up my hands. "Let's call it a night. You're too wound up, and you're getting sloppy."

The third night proceeded like the other two, though she did her best to keep a level head—and by the very end, she was able to hang onto her knife a lot longer than before, earning her some high praise from me.

She beamed as she picked it up, staring at it with a sad sigh. "Maybe one day I'll learn how to use it."

"If you don't mind me asking," I said, making sure Cade was out of earshot, "were you not trained in the Erlking's castle?"

"The fae are above such things," she said. "The 'civilized fae' deal with disagreements with discussion and compromise, not swordplay."

"Still, there was no training?" I asked. "You seem like the kind of person who'd want to sock someone in their nose."

She snorted. "Perhaps that's the reason I wasn't ever trained."

I smiled. "What is it like there? In the civilized part of the fae realm?"

"Similar to the human realm," she said. "Villages and people living their lives. But the Erlking's castle is always fascinating. Fae come and go, jockeying for position in his court. Very political."

"Is that where you grew up?"

She nodded. "My parents were distant cousins of the Erlking, and when they died, he brought me into his home since there was nowhere else for me to go."

"That was fortunate," I said. "My brother was happy to be rid of me as soon as he could sign me up for a job."

"Isn't that because you were a hooligan?" Cade asked from the other side of the fire.

Riona's face fell, realizing that he'd been eavesdropping. I nudged her a little. "I know you hate him, but it's not a surprise to any of us that you haven't had a lick of training."

"I don't hate him," she muttered. "I just don't like him knowing how vulnerable I am."

"He happens to think you have this great well of power somewhere in there," I said, poking her and earning a look of surprise from her.

"He does?"

I shrugged. "I think he just wants to help you. If you'll let him." I cracked a grin. "Maybe you can focus all your brimming dislike of him into throwing him on his ass. I would like to see that."

She shivered, although it wasn't that cold. "No. I don't... I don't want to do that. Let's just keep it the two of us."

At least I tried.

Chapter Thirty-Eight

Cade

Since that first night, I kept my silence as Ward taught the fae girl how to use her knife. It seemed she wasn't keen on showing off in front of me—or at all—so the flashes of magic I did see were quickly tamped down. Unfortunately, she was too distracted to concentrate on both efforts, so her knife training faltered while she kept her magic locked away.

It was starting to grate on me, to have this fae believe me such a monster. Not only that, but someone clearly gifted with magic keeping it hidden like it was something shameful was wrong in my mind. Ward insisted that he was working on softening her perception of me, but it didn't seem to be getting any better.

So instead of involving myself, I returned to my book. I'd gotten fairly far, though it was starting to become repetitive again. What, in the human realm, had been a long study of wizards and their accomplishments was now wizards *and* fae. There were still no dates associated with any of the conquests, and no sign of the *seod croí*, or why the hundreds of wizards that had once been in existence had disappeared to one a generation. But since I wasn't welcome to participate in the nightly training sessions, the only thing I could do was read.

We'd been in the wildlands for nearly a week, and the climate had grown decidedly colder as we ventured closer to the *sidheog* lands, which Riona said were in something of a perpetual winter.

"Once we see snow," she said, "we know we're close."

It took a few days, but eventually, big, puffy flakes fell from the sky that melted once they hit the ground. Our clothes weren't made for such terrain, so I charmed my cloak to be impervious to the wet and cold and did the same for the knight. But Riona…

"I don't need it," she snapped, wrapping her thin cloak tighter around herself and marching forward.

"Still?" Ward said with a sigh.

"I can charm it myself," she said.

"Then do it," I said. "Charm it."

She stared at me and tilted her head. "Done." But no magic sat on her clothes, and her teeth still chattered when she spoke.

Ward rolled his eyes, putting his hands on his hips. "I don't think I've met a more stubborn person in my life."

"I have," I said with a wry smile. "She could challenge Ayla for that title."

"Can't you just…I don't know, sneakily charm her clothes while she's asleep?"

"I could try. She'd probably know, though, and throw another temper tantrum."

"I don't throw temper tantrums," she called from twenty steps away.

Things didn't get much better when the sun disappeared, and we had to set up camp. The fire was warm, but a cold wind gushed through the nearby rocks every so often, threatening to undo the charms I'd cast on our clothes. Riona's lips were a little blue, but she angrily rebuffed Ward's suggestion that I help her and demanded they continue their nightly training sessions.

But with frigid fingers, she was clumsier than before, and Ward knocked the knife from her hand without much trouble.

"Focus," he said.

"Easy for you to say," she snapped, shaking herself. "Again."

"Why don't you let the wizard—"

"Don't." She shook her shoulders. "Let's go."

I rolled my eyes and pulled out my book to read in silence, trusting that Riona wouldn't display any major feats of magic tonight.

"Argh!"

I looked up quickly—Riona's had been one of extreme pain. Ward had her knife in his hand, the tip of it bloody, and a horrified look on his face. Riona was clutching her right arm with a grimace.

"Are you all right?" Ward said, stepping toward her.

"Fine," she said through clenched teeth. When she removed her hand, her shirt was already soaked with blood. "It will be fine."

"That looks bad," I said, putting the book down and grabbing my staff. "Let me—"

"Absolutely not," she snapped, glaring at me. "I don't want your magic anywhere near me."

"Riona, this is ridiculous," I said. "That cut could get infected—"

"No, it won't." She stood quickly and disappeared into the forest.

Ward looked at me with an exasperated sigh. "Stubborn."

I stared after her with a little distaste in my mouth. Bumps and bruises were one thing, but that gash had been deep. Was she so insistent that she'd rather bleed to death or die of an infection than accept help from a wizard?

"I'll work on her," Ward said after a moment.

Riona arrived back an hour later with a bloody arm covered in some kind of muddy mixture and ignored any questions about what it was or how quickly it might heal. Ward made some half-hearted attempts to convince her to accept my help, but at least for the moment, she was set in her mind.

The next morning, the mud had caked on her arm, her teeth chattered, but she stubbornly refused either Ward's or my aid. But as the day wore on, her pace kept falling behind, and her cheeks became flushed as if she were feverish.

"Riona," I said, finally growing annoyed and stopping. "You have an infection."

"No, I don't."

"I can clear it from your body if you'll just—"

"*Keep your magic away from my body.*"

She stormed off toward Ward, who'd already passed the next hill, and I glared at her retreating back with all manner of comebacks on my lips. Instead, I just cursed her under my breath and followed.

⇥ ⇥ ⇥ ⇥

That evening, when we set up camp, she was too weak to venture out to find food, so we snacked on the dried meat from Ward's pouch. Riona took none of it, muttering to herself about wizard trickery, but I knew it was because her fever had gotten worse. Neither Ward nor I attempted to persuade her to accept my help, but something told me she'd take it sooner or later.

Riona fell asleep before we'd even finished eating, and I offered to take the first shift. I settled in with my book and, without the distraction of the nightly training matches, managed to read a few chapters. More information on famous wizards of the past, more tales of conquest and battles and magical miracles. And oddly enough, as the time marched closer to the present, more discussion of how wizards and fae used to not only get along but live amongst one another in the human and fae realms.

"No..."

I looked up, my hand on my staff, then relaxed when I realized the sound had come from Riona. She was curled into a ball, her sweaty face toward me, and her eyes shut. Her cheeks were bright red with fever, though—a worrisome sign.

She kept muttering to herself, dreaming. I ignored her for as long as I could, but when she cried out in pain, I finally rose to check on her. Her skin was on fire, and when I peeled back the crusted shirt near her cut, the skin was violently red.

"Riona," I said. "Wake up."

She didn't oblige, and I sighed, pinching the bridge of my nose. She would be angry with me when I finished, but at least she'd be alive.

I closed my eyes and drifted my magic to the wound, expelling the dirt, grime, and infection and closing it up so tightly there wouldn't be a scar. Slowly, the skin grew pink then paled to match her skin. Her eyelids fluttered for a moment and she sat up.

Immediately, she cried out in fear and scooted back. "*What did you do?*"

"Saved your life," I said with a sigh, looking back at Ward, who was still sound asleep. "A thank you would be appropriate."

She curled into a ball as if I'd violated her in the most intimate way, and annoyance settled on my brow.

"What's your problem with me, anyway?" I snapped, losing my patience. "We've walked together for almost a fortnight. We've saved each other's life, we've slept next to one another, we've fought together. And yet you still think I'm as trustworthy as a snake." I shook my head. "Even if Eoghan is the monster you think he is, I'm not. I want to help you."

As if to prove a point, I pointed my staff at her clothes and warmed them. I expected her to throw another fit, but she loosened a breath of relief and rubbed her hands together.

"Thank you," she said, closing her eyes. "That does feel better."

I took the opportunity to sit down next to her. "You are a stubborn ass, you know that?"

"I've been told that before," she said, rubbing her nose.

"Will you please let me help you with your magic?" I asked. "Apparently…" I chewed my lip. "Apparently, it used to be the norm for fae and wizards to learn from each other."

"More wizards from fae, but yes," she said, looking down at her clothes. "Once upon a time."

"So why not now? At the very least, you know that if you use your magic against me, I can defend myself. As much as I enjoyed seeing Ward get thrown around the other day, I think you would find more value in training with me."

She looked up at the sky. "Perhaps."

I couldn't help my curiosity. "Why haven't you been taught anything?"

"Politics."

I had to smile. "Such as?"

She cast me a furtive look. "My presence wasn't…welcomed by all of the Erlking's children."

"Like Aldrick?"

She nodded. "The Erlking wanted me to be as docile and nonthreatening as a newborn lamb," she said, looking up at the sky. "My studies were all academic, up until this point."

I just had to laugh. "And you thought it a good idea, with all this lack of training, to run away from home and join a wizard and knight on a journey through the fae realm to retrieve the stone?"

"I didn't expect we'd be going through the wildlands," she said with a sigh. "I thought we'd be happily sleeping in beds in the forest realm." She tilted her head back. "Hopefully, we'll find somewhere warm in the *sidheog* lands."

"And in the meantime," I said, "why don't you and I see what sort of power I can draw out of you?"

She shifted, some of that fear coming to her gaze again.

"Let's start with something simple," I said quickly, hoping I wouldn't lose her again. I grabbed my staff and removed the charm from her clothes. "Warm your clothes."

"I don't know how—"

"Magic is all mental, Eo—" I swallowed, not wanting to bring up my master. "It's all mental. You just have to urge your magic to do what you want. For me, I push that urge through the magic into my staff. For you, I'd wager it flows a little more naturally."

"It…" She cast a glance at my staff, as if she wanted to say something. "Okay, I'll give it a try."

She closed her eyes and concentrated, putting her hands on her clothes. The scent of honey filled the air, and I smiled as her hands glowed. But I jumped to action when the scent of honey turned into burning cloth and her cloak caught fire.

"Ah!" she cried as I pulled the fire away from her and extinguished it. A red welt was visible on her bare skin, and I winced.

"That looks painful," I said. "Here."

I healed it quickly, mending the cloth, and she visibly relaxed, but a defeated look appeared on her face. "I don't think I'll try that again."

"Why not?"

"Because I just—" She trailed off at my curious look and seemed to change her mind. "Very well. How do I…not set myself on fire?"

"Don't set yourself on fire."

She scowled. "Funny."

"Serious."

She closed her eyes and took a deep breath, resting her hands on her arms and concentrating. The scent of honey filled the air once more, and I held my staff, ready to step in if needed. But this time, she was successful.

"Wow, that feels so much better," she said, opening her eyes and smiling at me, and my entire chest filled with something like pride.

"We'll keep practicing," I said. "If you'll trust me."

She licked her lips. "I suppose I can do that."

Finally. "Go back to sleep. I'll wake you when it's your shift."

I rose to leave her to it, but she softly called my name—perhaps the first time she'd ever used it. "Thank you."

I smiled over my shoulder. "You're welcome, Riona."

CHAPTER THIRTY-NINE

WARD

When I awoke the next morning, Cade and Riona were decidedly more friendly toward each other. Riona's arm was healed, her clothes seemed to be charmed as ours were, and peace had finally come to our traveling party. And not a moment too soon—at mid-morning, we finally reached the *sidheog* lands.

Or rather, a large river that separated the wildlands from the civilized domain just to the north.

"I think I might cry from happiness," Cade said.

"Hold back your tears," Riona said. "I have a feeling crossing it won't be an easy feat. The *sidheog* obviously don't want the lesser creatures encroaching on their lands. So we'll need to tread carefully."

We walked cautiously toward the river, but there didn't seem to be much in the way of obstacles. The current was swift, filled with small chunks of ice that would make any sort of forging difficult. And when Cade cast a spell at the river, it was knocked back, just as it had been in the forest realm.

"Is this the Erlking?" I asked Riona.

"No, this is Clíodhna's doing," she said. "The *sidheog* queen. Almost as powerful as the Erlking himself. We won't be getting past that barrier magically."

Cade rubbed his chin. "I can perhaps construct a raft of some driftwood, but it will be hard to steer directly across with the current as strong as it is—and there's no guarantee the charms on the water won't disintegrate my spell."

"You need passage across the river?"

My hand flew to my hilt, and Cade's staff lit up with magic as we searched for the source of the new voice. To my left, to my right, nothing but wildlands. Was the creature invisible?

"Down here."

I tilted my head down and nearly recoiled in fear and disgust. A large frog-looking demon, no higher than my knee, was staring up at us with wide eyes and a smile that stretched from ear to ear—if he had ears. He was a muddy green color, his skin scaly and slimy, and his legs bent at an odd angle as he sat on his haunches.

"W-what?" Cade stuttered to my left.

"I asked," the frog said, his mouth moving in an unnatural way, "if you needed a way to cross the river?"

"We do," I said, still in shock that a frog was actually speaking to us. "Can you help?"

"I have horses that are up to the task," he said. "And you can take them beyond to wherever your final destination is in the *sidheog* lands."

Oh, but that did sound inviting. After so many days of walking, it would be nice to let something else do the hard work for a change.

"What's your price?" Riona asked, a frown on her lips.

"I could go for a great many things," he said, rocking back and forth. "Your human, he has a nice head. I'd like to have it for my collection."

I blanched and took a step backward, earning a snort from the wizard and an eye roll from Riona. "His head isn't for sale. Try again."

"Oh, well…" He sniffed the air, his beady eyes lighting up with joy. "I smell gold on you. Do you have any? Three pieces would suffice."

"I think that's a fair price," Cade replied with a nod. "For horses."

"Agreed," I said. They were at least five apiece in Pennlan. "Riona?"

She was staring at the frog man with a little suspicion. "What will you do with gold out here?"

"The *sidheog* trade in it, of course." He chuckled. "I have little magic of my own, so I buy a spell here and there to keep me warm in these cold lands. But it's not often I get travelers on this side who have it to spare, so I'm willing to give you a deep discount."

"What sort of horses can cross this river?" Riona asked. "The fae have enchanted it."

He smiled. "Come with me, and I'll show you."

We followed him farther down the banks than we'd traveled, and some ways back south, until we saw a paddock of beautiful white horses with orange manes standing in a field. They were the healthiest horses I'd ever seen, gleaming in the drab sunlight, their tails flickering.

"Incredible," Cade breathed. "I've never seen such colors before."

"Hm." Riona still didn't look convinced. "And you say these horses are enchanted?"

"They are, dear fae traveler," the frog said, hopping up on a nearby fence post. "They have been enchanted by the *sidheog* themselves to allow fae to cross the river."

Riona's scowl deepened, but Cade and I shared a grin. "And you'll let us cross for only three gold coins?" I asked. Cade's hand was already in the coin pouch hanging from his neck.

"Aye."

"Are they just to cross?" Cade asked. "How much to keep them?"

He made a face, rubbing his hand. "I could part with three for six gold coins. More than enough to buy more from the *sidheog* across the way."

"Do you know how to ride?" I asked Riona, who still looked skeptical.

"I do, but..."

"Ignore her," Cade said, looking at me. "Pay the man...I mean, frog, I mean... Pay him and let's get on our way."

>-→ >-→ >-→ >-→

"Well?" I asked, settling into the saddle. "This is lovely."

"I'll say."

"It's convenient," Riona said, glancing behind her. "Nothing is convenient in the wildlands."

"Yet you're still on the horse," Cade said.

She had nothing to say in response to that, so I kicked my horse to spur him forward. He took off at a hearty gallop, giving me the sense it had been a while since he'd gotten to run this freely. He pointed his nose at the river without prompting, and I bent down to allow the cool wind to pass over me easier.

We approached the river without stopping, and where I expected a splash of water to rise from the banks, there was nothing. The beast was, in fact, *walking on water*. I leaned to the right to watch her hooves land on the top of the water as if it was sand.

"Do you see this?" I called back to the others.

"Amazing," Cade said with a relieved smile. "Best gold I've ever spent."

"Good horse," I said, patting her mane as she came to a stop. I kicked to goad her forward, but it didn't do much good. Not only that, but…my hand seemed to be stuck on her coat.

"Ward?" Cade called. "What's wrong?"

"I don't know." I tugged harder, but my hand wouldn't budge. "My hand is stuck."

"Let me…" He grunted. "Mine's stuck, too."

The horse began to walk again, but to my horror, whatever magic had been keeping it above the waves had disappeared. She was actually walking *into* the water.

"Do something, wizard!" I cried.

"I…can't. Not without my hands free. I can't reach my staff."

Damn that staff. "Riona," I barked, turning as best I could. "What the hell is this?"

But she was in the same boat, both her hands stuck on the mane. "I don't know. I've never heard of such a beast—"

Something dark jumped from the water below, and I only just registered it as the frog who'd sold us the horses. He smirked and perched on an iceberg, tilting his head toward us.

"I see the kelpies have taken to you," he said. "Strange creatures, these. It's been a long time since they've had a human to devour."

Dread slipped into my stomach. "Devour?"

"Yes, you see, kelpies have a particular way about them. They will entrap humans such as yourselves and drag them under the water until they're dead. Then they'll take their time devouring your body, leaving nothing but bones." His gaze tilted. "But the fair folk are impervious to their magic. Which begs the question…"

He leaped from one iceberg to another to another, until he landed feet from where Riona was struggling.

"What are you, exactly?"

"I'm fae, you stupid frog," she growled.

"Not wholly," he said. "You have some human in you."

She froze, staring at him as if he'd spoken some horrible secret.

"Not just some, hm?" He chuckled. "The fae don't like mixing blood. I'm sure they consider you an abomination. Half and half, are you?"

"Shut…up…" She growled, tugging at her hands. "You don't know what you're talking about."

"The kelpie magic doesn't lie, but you do." He smiled. "I hope they will leave me your head. It will make a fascinating addition to my collection."

And with that, he was gone—and the kelpies dove head-first into the water.

Cold rushed over me, sending my senses into overdrive, but just as soon as it started, we were back up, and I was gasping for breath. Then we dove back down again. The kelpies seemed keen on torturing us before killing us… or at least that's what it felt like.

When we broke the surface again, I took my chance. "Riona," I coughed, between gasps for air. "Can you break free?"

"Don't you think I would've—"

Down again then back up. This time, I had enough wherewithal to take a breath, so I could make the most use out of our above-water time.

"You still have some fae in you, so use it," Cade said.

Into the water, this time for longer—so long I thought I might lose consciousness, but we came back up.

"I can't," she said, her voice high and panicky. "I'm trying."

"Focus, Riona," Cade called to her. "You don't have to hold back anymore. There's no more politics or anything else to worry about. Show us everything you have."

We plunged once more, and this time, it seemed that it would be it. The kelpie kicked its legs and we descended further into the icy, murky water. My charmed clothes lost their warmth and ice covered every inch of my skin. My pulse began to slow, and I prayed Cade's words got through to Riona.

My eyelids were getting heavy as my chest burned, and I opened my mouth to release a breath. Bubbles floated around me—no, not bubbles, butterflies. They wiggled between the kelpie and my skin, freeing me from the magical grasp, then pushed me up toward the surface. The freezing air hit my skin, and I sucked in as much as I could, barely recognizing that I was still flying over the river. Gently, the butterflies placed me on the shore, where I rolled over onto my side and coughed up water.

Cade soon joined me, and I was actually grateful to hear him throwing up water. Finally, the fae girl—half-fae girl—landed next to us, her hair dripping and lips a bluish color. She looked at her hands for a moment, closing her eyes and clenching her fists.

"Riona..." I said, pushing myself to sit. "You did it. That was amazing."

"You're half-fae?" Cade, still dripping wet as he stood.

"I'm not," she said, coming to her feet. "I'm full fae. I don't know what that frog was talking about."

"Is that why the Erlking didn't want you taught? Is that why—"

"No more questions," Riona barked. "I'm fae, that's all there is to it. That frog was lying."

And with that, she marched toward the village, leaving a puddle in her wake. Cade said nothing as he followed, skepticism plain on his face.

"Good job, Riona," I said, weakly, bringing up the rear. "Way to save our lives. Glad you've got a handle on that magic. I'm so happy we've come to a nice place of friendship and there's no more distrust between us."

CHAPTER FORTY

CADE

Half-fae. Riona's parents weren't distant cousins of the king—at least, one of them wasn't. She'd lied to us. She wasn't supposed to be able to do that.

It seemed every bit of trust I'd built up when it came to her evaporated. Her inability to control her magic, the way Aldrick had so clearly thought her inconsequential. All of it could very easily be explained by her having one human and one fae parent. And I didn't know what it meant for us or our journey to date, but my suspicions about her true intentions returned with a vengeance.

For her part, Riona said nothing about it—or to us, for that matter —and trudged along with an exhausted sort of determination until we crested a hill and came across a well-worn road filled with pointy-eared travelers.

"Real people," Ward said with a relieved sigh. "We made it."

"Before we go down there," Riona said. "I need to change your appearance. Two humans would attract more attention than we want."

"How are you going to do that?" Ward asked.

"Glamour," she said, looking down at her hands—now covered in a silky, silvery material. "Come here."

Ward stepped up first, and she pressed her hands onto his ears. I half-expected something to go wrong, but clearly glamour was something she had experience in. Perhaps a handy skill for a half-fae in King Birch's castle.

When she finished her work, Ward looked mostly the same—save the golden eyes, pointed ears, and perhaps smoother skin. The scraggly beard that had started to show on his face was gone as well, leaving nothing in its wake.

"Well?" he asked me. "How do I look?"

"Like a fae," I said with a shake of my head. "Why the golden eyes?"

"More common," Riona said, walking over to me. "Your turn. Sit down."

I hesitated, but only for a moment. She'd let me heal her; I could let her change the shape of my ears. "All right."

She pressed both of her warm hands to my ears, rubbing them. The skin began to tingle, but not unpleasantly, and the scent of honey filled my nose once more. My eyes burned as if I'd been standing out in the sun, and the magic settled on my skin like a sheer veil.

She removed her hands and looked down at me, nodding at her handiwork. "That'll do."

"I think you need to try again," Ward said. "He still looks too human, scowling like that."

"Funny."

I rose from the stump and conjured a small mirror to look at myself. I did look the same, but also…different. Not just my eyes, which had been lightened to a golden-brown color. My skin was smoother, with deeper reddish-brown undertones. My jaw was a little more pronounced, my cheekbones a little sharper, my lips not nearly as chapped as they felt.

"Are you done gawking at yourself?" Riona asked.

I turned then took a step back—her bright green eyes were now a golden color.

Half-fae. The green eyes were from her human parent. No wonder I hadn't seen another with them on this journey.

"What's our plan once we get in there?" Ward asked. "I hope it's to head straight to an inn and get some dinner."

"That's about the long and short of it," Riona said. "And hope we don't get noticed."

⭢ ⭢ ⭢ ⭢

The village wasn't too far, and before we knew it, we were passing wagons filled with produce along a dirt road, manned by farmers with pointed ears and golden eyes. The village appeared on the horizon, and my pace quickened. A good night's sleep, a bowl of actual stew—I'd never been so excited in my entire life.

If I hadn't known any better, I would've thought we were in a human village—except that there were all manner of creatures hopping, buzzing, and standing around speaking with each other. I couldn't help but gawk a little as a small human with wings fluttered by, leaving a trail of sparkling dust that evaporated into the air.

"This is certainly…a place," Ward said, craning his neck.

"Will you two quit lollygagging and follow me?" Riona snapped, appearing in the crowd.

She led us to a small inn, where they did, in fact, accept gold. Ward paid for three rooms and meals, although there was nowhere to get a bath, I was still grateful to have a place to lay my head that wasn't the cold ground. While he finalized the details, I walked over to the hearth and extended my hands to the fire, which had a greenish tint.

"Here's your key," Ward said, handing me a small…coin? "I think. Not exactly sure how this works."

"I'll show you," Riona replied softly. I hadn't even noticed her walk up on Ward's left side. "C'mon, before someone sees you."

We followed her up the stairs, each of us dumbly looking at every inch of the place. Portraits on the wall told stories of fae heroes and mythical creatures, and the wood was an ashen color, instead of the dark wood of Pennlan. The stair railing was intricately carved with a design, and seemed almost alive under my hand. There wasn't one thing in this land that was exactly the same as in the human world.

"Listen to me," Riona said, as we stopped in front of three doors.

"You'll need to stay close to the inn. I don't think there are any *daoine maithe* here, but until we know for sure, it's best to keep a low profile."

She demonstrated how to use the enchanted coin against the brass doorknob. It fit perfectly in the center, and somehow instructed the door to turn on its own and open. It was absolutely fascinating, and even my dislike of fae couldn't stop me from spending a few minutes examining the doorknob.

The room was small, and the bed cramped, but it was the softest thing I'd ever laid in. I inhaled deeply, face-first into the pillow, catching the scent of lavender. I could've fallen asleep right there, except my stomach was rumbling.

With my golden eyes and pointed ears, I was more confident walking downstairs into the mess hall. The room was much larger than it looked from the outside, another reminder that the fae had imbued magic into every inch of this place. My stew was delicious, and I didn't even have to magic myself another bowl. Perhaps a fortnight on the road and eating nothing but dried meat and roots had finally made me hardier than the wizard who'd left the castle.

I remained in my perch in the corner, gazing at all the different fae who came and went. Some looked like Riona, except with golden eyes. But others were short with brown, knobbly skin and straw hair, and still others were gray-skinned and as short as the frog who'd nearly drowned us. Riona had said that most of the fae in this tavern were civilized, but I still couldn't help but think there might be a few wild ones in the bunch.

"Oh, this looks delicious." Ward had appeared in front of me and sat down with a spoon, a bowl, and a tankard of beer. To my curious look, he swiped the tankard off the table and took a long gulp. "Riona said all the food was fine. I assume that extends to drink, too."

"If you say so," I said, sitting back. "Do you think we can trust her still?"

"Oh, this again?" He put down the mug and dug into his stew.

"If she's half-human," I said, keeping my voice low, "that means she not only *can* lie but has been lying this whole time."

He made a face. "Did we explicitly ask her if she was half-fae?"

"She said she was fae."

"She is, clearly."

"Don't split hairs," I snapped, earning me a snort of derision. "Look, I don't like finding out new information so far into this journey —especially when it was clear she would never have told us."

"She has her reasons. And is it pertinent to our journey at all?"

I sighed. "It is if she's capable of retrieving the stone herself. She said she needed a human to do it, which was the whole reason she joined us. But now…"

He considered my words. "Perhaps her fae blood disqualifies her. I don't think this is the big revelation you're making it out to be."

"I think we should be cautious."

"I think we should just let it go," he said, rising from the table. "I'm going to bed. I suggest you quit worrying and do the same."

⤐ ⤐ ⤐ ⤐

I thought I'd have trouble sleeping, but the bed was inviting, and I slept dreamlessly. When I awoke, a light dusting of snow had fallen, and I was grateful I wasn't out in it. The rooms had been enchanted to stay warm, and even the wash basin water was a comfortable temperature.

I was somewhat surprised that Riona's magic still held, even overnight. What, exactly, half-fae meant in terms of how much magic she had remained a mystery. She was adept at glamour, that much was clear. Did her heritage explain her inability to use magic? My gut told me she was far more powerful than she'd let on. More questions, few answers.

I walked to the window, watching the sun slowly creep over the land. I thought about about home—and what would be waiting when I returned. It felt like we'd come to the end, but we were still at the beginning of a journey of unknown length.

It was starting to become apparent that I'd miss Ayla's coronation, and for that, I was truly sorry. But it redoubled my dedication to completing this quest—whatever it took.

When the sun came up and melted the frost, the city awoke, and I put on my charmed clothes and ventured out of the inn. Before leaving the safety of my room, I changed my staff into a small pocket watch, just in case any of the fae could recognize a wizard's staff. Riona was right; we needed to keep a low profile.

The shops were unlike anything I'd ever seen. They sold potions and all manner of magical ingredients, most of which were foreign to me, as well as charmed goods and even a vial of glamour.

The smell of roasting nuts and cinnamon drew me to a small merchant (and by small, I meant rising only to my mid-thigh) who was cooking what appeared to be a delicacy over the fire. He offered me a bag of them for a small copper, but I declined.

"I wonder if you could answer a question for me. We're searching for…" I considered my words carefully. "A magical object that might've come through here fifteen or so years ago. Have you heard anything about that?"

"Lots of magical objects come through here," he said with a chuckle. "You'll have to be more specific. A scepter? A sword? What about a staff?"

"I suppose it would look like a gemstone," I said.

He rubbed his chin. "Nothing comes to mind."

"If there were such an object," I continued, "where would someone hide it?"

"Perhaps in the wastelands to the south," he said. "Not much down there other than monsters and death."

"Great, thanks." I paused, looking down at his wares again. "On second thought, I will take a bag."

It was the most delicious thing I'd ever eaten in my life, and I savored every bite as I made my way back to the inn. I was starting to dread the new task ahead of us, and how very little we had to go on. We could travel this land for years and still not find anything.

Riona and Ward were seated in the dining hall, talking in low voices and eating bowls of what appeared to be gruel. I joined them at the table, and they nodded to me before continuing their conversation, identifying the various patrons in the dining hall.

"And that dog-looking one is a…what'd you say?"

"A *cù-sith*," Riona said under her breath. "They live in the forest."

He pointed to a fish-looking creature standing near the bar gulping water. "And that over there?"

"A *fuath*. They normally live near water, so I'm not sure what they're doing all the way up here."

"What about the *sidheog*? Do they look like humans?" Ward asked.

"Sometimes," Riona said, eyeing me. "You look troubled. What's wrong?"

"I was just conversing with a merchant out in the village—"

She paled. "You went out into the village? I told you to stay close."

"I can't see the problem with me venturing out. Your glamour has held, so—"

But commotion echoed from the front room, and Riona made a small noise. Before we could do anything, soldiers stormed inside, and I was very strongly reminded of Aldrick's fae guards who'd accosted us at the border. These fae wore different colors, blue instead of purple, but their weapons seemed just as sharp. Ward put his hand on his sword, but Riona shook her head.

"Trespassers," the lead soldier said. "You are coming with us."

CHAPTER FORTY-ONE

AYLA

Captain Gabhann scoured every inch of the castle in search of the fae and came up empty. They must've left once their mission failed. It didn't give me much comfort; they'd probably be back to try again. That the Erlking had simultaneously sent that cordial letter and an assassin made absolutely no sense. But perhaps that was because I was a decent person who valued life.

I didn't sleep for days, and the sleep I did get was punctuated by visions of a long-haired, sharp-toothed fae standing over my bed. I was so close to asking someone to sleep *in* my room, but that would be weak. And I was trying to show strength—at least until Eoghan came back. But I was irritable and jumpy, refusing Lady Enid's overtures to study and insisting that I remain in my office, my gaze jumping between the door and window.

It took an excruciatingly long three days, but finally, my wizard returned. He blew into my office, his coat dusty from travel and his frown severe.

"Are you all right?" he asked.

To anyone else, I would've said yes. But to Eoghan… I jumped to my feet, rushed over, and fell into his arms, sobbing quietly, the way I'd wanted to for days. He patted my head and whispered words of calm. This must be what a father would do to a frightened child, because within minutes, my soft cries dwindled. I stepped back, wiping my eyes.

"I'm sorry," I said, sniffing loudly. "I just…"

"I know you were scared," he said. "I never would've left, had I known…" He swept to the window and stared out, as if blaming the plains themselves. "I don't know why Cade and that guard haven't returned yet. I'm worried."

"Me too," I said, sinking back down into my chair. "Isn't there some magic you can use to locate them?"

He turned, smiling warmly at me. "I can look in my texts. But we can also send some of Gabhann's guards along the path they were sure to have taken. If someone saw something…"

"You don't think…" I rubbed my hands together, curious. "Do you think maybe they found out something from the fae in Críoch and… continued on into the realm itself in search of the stone?"

He chuckled. "I confess, I had a hunch they might've done something like that. Cade was eager to prove himself a wizard able to stand on his own two feet. What better way than finding the Pennlan stone for you?"

"I would rather he just come home," I said. "The stone isn't that important."

"Isn't it? If you'd had it around your neck the other night, you could have saved yourself from the fae creature instead of screaming for help."

I twitched, knowing he was trying to help, but unable to shake the way his words settled in the pit of my soul.

"But I'm here now," he said. "And we will get back to the business of preparing for your coronation. After all, we only have a fortnight until the big day."

Had it already come so soon? "Yes, of course."

⇥ ⇥ ⇥ ⇥

Eoghan seemed keener on sharing the details of my coronation with me, perhaps hoping the effort would soothe my nerves and build back my confidence. I did sleep better knowing he was back in the castle, but there was still a part of me, a small part, that chafed at the idea of needing him so much. Other sovereigns didn't have a wizard at their beck and call, and they still managed to rule effectively.

But I had other things to contend with, namely reviewing the stacks of papers and choices that had been made for me for my coronation. Colors and cake flavors and even the design of my dress—white, with pearls sourced from Nesuria's blue waters. All of it had been signed off months ago by Eoghan.

"This is a lot," I said, looking at Eoghan from the other side of the table. "So many choices."

"Which is why I felt it best to keep that from you," he said. "I didn't want to overwhelm you."

"Just yourself."

"Hm?"

"I meant…you didn't mind being overwhelmed," I said.

"It wasn't overwhelming to me. Considering I've been making such decisions for the past sixteen or so years." He smiled warmly. "It's no issue for me."

There hadn't been *that* many parties, but I supposed I'd always assumed the dinner parties and small gatherings had been handled by someone else. That Eoghan had taken them on, had dictated everything from the menu to the seating arrangements, was a little disconcerting. It didn't seem like the sort of thing a wizard counsel should've been doing.

"This dress is expensive," I said, looking up from the dress design. "Are you sure this is a wise use of money?"

"There's plenty in the coffers," he said. "And this kingdom is looking forward to a bright new chapter. This is as much for the country as for you."

I couldn't argue with that logic, but I still wanted to know how much we'd spent on something as silly as a dress I'd only wear once.

"Would you like to see it?" Eoghan asked. "The dressmaker has been working on it in a room in the castle. He's nearly finished it, in fact, and will need to see if there are any last-minute alterations. I was hoping to keep it a surprise, but if you'd like to see it today..."

To be honest, I wasn't interested in seeing the dress at all—more curious about the total cost of this day and what other decisions were buried in the midst of all these papers. But Eoghan was insistent, so I allowed him to lead me out of the vault. He was excited about the dress, describing the various deals and alliances he'd made in order to source it.

"The pearls, of course, come from Nesuria. The lace from Driwania. The fabric from Konevell. Your shoes were made in Sudaemor."

"It's a very international dress," I said, casting my gaze out the window to the stormy skies above. "But why did you go outside our borders when we have dressmakers here?"

"We will have envoys from each of the four kingdoms in attendance. It's a show of solidarity to have them represented on your coronation dress. A symbol of your willingness to ally yourself with them."

I nodded. It still felt a bit superficial—and something of a waste of money, as we had to pay all these kingdoms for their craftsmanship. But I kept quiet as we continued toward a small room on the first floor. Eoghan waved his staff across the knob, unlocking it, then pushed the door open.

My breath left my chest at the beautiful, white dress hanging from the rafters. The train was long—laid out across the floor and nearly reaching the other end of the room. There was a matching veil next to it, and the white leather shoes Eoghan had mentioned.

"Eoghan..." I said with a frown. "Why does this look like a wedding dress?"

He licked his lips, turning to me with something of a guilty expression. "Wishful thinking?"

"You thought I'd combine my coronation day and wedding day?" I asked. "When I explicitly told you I wasn't looking to do that?"

"You said it. I didn't say I agreed with it."

I blew air out between my lips, cautiously approaching the dress and running my fingers along the intricate lace. This wasn't something he'd done on the spur of the moment. Lace like this took months to sew. The small pearls were scattered along the train, too.

"I'm not ready to be married to a stranger," I said.

"You aren't ready to rule, either," Eoghan said.

I jerked my head up, staring at him with an open mouth. "I'm sorry?"

"I'd hoped you would somehow grow into your role, find the sort of maturity I've been seeking from you for the past few months. But all it took was one fae infiltrating the castle, and you fell apart."

I took a step backward, his words like a dagger in my chest. "I… The thing… *It tried to kill me.*"

"And a real queen would've brushed it off and moved on," he said, his dark eyes steely and unforgiving. "Instead, the first thing you did when I returned was jump into my arms and cry."

"Because…" Because what? I was scared? I couldn't deny his claims. I hadn't been very strong. At the same time, I couldn't help but ask, *Who would be strong after waking up with a murderous monster looming over them?*

"I have four marriage proposals," he said softly. "Even Lord Weymouth has said he would be willing to marry you, which frankly surprised me after your behavior toward him."

"I don't want to marry any of them," I said, finding my voice.

He sighed, and I got the distinct impression he was getting annoyed with me. "You have four choices. You need to make a decision in the next few days or else there won't be enough time to change the flags and colors to match whomever the groom will be."

"Eoghan," I said, a little firmer. "I don't want to get married to any of them. I don't want to get married right now."

"You don't have a choice," he snapped. "So I suggest you grow up, understand what you need, and pick the one you can stomach."

He left me there in the room, and all I could think was…

Why?

CHAPTER FORTY-TWO

WARD

I was smart enough to know when a fight was fair, so I let the *sidheog* soldiers take my weapons, including the knife hidden on my person, and put me in some sort of magical cuffs. Cade, however, wasn't as keen, pointing his staff at the fae.

"Back off."

"Cade," Riona snapped. "Put down your weapon and give it to them."

"Absolutely—" But before he could say another word, two of the fae soldiers shot him with what appeared to be a magical lightning bolt and he staggered backward, the staff falling from his hand. He let out a yelp as one of the fae picked it up and held it out of arm's reach while the other cuffed him with the magical bands.

Riona remained uncuffed, but had her arms crossed over her chest. "It's not illegal for three fae to walk in these lands, is it? Did I miss a decree from the Erlking?"

"Three fae, no." The fae who wore the finest armor of the group stepped forward, a calculating smile on her mahogany lips. "But a human, a wizard, and a fae do draw some attention."

Cade and I gave each other a look, then turned to Riona. She looked uncomfortable for the first time. "I don't know what you're talking about."

"Your magic isn't as potent as you think," the lead said. The magic that had been sitting on my skin for the past day slid to the floor and

Cade's pointed ears and golden eyes disappeared. "Now, if you're done holding us up, we will get moving."

"By whose authority?" Riona asked.

"Clíodhna, queen of the *sidheog*," he said.

In a second, all the fight left her body, as her eyes widened and her mouth dropped open.

"And where are we being taken?" Cade asked as the soldiers moved in.

"You don't get to make demands of us, wizard," the fae said, and those watching muttered curiously. "Let's go."

Whether I wanted to or not, I was frog-marched out of the inn and into the cold air outside. Two black carriages were waiting—or rather, one carriage and what appeared to be a prison wagon. The *sidheog* opened the door of the carriage and motioned for Riona to get inside.

"And my companions?" she asked, standing firm. "You can't expect them to travel in a cage."

"You don't get to tell us what to do," the fae said. "Now get inside the carriage."

She offered us an apologetic look before stepping inside, and I couldn't help but wonder what kind of power this Clíodhna had if she made Riona cower and follow commands.

"As for you two."

Cade and I were unceremoniously stuffed inside the barred wagon, made to sit on a pile of cold hay that barely offered comfort. My head scratched the top of the carriage, and Cade had to hunch over just to sit. He cursed under his breath in that native tongue I still hadn't picked up.

"She screwed us, just like I thought she would," he said.

"Looks to me like she's just as captured as we are," I replied, trying to find a comfortable spot as the carriage lurched forward. "Except her ride is a little more cushioned."

I braced myself against the metal bars for the slow slog down the road. But the beasts pulling us began to gallop, then moved faster than I would've thought possible. The world whizzed by, the cold air blasting my skin and chapping my lips in seconds.

"What…is…happening?" Cade heaved, pressed against the back of the carriage. The skin on his face rippled under the wind and his cloak was nearly flying out behind him. I dragged my hand along the bars, trying to peel myself off, but the force of the wind was too strong.

Then, the beasts stopped so abruptly that both Cade and I went flying forward, nearly slamming into the bars on the other end of the carriage. I gingerly pushed myself up, my face so numb it might never regain feeling again. Before I even had time to think, the fae arrived and yanked us out of the carriage.

I blinked and looked up, my jaw dropping. We were in some kind of ice-covered village, and beyond us was a castle made of beautiful crystal that rose to the sky. It glimmered even in the weak sunlight, providing its own glow to the lands beyond.

The frigid temperatures finally broke through my distracted mind, and my teeth began to chatter. It was colder than the coldest day in Críoch, when even the fountains froze mid-stream. Maybe we'd find some kind of relief wherever they were putting us. But I wasn't very hopeful.

"Damn her," Cade said, his breath puffing around his face and his nose and cheeks a reddish hue from the wind. "Got to travel in a carriage."

I followed his gaze to the carriage in front of us, where Riona had stepped out. She winced when she saw us but was quickly escorted away by the two guards.

"You."

I looked up—the lead guards had come for us, or more specifically, me. "What?"

"You're coming with us." She reached for my arm and yanked me forward, tossing me into the waiting arms of the other fae.

"What about him?" I said, nodding to Cade.

"The wizard will be put into his own prison until we can be sure he's to be trusted," she said with a smirk. "We have a special place for you."

"What the—Ward!" Cade barked as the fae cuffed him and dragged him away.

"And where am I going?"

"To see Clíodhna."

>→ >→ >→ >→

In very short order, I was all but dragged into the castle. At least it was warm, though I feared what they might do to the wizard. He was a pain in the ass, but I didn't want them to kill him. I just hoped wherever Riona was, she was using her limited influence to convince whoever had captured us that we could be trusted.

I hated to admit it, but this fae castle put Pennlan to shame. Like the tavern back in the village, everything about it seemed alive—even the walls. The flames that lit our path were an ethereal white glow versus a warm yellow, and the stones beneath our feet were smooth and black.

"Where are we—"

"Quiet, human."

I clammed up immediately and allowed them to keep marching me forward.

Finally, we rounded a corner into an antechamber of sorts, and I heaved a sigh of relief when I saw Riona standing there. She was surrounded by the fae soldiers, including the lead soldier who'd taken us, but she was still uncuffed. When she saw me, she smiled—until she noticed I was alone.

"Where's the wizard?" she asked the tall fae woman.

"None of your concern."

"He's my concern because he's my traveling companion," she huffed. "Where did you put him?"

"He's being held in a prison until Clíodhna decides what to do with him."

I finally noticed the large wooden doors in front of us, stretching toward the ceiling so high I had to crane my neck. Perhaps the infamous Clíodhna was beyond these gates.

"So who is this woman?" I muttered, once I was close enough to Riona. "Clíodhna?"

"The second most powerful fae, next to the Erlking."

"Was this part of the plan?" I asked.

She glared at me, but before she could say anything, the doors opened, scraping loudly against the pristine stone floor. Riona sucked in a breath, and I couldn't help but brace myself. If she knew what to expect, and was worried, that didn't bode well for us at all.

The tall fae woman stood behind us and pushed us forward with the heels of her hands. The room we walked into was magnificent, covered in dark blue paint that shimmered like the night sky. At least, I thought it was paint. Tilting my head back, I couldn't tell the difference between the night sky and the top of this room.

"Watch your step," the fae grumbled, grabbing me as I nearly tripped over my feet.

At the front of the room sat a beautiful woman with long, silvery hair and a crown made of ice. Her golden eyes bore down on us, and in the brief moments her gaze landed on me, my heart dropped to my stomach. I had no knowledge of magic or powerful creatures, but I knew, in my bones, this fae was not to be trifled with.

So why did I get the impression we'd done just that?

"That's far enough," she boomed when we were twenty paces from her step. "I can smell you from here." She lifted her gaze to the fae behind us. "Leave us. And do not allow a soul to enter these chambers without my permission."

The fae guards nodded and left, closing the large doors behind them. Then there were three of us in this expansive throne room.

Clíodhna released a loud sigh, sounding more like a tired parent than a queen. "Have you completely lost your senses, Riona? You look like a wildling."

Riona, who appeared just as unsettled as I, swallowed hard and murmured, "We did just come from the…wildlands."

"The…" The fae sat forward in her chair, her thin brows rising. "Did you just say you came from the wildlands?"

Riona nodded.

"And what possessed you to take a human and wizard into such a dangerous place?" She tossed her hands in the air and shook her head. "Never mind. The more important question is: Does your grandfather know where you are?"

Riona stared at the ground. She looked like a child who'd been caught red-handed in the sweets jar.

"I asked you a question, Riona," Clíodhna said, her voice booming in the room and making my knees weak.

The fae girl mumbled something under her breath.

"I know Birch taught you to speak up. He's very worried about you."

"Birch?" I whirled on her. "Birch is your grandfather? The *Erlking?*"

She winced. Immediately, the implications swam in my mind. *Half-human, granddaughter of Birch…* My mouth fell open as Riona stubbornly refused to look at me, but her bright red cheeks told me everything I needed to know.

"I'm disappointed in you, child," Clíodhna said with pursed lips. "You know, I received a letter from the Erlking just a fortnight ago, asking me to keep an eye out for you. I was to let him know the moment you arrived, so he could retrieve you."

Riona swallowed, a hopeful look on her face. "But you won't?"

"What is your purpose here, child?" she asked. "The stone? You seek to claim it?"

"No, not for me," she said. "For my… For Ayla. I want to give it to her so she will kill the wizard Eoghan and bring order back to Pennlan and the fae realm."

I stared, seeing Riona in a new light. Not that I'd spent hours gazing upon Ayla's face, nor that Riona looked much like her, but there were similarities. The shape of her lips, the turn of her nose. I snorted to myself—the wizard was going to shit himself.

"That's a tall order. Are you even sure she will do it?"

Riona nodded. "When she knows the truth of what happened with Leandra."

"And you, human?" Clíodhna looked at me and I jumped at being addressed. "What is your goal in this quest?"

"I have been tasked by the princess to retrieve the stone," I said, leaving out that Eoghan was the one who actually gave me the mission. "I was told by Riona that only a human could retrieve it, so I'm here."

"And the," Clíodhna breathed loudly through her nose, "*wizard* that accompanied you? The one with fae glamour on his skin?" She tapped her hand on the throne. "Don't tell me you've accepted his help as well?"

"He's a close friend of the princess's," Riona said, almost pleading now. "And he has been a valuable ally. Please release him back to us."

"You are in no position to bargain with me," she said, pointing her finger at Riona. "Do you even know who he is?"

"I do." She swallowed. "But he's proven himself trustworthy."

Clíodhna sighed and rose from her chair, showcasing her impressive height and the shimmery material of her robes that dragged behind her. Her feet were clad in slippers as she descended the dais and came to stand before us. She looked down at Riona, pursing her lips.

"I'm afraid you've been told wrong," she said. "The Erlking left a series of enchantments, the strongest of this land. It will take more than a human to retrieve it."

Birch hid the stone? "Leandra was the one who hid it, didn't she?" I asked.

"She brought it to these lands," Clíodhna said. "But upon her death, the Erlking placed it under protections that would take a very skilled practitioner to retrieve. His intention was for no one to be able to retrieve it—least of all the wizard Eoghan."

"Please," Riona said, inching forward. "Grandmother."

Grandmother? I tried to connect the dots quickly. That meant Leandra was the daughter of the *sidheog* queen and Erlking. How, exactly, that happened…

"Please help us," Riona said. "We can rid the world of that wizard once and for all."

"The only thing you need help with is a bath and a good night's rest," she said, waving her hand. "And I will see to getting you a square meal. You are nothing but skin and bones."

"And the wizard?" I pressed. "Will you release him?"

The fae turned her golden eyes on me, narrowing them as she took me in. "You are certainly brave, human, to have traveled through the wildlands with a child as your guide. But the wizard has a power I don't wish to unleash upon my people. He will stay where he is."

"He's of no danger, as long as you keep his staff," Riona said. "I promise. Please, don't… Please let him join us."

Clíodhna sighed. "Fine. I will see to it that he joins us for dinner—provided he remains on his best behavior."

Chapter Forty-Three

Cade

I fought the fae as much as I could, digging deep into my magic and searching for something—anything—that would manifest it. But without my staff, I was as helpless as Ward. It was a situation Eoghan had often warned me about, and he'd drilled into my head that a wizard's staff should be more an appendage than anything else. I felt naked and exposed without it, but I still had my fists, if it came down to it.

The fae's supernatural strength kept me moving forward even as I dug my feet in, and before I knew what was happening, I was tossed into a dark cell and the door closed behind me.

"You are alive by decree of the *sidheog* queen," the tall fae said, smirking down at me. "But she didn't say anything about what state you should be in. I suggest you keep your tongue to yourself."

The fae left me there, and all I could do was release a filthy string of curses in my native tongue. It made me feel better, but not by much, as I was still stuck here, without my staff—without my *magic*. This was, perhaps, the worst outcome.

I gritted my teeth, cursing Riona and wondering if she'd planned this all along. After all, she'd lied about being half-fae. What else could she be hiding in that stubborn head of hers? Was this all in pursuit of getting the stone for herself?

Or, like Aldrick, was this just another miscalculation, the folly of youth from a half-fae girl who had no business being outside the safety of the Erlking's castle?

As much as I wanted it to be the first, I had a sinking suspicion it was the second. It didn't make me feel much better about my predicament. Though perhaps if it was, she might be able to convince whoever had thrown me in this prison to release me—especially since I had no way to harness my magic without my staff.

The bars were thick, and even as I rattled them and made noise, no one came. There weren't even prisoners in the other cells along the hallway; at least none that I could hear or see. Was this a prison they'd specifically set aside for wizards or was I just considered so dangerous they put me somewhere far away from anyone else?

A few hours passed, and I began to get antsy, spinning tales and theories that Ward and Riona had already secured their own escape and left me here, until the more logical part of my brain insisted that they wouldn't desert me so readily. It was exhausting work, and I was nearly ready to try my luck on the hard slab of metal that served as a bed when I heard the door swing open at the end of the hallway.

A solo set of footsteps whispered on the stone floor. I steeled myself, walking to the bars and readying myself for anything—torture, death, perhaps just taunting and goading from some guards. But when she turned the corner, my hands fell from the bars in shock.

She was the most powerful thing I'd ever beheld, a tall, willowy woman with long, silvery hair and a delicate crystal crown on her head. Golden eyes framed by dark lashes and age lines that somehow made her look more foreboding stared me down. Her robes seemed made of starlight, a silvery material that had its own glow in this dark, damp place. It seemed so wrong for her to be here, in the muck.

I tried to keep myself upright in her presence, even though every inch of me wanted to cower in fear as she surveyed me without a shred of emotion or inkling of what she was thinking.

"Wizard," she said softly after a few moments. "You're nothing but a boy, aren't you? A powerful boy, but a boy."

I found my tongue. "I'm eighteen."

"A boy," she said with a tight smile. "You have traveled a long way, haven't you? From where do you hail?"

"Pennlan."

"Your master did his best to stamp it out, but I can still hear the remnants of an accent." She tilted her head. "The southern islands, perhaps? Eoghan traveled a long way to find his chosen student, didn't he?"

"Not that far," I said, though my voice seemed to have lost its confidence.

She smirked. "He must've, because this land has been purged of wizards for many centuries. Eoghan isn't even from this continent. He hails from beyond the mountains to a land covered in thick forests. Far from the curse of the stone."

Curse of the stone? "He's from…Pennlan," I said, though it dawned on me that I'd never actually asked him where he was from.

"What lies has your master fed you, I wonder?" She chuckled. "Other than the obvious one, sending you here on a fool's errand."

I licked my lips. "It's not a fool's errand. I'm here to retrieve the object that your kind stole from my sovereign."

"Is that so?"

She watched me as if I were a child who'd just told some fantastical tale. I had to remind myself that while Riona could probably lie, this fae couldn't—but that didn't mean she wasn't well-versed at skirting the truth. It didn't matter that she knew who I was or Eoghan's lineage. She was perhaps trying to make me trust her to divulge something about Ayla.

"Are you here to gloat, or do you have some business for me?" I asked, gesturing to the cell around me. "Because as you can see, I'm quite busy."

"Riona has spoken of your assistance on the journey," she said. "So I won't have you killed."

"Great." I rolled my eyes. "Just leave me in here to rot, then?"

"The Erlking is on his way," she said. "He has much less patience for wizards than I do. I cannot promise that he will allow you to remain alive once he sees you."

"I hear a 'but'..."

She sighed. "I have held the *seod croí* in my realm for the past sixteen years, and you three are not the first to have been sent by Eoghan. The longer it remains, the more the wizard will try to retrieve it—and my people may begin to suffer. I would prefer it to be gone from these lands, but I cannot openly defy the Erlking." She leveled her gaze at me. "Therefore, if you and your human cohort were to escape tonight, I would look the other way."

I took a step back, shocked. She was letting me go? Not only that, she was going to let me go retrieve the stone? But the ridiculousness of the plan became apparent after just a few moments of thought.

"Escape to where?" I asked. "We don't even know where it is."

She waved her hand, and a rush of lavender scent came across my nose as a small slip of weathered paper appeared in my hand. On it was... a map.

My heart skipped in my chest. A map to the stone.

I wanted to believe it a trick, but...there was something that spoke to the magic in my veins. This was a true map, something that had been drafted with the purest of intentions. The *sidheog* castle was at the bottom left, too, giving us perfect directions to reach the stone.

"Why?" I asked, looking up. "What could you want in return?"

"One very important thing: that you leave Riona behind."

I furrowed my brow. "Leave her?"

"She's a child and should never have left the Erlking's castle." She sighed, shaking her head. "The risks she took leading you through the wildlands were absolutely inexcusable. I can't fathom why she would do such a thing."

"Aldrick saw fit to cut off our easy path," I said with a wry smile. "Or so she said."

The fae narrowed her gaze. "Careful who you speak ill of. Aldrick is
—"

"I can only tell you what Riona told us." I sat back. "But it appeared he was eager to drive us to the most danger. I think he was hoping she wouldn't come out alive."

Clíodhna whispered something under her breath, a word Riona had used often when she was angry. I was starting to think it was a fae curse. "He will be dealt with, in that case."

"For what it's worth, I didn't welcome her presence on our journey," I said. "You're right. She's a child. Her power isn't anything to speak of, perhaps because she's half-human."

"I'm surprised she shared that with you. It's not a secret she shares with many."

"It wasn't shared so much as spilled," I said.

"She will one day stand amongst us as the fiercest fae warriors in existence," Clíodhna said, so confidently I almost believed her. "But for now, she must return home with the Erlking. If she's not here when he arrives, it won't be pleasant for anyone in this castle."

I looked down at the map, hoping I could make heads or tails of it when we set out. It was downright suspicious that the fae queen would give me directions to the stone, especially considering their hatred of wizards. But her secondary warning was something of an explanation. Perhaps she was confident Birch's charms on the stone would do me in, and Ward would be able to retrieve it for himself. Or maybe she was actually ready to be rid of the thing once and for all, and the burden of protecting it from interested parties.

"Well? Do we have a deal?" she asked.

I ran my fingers along the map. Riona had been a pain in the ass, but she was still more knowledgeable about this land than either Ward or me. But if this was our one chance at the stone, our one chance to escape...

"I can't possibly attempt this without my staff," I said, looking up at her.

"Are you sure?" Clíodhna said with a snort. "That thing is not meant for you."

"There's no other way for me to harness my magic," I said with a bit of heat. "I'm not fae."

She sighed. "Your staff will be placed amongst my most prized possessions, across the hall from my throne room. *As long as* you promise to leave Riona behind."

I couldn't say no to that. "Very well."

"There is one more thing." She clasped her hands in front of her. "And it is only because Riona spoke so passionately of how you saved her life in the wildlands that I tell you this: There are enchantments on the stone that are especially fatal to wizard magic. There is a good chance that if you leave here to pursue the stone, you will die."

"It's been a possibility this entire journey," I replied, my voice small coming from my throat.

"I don't think you understand," she said. "The bodies that are scattered there are fae and human alike. No one, not a single person, has been able to break through the final spell."

"Final?" I furrowed my brow.

"There are three enchantments. The first is a maze that has felled more humans than not. The second, a creature that will tear you limb from limb. The final trial is a lake that has drowned even the strongest fae. Not even King Birch will go near it." She pursed her lips. "It would be suicide for a wizard such as yourself to attempt it."

"I don't have a choice," I replied. "Ayla needs it."

"For what?" Clíodhna smirked. "To protect her from the horrible, horrible fae who lurk across the border? Or for something much closer to home?"

She was mocking me. "The fae killed her father—Leandra would've killed her, too, had Eoghan not stepped in. Besides that, the stone belongs to her. It's her birthright."

"So sure of yourself," Clíodhna said with a smile. "Very well, my conscience is clear. But know this: there's a reason your master hasn't come to seek the stone himself—and perhaps the very reason you were plucked from that small island where you were born and given a life of training. Eoghan is a very patient man, and if the whispers on the wind are to be believed, he has very nearly completed his long task."

"What task is that?" I asked, finding my courage. "Ayla is the only one who can use the stone."

The fae smiled, and there was pity there. "I will be sending my attendants to retrieve you, to clean you, and you will dine in my company tonight, after which you will be sent to a room next to the human. What you endeavor to do after that is up to you."

Chapter Forty-Four

Ward

I was still reeling from what I'd found out from Clíodhna about Riona, but I didn't have much time to process it. The fae led us to a set of bedrooms, and Riona and I were separated again. I barely had a chance to gawk at yet another room before a pair of fae arrived wearing white robes and dragged me into a bathroom with a steaming tub and fluffy white towels. I'd heard that such things existed in the richest humans' houses and that Ayla boasted her own private bath but, having spent most of my life bathing in ponds or in shared bathhouses, the hot water was a revelation.

"How—" Before I could ask questions, I was stripped naked and dunked into the water. The fae took brushes to my nails, my hands, my arms, my legs—but I drew the line when their rough handling reached my tender parts. I was submerged under the scalding water repeatedly until all the bubbles were gone, then tugged from the water and wrapped in a robe that was the softest thing that had ever touched my skin.

Then they left me in the large room with fresh clothes. My dirty shirt, trousers, and cloak were long gone. I probably would never see them again, to be honest. But perhaps that wouldn't be the worst thing. The fae silk sat on my skin like a cool breeze.

I walked around the room, amazed that such a space existed for someone as unimportant as myself. Golden curtains hung from the window, framing the dark night beyond. Every wall had a beautiful painting of some fae battle—including what I recognized as a griffin fighting a fae warrior. The rugs under my toes were soft and intricately designed. Even the bed was ornate, with a soft mattress and vine-covered posts that rose to the ceiling.

What must Clíodhna's chambers look like, if this magnificence was reserved for a lowly human?

There was a soft knock at the door, and Riona poked her head in. "Are you decent?"

"Decent, but still in shock," I replied.

She let herself in, wearing a new frock similar to mine, though she had the same silver slippers that Clíodhna had been wearing.

"I wanted to tell you that you've been invited to dine with Clíodhna," she said, looking at the ground. "And she has... She has considered my request to release Cade from prison. I told her he was useless without his staff, so she was a bit more amenable."

I nodded. "Shall we also discuss the interesting fact of your lineage?"

She stiffened, looking at me with fear in her eyes. "Whatever you think, don't speak it aloud. Even the walls have ears around here." She swallowed hard. "I would be in grave danger if more put together the pieces."

I nodded. "So, why are you here? Do you want the stone for yourself?"

"Absolutely not," she said with a swift shake of her head. "I don't... That kind of power hasn't ever appealed to me."

I quirked a brow. "Really?"

"This might sound mad, but..."

"I'm in the *sidheog* castle with a half-fae girl," I said with a laugh. "Nothing you can tell me is mad."

"I guess... Leandra never wanted that sort of power, either. She was the daughter of the *sidheog* queen and the *daoine maithe* king. She could've taken either throne. Instead... She chose who she chose."

I ran my hand over the stubble on my chin. "How...does that

work? The *sidheog* queen and *daoine maithe* king?"

She made a face. "The same way humans make children, I assume…"

"No, why would a king and queen from different lands…" I cleared my throat. "In the human world, the royalty usually marry before they start making heirs."

"Marriage isn't necessary to the fae, and the Erlking doesn't pass down to his children, usually," she said. "As I said, Leandra could've been the exception to that rule, but she didn't want it."

That flew in the face of the stories I'd been told. "What did she want, then? Why go to Pennlan? Why marry the king?"

She lifted a shoulder in a shrug. "They were in love."

I opened and closed my mouth, unsure how to react to that.

"Leandra would have all sorts of dreams. Premonitions, feelings. Instincts about people. It's how she knew to reach out to Bresal when his wife had died. It was like she could feel his pain from across the…" She stopped. "Anyway. I don't have any of that, but I did… She came to me in a dream. Told me that I needed to find a pair of travelers sent from Pennlan castle to retrieve the stone. So…I left and happened upon you in that first village. It seemed to be fated."

"You left the safety of the Erlking's castle because of a *dream*?" I blinked incredulously.

She glared at me. "Yes."

I swallowed my laughter.

"The Erlking made it clear that it was dangerous for me to leave," she said. "I know it was stupid. But… There was something about that dream that just made me feel like this was what I was meant to do. That helping you get the stone and bringing it back to Ayla…might help mend the gap between our lands."

"So as long as nobody knows you're—"

"Don't say it out loud," Riona said.

"And you still think I'm the only one who can retrieve it?"

She nodded. "The legends I've been told are that only a human can retrieve the stone—no more, no less than that. I just put two and two together when I had the dream."

"And you think that if I get the stone for Ayla, she'd use it on Eoghan?" I asked.

She nodded.

"I think you underestimate how much she relies on him for…well, everything," I said. "Getting her the stone would put it within reach of him."

"But he can't *use* it," she said then, barely audible, added, "As long as I stay far away."

Finally, the reason for her fear of Cade, that compulsion spell, and everything else became clear. "Eoghan used that wizard coercion magic to force Leandra to take the stone, didn't he? Because, by nature of her marriage to the king, she was allowed to use its power."

"Exactly," Riona said in a low whisper. "And he could…" She gestured to the air and to herself, her meaning clear. "I couldn't live with myself if he used me for that purpose. Leandra… Well, she couldn't either."

Her words hung in the air around us for a moment, and I just stared at her, wondering if I believed her. "So who knows about your… little secret?"

"No one in the *daoine maithe*," she replied. "I was born here, in the *sidheog* lands. Clíodhna is the only one who knows the truth. Though there are those who suspect." She gestured to her eyes. "These tend to give my parentage away."

That certainly explained Clíodhna clearing the room earlier.

"What do we do now?" I asked. "Cade is in prison, so are we basically, and there's no way for us to get out."

"Leave the second part to me," she said. "And as for the first… my hope is that my plea to Clíodhna will work, and he'll be joining us for dinner." She licked her lips. "But you cannot tell the wizard what you've learned today."

"After all this time, you still don't trust him?" I asked with a wry smile.

"Eoghan is his master, almost like his father." Riona shook her head. "Even if I thought I could, I won't be the one to shatter his illusions." She turned to me. "And he will most assuredly tell Eoghan about...me." She shook her head. "He would be absolutely unstoppable then."

I exhaled. "Fine. I will take your secret to my grave."

⤞ ⤞ ⤞ ⤞

Riona was apparently enough of an escort, because we went alone through the castle. I burned to ask more questions about the new information I'd learned, but out of respect, I kept my mouth shut. I didn't know who or what could be listening—could the walls share what we'd discussed? Either way, I was looking forward to a hot meal.

When we rounded the corner, there was already a crowd waiting, including—

"Cade?" I blinked. "Is that you?"

The wizard seemed to have had the same scrub-down treatment as I had, as his hair was still damp, and his clothes were new. But the expression he wore was closer to that of a wet cat than a freshly-laundered human.

"This place sucks," he snapped when we joined him.

"I'm sorry I couldn't get you out sooner," Riona said with a wince. "But at least you're here now. They didn't treat you poorly, did they?"

He gazed down at her, something new in his gaze. "Not until they started cleaning me. I know how to bathe myself. There was no need for the assistance." He rubbed his arm. "Though the clothes are nice. What are they made from?"

"Star silk," she said, nodding to the closed doors. "I will announce our presence."

She approached the doors, placing her open palm on the wood for just a moment. The wood shuddered and, as before, began to open, revealing a large dining hall with a long table. The place settings were limited.

"The Erlking is displeased," Clíodhna replied. "He's on his way this evening."

Riona looked up, the color draining from her face. "What?"

"As his ward, you are his responsibility. He will be here in the morning to take you home." She glanced at Cade and me. "And has agreed to escort the humans to the border so they can return to their lands."

"But we haven't gotten the stone," Riona said, her brow furrowing. "We can't turn around now. We're so close."

"You don't even know where it is, child," Clíodhna replied. "You will return to the Erlking's side and accept whatever punishment he has in store for your insolence."

I expected more from Riona—arguments, bargaining, or maybe even some pleading with the fae queen, perhaps mentioning her dream— but she merely sat quietly, staring at her plate. But I'd known her long enough to sense when she was scheming.

"Since you are here at my table," Clíodhna began, "I will entertain you with a tale. What do you know of the history of the stone you seek?"

I frowned and shook my head. "All I know is that the sovereign of Pennlan can use it and no one else."

"It was gifted to Pennlan by a wizard a long time ago," Cade replied.

Clíodhna snorted. "You know so little, wizard. The stone was made by a fae, in fact, for her wizard lover," she said. "Some say it was made *with* him. But the power corrupted the wizard, driving him mad and sending him into a chaotic, murdering frenzy. He decimated the entire wizard population on this continent, breaking magical lines that were older than the lands themselves. It's why your wizard master Eoghan comes from across the mountains, and you, boy, from the southern islands."

I glanced at Cade to see if he was surprised by her knowing this, but his face was passive.

"The wizard made sure no one else would lay claim to the stone, but he didn't expect his fae lover to turn on him," she said. "There was an epic battle, and just when it seemed all was lost, the fae found a way to enchant the stone so it couldn't be used by anyone else. She enchanted it to allow it to be used by a human—and not just any human."

"The royal family of Pennlan," I finished. "But why them?"

"Proximity to the *daoine maithe* lands, first of all, but also, the Pennlan soldiers aided in the fight against the wizard. They paid a large human price for it, too. So the Erlking back then gifted the stone to them, enchanting it so only the sovereign of the kingdom could use it."

"Could a wizard break that enchantment?" Cade asked. Clíodhna's eyes narrowed and he held up his hands in surrender. "Not that I would, just…curious."

"It's possible, perhaps, given enough time. I'm sure your master Eoghan tried in the years before he realized that it was folly. There were much easier ways to achieve his goals." She cast a short look at Riona, who wilted a little under her stare.

"You have such a low opinion of him," Cade said, lifting his gaze. "I hope he would prove you wrong."

I expected her to retort, but she merely smiled. "Shall we call for dessert?"

⤞ ⤞ ⤞ ⤞

Almost as soon as the last bit of food had disappeared from my plate, the fae guards were back to escort us back to our room—but just us.

"Riona, I would like to have a word with you before you retire," Clíodhna said.

She started. "Another one?"

"Several, in fact." She nodded in our direction. "I expect the

Erlking will be here within the next few hours. I would rest while you can."

"Thank you," Cade said, surprisingly. "We will do just that."

He rose without another word and made to follow the guards out of the room. I gave Riona another look, unsure if I wanted to be parted from her in this place, or what our next move was going to be. Perhaps that was part of Clíodhna's plan. She knew her granddaughter well enough.

"I'll see you in a few hours, I suppose," Riona said, making a show of looking defeated.

"I suppose you will," I said, hesitating. "I—"

"Go." Clíodhna wasn't asking.

I stood as well, giving Riona one last, lingering look before pushing my chair back under the table. There was more that needed to be said, more that we needed to discuss. But for now, I simply nodded and joined Cade and the guards at the door.

Silently, they walked us back to the room where they'd retrieved me. Cade said nothing, and the fact that he didn't look surprised or concerned at anything gave me pause. For a moment, I thought he might've been one of those changelings again.

But once the guards deposited us inside the room, the wizard lost his stoicism and smirked at me. "We've been given a gift."

"I don't see how any of this is a gift," I said, gesturing to the room. "The Erlking will be here in hours to kill us both, most likely."

"We won't be here when he does."

"And how do you expect us to do that?"

He pulled something from his pocket, a piece of paper.

"What's that?" I asked, narrowing my eyes.

"A map to the stone," he said, as his grin widened. "Given to me by Clíodhna herself."

I blinked. "Why the hell would she do that?"

"It was given to me under one condition," Cade said, folding the map up and tucking it back into his shirt. "We leave Riona behind and continue without her."

I rubbed my jaw, my mind working in two tracks. On the one hand, I couldn't fathom why Clíodhna would defy the Erlking to give us the *map* to the stone and let us walk out of her castle without a second look. But on the other, her bargain with Cade was understandable. Riona had no business continuing the journey. And all this time, it seemed that Riona, not us, was the one they were worried about.

"Well?" Cade said, walking to the door and finding it unlocked.

"What do we do first?" I asked.

"First, we need to find my staff," he said. "Then we get the hell out of here."

CHAPTER FORTY-FIVE

CADE

We ventured out into the empty hallway and started the next leg of our journey. Ward promised me he knew where to find the throne room, and by extension, the treasure room Clíodhna had spoken of, so I had no other choice but to trust him. The sooner I got my staff back in my hands, the less vulnerable I'd feel.

There was no one around, so it was easy to slip out unnoticed—perhaps part of Clíodhna's plan to allow us an easy escape. Ward led us down the hallway, taking a left then a right then another left. I had no concept of where we were, but eventually, we ended up in another long corridor that seemed to be the central hub of the castle.

"Where are all the guards?" Ward muttered to himself.

"Let's not look a gift horse in the mouth," I replied as we turned another corner. Two ornate doorways stood on either side of the hallway, one with a very intricate lock hanging on it.

"The throne room," Ward said, pointing to the unlocked door. "And I'd guess…"

"The treasure room." I sighed as I walked toward it. "I don't understand why it's locked."

"Are you sure Clíodhna said treasure room?" Ward asked.

I nodded, tugging on the lock. It wasn't just a mechanical one, it was imbued with magic—the sort Eoghan placed around the vault. But this was even more confusing than even his, and without my staff, I wasn't sure I could untangle it.

"Well?" Ward said, rocking on his heels as he looked up and down the hall. "I don't think we'll be able to stick around here unnoticed for long."

"I'm thinking," I snapped, closing my eyes and wishing—praying—my temperamental magic would behave. I rested my hand on the metal lock, and the taste of lavender washed over my tongue. Clíodhna herself had enchanted this. Power stirred deep in my veins, searching for an outlet and bumping against the confines of my body. This lock seemed to invite it forth, offering an open door—if I was brave enough to step through.

"Hurry up," Ward said, looking around. "There's bound to be someone walking by any minute now."

"This doesn't happen immediately," I snapped back. Though the magic under my fingertips seemed to disagree, jumping at the thought of being released into this new conduit. I hadn't ever used anything except my staff to wield magic, but this…this was like breathing. Power released from my palms, sinking into the metal and melding with the lavender-scented magic Clíodhna had left. Hers almost *guided* mine by the hand, walking me through the path she'd created.

But the part of me that still distrusted fae hesitated, unsure if allowing myself to dive headfirst into this new sensation wasn't some elaborate fae trap.

"I hear someone coming, so we'd better open that thing or hide."

I breathed a curse at him and refocused my attention to the door in front of me. I released the last bit of hesitation, and Clíodhna's magic grabbed mine, pulling it farther into the lock.

"Cade…"

A hundred different intricate gears moved and turned until finally, the latch on the top clicked open. My mouth fell open in surprise, but Ward was faster, removing the large lock and opening the door, practically dragging me into the room.

We pressed ourselves against the door, and it was only then that I heard the sound of footsteps outside the room. I got a whiff of two new fae scents, and I exhaled.

"Cutting it a little close," Ward muttered, glaring at me. "What the hell was that?"

"I don't know, exactly," I said, looking at my hands. "But I—"

The words died on my tongue as I took in the room behind us. Artwork, sculptures, vases, rubies the size of my head, gold coins in piles —this was certainly a treasure trove. Even bejeweled swords and spears. All of them, on display in this room as if for an audience.

Ward seemed to have lost his smirk, his gaze landing on the gold and lighting up. "Wonder where all this stuff came from?"

"Conquests, perhaps." I didn't want to think about it. "C'mon, we need to hurry."

We split up, walking through the treasure room and searching for the staff. I'd hoped it would be up front for easy retrieval, but I still had hope it was somewhere around. I could spend hours in here, trying to map each item to a fable, admiring the history behind it. But we had a goal, and the longer we lingered, the more danger we were in. The last thing I wanted was for the Erlking to find us amongst fae treasures.

"There!" My heart lifted to the sky as I saw my beloved staff sitting against a shield in the back of the room. I picked it up, the magic in my veins coming alive immediately. I could've kissed it, I was so relieved.

But my gaze fell to the shield it had been standing on—the Pennlan crest was etched onto the metal. I bent down to examine it, running my fingers along the crest and the empty slot above it. Jewel-sized, in fact— and there were three more openings at the cardinal points of the shield.

"Oh, you found it." Ward came up behind me. "What's that?"

I felt the urge to take it, sensing it might be important one day, but I shook my head. "Nothing. Let's get out of here."

⇥ ⇥ ⇥ ⇥

With my staff, I was able to use my locator spell to chart a path through the castle that would be mostly free of fae guards. It took a little longer, perhaps, than the way Ward would've taken us. But instead of walking through the front doors, we found ourselves looking at a nondescript door to what I could only assume were the kitchens.

"There's someone in there," I said. "A couple someones."

"What do you want to do?" Ward whispered.

I cast another locator spell searching for an alternative exit, but my magic kept bringing me back here. This was the easiest way out of this castle.

"I don't want to cause a scene," I said. "But I don't know how else we can get through there without being noticed."

"I can glamour you."

The words came before the scent of honey hit my nose, and I nearly jumped out of my skin. Riona stood behind us, a frown on her face as she surveyed the two of us.

"Where do you think you're going?" she asked. "And why were you going without me?"

"Clíodhna told me to leave you behind," I said, holding onto my staff as if the fae queen herself would materialize and remove it from my hands. "Ergo, that's what we're doing."

"And then what would you do?" she asked, tilting her head.

"We'd figure it out—"

"Clíodhna gave Cade a map," Ward said, earning a scowl from me. "We were going to follow it."

"She…what?" Riona blinked. "Why would she do that?"

"Look, it doesn't matter why," I said. "We can't take you with us. I promised her."

"You promised her you'd leave me, not that I wouldn't tag along," Riona said, putting her hands on her hips. "Ergo, you didn't break your promise."

Ward snorted and looked at me. "She has a point."

I shook my head. "Clíodhna won't see it that way."

"She won't have a choice because we're going to get to the stone before she even knows we're missing," Riona said with a mischievous gleam in her eye.

"How do you plan on doing that?"

"We'll steal the *donn cúailnge*," she said.

"The…what?"

"Clíodhna's horses, the ones that got us halfway across the *sidheog* lands in an hour versus three days," she said, smirking.

I shared a look with Ward, hoping he might have something to say to dissuade her. He stared at her as if he were communicating something secret with her.

"Are you absolutely certain this is what you want to do?" he asked. "Clíodhna said the enchantments on the stone are deadly—the Erlking wanted no one to go near the stone, ever. You would be risking a lot if you continued with us."

"I'm already in a load of trouble," she said with a half-smile. "Might as well see the journey to the end."

Ward looked at me as if that were a satisfactory answer, and I just shook my head. "If this comes back to bite us in the ass—"

"It won't," Riona said, confidently. "Now come here and let me glamour you."

She worked quickly, changing our appearance and clothes so we'd better blend in with the fae servants, then did the same to herself.

"Follow me."

With a confident air, she walked toward the kitchen and opened the door, allowing us to walk in first. I held my breath, but the magic seemed to do its duty. None of the fae maids or chefs gave us a second look as we walked through the chaos and out the back door.

The night was cold, but we didn't stop until Riona led us to the stables. There, we found the two giant beasts that had so very swiftly carried us across the *sidheog* lands. They didn't appear to be much at all, more like the wooliest, tallest horses I'd ever seen.

"She only has two of them?" Ward asked.

Riona nodded. "So if we take them, she'll be at least half a day behind us."

"And the Erlking?"

"He can travel fast, but not that fast," she said. "Now help me find their saddles."

No sooner had she spoken than a horrible screeching echoed from the castle beyond. It was otherworldly, like the sound those revenants had made in the *aos sí*.

"I think they realized I'm not in my room," Riona said with a frown.

"What do we do?" Ward said.

"We don't have time for saddles, I guess," she said. "C'mon—we have to hurry. Give me the map."

I hesitated then handed it to her. She showed it to the animals and spoke in low, hushed tones. Whether they understood or not, I hadn't a clue, but she seemed confident as she mounted.

"I'm riding with her," Ward said, scrambling up after her. "Cade, you get that one."

"How does this thing work?" I asked, pulling myself up by its mane.

"Just hold on."

That was the last thing I heard before it took off, and it was all I could do to cling to the hair on its neck. As before, the wind ripped at my clothes. The world flew by, and since I could no longer keep my eyes open, I shut them and hoped I wasn't needed to steer anything. I couldn't hear a thing over the roar of the wind, and my exposed skin grew numb as the minutes ticked on. How the thing knew where we were going, I hadn't a clue, but I hoped Riona knew what she was doing.

Too late, I felt the beast slow then come to a complete halt. I somersaulted over its head, and it was only thanks to my staff that I didn't land squarely on my back. I took a couple breaths before lowering my feet and coming to stand. Riona and Ward were dismounting nicely, and the beasts showed no sign of exertion. If anything, they looked bored.

"Are we here?" I asked, looking around. There didn't seem to be much—it was nearly pitch black, save for the stars twinkling above our heads and the black rock under our feet.

"I think so," she whispered, a determined look on her face. "C'mon, we don't have a lot of time to waste."

CHAPTER FORTY-SIX

AYLA

I told Bronwen I was ill and unable to leave the room for the day, but in reality, I wanted to avoid...*everyone*. Including and especially Eoghan. As I spent the morning pacing, my chest was constricted, my hands clutched at my dress, and nothing I tried would give me peace. I didn't understand *why* marriage was suddenly a decision I had to make now, to become a queen and a wife at the same time. And I certainly didn't like any of the options Eoghan had said were the only ones available to me.

I kept going to my window, wishing with all my might that Cade and Ward would be coming across the plain. So far, there had been no sign of them, except for reports of their stops along the way. By now, I'd accepted that my two intrepid travelers had continued into fae country. Out of my reach, and with no way to get news to or from them until they crossed back. Whether they'd ever do that...

I had to have faith. Otherwise, I'd fall into a deep state of depression. I couldn't lose my best friend and my independence all at once. It would be too much.

Mid-afternoon, there was a knock on my door. "I apologize for the interruption, my lady. But it's important."

"Come in," I said, turning away from the window.

Captain Gabhann strode in, her hand resting on her sword. "They tell me you're not well. Shouldn't you be in bed recuperating?"

"I thought a bit of fresh air would do me some good," I said with a half-smile. "You said it was important? What's wrong?"

"I've just received news from Críoch."

My heart soared. "And?"

"They arrived weeks ago," she said, her face grim. "They left their horses there—we've brought them back. The garrison commander says they were there on Eoghan's orders to interrogate fae that were never there in the first place."

"Never…there?"

"No, apparently," she shifted in her boots, as if she were about to tell me something unpleasant, "the garrison commander says he's never received a letter from Master Eoghan. They haven't had a fae in Críoch for years, either."

"Haven't had…" I shook my head. "What about Caecarcem? I was told that every fae they capture was sent there?"

"I was told the same," she said. "But I've never laid eyes on the prison myself. Eoghan always dismissed my requests to pay it a visit. So I sent two guards to the south to see if it even exists."

I took a step back. "If it… Surely, it exists. Why would it not?"

"I have suspicions," she said. "I hope they're unfounded."

I waved my hand, hoping for the same. "Never mind. What of Cade and Ward? You said they left Críoch weeks ago?"

"No one knows exactly where they went, but…" She grimaced. "They were asking how to cross into the fae realm."

I nodded. If I wanted answers, I would have to gather my courage and face Eoghan again. "Thank you. If you hear anything else…"

"As soon as it reaches my ears." She bowed then paused. "Are you all right, Ayla?"

"No," I said with a shake of my head as I looked out the window. "But I will be."

⤜⤜ ⤜⤜

"Captain Gabhann tells me they haven't captured a fae in Críoch in years," I said, barging into the vault where Eoghan was reading.

"What?" He looked up. "What are you talking about?"

"We just got word back from Críoch," I said, blood pumping in my ears. "The garrison commander says Cade and Ward showed up a few weeks ago then disappeared. They left their steeds there. Apparently…the commander has never received a letter from you. And they haven't seen a fae on their side of the border in years."

"Well." Eoghan slammed the book shut and stood. "Clearly, we need a new garrison commander in Críoch. You, yourself, saw there were fae in Pennlan. If he can't keep them in check—"

"Eoghan," I snapped. "What's going on? Did you even send him a letter? Where are Cade and Ward?"

"The fae country, I'd wager," he said, impervious to my rising anger. "Sounds like they didn't find what they were looking for and continued on."

"On a quest *you* sent them on," I said. "Under what appears to be false pretenses."

"False?" He tilted his head. "In what way?"

"There were no fae at the garrison," I said. "Is there even a prison called Caecarcem?"

"Of course there is," he said with a smirk. "Why would I lie to you about that?"

I opened and closed my mouth, unable to come up with a reason, but knowing, in my gut, that I was right. "*Why did you send them?*"

"Fine, I'll admit, I told you a little white lie to soothe your heart," he said, holding up his hands. "They were tasked with going to the fae country to retrieve the stone. I only told you the Críoch story so you wouldn't be upset with me. I doubt they'll be back before your coronation."

"If they're back at all!" I took a step forward, emotion welling in my eyes, but it wasn't sadness. It was anger. "You can't lie to me about these sorts of things."

"I was only trying to protect you, so you wouldn't spend the last few weeks distracted when you should've been preparing to become queen."

"Preparing to become a *wife*, you mean," I said, narrowing my eyes at him. "Because that's all you want from me."

"Ayla, don't be a child," he said. "Your marriage will *help* you. It's not a punishment."

"It's not a punishment, it's an order," I said. "Which is the sort of thing a *queen* should be giving her subordinates, not the other way around."

He lifted his gaze to meet mine, amusement there but also something else—warning. "Am I your subordinate, Ayla?"

I swallowed hard, all my confidence leaving my body. "You are…"

"Am I, the wizard who raised you, who protected you, who has made every decision in this kingdom since you were too young even to speak, your *underling*?" He rose from his chair. "Do you think so little of me?"

"Of course not," I said. "But you can't dictate to me when and whom I should wed."

"Dictate, no," he said with a small shrug. "Help you avoid a gigantic mistake that could destroy this kingdom and everyone in it? I'd like to think so."

"I'm not making a mistake."

"Then why do you sound so hesitant when you say so?" He stepped forward. "What has caused you such unease? Is it the choices I've laid out for you?"

"The choice to *not* marry doesn't seem to be there," I said, losing my grip on the conversation but holding on for dear life. "I shouldn't have to marry."

"It's as I said—you aren't ready to lead. You don't even know anything about the world beyond this castle. You need a partner to guide you in these early years to continue what I've started."

"I don't agree," I said. "I think I can handle it."

"Do you?"

The question hung in the air, and I wished with all my might my tongue would work. But under his intense stare, all I could do was drop my gaze to the floor.

"You know, I have been thinking about your complaints, and I have a solution that might be amenable to you."

I hesitantly lifted my gaze. "What is it?"

"You and I should wed."

"I'm sorry...*what*?" I blinked at him. "Very funny."

"I'm being serious," he said. "I have been as much as running this country for your entire life. It would be no great change for me to assume the throne by your side."

My skin began to crawl at the thought. I cared for him deeply, but not like that. Nowhere near close to that. "I don't..."

"Do you not appreciate the effort I've put in for you?" he asked, taking a step toward me. "This kingdom would've been overtaken by the fae years ago had I not stood here. Clearly, my presence is necessary."

I licked my lips, shaking my head. "Presence, but marriage is—"

"Don't be immature," he said with a wave of his hand. "It is the best thing for this kingdom and for you. Only I can manage your temper and moods."

I didn't have a temper, nor did I have moods. "I can manage myself. And I don't think I need you—"

"Don't you?" Another step toward me. "Was your first instinct not to call for me when that fae arrived to kill you? Didn't I rush to be back by your side? Didn't I solve the problem?"

Yes, yes, and yes—but every fiber in my being was uncomfortable. "Eoghan, your service has been appreciated, you know that. But...this isn't..."

"It wouldn't be a marriage of passion, of course, but of protection and convenience. You don't want to marry a stranger, and I'm most assuredly not a stranger." He tilted his head. "I'm also much younger than any of the others I've proposed."

It was getting hard to breathe again as the world seemed to be spinning out of control around me. I shook my head, fumbling through my thoughts as all I could think was *no, no, no, no*. This wasn't my only path, it couldn't be, so why did it feel like I was being dragged that way?

"Spend some time thinking about it," he said. "But if you do not opt for any of the others, I will begin the preparation for our wedding on your coronation day."

⤛⤜⤛⤜

Somehow, I stumbled out of the vault all the way back to my room. I found myself locking the door behind me, something I'd never done before. As I pressed myself against the door, I closed my eyes and couldn't believe what I'd heard—couldn't believe what was happening.

But who could stop this?

Eoghan was a wizard. No one else in the kingdom could come close to matching his power. And if he left, everything he'd set up would fall on me. Would he leave if I denied him? If I used my voice to tell him *no*, to say that I didn't agree with his plan?

But I'd said no repeatedly, and it had been ignored. Eoghan seemed keen on marrying me off as quickly as possible—or to *marry me* as quickly as possible. My stomach came to my throat, and I forced it back down with a heavy swallow.

I paced my room, wishing I had someone else I could speak to. But even Gabhann deferred to Eoghan, and she would perhaps say that he had my best interests at heart, and I should just let him stick me in a white dress and marry me.

Was this his plan all along?

The small voice in the back of my mind was scared, quiet, but I couldn't deny it had a point. Everything seemed to be driven by Eoghan, down to the choices he'd picked. Perhaps they'd been intentionally boorish, to make himself a better man by comparison. He'd sent away Cade, my only confidant, so I would be left to my own mind and insecurities. Ward, too, had served as a temptation to my heart (if only briefly). There was more to the story of their journey to Críoch, and I was starting to doubt the idea that it was due to Cade's wizard trial.

And if he were to marry me, and they *found* the stone…

My hands gripped the folds of my dress as more pieces fell into place. But I couldn't bring myself to believe the man who'd raised me, who'd mentored me, who'd been my rock in a sea of uncertainty could have done *all* that he did just so he could have the Pennlan stone.

It was a truth too horrifying to even think about.

Chapter Forty-Seven

Ward

I kept my hand on my sword, ready for anything to jump out of the shadows, but as we pressed farther into the land, there didn't seem to be anyone but us. Cade had cast a directional spell, the compass casting a warm glow around us, but even that light seemed dwarfed by the darkness. Still, he felt confident his magic was leading us in the right direction.

"What even is this place?" I asked, tilting my head back to take in the blanket of stars above us. One, in particular, twinkled brightly over the horizon in the distance. I hoped it was an auspicious sign, since we seemed headed in that direction.

"The very end of the known world," Riona replied softly.

"That's…not terrifying or anything," I replied with a small shiver. "What's beyond the known world?"

"Nobody's ever returned to tell the tale."

"Great." I pulled my cloak tighter around myself. I didn't think the chill in my bones was from the air anymore. "What are we looking for?"

"Clíodhna said the first trial was a maze."

Riona and I both turned to him. "A maze?" she asked. "Like…an actual maze?"

"Your guess is as good as mine," he said. "She said there were three trials. The second was supposedly a bloodthirsty monster who could rip me limb from limb, and the final was an enchantment so powerful the Erlking didn't even attempt to broach it." He paused then added, "And that each of the trials were particularly dangerous to wizards."

"Wonder why," Riona muttered under her breath.

"What could this final enchantment be?" I wondered aloud. "And didn't the Erlking set all these traps? Why would his own magic be a danger to him?"

Riona shrugged. "Clíodhna is a few hundred years old and knows exactly how to phrase the truth. Perhaps it's not necessarily that the Erlking doesn't want to approach it because it's so powerful, but because the stone itself is such a danger."

"Or maybe it's a human who needs to retrieve it," I said.

She nodded. "Clíodhna said that wasn't true, but I don't know if I believe her. Leandra told me I needed to find the pair of travelers sent by the princess—"

Cade stopped short. "*Leandra* told you?"

She turned to him, completely serious. "In a dream, yes."

He shook himself, looking at me. "W…What's this about? You had a dream about the fae who stole the stone?"

"Leandra came to me in a dream a few weeks ago. She told me I needed to leave the Erlking's castle and find a pair of travelers sent by Princess Ayla and guide them to the stone." Riona glanced over her shoulder, expecting him to blow his top.

But surprisingly, he nodded slowly. "Well, that explains a few things. She didn't offer anything else helpful in these dreams, did she?"

"No," Riona said with a sigh, looking toward the front. "She didn't even show me your faces."

Cade grew quiet, lost in thought, and I was surprised he didn't press more. I certainly wouldn't have dropped everything and left home if I'd had one nightmare.

Our pace was slow but steady, but as the minutes drew on, I began to worry that maybe Cade's magic was yet again causing him problems. But Riona scampered ahead, narrowing her gaze and pointing.

"I think I see something. Can you cast a brighter light?"

Cade complied, and I began to make out what Riona was seeing. It was nothing but a dark mound in the distance for now, but it was new. I tightened my hold on my sword as we quickened our pace, eager to see what the first of these so-called challenges would entail.

"It's…a hedge maze?" Riona got there first, standing in front of the opening with her shoulders slumped. She turned to look at us, confused. "Seriously?"

It looked innocuous, just a hedge with a split in the middle for us to enter. "This isn't so bad," I said. "Or maybe it's the worst thing in the world."

"What do we do?" Cade said.

"Walk through it, I suppose," Riona said, inching up to the hedge on either side and gingerly touching the leaves. They didn't react. "Maybe the challenge is waiting inside."

"Either way, I can cast a directional spell to get us through," Cade said.

Riona cast a nervous look at me. "I don't think that'll work here, Cade."

He walked up to the front of the maze and cast the spell he'd been using to guide us to this spot. The gold compass appeared on the top of his staff, but instead of pointing forward, it began to spin wildly, as if it weren't sure which way was up.

"Hang on."

He cleared his throat and straightened, casting the spell again. But as before, the compass tilted and spun, and Cade released a growl of frustration.

"Well, maybe I'll just blow a hole through it."

Before either of us could stop him, he released a large gold fireball toward the maze. It burned a hole through the first wall, then the second, then the third…then it stopped—and came zooming right back out.

"Look out!" Riona cried as the magic headed right for Cade's head. He only just ducked in time—and the ground behind him exploded in rock and dust. And by the time I looked back to the edge, all the damage to the hedge had been erased.

"So that won't work," I said.

"I could've told you that," Riona said with an impatient sigh. "Remember, the Erlking magicked this against a wizard. He's not so sloppy that he'd just let you blast your way through. Your magic's no good here."

"I don't hear you offering ideas," Cade muttered as he gingerly got to his feet.

"The last thing we need to do is get lost," I said, rubbing my chin thoughtfully. "So…maybe we just keep taking lefts."

"Lefts?" Riona asked.

"If we reach a dead-end, we can backtrack," I said. "And eventually, we should reach the end."

"How long is eventually?" Cade muttered.

Neither of my compatriots had another idea, so together, shoulder to shoulder, we walked into the maze. I held my breath until we were inside, and when nothing happened, I exhaled loudly—joined by Riona and Cade. We shared a shaky smile.

"Shall we?" Riona said, stepping forward. "To the left."

My method seemed intelligent enough. Clíodhna had warned that this maze was treacherous, but so far, it seemed to be just…a maze. Every corner we turned, I was ready for a beast or monster to jump out and attack, but it was just another corridor of hedges. I glanced up at the stars. The bright star I'd seen was jumping from the east to the west, and I averted my gaze. Lefts, lefts, lefts. I wouldn't put it past the Erlking to flip the stars to confuse people.

When we'd reach a dead end, we'd turn back around, taking the next right then continue to turn left. Time was ticking by, and I found myself glancing toward what I hoped was the east, looking for the sun. But that might've been hours away. Or this place was just in perpetual darkness.

Finally, we turned a corner and saw…*something*. I stopped short, narrowing my gaze at the shadowy lump in the darkness.

"What is that?" Riona asked. "Cade?"

Cade shone his staff in that direction, casting a bit of light, revealing a skeleton. We all took a step backward, perhaps the other two remembering those *aos sí* revenants as I did. Cautiously, gripping my sword hilt, I inched toward it, ready for it to jump up at any moment.

But it remained where it was, and as Cade's magical light grew closer, the familiar color of the skeleton's tattered clothes became apparent. The same dark red color I had very recently become accustomed to—the Pennlan royal guard uniform.

"What is it?" Cade asked.

I didn't answer right away, still waiting for some kind of surprise attack. After all, why else would the Erlking leave a Pennlan knight in the maze? A warning? A trap?

Cade exhaled loudly above me. "That's…"

"Yeah."

"What is it?" Riona asked.

"It's a Pennlan royal guard," I said, staring at the white bones and trying to imagine what this soldier had looked like. "At least the uniform is." I turned to her. "Any idea what they're doing here?"

She shrugged. "There aren't humans this way. At least, none that I know about."

I took a chance and poked the skeleton, but it just slumped onto the ground, the jaw falling off. I winced and picked it up, trying to set it back in place respectfully. If this was a Pennlan guard, it was the least I could do not to disturb his gravesite.

"I wonder what killed him?" Cade shone his light brighter over the bones. The uniform was tattered, but there didn't seem to be any broken bones or signs of distress.

"Maybe starvation?" Riona offered.

I craned my neck at her. "Seriously?"

"If the maze is designed to trick people, perhaps he wandered until he couldn't anymore," she said softly.

Neither of us spoke for a few moments, and I couldn't help the shiver that came across my chest.

"We should keep moving," Cade said.

There was a tenseness in the group as we continued, and for my part, I began to worry that these lefts were, in fact, the wrong direction. That blasted star kept moving every time I looked at it, but for my companions' sakes, I would keep my head about me.

Until we came back to the skeleton on the ground.

"Is that…" Riona said, releasing a sigh of frustration. "Seriously?"

"It might be a different one," Cade said, perhaps more for himself than for us. But its jaw was set at the same awkward angle, and there was no denying the truth.

"How did this happen?" I said. "I—"

But out of the corner of my eye, I saw the hedge move; no, not move—grow and fill in the path we'd come, opening a different path a few paces to the right.

"This maze is reconfiguring itself," Riona said with a loud sigh.

"No." Cade tilted his head toward the sky. "Please tell me that hasn't been happening this whole time."

But when we tested that theory by taking another three lefts then backtracking and we *didn't* find our skeletal friend, I released a sigh of frustration.

"So much for my plan," I said, shaking my head. "I have no idea where we are or how to get to the other side."

"The starvation theory is starting to have some merit," Cade said, rubbing his chin. He looked at his staff. "I could—"

"*No*," Riona and I said in unison.

"I don't want to risk this maze swallowing us whole," she said.

"Let's just take a minute to rest and reconsider our strategy," I said.

We took spots on either side of the hedge, each of us wearing a dejected look. I couldn't help but blame myself for getting us lost, though I didn't think there was a better idea. We perhaps should've known there was more to this maze than a simple plant.

I tilted my head backward, gazing at the stars and finding that one, bright star that had been flip-flopping. I should've stopped us the first time I'd noticed it was different.

"Wait a minute…" I got to my feet, earning curious looks from the other two. "C'mon. I have another idea."

I kept my gaze on the star, taking rights, then lefts, until it was squarely center in my point of view. When we came to another corner, I would judge based on which path kept it the more centrally located in the sky. Sometimes that meant taking a left, sometimes it meant taking a right, but as long as the star remained where it was supposed to be, I had faith I was leading us in the right direction.

"This doesn't seem to be working," Cade said with a sigh. "Are you sure you know what you're doing?"

"Not at all," I said, looking up to check that bright star again. "But this is better than us wandering around until we become skeletons ourselves."

We turned a corner, and all three of us released a collective sound of surprise.

There was no more maze—just dark plain beyond.

"You…did it," Cade said, looking impressed. "Well done."

"What were you looking at?" Riona asked.

I pointed to the star in the sky. "That."

She snorted. "The fae call it Aoibheann—Laughlan's fae lover who enchanted the *seod croí*. Some legends say after she betrayed him, she was so heartbroken, she asked to be placed among the stars because the earth couldn't hold the depths of her sadness."

"Well, it's super bright," I said. "And it's been more or less the way we've been going."

"Guys," Cade said, his face lighting up with joy. The compass atop his staff was now pointed very strongly to the north, following the same path. "My staff is working again."

"Don't let your guard down," Riona said. "That was supposedly the easiest of the three trials. I'm afraid to find out what the other two entail."

Chapter Forty-Eight

Cade

I'd hoped that once we left the maze, the unsettled feeling that sat deep in my bones would disappear. Clíodhna was right; this was no place for a wizard. Everything about it felt wrong, and I was just grateful a simple directional spell was functioning again—for however long the Erlking's enchantments would allow it.

Once again, we found ourselves on a dark, desolate, rocky plain, accompanied by nothing but stars and the faint glow of my staff. I couldn't stop thinking about the Pennlan knight's skeleton. It was another question in my mind, another seed of doubt that Clíodhna had planted about my master.

"He has very nearly completed his long task."

It was nonsense, designed to turn me away from Eoghan. But her words buzzed between my ears, unsettling me and making me question everything I knew to be true. She'd painted my master as an evil schemer who'd stop at nothing for the ultimate power of the stone.

But that power isn't available to him. He wasn't the sovereign of Pennlan, and he never would be.

Right?

I shook myself. It was probably a trick of the fae to unnerve us.

"Where's the next challenge?" Ward asked as we continued walking through the nothingness. "This is taking too long."

"Hush," Riona barked at him. "You don't want to invite it any sooner than it'll come."

"Except, you know, the Erlking is on his way. And I'm sure he'll be able to wilt that maze to the ground," Ward said. "Since he made it."

Before Riona could respond, two torches roared to life, and I jumped back three feet, my staff at the ready, even though I wasn't going to be using it. Ward had drawn his sword and Riona had even pulled her knife. But it was nothing but a pair of torches and a stone wall that stretched as far as the eye could see.

"What is this?" Riona said, walking up to touch the stone.

"Maybe we have to climb over it," Ward said. "Or find a weak spot."

But my directional spell was pointing to the east now. "There might be a way through over there."

We followed the wall closely, torches lighting up as we passed close to them, then extinguishing shortly afterward. It was convenient to light the way, though it concerned me that something in this land was making our journey easier.

"It looks like a gate," Ward said, excitement in his voice as he picked up his pace. "C'mon."

But he stopped short as he reached it, and when I joined him, I saw why. No fewer than a hundred large griffins stood guard beyond the large stone wall. They stared at us with golden, clear eyes, as if daring us to walk through the open gate and into their lands.

"Second challenge," Riona said with a little nervousness. "I don't think I've ever seen so many griffins before."

"Why aren't they attacking?" Ward asked, holding his sword aloft. "What are they waiting for?"

"Us to cross through the gate," Riona said with a grimace. "Is there any other way around?"

My compass was very clearly pointing straight ahead. "I don't think so."

"What do we know about griffins again?" Ward asked. "Can they be reasoned with?"

"They're highly intelligent," Riona said. "And they follow their leader." She pointed at one of them that seemed a little bigger and taller than the others. "That one looks like the leader."

"So maybe we try talking with him."

"Her," Riona said with a heavy swallow. "I'll go. They might be more amenable to a fae."

I gripped my staff, ready to step in if needed, and Ward stood poised to run in after her. Riona passed under the threshold, and the griffins stirred restlessly. But none moved as she cautiously walked up to their leader.

She bowed low. "Esteemed griffin, I—"

The griffin opened its beak and let out a loud squawk that echoed across the land. The other griffins lifted their heads, all of them staring at Riona with a murderous glare.

"We mean no harm—"

But that didn't seem to matter as the griffins unfurled their wings, advancing on her. Riona tried to reason with them, her hands up, but Ward ran forward, grabbing her by the waist and dragging her back through the gate. I stood ready to strike any griffin who threatened, but once Riona and Ward were on the other side, the beasts calmed down immediately.

"That didn't work," Ward said, putting Riona down. "Now maybe we try the sword idea?"

"I'm not interested in slaughtering a hundred griffins," Riona said, adjusting her cloak with a glare. "There has to be another way."

I glanced at the leader, who had returned to her calm observance now that the intruders were gone. "You said that if the leader were convinced, the others would follow?"

"Yes, but I don't see how we can convince her if I can't even speak with her," Riona said.

"I might be able to convince her, but…" I winced. "You might not like it."

"Why, what are you…" Her eyes widened. "No. Absolutely not."

"What?" Ward asked. "What are you thinking?"

"I'm going to use a compulsion spell on the leader," I said.

"You *cannot* use that ghastly spell on these magnificent creatures," Riona said, glaring at me. "It would be absolutely—"

"Would you rather we kill them or they kill us?" I shot back. "I promise, I'll just compel the leader and as soon as we are safely past them, I'll let her go. I won't even make her do anything except not…well, not rip us limb from limb."

"Riona," Ward said with a look. "It sounds like it might be the easiest solution."

She licked her lips, still uncertain.

"I won't hurt her," I said, catching Riona's gaze. "I promise."

The sincerity in my face must've softened her hatred. "Just be… careful."

I approached the golden gate, feeling the air around me shift. Something very powerful was keeping these griffins on their side, something even more powerful than Clíodhna's magic. This was the Erlking, and I was glad I wouldn't be meeting him anytime soon.

Inching closer to the gate, I caught the attention of the closest griffin, and he narrowed his golden eyes in my direction. The leader was some ways away, but I could very easily find a vein of magic in the ground to spread the spell through.

"Cade…" Riona stood next to me.

"It'll be fine. I'll just compel her to leave us be," I said.

She clenched her jaw. "Do it."

I closed my eyes and felt the spell gather in my body, whispering the words I'd learned so long ago. The magic slipped through the ground, running through the veins of magic, bypassing all the other griffins, until it reached the taloned hooves of the leader. It crept up her body, and although I was sure she felt it, she remained absolutely still until it had captured her mind.

Immediately, my own perspective shifted and I began to see what the griffin saw, to know what she knew. She was older than even the Erlking, a proud beast who'd been driven from her home in the *aos sí* when the fae had gone to war with each other. The Erlking—not Birch, someone much older—had allowed her entry into his lands, and she'd grown her flock from a handful to the great numbers. Birch had come to her years ago, requesting a repayment of the favor, and she'd resettled her flock here…

"Are you there?" Ward was waving his hand in front of my eyes. "Cade?"

I shook myself. I must've fallen into her mind. "Sorry. Yes, we should be good."

"What happened to you? You went blank for a few minutes," Ward said.

"I could…" I glanced at the griffin again, licking my lips. "I could see inside her mind. It was magnificent."

"You can see inside their mind?" Riona asked, a little horror on her face.

I nodded. "But it's different. It's like she…she pulled me in to show me something. I've never experienced anything like that before."

Even now, I could hear her calling me, dragging me back toward the vision. Before I could stop myself, I was back in her mind, and she was revealing the battle of the *aos sí* to me, how the fae battled against each other. But it wasn't just fae. It was humans, trolls, *fuath*—and more creatures I couldn't even begin to name.

In the middle of the melee, there seemed to be a great source of power somewhere in the middle. Through her eyes, I flew high above the chaos, finding the power source.

It was a wizard with a brightly-lit gem around his neck, and a cavalcade of fae and human alike being unceremoniously killed by the power emanating from that gem.

"*Cade.*" Ward's voice broke the trance. "Quit screwing around and let's go."

I took a step backward, clutching my pounding heart. "I'm not sure what…"

But I was sure of what I'd seen. This griffin was showing me a past that I'd only gotten scraps of before.

Ward grabbed the sleeve of my shirt and dragged me forward into the thick of the griffins. None of them stepped up to attack, calmed by the fact that no one had ordered them to strike. My control over the leader remained, and in the back of my mind, I could see her watching us. See her offering more of the story she'd only begun.

But with Ward's rough handling, she wasn't able to draw me back in.

"How many damn griffins are there?" Ward asked as we kept walking.

"There," Riona said, nodding toward the front. "I can see another one of those gates." She glanced at me. "Is she okay?"

"She's patiently waiting for me to release my hold," I said softly.

"Have you peered any more into her mind?"

"Not if I can help it." Though she certainly wanted me to try. The promise of more information, more secrets unveiled, more…more…

Someone yanked my face in the other direction and I was staring into a pair of green eyes. "Focus, Cade. Clearly, this is part of the challenge."

"Part of…" I blinked. "What are you talking about?"

"It's no coincidence the Erlking put a griffin here. They're highly intelligent, and I wouldn't be surprised if they were able to flip that compulsion spell back on you." She released my face. "You're supposed to be the one in control, not the other way around."

"I'm in control," I said.

"No, you're not," Ward replied, sticking his thumb at the griffin. "You've gone glassy-eyed three times already."

"Clíodhna said these trials were specifically designed to entrap wizards," Riona replied. "And I bet the Erlking assumed Eoghan would use the compulsion spell, just as you did."

"Meanwhile…" Ward said, eyeing the griffins around us. "How long until they decide their leader is under a compulsion spell and eat us?"

"Let's just get through the gate before we find out." Riona placed her hand on my shoulder and pushed me forward. "No more mind-gazing."

I turned toward the front and walked with purpose, but the temptation was so strong. It seemed almost like this creature knew *my* greatest weaknesses and was tempting me in the worst ways possible. But Riona's hand on my shoulder was a grounding force, and I focused on Ayla, getting the stone to her, reaching the final trial and the stone. We were so close. The mysteries of the past could remain that way.

The gate drew nearer and the pull on my mind grew more insistent. This griffin didn't want to let me go—so much so that I worried perhaps I might not be able to let *her* go. I didn't dare break the compulsion spell, though, as it was the only thing keeping us from the rest of the griffins.

Finally, we passed through the threshold, and as before, a new feeling rose from my toes to my head. We were in a different realm once more.

"Let her go," Riona said.

I nodded and to my relief, the compulsion spell released with ease. The griffin, still on the other side of the open field, caught my gaze and bowed her head. What that meant, I had no idea, but I hoped I'd earned her respect. One day, I'd like to come back and ask her—

"*Cade*," Ward said, impatiently.

"Sorry," I said, shaking myself. "I'm ready."

"I told you that spell was evil," Riona said, matter-of-factly.

"I didn't even realize it could go the other way," I said, using all my mental prowess to keep my mind in the present moment. "She showed me some things… Very curious things."

"Don't think about it anymore," Riona said. "Or she'll drag you back into her trap."

"What kind of things?" Ward asked.

"She showed me the battle of the *aos sí*," I said softly. "But it wasn't...it wasn't the fae you said it was. Laughlan was a wizard."

"That vision was specifically designed to entice you into staying there and learning more," Riona replied, eyeing me suspiciously.

I held up my hands. "I don't want that power for myself, I swear. But I just...the history..."

"You can ask Clíodhna," Riona said. "But in the meantime, we have one more trial to overcome, and may I remind you that the Erlking can very easily walk through these trials as he's the one who made them. So let's quit standing around and thinking of the past, and *get a move on*."

Chapter Forty-Nine

Ward

The farther we walked from the griffins, the less distracted Cade became. We were on yet another desolate plain, and the darkness overhead seemed almost permanent. I wasn't sure how long we'd been here, but morning should've started breaking by now. Unless it just didn't in this land.

"This is the last trial?" I asked Riona.

"Should be," she replied with a wry smile. "Unless Clíodhna was lying, and there are five more."

"Don't say that," Cade said on the other side of her. "I'm not sure what else I can take today."

"Just remember we have to walk *all* the way home," I said over Riona's head. "And avoid the Erlking while we're at it."

Riona actually giggled. "The trip might be faster with the *donn cúailnge*."

"If the beasts are still there when we get back," Cade said. "They might've returned to their stables."

A nervous silence descended.

"Let's just focus on surviving this last test," I replied.

With the star and Cade's staff guiding us, we kept on the same path until another dark shadow emerged. As we drew closer, it revealed itself to be a large mouth of a rocky cave.

"This looks promising," I said, though I didn't mean it. "Maybe there's a giant slug in there that wants to eat us."

"We've already fought creatures," Riona said with a shake of her head. "And the second was a test of mental strength."

"Supposedly, this is a powerful enchantment," Cade said.

Riona nodded distractedly. "Supposedly."

The cavern opening very quickly narrowed to a hallway of sorts, and the incline was steep. We descended slowly, bracing ourselves on the slippery walls. Water was dripping from somewhere ahead, and more than once, something wet fell on the back of my neck. But we kept walking, holding our breath as we waited for the challenge to present itself.

"Up ahead," Riona said.

Light was shining on the ground from what appeared to be an opening. I put my free hand on my sword, though the path was so narrow I didn't think I could even get it out of its sheath. Riona stepped into the light first, a frown coming to her face.

"There it is," Cade said, coming up behind her.

It wasn't until I joined them that I realized the path had ended. Far below, crystalline water shimmered from some unknown light source—or perhaps from something within the lake itself. There didn't seem to be any dry land in the crater below, either, other than this small overhang.

"Where is it?" Riona asked, a little impatiently. "It's supposed to be here?"

"Maybe it's at the bottom of the lake?" Cade offered. "Should we dive in and find out?"

"Who's the strongest swimmer?" I asked. "I'm fairly good—"

"It wouldn't just be in a cave anyone can jump into," Riona pointed out with a little huff. "There's something wrong with this lake. I can feel it."

But nothing happened the longer we stared at it. There wasn't even a ripple in the water, just the ever-present soft glow from whatever had lit it up.

I got down on my knees to look directly below. "There seems to be a small area down there we can stand on." With care, I lowered myself off the overhang, grabbing onto a jagged rock, and shimmying down the side of the cave. When I reached the bottom, I landed on a very small beach of gravel, the water mere steps away. The other two followed, neither wanting to use their magic in this place.

"Well," I said, unhooking the clasp around my traveling cloak and dropping my sword from my waist. "No time like the present."

"Are you sure?" Riona said.

"You said I was the one to get it," I replied.

"Clíodhna said she was misinformed," Cade drawled, taking off his cloak and leaning his staff against the wall. "So maybe I should go get it."

I narrowed my gaze at him. "You just want to tell Ayla you got it for her."

His scoff of disbelief was almost a little too rehearsed. "I do not. I just think it's better if I go instead of you. Clearly, there's nothing in here preventing me from using my magic—"

"Why don't you try putting your toe in before you dive in?" Riona said with a hearty roll of her eyes. "Besides that, I don't think Ayla will care which of you *actually* got the stone out of its hiding place. You both went on this quest to retrieve it. It really doesn't matter."

I disagreed, and based on Cade's expression, he did as well. But I also couldn't argue that it was safer to test the waters before diving in. I pulled off my boots and winced as the gravel cut into my bare feet. But with care, I approached the water—Cade right beside me.

"Shall we?" I asked, the water lapping inches from my skin.

"You first."

"Brave of you."

"I'm also the one who can pull you out," Cade said, sticking his staff into the ground.

"Well, you have a point."

I inched closer and stuck my toe in. The water was somehow refreshing, even after hours in the frigid landscape above. When nothing happened, I pushed my whole foot in then my other, then waded up to mid-calf.

"Seems like—"

I didn't know *how* but something rose from the water and tugged me under. I fought and kicked against an imaginary foe, unable to find who or what had grabbed me. Gold magic flew through the water, surrounding me and lifting me into the air. Once I broke the surface, I gasped as much air as I could, and once back on the beach, I spat up and coughed out whatever I'd breathed in.

After a moment, I looked up at the other two, horrified. "What the hell was that?"

"I don't know," Cade said, his face pale. "Something invisible grabbed you and dragged you under."

"It didn't even seem possible," I said, slowly coming to my feet as water dripped from my hair. "I was a few inches in. How does someone drown in a few inches?"

"Because it's an enchanted lake, obviously," Riona said. She still had her shoes and cloak on as she watched the water. "So we just need to figure out how to get past the enchantments."

>⋙ >⋙ >⋙ >⋙

Unfortunately, nobody had any good answers.

Cade attempted a few spells, and while it didn't bring the entire cave down around us, whenever his magic reached a certain depth, the lake would spit it back out and it would bounce around until Cade called it back to himself. The third time he tried it, and a chunk of the cave fell down, Riona barked at him to knock it off.

"Clearly, that's not working," she snapped. "And I'd rather not die in a cave-in."

"Fine." He gestured to her. "You give it a try."

But she remained where she was, watching the water as if it would give up its secrets any moment. Cade scoffed and sat on the other side of the small beach, crossing his arms and scowling at the water. Then there was silence and stillness.

I ventured over to Riona, who wore a curious look on her face, and sat down next to her.

"What are you thinking?"

"I don't have a clue," she whispered. "I'd hoped that once we got here, the answers would make themselves visible to me in some way. I couldn't..." She shook her head. "I'm starting to wonder if that dream I had was just that..."

"Seems to have worked out so far," I said. "We did make it here."

"Only to be thwarted."

"Not yet." I nudged her. "What was in that dream? Describe it to me."

She exhaled. "I was in a forest somewhere, walking in the darkness. I heard Leandra calling to me, but I couldn't find her. I came out of the forest into the human realm, staring at the Pennlan castle. It was dark and ominous, as if there was an evil lurking in the walls." She paused. "There were two shadows leaving, and the voice said I was to find the travelers and together, we'd find the stone." She straightened, looking at me as if she'd just realized something. "*Together*, we'd find the stone."

"Yes, and?" I gestured to the lake. "Do we go in together?"

"No. We did find it together, but..." She rose and unclasped her cloak. "It's me. I'm the one who has to get it."

"Wait, what?" Cade jumped to his feet and walked over. "Why?"

"Because..." She swallowed as she walked toward the water. "I just know."

I pulled her back from the water and made her look at me. "Riona, whatever's in there is dangerous. You have to be very sure you know what you're doing. We don't even know if the stone is down there—you could drown for nothing."

"I won't drown."

"Everyone just hold on a second," Cade said. "Did I miss something?"

Riona gave me a look that very clearly reminded me of my promise to keep her lineage to myself as she pulled her boots off. "I'm going in."

"Hang on—" Cade grabbed her arm as she walked toward the water. "You can't."

She put her hand over his and smiled. "Trust me. Besides that, if I'm wrong, you'll just be rid of me."

"Nobody wants that," Cade said with a frown. "Are you sure?"

She nodded and he released her, but not the look of concern on his face.

"If you get in trouble, I'm pulling you out," he said. "Even if it brings down the cave. Understood?"

"Try not to do that," she said with a wry smile. "But understood."

He stepped back and let her continue, and I joined him on the shoreline as she put one bare foot into the water then the other. I held my sword hilt tightly, knowing it would be no use against whatever magical force had dragged me under. But she continued into the water, wading up to her hips without any problem.

"Are you all right?" Cade asked.

"Yeah," she called, giving us a look over her shoulder. "Going in."

She went under then resurfaced, popping up every few feet to take another breath as she made her way to the center of the lake.

"So far, so good," I muttered.

Cade nodded, but the tip of his staff was bright gold nonetheless.

Finally, she reached what was perhaps the center of the lake. "I think I see something down there," she called, her voice echoing in the cave.

"Be careful," I called.

She waved at us, took a deep breath, and dove in.

"Good luck, kid," Cade muttered. To my curious look, he shrugged. "Seriously. I hope she finds it down there."

"Just be ready to grab her if she doesn't resurface," I said.

He gripped his staff and nodded.

The seconds passed, and my pulse quickened, worried that something had grabbed and kept her down, that there was one more surprise waiting for us. That Riona would fall victim to something horrible.

I released my breath when I could hold it no longer. "Cade…"

"I know." He released a ball of magic across the water. It rippled as it traveled along the water, but before it reached the center, it was swallowed by a large wave that seemed to come out of nowhere.

He cursed and tried again. I inched closer to the water, knowing I could do nothing to help. More spells went across the water, and all of them had no effect.

"Ward, you can't go—" Cade said, grabbing my arm as I ran toward the water. "You'll drown, too."

I knew that, but I couldn't just let her die. "We have to—"

A loud splash drew our attention, as Riona resurfaced, spraying water and coughing as she bobbed. Cade cast another spell across the water, this time a successful one that carefully cradled her out of the water and carried her back toward us. She landed softly on the ground on all fours, coughing and spitting up water.

"Are you all right?" I asked, firmly hitting her back to help the water come up.

She nodded, though she couldn't yet speak.

"Did you find it?" Cade asked.

"Give her a moment," I snapped.

But as she continued coughing, she tilted her head up and turned her palm over, revealing a large, blue gem that glowed ominously.

"You…" I blinked, unsure I was seeing what I was seeing. "You found it."

"Told you," she huffed with a proud smile. "I was the one. It wasn't that you needed me to get here… *I* needed *you* to bring me here. That's what Leandra meant."

"Is that really it?" Cade knelt on the other side of her. He made no

move to take it from her, merely ran his fingers along the top. "It feels…
I've never felt power like that before."

"It's the real thing," she whispered. "Ayla will be so happy to have it
back."

"That she will. Well done, all three of you."

Chapter Fifty

Cade

I was sure my mind had become bewitched by a spell. Because that sounded like the voice of my master.

But he was all the way back in Pennlan.

How he could've made it to the very northern part of the fae realm, to stand here with us?

And yet, Riona's gasp of surprise and Ward's bugged-out expression told me perhaps it wasn't as far-fetched as I'd thought.

I turned slowly, my heart pounding in my chest. Eoghan stood in front of a large magical circle, beyond which was…the vault. Home. Eoghan had created a door between realms and walked right through.

Out of the corner of my eye, I saw Riona scramble to her feet and disappear in a puff of butterflies. But Eoghan was faster.

"I don't think so," he said, casting a spell I'd never seen before and pulling her back down to the gravel beach between him and us. She rematerialized with a cry of pain, and the stone fell from her hand. She scrambled to pick it up, but it disappeared and reappeared in Eoghan's hand—now a lifeless, dull gem.

"What…" Ward couldn't even form words. "What are you doing?"

"I confess, this last trial has confounded me for the better part of a decade," he said, examining the stone closely. "I can't tell you how many knights have drowned trying to get into it." He glanced at Riona. "I wonder why you're so special."

Knights have drowned. "You've…" I blinked. "You've been here before?"

"Of course," my master said, pocketing the gem as if it were a mere trinket.

"How…" I shook my head, still not quite comprehending what was going on. "How did you do this? I've never seen this spell before."

"Boy, your knowledge of magic is as thick as a piece of paper," he said with a hearty sigh. "You know the skills I needed you to know to make this journey."

Riona seemed to have come back to her senses and tried to escape once more, but Eoghan pulled her back down, this time onto her back.

"How did you do it?" Eoghan asked, walking closer to her. "Is it because you're a fae? I have compelled a hundred fae to swim these waters. All of them died."

She rolled onto her side, gripping at the pebbles as her jaw clenched. Then she tried to escape again, only to be brought back down —this time, with a spell wrapped around her to keep her in place.

"I asked you a question, you little piece of—"

"Eoghan," Ward snapped. "Let her go. She's unimportant. She got you the stone, that's all you need to know."

"Is it?" He narrowed his eyes at the knight, straightening as Riona struggled against his bonds. "Did you and the fae girl become friends while you were out in the wilderness together? Do you find her youthful indiscretions endearing? Ayla will be sad to hear your heart has been so easily turned toward another."

"She's a child," Ward snapped.

"Master," I said, finally finding my tongue, "he's right, she's of no consequence. We have the stone. That's all that matters now."

"Do you, apprentice?" Eoghan narrowed his gaze at me. "What sort of secrets has this fae girl shared with you?"

I licked my lips, looking at Riona, whose pleading eyes stared into mine. The only thing I knew was that she was half-fae…and somehow, I didn't think that was something she wanted Eoghan to know.

"I don't know any secrets, master. She's…she's just a child who showed up to help us on our journey."

"You're a terrible liar," Eoghan said with a roll of his eyes as he stamped his staff onto the ground. "But there are ways of getting the truth out of fae."

"*No!*"

Ward rushed forward, but Eoghan cast a spell and flung him backward to the cave wall, which he'd enchanted to become almost liquid. Ward sank almost completely into it then it hardened fast—only his head was visible.

"What the—*Cade, do something!*" he bellowed.

I took a step forward, but Eoghan pointed his staff at me, his gaze full of fury and fire. "Stand down, apprentice."

My attention bounced between Ward and Riona, the latter of whom had gone stark white with fear as Eoghan approached. "Master, I don't know what you think you'll get out of her, but it's not—"

The magic hit my midsection before I even knew what was happening, and I flew backward, landing on my rear and coughing as I struggled to catch my breath. I tilted my head up, wincing in pain as Eoghan approached Riona, his staff already filled with the compulsion magic.

"Now, as for you." Dark magic wrapped around her legs first, slowly drawing up as she fought against the magical bonds keeping her in place.

"N-no," she whispered, her eyes wide as she struggled against his binds. But all she could muster was a single butterfly that dissipated when it got a few feet from her.

Tears splashed down her cheeks as she cried out in fear, for me, for Ward, for anyone to help her. But as the darkness reached her eyes, the struggling stopped. Her green eyes turned black, and her hands became limp as her head tilted forward.

"Now, that's better," Eoghan said, pulling his staff upright. "Will you behave now?"

She nodded, and the bonds keeping her in place released. With ease, she pushed herself to her feet, then stood obediently with a blank expression on her face. It was at that moment that I finally understood *why* this compulsion spell had so terrified her. In the wrong hands...

"What did you do to her?" Ward snarled. "Let her go!"

"Not until she answers my question," Eoghan said, a smile curling onto his face as he walked up to her. "Now, child: what is so special about you?"

"Nothing. I'm no one." Her voice was monotone and lifeless.

"Strong, aren't you?" He twisted his staff, and another spell crawled toward her.

She jerked, almost involuntarily, before stilling again.

"Who are you?"

Her jaw tightened, as if she were using every bit of energy she had to fight the compulsion. A solitary tear leaked down her face.

"Eoghan," I croaked, getting to my feet again. "Let her go, please. She doesn't—"

Before I could finish, he cast another spell. This time, I landed hard against the other side of the cave, and the same spell that had Ward now entrapped me.

By the time the stars cleared from my eyes and the air returned to my chest, I heard Riona speak.

"My name is Riona of the *daoine maithe*, daughter of Leandra and King Bresel."

"*What?*" My word echoed in the cave, and I couldn't believe my own ears. It had to be another fae lie, a spin of the truth. There was no way...no way this girl could be Ayla's half-sister. It was impossible. Except...

Except it wasn't.

I stared at the blank-faced girl I'd traveled with this whole time, my mouth hanging open in shock. It wasn't even the physical attributes that stood out to me, but the personality. They were both loyal, stubborn, at once reckless and self-defeating. I'd been so blind this whole time to have not seen it.

"How very…wonderful," Eoghan said with a gleaming smile. "You may not know this, child, but you've made my plans much easier—and your sister's life that much better. She will no longer have to marry me."

Marry…

"*What?*" Ward barked from the other side of the cave. "Why the hell would Ayla marry *you?*"

"How else would I gain access to the powers of the stone?" Eoghan asked.

"She's not Ayla's sister," I said, wishing I sounded more convincing. "She's just some fae girl who wanted to help."

"Well, there's really one way to find out for sure." He plucked the stone from his pocket, and Riona put out her hand. The stone landed in her hand, and I exhaled a breath of relief when it remained dormant. Just a beautiful, misshapen—

The stone began to glow, a beautiful, powerful, magnificent blue that cast an otherworldly look on Riona's face. My heart sank into my stomach as Eoghan's smile widened.

"Show me what you can do, little fae," he whispered, his staff lighting up.

The beautiful glow turned into a white-hot light. Magic flowed around her, both from the stone and her own—the strong scent of honey permeated the air, lifting the hair from my arms. Through Eoghan, she was drawing into the deep reserve of power I'd always suspected was there, but she'd never managed to tap into.

"She will one day stand amongst the most powerful fae."

Clíodhna had been right. But it took someone with much more knowledge of the depth of magic to bring it out of her.

She gathered her magic into a concentrated ball in her hands, and this time, there were no butterflies, no smoke and mirrors, just power.

Then the power shot upward to the top of the cave. I winced as a loud *boom* echoed around us, my ears ringing, and my eyes blinded by the light. The cave began to crumble around us, large rocks falling into the water with loud splashes. I could barely breathe, watching this massive cave disappear in the face of this magic from a girl who could barely defend herself.

When it was over, there was nothing left of the cavern ceiling, just the night sky and that damn star that Ward had been following this whole time. I became aware of the sound of my own breath coming out in small puffs.

"The power of the stone," Eoghan said, resting his hand on Riona's shoulder. "Only accessible to a member of the Pennlan royal family. In some ways, perhaps it's poetic that Bresel mated with one of your kind and created you."

He lifted his hand to cup her face, and I could practically feel the disgust radiating off her, even completely under his control.

"This is why your mother hid the stone. It wasn't to save herself. It was to keep you from me, wasn't it?" Eoghan said with a condescending chuckle. "Don't worry, child, we'll return to Pennlan, and you'll get to meet your beloved sister, just as you've always wanted."

"Eoghan," I said, trying one more time to reach him. "This… You can't…" I swallowed. "What about Ayla? You *raised* her. You can't do this."

"*This* has been the only thing for longer than you've been alive," he snapped, looking at me with a fire I'd never seen before. "Everything else has been a distraction, something to pass the time until Ayla came of age. But now…" He looked down at Riona like a farmer would his prized pig. "Now there's no need for that plan."

"You're disgusting," Ward spat. "She's half your age."

"Merely a means to the end," he said, impervious to his derision. "But as you can see, I've found a better option. Your Ayla is free to be with whichever of you she deems fit."

"So you'll leave her alone?" I asked, hopefully. Perhaps my master wasn't that much of a monster.

He glanced at Riona and tutted. "On second thought, perhaps not. I don't like leaving anything to chance. I will send your regards before I have her killed."

"Riona won't hurt her sister," Ward growled, struggling against his bonds. "She risked everything to try to help her. Her mother broke your spell, and Riona will, too—"

My jaw dropped. "You… *You knew*? You knew who she was? How long have you known?"

"I see the journey has done nothing to dispel your petty dislike of one another," Eoghan said with a sigh. "I'd had higher hopes for you, apprentice. But it's clear you've outlived your usefulness." He turned to the fae girl staring blankly by his side. "Take care of it."

The stone lit up once more, and a spell released, hurtling toward me. I braced myself for pain, for death, for whatever came next. But the burst of magic dropped at the last minute, and I realized with horror that it wasn't meant for me.

My staff, laying feet from me, exploded, and I vaguely heard my scream of horror as the magical object that had been by my side since I was a boy was obliterated. When the dust cleared, there was nothing left except a pile of splinters.

"Good girl," Eoghan said. "Now, come with me. We have work to do."

CHAPTER FIFTY-ONE

AYLA

I stood in front of the vault door, licking my lips.

I'd spent the day thinking about Eoghan's proposal, and my stomach was sour with unease. He was more a father, an uncle. A husband?

Absolutely not.

The decision hadn't come without second-guessing, though. I'd spent all morning ruminating, thinking, replaying conversations and trying to be secure in my own mind before I even attempted to leave my room. I wanted to be firm and clear when I spoke with Eoghan.

I would not marry him, or anybody, until *I* found a match suitable for this kingdom and myself.

Now I just had to convince my wizard counsel of the same.

Ever since Eoghan had told me the "right" way to open his vault, I'd practiced and rehearsed the intonation I'd used to open it in his presence. Just to be sure, just to trust my own mind. Because in my mind… No, I wouldn't discount him until I knew for sure. I owed him that much.

"I, Princess Ayla, sovereign of Pennlan and soon-to-be queen, demand that you open for me."

I put my hand on the door, and to my joy, the lock turned, and the door opened. But just as soon as my heart lightened, it sank into my stomach. So Eoghan hadn't been lying, which meant I would have to consider…

"Ah, excellent timing."

Eoghan stood in the center of the room, but there was something behind him—a magical circle hanging in the air, almost a window into another world. But it closed before I could see exactly what it was. A girl stood by his side with blank, expressionless eyes.

I took a terrified step back—she was *fae*.

"Who…" I shook myself. "Eoghan, who is *that*?"

"Oh this?" He glanced down at the girl. "This is your sister, Riona."

"S-sister?" The word was somehow foreign on my tongue. "I don't have a sister."

Especially not one who was…

"I confess, I had no idea either. Leandra was a tricky creature, it seems." He was talking as if we were discussing the weather, not my entire world tilting on its side. My lungs forgot how to breathe as I took her in, unable to accept the strangeness of the situation and at the same time, repeating this strange word in my mind.

Sister… Sister… Sister…

"I don't understand," I said, finally.

"I wouldn't expect you to," he said. "Your father and the fae Leandra had a child together. Leandra hid that child in the fae realm under a false identity." He glanced at the girl. "But it seems she was compelled to help your friends find their way to the stone." His smile grew cruel. "She wanted to help her sister."

Your friends. "She traveled with Cade and Ward?" I asked slowly. "She helped them?"

"Oh, they've had quite an adventure, she tells me. They traveled through the fae wildlands, fighting ghosts and monsters and fae alike." He smiled at her, much as he used to do with me. "Became quite the trio, didn't you?"

The girl stood still, but there was something in the back of my mind that urged me to intervene. She was far too quiet, her face too expressionless. It was almost as if…

A compulsion spell.

I shook myself, needing to distract and delay in order to get my thoughts together. "Are they all right? Cade and Ward?"

"Wouldn't you rather know if they were successful?" He wore an enigmatic smile. "Riona. Show her."

The fae girl reached into her pocket and pulled out a small, blue stone. Once again, the reality that I'd known slipped sideways.

They'd done it. They'd found the stone.

It called to something deep inside me, to my very soul. A knowing that while it rested in someone else's hand, it belonged in mine.

And that Eoghan wasn't going to let me have it. Slowly, understanding came over me and my pulse quickened. The truth I'd been so keen to avoid facing was staring me in the face, with blank eyes and a vacant expression.

"My… You…" I shook my head, my thoughts running too fast to keep up with them. Everything was now different, the story of my life as I knew it was changing in front of me. Things I'd been certain of were now false and things that had seemed impossible were painfully obvious.

But one voice was very clear: I was very much in danger.

"I confess, I didn't send them expecting them to be successful. Cade had proven to be a lackluster apprentice and the knight was merely there to make sure he didn't starve to death," he said. "But I hoped Cade's training might've prepared him to endure the trials the Erlking left—perhaps it might've been the missing link in that final challenge that had befuddled me for so long." He shrugged. "In the end, it was only Leandra's own daughter who could retrieve it. And she did an admirable job of it."

He walked to the map on the wall, examining the countries he'd been visiting as my counsel. It had all been in preparation for this. If he'd never found this fae girl—my half-sister—he would've perhaps coerced me into marriage, and thus taken the power for himself. It was always about the stone.

His back was turned, and the power he'd found for himself was steps from me. If I could get it back, I could stop him. It was the only thing that would save my own life.

I dove for the girl, but she disappeared in a puff of butterflies, appearing at Eoghan's side without as much as a flicker of life as she stared down at me.

Eoghan chuckled and patted her on the head. "Good girl."

"Eoghan," I said, coming to my feet. "You can't do this."

"I can do whatever I want," he said, looking over his shoulder. "I'm the holder of the most powerful object in existence."

"It isn't." The girl's voice was soft.

"What do you mean, it isn't?" Eoghan said, his gaze flashing at her. "I have studied this more than anyone in these lands. This stone is—"

"This is not Laughlan's stone." She stared at the floor. "It is merely one piece of it."

He turned fully, as if he didn't quite understand what she was saying. He yanked the stone from her hand and examined it closely. The moment it left her hands, it turned lifeless and gray.

"You little…" He looked at her. "Did your mother destroy it?"

"No," she said. "It was destroyed before it was ever given to the Pennlan house."

He tapped the stone to his chin, a smile coming to his face. "Please, child, enlighten me as to what secrets your grandfather has kept from the world."

"The stone was deemed too powerful by Aoibheann," she said. "She couldn't destroy it, so she divided it and sent the pieces away. One to the humans in Pennlan, one to the mountains, one to the sea, and one to be buried in the aether."

"Hm." He placed the stone back in her waiting hand where it lit up once more. "Then I suppose you and I have a journey to make. But first, we must settle things in this realm." He glanced at me. "And with her."

My heart pounded in my chest as I realized what he meant to do.

"Eoghan, you can't—"

"I can do whatever I want," he said. "Kill her."

The girl turned on her heel, the stone glowing bright blue in her hand. But there was something else, a white magic infused within it. Eoghan was making her use both, it seemed.

"Perhaps all those nightmares of a fae woman coming to kill you were premonitions," he said with a cruel smile. "It hasn't been a pleasure to raise you."

I backed up as far as I could, putting my hand on the doorknob but finding it locked once more. No words I could summon would open it, either. I faced the girl—my *sister*—with a straight back. The power gathered in her hand raised the hair on my arms and neck and I steeled myself.

"Tell me one thing," I said, looking at Eoghan. "Did Leandra kill my father?"

"Of course she did," he said with a smirk.

"Under your spell," I snapped. "Did she even try to kill me, too, or was that another lie you told to scare me into submission?"

"I told her to, but she was resistant to it." He tutted. "She was quite fond of you, actually. But I won't make that mistake again." His staff lit up as the fae girl walked closer. "Make sure to finish the job. I don't feel like cleaning up a mess."

My back straightened against the door, and I stared into the eyes of this fae girl approaching me slowly. There was nothing there, but deep down, I knew I could reach her.

"R-Riona, was it?" I said, my voice soft. "You don't want to do this. I know you don't. If you wanted to get me the stone to help—"

"Riona," Eoghan said, his staff glowing once more. "I'm tired of hearing her talk. End it now."

But the girl had stopped, her cheeks wet with tears. Eoghan tapped his staff against the ground, and the tip lit up brighter. But she remained where she was, her hand shaking as she held the magic aloft.

"That's it," I whispered, staring deep into her eyes. Somewhere, deep inside, was a very strong will. "You can fight him the way your mother did."

Something powerful and painful landed in the middle of my stomach, and I doubled over as a scream of pain left my lips. I looked up. Riona was still holding the magic—the spell had come from Eoghan. He actually looked angry with his little fae pet.

Good.

"Then I will do this myself," Eoghan said, gathering another spell in his staff.

But the fae girl took a large step forward, standing between me and him—the power of the stone now pointed at him.

"Is this a bargain?" He chuckled. "You would sacrifice the world for your sister's life?"

I couldn't read her expression, but I could see his, and he knew when he'd been defeated.

"Fine," Eoghan said with a sigh. "You're stronger than your mother, it seems. No one will know to find her down here."

This seemed more amenable to the girl, as she absorbed the magic back into her body and walked forward, yanking me up and dragging me by the arm. I didn't fight, knowing that this was preferable to death. If I were still alive, I could try to escape.

Riona's expressionless eyes were the last thing I saw before the door slammed shut. I spun around, realizing I'd been locked in Cade's room. I ran to the door to jiggle the handle, knowing it was locked and I wouldn't be able to get out anyway but needing to try.

The voices died in the room beyond the door, or perhaps it had just been enchanted so I wouldn't overhear—and perhaps so no one would be able to find me. It didn't matter; no one would be able to hear me all the way down here with all the doors locked.

But I was still alive. And as long as that remained the case, I would do whatever I could to get the stone and free my sister from the clutches of that evil wizard.

Because if I didn't, no one else would.

Chapter Fifty-Two

Ward

I closed my eyes, taking stock of our situation.

Eoghan and Riona were gone with the stone.

Cade and I were stuck in the walls of a cave.

Cade's staff was in a pile of sticks on the ground.

And my wizard friend seemed to have mentally left this realm.

Not the best scenario.

"Cade, buddy," I said, struggling against the rock that surrounded me from the chest down. "Are you still with us?"

"My staff. He destroyed my staff."

"Technically, he made Riona do it," I said, sighing as I rested my head on the rock behind me. "This is great. Can you get us out of here?"

"My staff…"

"Yes, your stupid staff is gone," I said. "Get it together, man. Ayla's in danger."

Even the mention of his precious princess wasn't enough to draw his attention from his obliterated piece of wood, and I tugged harder at my hands until it felt like they might fall off. They weren't budging.

"We have to get back to Pennlan," I said, but even then, it seemed like an unbelievable feat. Assuming we could free ourselves from this cave wall, we were at the very northern tip of the fae realm. It would take us weeks to cross, assuming we didn't die in the wildlands this time, and even longer to reach Pennlan. Eoghan seemed to be able to move much faster.

He was already back in Pennlan. Ayla might already be…

I couldn't think about that. There would be another solution.

"Cade," I said. "Listen to me. You don't need that thing. You saw Eoghan use magic without it. Surely you can learn too, huh? Or we'll find you a new one. It can't be the only staff in the world."

He murmured to himself, his gaze far away.

"Did it break your brain?" I barked. "Grow up. We're the only people who can stop her. You're a damn wizard and I'm…" I shook my head. "I'm going to help you pull yourself back together."

"I'm not a wizard," he said. "Not without my staff. I'm nothing without it."

"You still know magic," I said, a little softer. "And maybe you can try to figure a way out of this rock so we can make an attempt to rescue our princess before your evil wizard master gets ahold of her."

"I didn't know," he said, looking at the ground before something like anger flashed across his face. "But you did. You knew who Riona was."

"I've known for about a day," I said with a sigh. "She made me promise not to tell you. Clearly, she was worried about Eoghan finding out."

His eyes, which had seen a small spark of life for a moment, fell back into desolation. "I can't believe he did this… I can't believe he was able to just show up here. There's so much I don't know…" He closed his eyes. "And I never will—"

"Yes, because your staff is gone," I said, a little exasperatedly. "Focus. How do we get free?"

"I don't know," he said. "I don't know anything."

I let out a growl of frustration and thrashed as much as I could, wincing as my skin tore. But even with my strength, I was no match for the solid wall holding me in place

"So that's it, then? We'll just be stuck here forever? Hopefully a fae monster will come by soon and eat us. Save us the frustration of being in each other's company for much longer." I shook my head. "I knew that wizard couldn't be trusted. Damn him. *Damn* him."

Cade lifted his head, his brow furrowing as he tilted his head upward. "Maybe you'll get your wish sooner than you'd hoped."

I followed his gaze to the sky. A black cloud was headed this way. But as it drew closer, I sensed the reason for his concern. It wasn't a cloud; it was a swarm. Fae.

I tugged harder. The civilized fae would be worse than being eaten by a monster. A monster would simply tear my head off; the fae would torture us for what we'd done, even though we hadn't done it. The pressing concern seemed to have awoken Cade, as he was now trying to release himself from his bonds. But it didn't do either of us any good.

The swarm landed in the center of the clearing, materializing into not one, but *twenty* fae. Among them was Clíodhna, Aldrick, his fae guards and…

If I hadn't known it was the Erlking from the crown on his head, woven from what appeared to be twigs dipped in gold and shimmering even in the scant light, I would've known from the magic that filled the space and drew the breath from my lungs. He seemed ready to fight, and I swallowed hard.

"Where is he?" he said, turning around. "Where…" He spotted us against the cave walls, and where I expected fury, I saw fear. "He took her, didn't he?"

I had no choice but to nod. "We tried to stop him—"

"It isn't him you should've stopped, human," Birch snapped. With a wave of his hand, he released us from the rocky prison, and both Cade and I fell forward onto our hands and knees. I expected the fae king to come for us, but he whirled on those gathered behind him.

"Are you pleased with yourself, Aldrick? Clío? You have brought this horror on our people," he snapped. "This wizard will use the magic to eradicate us, and anyone else who stands in his way. And Riona will be his weapon." He ran a worried hand over his face. "That poor child."

Aldrick looked chastened, but Clíodhna stared firmly at him.

"It was bound to happen sooner or later," she said. "And these two are still here. They can help."

"Can they?" Birch asked. "A human and a broken wizard."

I opened my mouth to argue, but one glance at Cade and I couldn't help but agree with the assessment. The wizard stumbled to the pile of kindling where his staff had once been and knelt before it.

"It's…" he whispered, picking up the pieces. "I can't believe…"

"Believe it," Birch said. "Your master has been a plague on these lands since he appeared, seeking the stone for himself. Leandra knew he was trouble the moment she set eyes on him."

But the wizard wasn't listening, merely picking up pieces of his staff and putting them together. I moved toward him, but the fae king was faster. He placed a comforting hand on Cade's shoulder, squeezing.

"I know it hurts to be betrayed," he said.

"My staff," he whispered, holding up the pieces. "He destroyed my staff."

"What's broken can be replaced," Birch said. "But if you want any chance of saving your princess's life, you must come with us now. There isn't much time to waste."

This mention of Ayla finally seemed to draw Cade from his sorrow, and he nodded, coming to his feet slowly. "What hope do we have against him now? He's got the stone, and Riona is under his control. He can do whatever he wants."

Birch squeezed his shoulder. "As long as your princess draws breath, there is still a chance. But it will require you to trust me."

⤞ ⤞ ⤞ ⤞

I'd never traveled by magic before, and I could honestly say it was something I hoped I'd never experience again. The Erlking's magic surrounded me and lifted me from the ground, carrying me across the fae lands. I wasn't necessarily afraid of heights, but we were up in the clouds, so high up that if the fae decided to drop me, I would be nothing but a splatter on the fields below.

I was heartened that the wizard seemed just as terrified as I was, in the glimpses I got of his face as the magic whirled around the two of us. The fae had turned into their ethereal forms, so I didn't even know which fluttering thing belonged to which person. But I couldn't deny it was much faster than walking.

We crossed the forest we'd tried to pass through on our way to *sidheog* then began to descend toward the ground in slow motion. A large, black stone castle rose in the distance, and my heart beat faster. The fae were taking us to their stronghold.

I thought we would land in a garden, perhaps a small space outside the castle. But the swarm continued toward the castle, showing no signs of slowing down. As we drew closer, it looked like we would make a direct hit on the hard stone, and I prayed the fae remembered they had a weak human in their midst.

The castle drew up on us and I closed my eyes, bracing for impact. But when impact didn't happen, I weakly opened my eyes then straightened in shock. I was standing in a large room that looked appropriate for strategizing. Maps of the fae lands hung from the walls, framed by statues wearing fae armor, and in the center of the room was a circular table.

"Are you going to sit?" Aldrick asked, a smirk on his face. "Or are you still about to wet yourself?"

"I wouldn't be so cocky, considering the Erlking has stripped you of your guardianship," Clíodhna said as she passed him.

Aldrick scowled. "And you're the one who gave them a map to the stone."

"I'm not under the Erlking's purview," she replied with a catty look.

"Clío," Birch said, interrupting them. "Take the wizard to the grove to find a new familiar."

For not being under his purview, she did as she was told, putting her hand on Cade's shoulder and turning him. "Come with me, boy."

"Where are we going?" he said, looking at me nervously before they disappeared through the door.

"Human." The Erlking was speaking to me now. "Come closer. We don't have much time."

"Is Eoghan back in the castle?" I asked. "What about Ayla?"

"I don't know. My spies can only get so far before they're disintegrated by the wizard's magic. I wish I could give you more before I send you into the lion's den."

Send you. "You mean to tell me you aren't coming?" I asked. "Why the hell not?"

The fae around us shifted, as if ready to throttle me, but the Erlking settled into his chair.

"Could you imagine what that wizard could do if he managed to control *me*?" Birch asked, but there was little heat in his words. "Likewise, if I were to send twenty of my best fae warriors with you, he could turn them against me." He sighed. "As much as you might think otherwise, it's better for you and the wizard to go alone."

I could see his logic, but it still seemed…hopeless. "What can we do against him?"

"You and the wizard managed to outwit my maze and the griffin, not to mention travel through the most dangerous parts of the fae realm," Birch said, tilting his head to the side. "You are also supposedly one of the best warriors in Princess Ayla's guard."

That was all true, but I'd seen what that stone could do.

"Your weakness will be to your benefit," Birch said. "The two of you will be able to sneak into the castle much easier and find the princess. She is the key to stopping Eoghan."

"Get the stone to her," I said. "Easier said than done."

"I didn't say it would be easy. I simply told you what you should do."

"And what if Eoghan has killed her already?" I asked. "Or kills us?"

"If you fail," Birch continued, "Eoghan will spread across these lands like a plague. He will not stop with the humans—he will find his way to the fae realm, through the human kingdoms, and beyond. He will be unstoppable."

"So no pressure," I muttered. "Eoghan has complete control over Riona, you know. Getting the stone out of her hand is going to be damn near impossible."

"His control is not complete, not as long as the fae has some fight," Birch said, his gaze growing sad. "And that my grandchild has in spades. I have faith she will do her best to help—even under his total control."

Chapter Fifty-Three

Cade

I was somewhat convinced the past few hours had been a dream. That somehow, I'd slipped into a nightmare where Eoghan had turned into a stranger and destroyed my most sacred possession, that he'd taken possession of Riona and the stone, and, most unbelievably, Ward and I had flown across the lands that we'd just spent weeks walking through to land in the castle of the Erlking.

But as I followed the *sidheog* queen into a small grove outside the castle, pinching myself repeatedly, I slowly came to accept that perhaps this was all…really happening.

"I can't believe Eoghan…" I said. "He *raised* me."

"He *stole* you from your home would be my guess," Clíodhna said, stopping to look at me. "Don't fret, child. He's hoodwinked mages far more powerful than you. Eoghan has lived longer than any man should. When he appeared in these lands, he was already too knowledgeable about the *seod croí* for his own good—and the mastery of magic he held was far beyond what any mortal wizard could have learned in their years."

Your knowledge is as deep as a piece of paper. "So it's hopeless."

"With that attitude, sure," Clíodhna said with a scowl. "But one thing you will have that he won't is a true familiar, the kind that comes from the Erlking himself. That will allow you to tap into the kind of magic you've never known before, and might be enough to change your fate against your master."

Might. "The book I have…" I reached into my bag, still slung around my shoulder and flipped the book open to the page I'd dog-eared to show her. "It talked about such a grove in this castle, but I hadn't believed it. Are you telling me that everything in this book is…real?"

"Where did you get this?" Clíodhna asked softly, gazing down at the book with curiosity.

"I found it in a library in the human realm." I looked up at her. "Why? Where is it from?"

"Little trickster," Clíodhna said, running her hand across the pages. "This came from the Erlking's library. Riona must've cast glamour on it to entice you to take it."

So I was right. "Why give it to me?"

"Perhaps she wanted you to know more than your master told you," she said. "And knew that if it came from her lips, you wouldn't believe it."

That was true. It had taken me a while to even feel comfortable sleeping around her—and had the book been in its true form in the human realm, I would've probably burned it. But a history of wizard lore? I'd practically salivated at the chance to read more about my kind.

She was rather clever, that Riona.

"The glamour must've faded, or perhaps she realized it was time to reveal the truth to you." Clíodhna tilted her head. "Did you discuss it with her?"

"No, I was…" I couldn't even justify my own behavior. Not now.

"It takes time to overcome the prejudices our mentors imprint in our brains," Clíodhna replied. "But if you are over yours, you must find a new familiar. We don't have much time."

We walked through the grove, but I got the distinct impression Clíodhna was waiting for me to do something.

"How do I pick one?" I asked, looking at the trees.

"You don't pick it, it picks you," she said. "I'm just waiting for one of the trees to call your name."

"Will I hear it or…?"

She grew silent, smiling as we strolled through the grove. There had to be at least a hundred trees here, different sizes and shapes, all of them…magic.

"Back in the *sidheog* lands, you told us about the stone." I swallowed, unsure if she'd talk to me about it. "About a battle that eradicated all the wizards."

"Not just a battle."

"But it took place in the *aos sí*, didn't it?" I replied. "I saw it… The griffin gave me a vision when she was trying to bewitch me to stay in her challenge."

Clíodhna smirked. "You managed to resist the charms of Niamh? I'm actually impressed."

"Friends help," I said, embarrassed at the way Ward and Riona had practically dragged me out of there. "This wizard, the one you said killed every other wizard and broke blood lines…that wasn't Eoghan, was it?"

"Of course not. That wizard is long since dead," she said. "But the damage he did lingers. Now quit talking and go find your familiar."

She pushed me forward to walk alone, and I wasn't sure what I was looking for. Eventually, I lost her in the grove, meandering aimlessly from one end to the other. Clíodhna seemed to have faith I would find something, or something might find me, but I didn't. I wasn't even from this land—why would an ash tree grown in the fae realm call to *me*? What could—

I stopped short. *Something* was calling to me. Something soft and sweet, like my mother's almost-forgotten voice. I walked away from the sidheog queen, pressing my hand to each of the trees as I searched for the source of the sound.

I couldn't explain why the tree spoke so clearly to me, or why I knew that it was the one. But with it in my hands, I would become much more powerful.

"Once upon a time," Clíodhna murmured, appearing behind me. "Wizards and fae weren't so dissimilar. It was a fae who gave a wizard their first staff from an ash tree, who showed them how to harness the power untapped in their veins. That tradition was lost when the stone was forged, and wizards became powerful in their own right. This ash forest was protected by the Erlking to make sure only the worthiest wizards were able to gain a staff."

She opened her hands, and the tree lifted from the ground, roots and all, floating a few feet above us. Clíodhna's eyes were closed, but her hands moved in the air as if she were touching the tree itself. It shrank and turned and changed, the roots crawling back up into the trunk, the limbs shrinking as well. And then the thick trunk began to morph and twist in the air, growing smaller and thinner until it fashioned itself into a staff.

It was simple, but beautiful. No markings or carvings adorned this piece of wood, but there didn't need to be. It was magnificent as it was.

"Here."

She placed the staff in my hand and I couldn't help the breath that left my chest. My old staff was a distant memory now—this beautiful artistry was *made* for me. Whereas before, I had to ask and bargain with my magic to do what I wanted, this staff simply took my suggestion and ran with it. I conjured a ball of magic with ease, more powerful than I'd ever made before. I was humbled by my own ignorance, wishing I could stay in that grove for years to learn everything that had been from me.

Clíodhna beamed. "You may find yourself more capable without the shadow of your master standing over you."

⇥ ⇥ ⇥ ⇥

I followed Clíodhna back to the castle, but I stayed one step behind, mesmerized by my staff and the freedom it provided. No longer would it slip from my grasp in a battle, the staff *wanted* to stay with me at all times. Someone would have to sever my hand to get it off.

Ward and another fae were waiting at the front gates of the castle, and the knight quirked a brow at me. "Why are you grinning like an idiot?"

"Because he's been given a wondrous gift," Clíodhna said with an appraising smile. "What advice has the Erlking given you about Eoghan?"

My good mood evaporated. Eoghan. Riona. *Ayla*. This staff was going to get a trial by fire almost immediately.

"Not much," Ward said. "This fae will drop us off in the village as close as he can get, but after that…it's up to us."

"That's not a great start," I said. "Eoghan might've enchanted the whole place to keep us out."

Clíodhna looked at the fae. "The wizard will handle himself."

"I don't…" I shook my head. "I don't even know anything about —"

"And that's your first lesson," the fae queen said with a knowing smirk. "You will no longer be studying to learn what you can about your magic. You will just use it. If you want to fly, you will fly. If you want to break the enchantment, break the enchantment. We will begin the process of undoing the nonsense your master instilled in your mind today."

I opened and closed my mouth, looking at Ward, whose eyebrows rose. "Did I miss something?" he asked.

"If you survive," she said to me, "you should return to the fae realm to learn under a real tutor. A power such as yours shouldn't be hidden away under the mediocrity of a poor teacher." She bowed her head. "And for what it's worth, I hope you survive. I'd like to see the sort of mage you become one day."

And with that, the fae queen disappeared in a burst of snowflakes.

"What… Did she just offer to teach you?" Ward said, rubbing his forehead.

"I think she did," I replied.

"Are you going to take her up on it?"

"I don't…"

"Perhaps you should focus on surviving first," the grumpy fae behind us said. "And the clock is ticking—it will take some time to reach the human realm and our final destination."

I nodded and gripped my staff, the magic flowing between me and it so very perfectly. The fae said nothing as he put his hand on Ward's shoulder, lifting him off the ground in a swarm of what appeared to be conjured bluebirds. They were high in the air before I realized the fae would give me no instruction.

"If you want to fly, fly."

I exhaled and called upon my magic—and to my surprise, my feet lifted from the ground. Magic surrounded my entire body, making me weightless as I rose higher and higher. And with a simple thought, I turned to follow the knight and fae into the air.

The lands that we'd traveled on foot, spending weeks of bickering, pain, and sleepless nights flew by hundreds of feet below us. It was somewhat unfair that I'd had this power the whole time, I'd just lacked the proper familiar.

I wanted more—to take this magic as far as the horizon and to the heavens above. It was intoxicating, perhaps a little dangerous. It was clear why the fae wanted to keep this under lock and key. And perhaps a testament to how much they trusted me—or how desperate they really were.

I put aside all excited thoughts of training under Clíodhna as we flew over the border town of Críoch. How very easily the fae moved from this realm to the next. All the preconceived notions of Pennlan's security vanished. We had always been vulnerable to them. Though my thinking had somewhat shifted on the danger they posed.

The sun was rising in the east, casting a beautiful glow across the green fields beneath us—and Pennlan Castle rose in the horizon. My heart twisted at the sight, emotion welling in the back of my throat. Home. How long had I been praying I could get back there? To sleep in my bed, to walk the gardens with Ayla. To no longer have to spend the day walking miles through unfamiliar and dangerous lands.

But home would never feel the same again. Eoghan had made sure that everything I'd ever held dear would be irrevocably changed. And if he hurt Ayla, *I* would make sure he regretted it.

Chapter Fifty-Four

Ward

Cade seemed permanently enamored with his new stick—and I wasn't exactly sure why he could suddenly fly—but as Pennlan castle became visible, I bore down on the task ahead and began to formulate a plan.

We had a wizard in the castle who had a fae girl with an all-powerful stone—and Riona was pretty damn powerful in his own right.

The only way we'd survive the day was if we got the stone from Riona to Ayla, and Ayla used it to destroy the wizard.

It all seemed like a long shot, but we had no other choice. We weren't—I hoped—completely alone. I didn't know what Eoghan had done or said to Gabhann or the rest of the royal guards, whether they'd fallen in line under their new sovereign or decided to fight back. For this vague plan I was forming in my mind to work, we would need numbers, not necessarily magical skill. I was banking on Eoghan being unable to defend himself against a swarm of human force.

And if he somehow could…well, we'd figure it out from there.

We descended in the village near the castle, the wizard right behind us. Dawn was coming, but it was still very early. There didn't seem to be a soul out and about yet—or perhaps they were just too scared to leave their homes. It would make getting close to the castle easy.

My feet touched solid ground, and I exhaled in relief. The fae hadn't said one word to me since we'd left the Erlking's castle, his face a permanent scowl of distrust.

"Thanks for the ride. Next time, I think I'll take the horse," I said with a friendly smile.

But he was immovable, a frown on his face as he stared at the castle. "This is as far as I can take you. Best of luck—the entire fae race is counting on you."

Before I could respond, he disappeared in a column of birds and rose back into the sky.

"Thanks…" I said, quirking a brow as Cade came up beside me. "So what's the deal with your new toy?"

He scowled. "It's not a toy."

"Fine, staff."

"Just another piece to the puzzle Eoghan was content to keep from me," he said with a wistful sigh.

"What's that supposed to mean?"

"It means that I'm ready to get into the castle and use it on him," Cade snapped.

"What happened to the man who thought every word out of a fae's mouth was a lie?" I asked. "That everything they did was a trap? How do you know this staff isn't some fae trick?"

"Did you not just see me *fly* here?" He gestured to the sky behind us. "Besides that, my opinion shifted somewhat when the man I thought I trusted melded us to a cave wall, and the fae Erlking released us instead of killing us."

I couldn't argue with that logic and started walking toward the castle. "I've got something of a plan, unless you have a better one."

"I'm all ears."

"Find Gabhann first," I said. "Find out what lies Eoghan's told her and hopefully convince her to help us instead. She's loyal to Ayla."

He nodded. "She's always been a good ally. But what are we going to do with the royal guard? Eoghan could blast them into next year without breaking a sweat."

"Then let's not mention that," I said, picking up the pace again.

"So we're sending them in to die?"

I stopped and turned on him fully. "I don't think you understand. We *all* will if we don't stop him here and now. Besides that…" I gazed up at the castle again. "Somehow I don't think he's as powerful as he lets on. Somewhere in there, Riona's still fighting him. She's a stubborn little…"

"That she is…" Cade muttered. "First thing I'm doing when I see her again is apologizing. Clearly, I was fearing the wrong type of magical user."

We continued the rest of the way in silence until we reached the large wall surrounding the castle. There was a single, guarded door that connected the garrison to the village outside the castle. Thankfully, I recognized the man on duty.

"Morning, Chuck," I said, waving at him.

His eyes bugged out of his head. "W-Ward? Son of a bitch, is that you?" He stepped forward and clapped me on the shoulder in greeting. "We thought you were dead. Did you come from the fae realm? Did you find the stone?"

"So news hasn't spread," Cade said behind me. "We need to speak with Captain Gabhann immediately."

"Of course, of course." Chuck stepped aside and let us walk in. "She's in her room, probably."

I led the way, doubling my pace. What lies Eoghan had told about our journey, I could only guess, but if they thought us dead, seeing us alive might earn us some more trust in our wild story. Gabhann's room was at the end of the barracks, which had already started to come to life with the dawn. I stood in front of her door and rapped hurriedly.

A moment later, she opened the door, already dressed and ready for the day. "W-Ward? Is that you?"

"Yes, ma'am," I said, nearly forgetting to salute her. "I apologize for the early intrusion. But it's important we speak with you."

She waved us inside then shut the door behind her and pulled her sword.

I jumped back three feet, holding up my hands. "Ma'am?"

"Prove to me you aren't glamoured fae," she said, the end of her sword inching closer to my body. "Give me some sign."

"I'm not a glamoured fae," I said, looking at Cade, who was similarly confused. "I came here from Críoch—"

"All things a fae would know."

Cade stepped up, conjuring a fireball and flinging it at her desk then just as quickly, reversed it as if nothing had happened. "How about that? I'm a wizard. I can't be mimicked."

I didn't know how true that was, but it seemed to calm the good captain somewhat. "Then where the *hell* have you two been? We expected you back from Críoch weeks ago."

That story wasn't an easy one to tell, but I thought it best to be upfront and honest about everything. To her credit, Gabhann listened without interrupting, though her brows rose a few times—especially as I told her about Eoghan arriving in the fae realm, and the truths he told us there.

"He has often asked for soldiers," she said with a shake of her head. "Said he was sending them to Caecarcem."

"I don't think such a prison actually exists," Cade said. "At least, the garrison commander at Críoch had never heard of it."

"So there is a fae girl in the castle now, the half-sister of the princess?" she said. "And she's completely under Eoghan's control?"

"I know it sounds far-fetched," I said. "But it's the truth. On my honor."

"It certainly explains a few things," she said. "Namely why Eoghan asked every knight to vacate the castle last night. Said he was casting a few spells to protect it from the enemy in advance of Her Majesty's coronation."

"So there's not a single guard inside the castle right now?" I asked, a little shocked that she would allow such a thing.

"No, but believe me, I argued my point," she said. "There's only so much I can do against the wizard before that staff begins to glow ominously."

"That makes this a little more difficult, but not impossible," I said. "Eoghan is powerful as long as he has Riona and the stone, but if we can get the stone away from him and into Ayla's hands, we have a chance. The fae told us they suspect he's got her locked in the basement."

"Vault," Cade corrected. "He has all sorts of charms and enchantments to keep out unwanted intruders, so it's probably the most secure place."

"This is going to be a two-pronged attack," I said, nodding at him. "Cade, you go find Ayla and bring her to wherever Eoghan and the stone are. Your job is to protect her at all costs."

He furrowed his brow, as if confused by something, but nodded.

"Captain, you, me, and the rest of the forces will infiltrate the castle," I said.

"And do what?" she asked. "What hope does a contingent of humans have against a wizard?"

"If we're lucky, it'll be enough of a distraction that I can get the stone from Riona to Ayla," I said, looking at the wizard.

"This sounds all very iffy," Cade said. "Eoghan will probably see through all of it. Why not leave Ayla in the vault until we have the stone?"

"Because I don't think we'll have much time after getting the stone from Riona. There's going to be a lot of improvising." I surveyed him. "Do you think you can handle keeping her safe?"

He stared at me for a moment. "Eoghan will engage me, most likely. You know that, right? I don't see how I can protect Ayla and defend myself at the same time."

"You've got that nice, new stick," I replied. "I'm sure you'll figure it out."

⤞ ⤞ ⤞ ⤞

We didn't have much time to lose, so I led Cade out from the garrison and onto the greens, assuming he could find his way from there. But he hadn't taken more than a few steps outside the garrison before he turned to me, a curious look on his face.

"What is it?" I asked.

"I'm just surprised you want me to be the one to rescue Ayla."

I blinked, rubbing my face and hoping the fae hadn't addled his brain. "Yes, we've gone over this—"

"No," he waved his hand, "what I mean is… You don't want to be the hero?"

I stared at him, a little incredulous. "In what way?"

"Ayla's going to be overjoyed to see whoever opens the door in the vault and lets her out," he said, deadly serious. "I just… I would've thought you would've wanted it to be you. Since you like her and all."

Not this again. "You mean because I spent one evening in the garden with her?"

"You agreed to go on a dangerous quest to retrieve the stone for her," Cade said. "And I saw the way you looked at her. I guess… I'm just wondering why you're letting me get all the glory?"

I couldn't believe what I was hearing, so I walked up to him and leaned in close. "Are you seriously asking me this?"

"I am."

"You do realize there's a dangerous wizard in there, right? And we are all risking almost certain death for this idiotic plan?"

"Well, yes, but—"

"Then I don't have time to be petty about who gets to save the princess," I said. "My job is to rally the troops and get the stone from Riona. Your job is to unlock all those enchantments in the vault, get Ayla, then help us stay alive against Eoghan. I don't have magic—you do." I sighed. "And even if I liked her as much as you say I do, I would rather stick her with the person most apt to keep her safe."

He nodded. "I suppose I'll see you up there."

I clapped his shoulder and shook his hand. "And if I don't, it was a pleasure traveling with you."

"Agreed." He squeezed my hand. "Hope we never have to do it again."

"You said it."

And with that, I left him there. Forget being the hero, I was just hoping we'd all make it to nightfall.

Chapter Fifty-Five

Cade

Never had the castle seemed so intimidating. There was a new aura around it, something more than magic. My pulse pounded in my ears, and I braced myself to fight against a man who'd gone from father figure to stranger in a matter of hours.

The staff in my hand gave me some false confidence. Sure, magic was coming easier, and it seemed I could do more, but if Clíodhna was to be believed, Eoghan had lived several lives to my less-than-quarter of one. He'd conjured a doorway from Pennlan to the top of the fae realm with ease, and he seemed to know details about magic I could only guess at.

My path to Ayla started at the kitchen door, which I found not just locked but *magically* so. Eoghan's fingerprints were all over it, too. He must've been prepared for a magical user to attempt the castle because the lock was so intricate and complicated, it made my head spin.

But Clíodhna's words in my mind soothed my panic, and I placed my hand on the knob, magic flowing from me. It was similar to the lock I'd untangled in her castle, another reminder that fae and wizard magic weren't as different as I'd been told. Another in a long list of things I was having to relearn.

The lock clicked under my hand, and I smiled. Undoing a lock wasn't the same as defeating an old wizard, but at least this first challenge hadn't stumped me. Perhaps there was hope for me yet.

Once inside, I moved quickly. Eoghan had cleared the castle of people, and I didn't even see a scullery maid in the kitchen. From there, I went down the main hallway, keeping my footfalls light as I listened for sounds. As I approached the throne room, the hair on my arms stood.

Eoghan—and the stone—were there.

I pressed myself against the wall and listened, hearing nothing. But they *were* in there. Eoghan didn't have to communicate verbally to order Riona around, and she wasn't in any position to respond. With a soft sigh, I released a spell to the garrison where Ward and Gabhann were waiting. In my mind's eye, I picked up the quill on her desk and wrote, *Throne room* then let it drop.

Hopefully, it would be enough. Because I had bigger problems. There was only one way in and out of the vault, and it was right past the throne room. I couldn't continue without being seen.

I searched for some spell Eoghan had taught me and came up short. But perhaps I could take a page from his book anyway.

I stepped away from the wall and held out my staff, remembering what Clíodhna had said. *"If you want to do something, do it."*

I envisioned the spot just beyond the vault, an easier target than trying to conjure a doorway inside. Then I cast a spell toward the air just beyond me. Gold magic slipped from the tip of my staff, forming a spinning circle that grew larger and larger.

And to my surprise, the front door of the vault was on the other side.

"Riona, bring that to me."

I jumped, remembering that Eoghan and Riona were on the other side of the wall. I didn't have time to admire my own handiwork, so I stepped through and closed it behind me, exhaling loudly. I'd have to practice that more—assuming I survived the day.

Much like the front door of the castle, the vault was covered in locks and enchantments that only Eoghan could open—but he'd given me access to them as well. I unlocked the door and stepped inside. It looked and smelled of home, and for a brief moment, I let myself sigh in relief.

My bedroom door was closed, but immediately I heard someone screaming for help. I rushed forward, finding another—though this time very basic—magical lock. Holding my breath, I pulled it open.

"H—" Ayla had been mid-bang, and her beautiful eyes widened significantly when she saw me. My heart nearly burst from joy at seeing her unscathed, just *seeing* her again. She was magnificent.

"C-Cade?" She breathed, taking a step back. "It… Is it really you?"

All I could do was nod dumbly. "I'm here."

She took a step forward then practically jumped into my arms, clinging to me as if we were adrift at sea. Her body shook with sobs of relief, and I almost joined her, tangling my hands in her auburn hair and holding her tightly to me. The journey, the tribulations, the sleepless nights—every bit of it was worth it just to hold her like this.

"It's about time you showed up," she said, standing upright and wiping her eyes. "I was starting to think I'd have to save myself."

"I'm sure you could," I said with a half-smile. "Are you all right?"

"I don't know," she said. "Cade, tell me it isn't true. That girl, she can't be…"

"Riona?" I tilted my head. "Ayla, she can use the stone. I think that's a pretty good indication of her lineage."

"She saved my life," she said, turning away from me. "Eoghan was going to have her kill me, and she refused. Then he tried to do it himself, and she…" She shuddered. "Eoghan said she would bargain the whole world for my life."

I rested my hand on her shoulder, squeezing. "She's… Well, she's a pain in the ass. But she's a good person. A lot like you, actually."

She half-smiled. "I suppose I may have to rethink my hatred of all fae."

"You and me both," I said, already imagining what she'd say when I told her who rescued us from Eoghan's spell. "Look, as much as I want to tell you *everything*, we don't have time right now. Ward—"

"Ward?" Her eyes lit up, and I buried the pang of jealousy. "Ward is here, too?"

"He's with Gabhann. They're going to help us."

"Help us do what?"

But the scent of honey crossed my nose, and I flipped around, covering Ayla's body with my own, my staff lit up and ready. Not a moment later, Riona appeared a few steps from us, the stone in her hand, her dark, lifeless eyes unfamiliar.

"Come with me." Even her voice sounded wrong.

"N-No!" Ayla said, over my shoulder. "Cade, do something."

"I am," I said, lowering my staff. "We're going with her."

"But—"

"Trust me on this," I said, eyeing the stone in her hand. "We're better off complying. For now."

>→ >→ >→ >→

"So you managed to escape the cave?"

Eoghan looked very much at home on Ayla's throne. The only thing he was missing was her crown, but I assumed her tiara was too small for his large head. I held my staff tightly in my hand, keeping Ayla's body touching mine. Ward's direction to me was on repeat in my mind, *protect Ayla, protect Ayla, protect Ayla.* I assumed they'd wanted more time to rouse and arm the guard. I'd only given them minutes.

"I asked you a question, apprentice," Eoghan said.

"I think you lost your ability to call me that when you tried to kill me," I replied icily.

"I did nothing of the sort," he said. "I sent you on a dangerous journey. You survived, just like I thought you would."

"Liar," Ayla barked behind me. "You told me you expected him to die."

He ignored her, his gaze landing on my staff. "Where did you get that?"

"Picked it up off the ground."

Eoghan reached out, and I felt the tug of his summoning magic on my staff. But unlike before, where he could summon my staff at will, it remained in my hand, magically linked to my body. He narrowed his gaze and tried again, and when the staff didn't move, he let out a long breath.

"It seems you've been making some powerful friends," he said softly. "Did the Erlking come looking for his progeny? Will he be making an appearance tonight, or is he content to cower in his castle?"

I kept my mouth shut, hoping Eoghan's grousing would buy Ward and Gabhann more time to get in position.

"So you've decided to be taciturn," he said. "It doesn't matter. Even the mighty King Birch is no match for the power I now hold—and the power I will hold."

Will... "What do you mean?"

He summoned the stone from Riona's hand, holding up the gem with two fingers so it sparkled in the light. "You and I have been misled by the fae, boy. This jewel is merely one piece of what I'd been told was the *seod croí*, Laughlan's stone."

I narrowed my gaze. "What are you talking about?"

But he smiled, the same way he would when he was about to teach me some obvious life lesson. "There are *four* gems, each exactly like this one. Put together, *that* is the stone of legend, the *seod croí*—the stone Laughlan used to bring this entire realm to—"

Something whizzed through the air—an arrow—and knocked the stone from his hand.

"You talk too much," Ward said, appearing from behind one of the hanging tapestries. Almost instantly, the room filled with knights from doors seemingly out of nowhere—all of them holding bows and arrows pointed at Eoghan.

"Cade..." Ayla whispered.

"Don't worry," I said, taking her hand and squeezing it. "Just stay close. We have a plan."

But Eoghan merely smiled, sending chills down my spine. "This is pathetic. So now you've turned on me, Captain?"

The good captain stood in the doorway, her old eyes on fire. "It was you who betrayed Pennlan first."

I only had seconds to react as Eoghan cast a barrage of fireballs toward the guards, conjuring a spell to block most of them. But he was still faster, and half the knights fell to the ground.

Ward, one of the few I'd managed to protect, nodded, pulling his sword and stepping forward bravely. But against a wizard like Eoghan, he'd be dead in seconds—they all would.

"Let me handle him," I said to Ward, releasing Ayla's hand. "You stick to the plan."

"Oh, and what is this brilliant plan?" Eoghan asked. "Will you face me, apprentice, using what little skills I allowed you to learn, and defeat me? Is your new staff so powerful it will let you overcome your lack of knowledge?"

I let his criticisms roll off my back, magic pooling in my staff as I crossed the room toward him. Out of the corner of my eye, I saw the knights dash over to Ayla to protect her, and Ward was making his way toward Riona. She hadn't done much except stand there—Eoghan couldn't manipulate her and fight at the same time.

I hoped.

Eoghan stood facing me, clearly waiting for me to make the first move. I fired off a warning shot that he deflected without breaking a sweat.

"Is that all you have?"

I conjured another, but he was faster—so much faster. He moved in the blink of an eye, and it was all I could do to keep myself from flying across the room. Magic lit up the room, flying this way and that. I had to hope the guards had enough sense to avoid it, because I couldn't protect them and myself at the same time.

"Your new staff is impressive," Eoghan said. "You aren't nearly as disappointing as you have been."

I met his latest volley with one of my own, and together they careened toward the ceiling, blasting a hole in the rock. "Imagine what happens when a wizard has a staff that is *actually* meant for them, instead of someone else's castoff."

He narrowed his eyes. "Is that what the fae told you?"

I fired off another, this one actually making it past his defenses and glancing against his shoulder. "It's what I've seen with my own eyes. The world isn't as you described it to me. But somehow, I think that's been your plan all along. Construct a reality that suits your needs."

"You're catching on."

We exchanged another volley of magic, but I began to realize that Eoghan was merely toying with me. My power had become stronger, more focused with the new staff, but against Eoghan, it still wasn't enough. Given enough time, he would grow tired of playing with me.

But it wasn't about defeating him. I just had to distract him so Ward could get the stone.

CHAPTER FIFTY-SIX

WARD

Cade and Eoghan's light show was impressive enough, but I had my marching orders. The wizards would keep each other busy, and hopefully, Eoghan's hold on Riona would be lessened enough that I could pry that damned jewel from her hands.

I scanned the room, now full of broken stone and scattered, injured knights. Riona stood in the corner, holding the gem in her hand and staring off into space as if she were a doll. A fresh surge of hatred rose from my gut. She was many things—a pain in the ass, a half-fae overcompensating for her perceived weaknesses, an innocent kid who just wanted to help—but above all, she was fiercely independent.

Cade cried out in pain as he flew backward, stopping himself before he slammed into the wall. Even with his new stick, he wouldn't last very long.

I kept myself against the wall as much as I could, hoping to avoid being seen as I made my way toward Riona. I wasn't twenty feet from her when a column of white butterflies zoomed toward me. I twisted out of the way then had to twist the other way when she fired another one.

"So now you want to show me your magic?" I muttered, shaking my head.

Riona's dark eyes were focused on me now, though there was no emotion there. Eoghan had a tight grip on her, but she was a fighter.

I walked toward her slowly, holding my hands out. "Riona, can you hear me?"

Another volley of butterflies. This time, they caught the edge of my tunic, tearing it.

"Riona," I tried again. "It's me. You know who I am. You can fight this magic."

"I said to *take care of him*," Eoghan barked.

But the attack was another flock of butterflies, barely a tickle. Behind the lifeless eyes, she was still fighting. Still trying to help.

"I see you," I said with a nod. "Can you give me the stone?"

She hesitated, as if warring with the wizard as plainly as Cade was. She took a staggering step forward, holding out her hand with the stone in it. Her cheeks had grown red with exertion.

"That's it," I whispered. "C'mon, Riona, you can fight him. The same way your mother did."

A spark of green flashed across her eyes, and the stone was close enough for me to reach. I dove for it, but she disappeared in a puff of butterflies to the other side of the room, looking unbothered.

Eoghan sniffed angrily, and my stomach churned uncomfortably. He'd caught onto our plan.

I cursed under my breath and jumped to my feet. The other knights in the room attempted to grab the stone, but Riona would simply disappear and reappear. Eoghan didn't have to try hard to keep her from us—but he did have to pay attention while deflecting blows from Cade.

"If you don't think I can handle *all* of you, I've surely taught you nothing, apprentice." Eoghan conjured a massive fireball. "And now you've left your princess defenseless."

"*Ward! Grab her!*"

I dashed toward Ayla, magic at my heels pushing me faster than I'd ever run in my life. I tackled her just as the spell landed inches from where she'd been standing. I covered her body with mine as pebbles and dust rained down on my back, becoming aware of her labored breathing in my ear. When the barrage stopped, I carefully lifted my head, staring into those wide green eyes that had entranced me in the garden all those weeks ago.

"Are you okay?" I asked.

She half-smiled. "I'm fine. Thank you for saving me."

"Anytime. I—" I heard a loud crack above our heads and saw a piece of ceiling stone falling toward us. I grabbed her shoulders and rolled us out of the way; this time, she landed on top.

"Thanks again," she said, a little breathlessly. She got to her knees and held out her hand to help me up as she watched the chaos around us.

Eoghan and Cade were locked in what looked like an epic wizard battle, but based on Eoghan's smirk, it didn't appear Cade was going to win the day. The other knights were helping their fallen compatriots, and some were trying to make their way over to me. Riona stood in the corner, watching the fight without even the slightest hint of concern.

"We have to get the stone," I said.

"I don't even know what I'd do with it," Ayla replied softly.

"You'll know," I said, hoping I sounded confident. "Remember, you're not an ornament."

She flashed me a smile, and warmth shot from every inch of my body. But when she turned back to the scene before us, she was all business. "We can't hurt her. Riona, I mean. She's innocent."

"She'll hurt us first," I said, coming to my feet and helping her up.

Two knights rushed over to us, taking Ayla by the elbows. "Your Majesty, we need to get you out of here."

"No," Ayla said with a firm shake of her head. "Help Ward get the stone from Riona. Then get it to me."

They looked at me for disagreement but I turned on my heel. "You heard Her Majesty. I'll work on the fae girl. You two keep Ayla safe until I can get the stone to her."

They nodded and took her to a safer location, farther away from the flying spells. Cade was looking even more tired; he didn't have much more than he'd already given, not even with his new magic stick. He was running out of options—as were we all.

I spotted a bow and quiver of arrows lying near an unconscious guard and was struck with an idea. I dashed toward it, grabbing the quiver and putting it over my shoulder. Immediately, I released three arrows at Eoghan's head. They wouldn't do much, but they might help Cade gain the upper hand.

He deflected them with ease, but it did earn me a snarl of annoyance. A good start.

But he had Riona, I remembered almost too late. As butterflies came toward me, I scampered out of the way, grabbing another quiver from another fallen comrade and firing the arrows at Eoghan as I ran to avoid Riona's attacks. When that quiver was empty, I spotted another and dashed toward it.

Before I could get three steps, a fireball charred the ground in front of me. Eoghan snarled, able to conjure a shield to protect himself from Cade's attacks as he turned his attention to me.

"You've become a nuisance," he said. "All of you."

"Good," I replied, diving for the quiver once more. But Eoghan conjured another giant fireball destined for Ayla—and this time, I was too far to do anything about it.

Almost too late, a bright gold forcefield appeared in front of her—Cade had conjured one. But the distraction seemed to be the point, as Eoghan's spell landed in Cade's midsection and flung him backward toward the wall. He landed with a sickening thud, snapping his head against the stone wall then slipped down, a trail of blood behind him.

"*Cade!*" Ayla screamed.

I held my breath, waiting for him to get up, to shake it off, but he remained on the ground with his eyes closed. "C'mon, Cade, get up," I whispered. "Get up."

Eoghan chuckled, adjusting his sleeve as if everything had gone according to plan. "It was a valiant effort."

I lifted my bow and arrow once more. "I'm not done with you yet, wizard."

"What can your human weapons do against me?"

I didn't care, firing off another arrow that he dismissed with a wave of his staff. I wasn't going to die without a fight, even if it was useless.

"Pathetic," he said. "You should've stayed in that cave."

I fired another one, my second-to-last. "Probably, but then I wouldn't get the heroic death I've been angling for."

"Is it really heroic to die when you had no hope?" he asked. "The Erlking will be so disappointed in your performance."

I fired off my last arrow, which was easily deflected. Then, with nothing left except my blade, I pulled it from its sheath and stared at him, ready for his final blow.

Eoghan just shook his head. "It's a pity you won't stand down. I might even spare your life if you do. I could use someone stupid and loyal like you." He tilted his head toward me. "But I can see we're at an impasse." He conjured a fireball above his staff. "And there's no one in this world or the next who can stop me."

"I can."

CHAPTER FIFTY-SEVEN

AYLA

I'd watched the fight from a distance, wanting to help, but knowing that my part in this play was to remain alive long enough for them to retrieve the stone. But Cade wasn't moving, and if I didn't do something, Ward and everyone else in the room would soon be dead.

"You aren't an ornament."

"Your Majesty," Donnegan said, as I gently shook off their tense grip on my arms, "where are you going?"

"Stay close," I said. "I'm getting what's mine."

It was easy to slip around the room unnoticed. Ward was firing arrows at Eoghan, and the other knights were scrambling to catch the fae girl who kept disappearing and reappearing in a different spot. I hid behind a tapestry, waiting for the opportune moment.

And when Riona appeared less than a foot from me, I made my move, grabbing the stone from her hands.

The throne room disappeared, bathed in a bright blue light as I was mentally transported to another place. A beautiful cacophony of voices filled my ears—songs and legends of my ancestors. They whispered the secrets of the stone, the depths of its power, the instructions for how a sovereign such as myself could use it to protect her people.

The vision faded and I was back in the throne room.

"…no one in this world or the next who can stop me."

"I can."

The words had come from somewhere deep in my soul, and I felt no fear as I walked toward my enemy in the center of the room. Cade was awake, mumbling to Gabhann who was helping him sit up. Ward stood like a knight of old, ready to die for his kingdom, watching me with wide eyes and an open mouth. The other soldiers stood at the ready, but this wasn't their fight.

It was mine.

"Put that down, you stupid girl," Eoghan said. "You have no idea what you're messing with."

"I do," I replied. "And I'm not stupid."

I gathered the magic in my hands, knowing it would take a magnificent spell to end his life once and for all.

But did I want to end it?

My soft heart twinged. Eoghan had become a plague, but he'd raised me. Even in the face of his treachery, I couldn't shake the memories of him guiding me, teaching me, comforting me in my low moments. The relief I'd felt when he'd returned after I thought a fae had been in my room to kill me.

"Ayla!" Ward cried. "Any day now!"

I wrestled with this feeling, knowing I could end his life but unable to bring myself to do it. Perhaps this had been his plan all along, to make me so dependent on him that ending him would be impossible.

"Please," I whispered to the voices singing in my mind. "Give me some other option. I can't..."

"*Ayla*!" Ward bellowed. "*Do it now!*"

I opened my eyes as Eoghan gathered his own magic and sensed it was coming for me. There was nothing else to do, no other option. I would perhaps hate myself for it later, but for this moment, it was the only way forward.

"*I banish you.*"

The power exploded from my hands, flying toward the wizard and wrapping him in a blinding white light. Then he was gone, leaving nothing but the echo of a powerful spell bouncing off the walls of the throne room.

I exhaled loudly, taking a step forward as I came back to my senses. The jewel returned to a normal color, resting gently in my hands as if it were merely a bauble. I licked my dry lips and shook myself, vaguely aware that figures were running toward me.

"Ayla," Cade said, tilting my chin up to look at him. He had blood on his temple but seemed to be in one piece. "Ayla, are you—"

"Fine," I whispered. "Are you all right?"

"Nothing a quick healing spell won't fix," he said with a half-smile.

"Ward?" I said, turning to the other figure and smiling. "Are you all right?"

"How are *you*?" Ward asked, taking my other hand and turning it over to reveal the gemstone. "Besides awesome."

"You used the stone," Cade said with a proud smile. "I knew you could do it."

"I…" I swallowed, reality coming back to me. I should've killed him, but I was too weak. "He's gone."

"Ayla," Cade said, a little warning in his tone. "Is he dead or is he gone?"

A tear leaked down my cheek. "I couldn't do it. I banished him instead."

Cade brushed it away. "At least it's over for now. We can deal with the ramifications later."

"You did well," Ward said, taking my hand. "Now where's…" He looked over my shoulder. "Riona."

They hurried past me, and I spun around, finding the fae girl crumpled on the ground. Ward cradled her head as Cade waved his staff over her, perhaps checking for any remnants of Eoghan's spell. He nodded to Ward, who leaned in close.

"Riona," he said softly. "Can you hear me?"

She moaned and blinked, opening and closing her hands as if testing to make sure she had control over them. Her eyes shot open, and she shoved Ward away, backing up to the wall and taking heaving breaths. I watched the realization wash over her, perhaps that the spell was broken, that she was free once more. There was pain behind her eyes that twisted my heart. She'd been aware of what she'd been forced to do.

Slowly, her gaze lifted to meet mine, and my heart stopped as I saw myself reflected in a stranger. My eyes—she had my eyes. The particular shade of green that everyone said I'd inherited from my father. The shape of her lips was familiar, as were the lines of her cheeks. I'd thought I'd resembled my mother my entire life, but now…now I knew just how much I'd favored my father. Our father.

"You would trade the entire world for your sister's life."

I was a stranger, but she already loved me more than anyone else in this world.

Her breath was coming in short spurts. She seemed ready to flee but was almost trapped by my gaze. I didn't have the words to tell her not to be afraid, so I just said the first thing that came to mind.

"Hello," I whispered.

Her gaze darted around, landing on Ward and Cade before returning to me. "'Lo."

"I don't think we've been properly introduced," I said.

"No."

Cade came to stand by me, resting his hand on the small of my back. "She can be trusted, I promise."

"I know," I said with a half-smile. "She's my sister."

There was something about that word, so foreign on my tongue, that seemed to mean something important to her. She slowly came to her feet, her mouth parted, her gaze unsure. Cade nudged me forward gently, and I walked closer, taking in all of her.

"So…" I said, aware that we had an audience. "Hello."

"Hello," she breathed. "I'm sorry that—"

"It wasn't you," I said with a wave of my hand. "Besides, I suppose I have you to thank for finding the stone in the first place."

She nodded, swallowing.

The air was thick between us, neither of us seemingly sure what to do next. I felt a brush of magic at my back—Cade urging me forward again.

"May I hug you?" she asked, a tear spilling down her cheek.

"O-of course, I—"

She burst into sobs and flung herself at me. Out of the corner of my eye, I saw the guards move forward, but Ward held up his hand to stop them. She landed in my arms, and we embraced fiercely. It was so natural, so easy to hold her and know that even though we were strangers, we wouldn't be for long. Her body shook in my arms, her tears soaking my shoulder as I pressed my hand to the back of her head.

"I'm s-s-sorry," she stammered, stepping back. Her face had become quite red—much as mine did when I cried. "I've j-just always wanted to m-meet you."

She didn't want me to hate her. The words remained unspoken, but clear on her face. And she would've been right just a few days ago. But now…now my entire worldview had shifted. It would take time to reconcile the things I knew to be true with the things that were.

But her whole body went slack, and she turned to Cade, who nodded.

"I sense them," he said, turning around.

The throne room was immediately filled with a crowd of people, all of them tall, ethereal, and with distinctive pointed ears. My heart seized in my chest, the old fears Eoghan had impressed upon me coming to the forefront—especially as I saw the man leading the group.

"Riona? Where is she?" he bellowed.

"Crap, I'm in so much trouble," Riona muttered.

I looked down at her, amused. "Why?"

"I…might've run away from home," she said, inching out of my arms and toward the wall as she ducked her head.

"You did what?" I said with a laugh.

The Erlking marched forward, standing over Riona and myself as if unsure who to speak with first. In the end, he nodded in my direction. "Your Majesty, I do apologize for the intrusion. The wizard, he's gone? I don't feel his power in these lands anymore."

"Gone, but not dead," Cade said.

The Erlking turned to me, annoyance on his face as he cursed softly. I hadn't realized Eoghan was a threat to more than just me. A stronger queen could've done it, perhaps. But I hoped my act of mercy would be enough to keep him from coming back. "I'm… I'm sorry. I couldn't do it."

Where I expected a chiding, instead I got a warm smile. "You have done much in your short time as the owner of the stone. We may have to face him once more. But that is a problem for another day."

An older, female fae stepped forward. "Granddaughter, are you going to stay hidden against the wall, or are you going to properly greet your grandfather?"

"I was hoping to avoid it as long as possible," Riona squeaked from behind me.

"Come to me, Riona."

There must've been some magic in his words, because Riona rose and passed me, approaching the Erlking with slow steps. Tension radiated off her body as he stared down at her, looking more disappointed than angry.

"You have caused everyone in my court much angst," he said. "And you will be punished for your insubordination. But first, we will clean up the mess you made."

Magic flowed from his fingertips, circling the room and surrounding the soldiers laid out on the ground. Slowly, their wounds closed, and they moaned as they got to their feet. But my heart sank as more than a few remained on the ground, motionless.

Birch seemed to sense my distress. "I have healed those who still drew breath," he said to me with a nod. "Now, I will take my leave from your lands. Once you've been crowned, I hope we might discuss a reopening of our border. I will be in touch."

His magic shot out once more, this time wrapping around Riona. She looked back at me with pleading eyes, and I ran forward.

"Wait," I said, stepping forward. "Please."

The Erlking turned to me. "Yes?"

I wasn't even sure what I wanted to say. "Thank you for your generosity. But...if it wouldn't be too much, can you delay Riona's punishment?" I smiled at her. "I've only just learned I have a sister, and I'd like to get to know her a little before she's taken from me again. Perhaps until my coronation in a few days?"

"I will stay behind," the older, female fae said. "And ensure she makes it back to your court."

"Can I trust you after you let her escape your castle, Clíodhna?" the Erlking asked.

"She won't escape this time," the woman said with a knowing look. "I swear on my lands."

"Very well." He nodded to me then cast one more stern glance at Riona. "In three days' time, I expect to see you in my court, Riona."

She bowed. "Yes, Erlking."

Seemingly satisfied with the bargain he'd made, the Erlking, and all except Clíodhna, vanished.

Riona released a loud sigh as she stared at the ceiling. "Thank goodness."

"A delayed punishment is a punishment all the same," Clíodhna said.

"I confess, I'm a little lost," I said, weakly. "Does anyone care to fill me in?"

CHAPTER FIFTY-EIGHT

WARD

The five of us—myself, Ayla, Cade, Riona, and Clíodhna gathered in the somewhat cramped quarters of Ayla's office, along with Gabhann. It would be a while before the good captain would forgive herself for allowing the wizard so much leeway.

Riona was the first to speak, telling Ayla about the dream that had spurred her to leave the safety of the Erlking's castle, and how she'd found Cade and myself in the first village. From there, Cade and I took over, telling her how we'd arrived in Críoch and found no evidence of fae prisoners.

Clíodhna let out a snort of derision. "As if humans could capture fae in that way."

"It seems the prison was a facade for his schemes to send people to retrieve the stone," Cade replied. "Who knows how many lives he took in his pursuit."

"And I knew nothing," Ayla said, her gaze casting downward.

"Don't blame yourself for what that trickster told you," Gabhann grunted from the corner. Her scowl seemed somewhat permanent.

"Once we realized there was nothing in Críoch, we made the decision to continue," Cade said.

"Separately," Riona muttered under her breath. "Like idiots."

Ayla glanced at me, something like amusement in her gaze. "Why? Why wouldn't you stick together?"

"Because—" Cade began, but Riona was faster.

"Because they're idiots, as I said," she said as Cade scowled at her. "I found them just as Aldrick—he's the guardian of the border—was about to lay them out. Managed to trick him—"

"More like he let you go," Cade drawled. "Remember? Because he wanted you dead?"

"Yes, yes, anyway." It was Riona's turn to scowl, but she quickly continued with the rest of our journey through the *daoine maithe*, the attempts to cross into the forest realm—though I noticed her skipping over the details of the *aos sí* with a furtive look at her grandmother—and onto the wildlands. Cade and I interjected as needed with corrections, and occasionally Clíodhna chimed in with some comment about Riona's idiocy. Then, when she reached the point where we'd escaped from the *sidheog* castle, she looked sheepish.

"I was supposed to stay, but—"

"Yes, you were," Clíodhna said. "Had you stayed in the castle, Eoghan never would've been able to get his hands on the stone."

Riona twisted in her seat. "But then Ward and Cade... They would've died."

The old fae snorted and shrugged, as if that would've been a preferable outcome.

"But if Riona was the only one who could've retrieved the stone... Was the Erlking's plan to never let me have it?" Ayla asked, a curious look on her face.

Clíodhna softened. "It had nothing to do with you, princess. But we'd seen firsthand the sort of depths Eoghan would go to in order to get his hands on the stone. It was better safe in our lands until he was dealt with."

She nodded, pulling it out and staring at it. "When I used it, I felt... I don't even know how I knew what to do with it." She closed her hand and shook her head. "I should have killed him."

"You should have." Clíodhna nodded.

"Grandmother," Riona said, twisting in her seat. "You can't blame her."

"I can, actually—"

"What's done is done," Cade said, as Ayla's gaze filled with sadness and remorse. "Now we need to figure out what to do next—or if Eoghan can even set foot on these lands again."

"You said you banished him, girl?" Clíodhna asked.

She nodded.

"Then at least these lands should be safe," she said. "The Erlking will fortify the border to keep him out. But the magic of your stone is absolute, the most powerful thing in this realm."

"Until he gets the other three pieces," Cade said, a little dourly.

Clíodhna stilled, her old face growing slack. "Oh, Riona… You didn't."

Riona's face darkened as she crossed her arms over her chest. But she didn't look obstinate, or even annoyed. She looked disgusted with herself. "I didn't… I didn't have a choice."

"I'm sorry," Ayla said, raising her voice. "What are you talking about? What pieces?"

Clíodhna let out a loud breath. "The stone you hold is merely one piece of what we call the *seod croí*. Many, *many* years ago, it was deemed too powerful and split into four pieces. The other three were hidden far from these lands, while this gem was given to your ancestors." She glared at Riona, who melted even more into her chair.

"Riona told him…" Ayla said, understanding dawning. "I remember. One to the humans in Pennlan, one to the mountains, one to the sea, and one to be buried in the aether…whatever that means."

Clíodhna nodded solemnly. "If the wizard gets his hand on any one of the other stones, he will be able to wield it. There are no stipulations on their use. It was *hoped* that their location would be lost to time."

"*I'm sorry,*" Riona snapped, her face now the color of a tomato. "It's not as if I enjoyed having him…*in my mind.*" She shivered, and I placed a comforting hand on her shoulder.

"It's not your fault," I said.

"I disagree," Clíodhna muttered. "If you'd stayed in the castle—"

"What's done is done. Now, what do we do about it?" Ayla asked.

Silence descended on the group, as the answer seemed obvious but no one wanted to voice it—until Gabhann cleared her throat from the corner.

"Seems to me like we need to send out some search parties. The first two seem easy enough. Mountains and water. The aether…who knows?" She slapped her hands on her knees as she stood. "If we can get two or three to his one, we'll have the upper hand."

"Even two," Clíodhna said with an appraising look behind her.

"I will find my best knights and prepare them to leave immediately." The captain bowed and walked out without another word, leaving the rest of us in silence.

"Well, that…solves that," Ayla said softly.

"It doesn't even scratch the surface," Clíodhna said, rising as well. "But at least progress will be made. That's all we can do." She glanced at Riona. "I will go offer what knowledge I have to narrow the search. Don't even think about—"

"I'm not going to leave," Riona muttered, though I thought she might melt into the floor. "I promise."

"See that you don't." And with that, Clíodhna disappeared in a puff of snowflakes and we were left alone. Again, silence descended. Riona's face was still a deep red, her fists clenched in anger.

"I didn't want to tell him," she whispered.

I opened my mouth to reply, but Cade was faster, "You fought him well, Riona. Don't let anyone tell you differently."

She turned to him, a little surprise on her face. "Really?"

"Agreed. You saved my life," Ayla said. "Twice."

Riona turned to her sister, and I got the distinct impression that they perhaps wanted time for a private chat. So I rose, bowing at the hip.

"Your Majesty," I said. "I'm going to see if I can assist Captain

Gabhann. Cade, will you join me?"

"Actually," Ayla said, rising from her desk a little too quickly. "Cade, would you see to it that Riona and Clíodhna have accommodations in the castle. I'd like a moment to speak alone with Ward."

Cade's eyes clouded considerably, but he nodded. "It would be my pleasure."

"Will we..." Riona looked at Ayla with concern. "Will we get to speak?"

"As soon as I'm done with Ward, I'll come find you," Ayla said with a smile. "Perhaps I'll have the kitchens send up some food. It's been a long morning for all of us."

Riona's face brightened, reminding me she was a kid who'd just met her big sister. She practically skipped out the door.

Cade remained in place for a moment, as if he wanted to say something to Ayla. But instead, he nodded to her. "Let me know how I can be of assistance otherwise."

"Cade," Ayla said, as he was halfway out the door. "Thank you. I'm so happy to have you home."

It was something, but it didn't seem enough for him, because he cast me a dirty look as he closed the door behind him. I was sure I'd hear about it later, but I had no idea what Ayla could have to speak with me about privately, other than to offer her thanks for completing the quest.

But as I turned back, realizing that there was only her desk between us, I couldn't help but feel a flutter of excitement in my chest. After all I'd been through, my palms grew wet and my pulse quickened just being alone with her. That I was the *first* one she wanted to speak with.

"So..." Ayla began, licking her lips. "I hope that... This isn't the end."

I blinked. "Of?"

"Our...um." She cleared her throat. "Friendship, perhaps?" Much like her sister, Ayla's cheeks flushed bright red. "I mean, I don't... I want to… I don't want you to disappear into the garrison, and I never see you again."

"I think you perhaps have a lot to do with that," I said, then added, "Your Majesty."

"That's right. I'm in charge now," she said, as if the thought had just occurred to her. But she shook herself as she turned back to me. "You have saved my life, saved the kingdom, brought me my sister. I suppose what I'm trying to say is…" She smiled, and my heart skipped a beat. "Thank you."

"I think I should be thanking you," I said. "Since you're the one who saved mine."

"Then we'll just call ourselves even." Her gaze dropped to the desk as a little smile formed on her face. "But I'd still like to request that you…well, I don't think that knight is an apt role for you anymore."

"Then what role would you have me take?"

"I don't know." She shrugged. "But I want to see more of you."

The words hung in the air, bringing a smile to my face and earning me one in return. Our brief flirtation in the garden had clearly stayed with her as much as it had stayed with me, even after six weeks apart.

"Of course, Your Majesty."

>-» >-» >-» >-»

I headed straight for the garrison, needing a bath, a change of clothes, and to sleep for at least the next three days, even though my heart was light. The sun had risen over the land, and the birds were chirping. After being so long in the cold, frigid fae realm, it was a balm to sweat a little.

"So." Cade glared at me, his staff ominous in his hand. "What did you and the princess talk about?"

The princess. "She wanted to thank me for my help," I said, simply. "No need to get jealous."

"I'm not jealous," he snapped, though he clearly was. "Did she say anything else?"

"Only that she wanted to make sure my efforts to protect the kingdom were rewarded with a promotion," I said. *I want to see more of you.*

"I see." He folded his arms across his chest. "Will you leave to seek the other stones?"

I sighed, staring out the window. "Not today, if that's what you mean."

He clicked his tongue against the roof of his mouth. "Clíodhna has asked me to return with her and Riona."

I spun toward him. "What? Back to the fae realm? Why?"

"Because it was made clear to Clíodhna that my training has been insufficient," he said, looking down at his staff. "She would like to teach me herself, under the eye of the Erlking. When Eoghan shows up—and he will, I know him—it would be better if I were prepared to face him."

"And you…want to go?"

He shrugged. "No. I want to stay here. I suppose that's why I was asking what your plans were." He looked at me with a deadly serious stare. "I'd feel a lot better about leaving if I knew there was someone here to protect her."

"I think she's proven herself perfectly capable of protecting herself," I said.

"Not against Eoghan," he said. "He has a way of…twisting things. She needs someone with a good head on their shoulders to keep her from second-guessing herself. I'd say you're as good a person as any to fill that role." He cast me a wry smile. "After all, what was it you said? I don't have time to be petty about who gets to save the princess."

"I did say that," I said, with a chuckle. Then I stuck out my hand. "Good luck. I hope your education is swift. Ayla will certainly miss you."

He shook it then winced. "If you would, don't tell her. I'm not going to until after her coronation. I don't want her throwing things at me."

Chapter Fifty-Nine

Cade

Even if I'd wanted time alone with Ayla, there was no way to get it. The coronation festivities had started in earnest, oblivious to the chaos that had been in the castle just a day before. And when Ayla wasn't making last-minute decisions about things, she was taking long walks arm in arm with Riona in the garden. I couldn't find it within me to be jealous of the time they spent together, not when Riona looked so happy. Clíodhna, even, lost some of her scowling as she stood guard. I wasn't sure why the *sidheog* queen was so worried. Riona was exactly where she wanted to be, finally.

I spent my days untangling Eoghan's charms and enchantments on the vault, sometimes leaning on Clíodhna to help me work through the trickier things when she wasn't keeping an eagle eye on her granddaughter. There were rooms upon rooms that had been closed to me, research on the *seod croí*—but nothing on the other three. Eoghan, like us, was also starting his search based on folklore.

"It doesn't mean he won't use any means necessary," Clíodhna said. "Time is truly of the essence."

Gabhann had already sent a pair of travelers west to the mountains and south to the shore. Both would take time, and the traveling party visiting the mountains would have the trolls to contend with—if they even still existed. No one had seen them since the battle of *aos sí*.

"They were distant—very distant—cousins to the fae. Don't have much magic to speak of, other than what they can do in rock and metal.

Very jealous and distrustful of the fae, too," she said with a snort.

"That's not a good start," I said. "Hopefully, Ayla's envoys will make better progress."

"Indeed."

>→ >→ >→ >→

Dawn broke on coronation day with the ringing of the bells in the town. White ribbons streamed from every building, post, rooftop—anything that was stationary seemed decorated. Inside the castle, flowers filled the air with a lovely scent and the sound of the envoys from all four kingdoms filled the throne room where Ayla would assume her role as queen.

I dressed in my nicest tunic and polished my staff so it gleamed. My familiar seemed to enjoy the process, and I could've sworn it purred at me. Still, I delayed my exit from the vault as long as possible. By the end of the day, I would be leaving again. And I still hadn't told Ayla.

"You won't be gone for long," Riona said, wearing a white dress with ribbons in her hair. "And maybe you can master that portal spell and come and go as you please."

"I hope so," I replied, turning around. "How do I look?"

"Like a wizard," she said with a quirked brow. "How do you want to look?"

I summoned my staff from the other side of the room—wanting to practice that particular skill as often as possible, now that it was easier—and opened a small portal to the hallway where we were supposed to meet prior to the coronation.

Riona hopped off the table with a scowl. "Show-off."

"Just practicing," I said with an innocent look.

We stepped through, and I closed the portal behind me as we took our places in the queue. A whole procession of the leading Pennlan dignitaries had been thrown together at the last minute, with Ayla the last to walk out. There were so many people crammed into this small hallway, I couldn't even see if she was back there.

"Where's Ward?" Riona twisted around and bobbed on her toes. "There he is."

Ward was in the front of the procession, sporting a shiny new uniform. Ayla hadn't had to twist Gabhann's arm to promote him to her second-in-command, as he'd been the mastermind behind the plan to save the kingdom. He seemed somewhat uncomfortable in the dress uniform, the sword at his side a new, shiny decorative one instead of the well-worn weapon he'd carried on our journey. Somehow, I figured that sword was somewhere under his bed, ready for when the moment called.

He led the procession into the throne room first, followed by other high-ranking merchants and others Eoghan had selected as to be part of this day. Ayla had kept mostly everything the same, except for her being the last to enter.

"Are you ready?" I asked Riona, offering my arm to her. "This might not go over so well."

"After Eoghan, I think I can face anything."

Clíodhna had declined to be part of this event, but when Ayla had asked if Riona would serve as the Erlking's official envoy, she had immediately said yes. Ward had offered to escort her, but I'd overruled him, saying it would be a much more powerful symbol if she walked in by my side.

We stepped into the throne room, and almost immediately, a gasp of surprise rose from those closest. Riona's cheeks grew pink, but her hand remained firm on my arm. Perhaps she was used to her presence being something of a surprise, or perhaps she was just too happy to be included to care. The road to mending the relationship between the humans and the fae would take a while to travel, but this was a good first step—especially as we took our seats in the front row.

"That was awkward," Riona muttered under her breath.

"It'll get better," I said.

The annoyed mutterings ended abruptly, and I swiveled in the chair as Ayla appeared in the doorway. She was radiant, beaming from ear to ear as she walked. Eoghan had seen fit to design her something of a wedding dress, so she'd told Riona, but she'd embraced it. She strode with confidence, a sign to all the envoys gathered that she was under Eoghan's shadow no more. And when the crown was placed on her head, the applause was deafening.

Immediately after, I used my staff to clear the stairs, and the music started for the celebration. Food seemed to appear on tables out of nowhere, thanks to the quick work of the castle staff, and before too long, everyone had a glass of wine and was enjoying themselves. Some had even cleared a space in the center to dance.

I wove toward Ayla, but every time I tried to reach her, she was already engaging someone else in conversation or a dance. She seemed at ease, for once, speaking with dignitaries and representatives from other kingdoms. I hoped that without Eoghan standing over her, she would continue to blossom into a confident, sure queen.

A loud noise drew my attention, but the tension in my chest lessened immediately. Ward had grabbed Riona and was showing her how to dance, though she seemed as good at that as she had been at knife lessons. I winced as they ran into a table and knocked over a platter of food.

"Can't teach her anything, can you?" Clíodhna said, appearing by my side. She'd glamoured herself to look human; I almost hadn't recognized her.

"She's stubborn," I said, glancing at the clock on the wall and realizing how late the hour was. "I suppose it's time, isn't it?"

"I do have an oath to uphold."

Ayla had joined Ward and Riona, laughing with them as Riona made apologies for running into a rather stuffy-looking old man.

"It's all right. He's a bore," Ayla was saying once he was out of earshot. "But you really should learn to dance. Perhaps with a better teacher…"

"I'm a fine teacher," Ward huffed.

"I hate to break this up," I said, clearing my throat. "But..."

Riona caught sight of her aunt and her entire face fell. "It's time?"

"Oh, no," Ayla said, looking at her sister. "Please come back as soon as you can. We have so much more to catch up on. And as the official envoy from the fae realm—"

Clíodhna snorted. "The Erlking might have a problem with that."

But the sisters ignored her comment, embracing tightly and earning curious looks from those around them. Both had tears in their eyes when they stepped back.

"I'll be back as soon as I'm able. Though..." She glanced at Clíodhna. "It might be a few years."

"If you're lucky," she said. "Wizard, are you coming?"

Ayla released Riona and stared at me, her eyes wide. "What? You're going, too?"

"Can I have five minutes?" I asked. "Please?"

Clíodhna sighed. "Five minutes."

⇥⇥⇥⇥

I led Ayla to a small alcove where we could speak privately, my heart pounding. "Cade, why are you going with them?" Ayla asked, as soon as we were alone. Her eyes were already wet. "What possible reason could you have for leaving again?"

"Eoghan taught me nothing," I said. "And Clíodhna is offering to show me how to better protect this kingdom." I stepped forward and chanced a hand to her cheek. "I promise I won't be gone forever."

But it didn't seem to soothe her. "So you waited until the very last minute to tell me?"

"I didn't want to interrupt your time with Riona," I said, before heaving a breath. "Look, I..."

I wasn't even sure what to say to her. It wasn't goodbye for good, but somehow, I felt I wouldn't be back for some time. While I knew it was the right thing to do, it didn't make it easier to stomach.

"You have to quit doing this," she said, her voice thick with emotion. "Just leaving."

"You miss me that much?" I asked.

"Of course I do." She lightly punched my shoulder. "You're my best friend. Who am I going to talk to about things? I need..." She swallowed. "I was really lonely without you."

"Ward said he'd stay here to help," I said. "Just don't..."

"Don't what?"

Don't fall in love with him while I'm gone.

I forced a smile. "Never mind. Take care of yourself, Queen Ayla." I leaned in to kiss her cheek. "I'll be back as soon as I can."

And there I left her, joining the two fae at the edge of the castle and on to the next adventure.

ACKNOWLEGMENTS

Writing a book pregnant was tough, but writing a long, twisty epic fantasy in the third trimester was nothing short of miraculous. In fact, I delivered this book to my editor with nine days before my planned c-section.

Talk about a deadline.

For this book, I am so grateful to those who helped me along the way, including:

My beta readers, Bettina, Chelsea, Kristin, and MC, for helping me shape the plot giving me the best feedback.

My editor, Dani, who always manages to know what I'm trying to say and help me say it better.

My QA editor, Lisa, for finding all the little mistakes.

I'd also like to say a special thank you to my husband, without whom I wouldn't be able to continue writing, and to my daughter, who will one day read this book and know that she was there every step of the way in the drafting of this book.

ABOUT THE AUTHOR

S. Usher Evans was born and raised in Pensacola, Florida. After a decade of fighting bureaucratic battles as an IT consultant in Washington, D.C., she suffered a massive quarter-life-crisis. She decided fighting dragons was more fun than writing policy, so she moved back to Pensacola to write books full-time. She currently resides there with her husband and kids and frequently can be found plotting on the beach.

Visit S. Usher Evans online at:
http://www.susherevans.com/

www.ingramcontent.com/pod-product-compliance
Lightning Source LLC
Chambersburg PA
CBHW060944190726
48286CB00005B/1421